OWL
SONG
AT
DAWN

EMMA CLAIRE SWEENEY

Legend Pr   UE
info@legend-paperbooks.co.uk I www.legendpress.co.uk

Contents © Emma Claire Sweeney 2016
The right of the above author to be identified as the author of this work has
been asserted in accordance with the Copyright, Designs and Patents Act
1988. British Library Cataloguing in Publication Data available.

Print ISBN 978-1-7850796-7-2
Ebook ISBN 978-1-7850796-6-5
Set in Times. Printed in the United Kingdom by Clays Ltd.
Cover design by Simon Levy www.simonlevyassociates.co.uk

Emma Claire Sweeney has won Arts Council, Royal Literary Fund and Escalator Awards, and has been shortlisted for several others, including the Asham, *Wasafiri* and Fish.

She teaches creative writing at New York University in London; co-runs SomethingRhymed.com – a website on female literary friendship; and publishes features and pieces on disability for the likes of the *Guardian*, the *Independent on Sunday* and *The Times*.

Owl Song at Dawn is inspired by her sister, who has autism.

Visit Emma at
emmaclairesweeney.com
or on Twitter
@emmacsweeney

To Lou, who fills our lives with music, and to Elaine, Phil and Sarah, who always sing along.

'Human speech is like a cracked kettle on which we tap rhythms for bears to dance to, while we long to make music that will melt the stars.'

– *Madame Bovary* by Gustave Flaubert

And with the owls began my song,
And with the owls must end.

– 'The Idiot Boy' by William Wordsworth

PART
ONE

PART
ONE

CHAPTER ONE

I was in the Honeysuckle Room, doling out extra bedding, the day Vincent Roper returned. The most familiar of details seem so important now: the barbershop band rehearsing in our lounge; the pale yellow of the blanket; the airing cupboard scents of lavender bags, copper pipes, that smell of warm wool like a pint of milk about to turn; the toll the task had taken on my back.

Perhaps I *was* getting too old for all this. Maybe Zenka had a point when she mithered me about leaving all the housework to her. But, as usual, she'd shown up to clean Sea View Lodge in stilettos and a miniskirt so I'd set her to work in the kitchen, out of sight of our guests.

I allowed myself a breather since the Honeysuckle Room afforded a magnificent view of Morecambe Bay: the pigeon-grey sands stretching out for miles until they reached the charcoal waves; the sky the shade of smalls gone through the dark cycle by mistake.

When I spotted an elderly gentleman heading up our front path, I thought at first that he might be a Frenchman: something about the cut of his jacket, the loose coil of his scarf, the rectangular shape of his glasses. But the high polish of his cane and the way he bowed his head to the wind with an air in between defiance and defeat – these things were unmistakably English.

He paused for a long while, taking in Sea View Lodge, his hand on our front gate. Perhaps he'd noticed that our masonry could do with a lick of paint or that the gutters needed repairing.

When the man looked straight up at the Honeysuckle Room, a memory broke into my mind: a girl holding her sister above the waves, letting the water lap at the little one's toes; the child's elfin face all wonder as a wave-froth caught in her curls.

I froze, there at the window, Vincent Roper staring up at me, his blue eyes appearing even brighter now that his hair had turned white as a gull.

'Steph!' I called out. 'Len!' And then, shaking my head to rid myself of the memory, and trying to quell the panic in my voice, I added: 'Would one of you come in here?'

Steph arrived at the doorway, panting – the mauve quilt for the Lilac Room folded across her chest. 'Problem?' she asked, her hand clenching and flexing as it always did when she was distracted or distressed.

'I'm sorry, love,' I said, as she gazed up at me – her face full of concern. 'I didn't mean to scare you.'

Len bounded into the room, just as our doorbell rang.

'Would you tell our visitor that I'm not in?'

'You *are* in, Maeve!' she insisted.

'Remember how we run through it in front of the mirror, my love?' I said, trying to hide my panic.

Steph nodded and stood up tall. 'Welcome to Sea View Lodge. How may I help you?'

'That's right, my love. Hop to it.'

Len beamed at her. 'You are the best receptionist in the whole wide world!'

'You are indeed, my dear,' I put in. 'If the gentleman asks to see me, you're to tell him I'm out.'

'You're out?'

'That's right.'

'Oh no, you're not!' she exclaimed, as if we were rehearsing for a panto.

'Now's no time for honesty,' I snapped. Folk with Down's

syndrome – the term of choice nowadays – don't tend to go in for white lies.

Len studied his reflection in the mirror, pulling up the sleeve of his garish Christmas jumper to reveal his flexed muscle. 'I can carry the suitcases!' he proclaimed. 'I'm a fine figure of a man!'

'You're not to let the gentleman stick around, do you hear me? He's not to darken the door.'

Steph's chubby hand began clenching and flexing again, making me feel shabby for having snapped.

The doorbell rang for a second time. Vincent Roper had obviously become impatient in his old age.

'You'd be doing me a good turn,' I said, trying to sound calm, 'if you'd tell him that I'm not to be disturbed.'

As Steph and Len toddled off, I had to sit down.

The barbershop band started up an impromptu rehearsal in our lounge, so I waited there in the Honeysuckle Room for what felt like an age, unable to make out a word from downstairs. I kept my eyes trained on our front path, jumping each time the bass's voice rang out the high notes in their rendition of 'Auld Lang Syne'. And I girded myself all the while for Vincent Roper's knock on the bedroom door.

That memory crashed over me again: it was your elfin face that I saw, Edie – a face that, God forgive me, I'd managed to block out for some time. The suitcase out in the shed contained a photograph of me dangling you over the sea, capturing a time before you grew fearful of water. You looked about five in that picture but, judging from my height, we must have been at least ten.

When I saw Vincent Roper heading out of Sea View Lodge, his body braced against the storm, my own body seemed to collapse – sweat springing to my palms, my pulse rushing to my ears, a sigh escaping from my lungs – as if everything had held itself taut until I was sure that Vincent Roper had left Sea View Lodge once more.

Dear Maeve,

 Forgive me for showing up unannounced but, ever since I learnt of Frank's death, you've been very much on my mind.

How wonderful to find Sea View Lodge unchanged and still going strong with you still at the helm. I returned, I must admit, with some trepidation.

I've taken the liberty of booking in for a week. Steph has kindly allowed me to leave my case, although she tells me that check-in isn't until four. I'll head into town for a mosey around, and perhaps catch Mass at St Mary's. I'll keep out of your way until early evening, but I look forward to seeing you later.

With all good wishes from your old friend,

Vince

*

The wind thrashed around my face and billowed through my coat, but I forced myself out of Sea View Lodge. Vincent Roper was only by the Alhambra. I'd catch up with him in no time.

The lead singer from Aspy Fella A Cappella followed me onto the doorstep. 'Excuse me, Maeve,' he said in that robotic voice of his. 'Forgive me for keeping you.'

'I'm sorry, my dear,' I called over my shoulder as I made my way down the front path. 'We'll chat when I get back.'

Although Vincent Roper needed a stick, he was going great guns up Marine Road West. I couldn't afford to lose track of him now. By the time I reached the promenade, he'd almost got to the bowling alley and he increased his lead with every step. Who would have guessed that he'd end up the fittest survivor of our class? My own strides must have been fuelled by fury because I wouldn't usually have been capable of such unexpected exertion: I'd already climbed up and down the stairs like a yo-yo today, thirty-three steps each way; I'd already hauled five quilts and seven blankets out of our airing cupboard.

Vincent Roper paused by the Midland Hotel, which was all trussed up with Christmas lights. On the odd occasions I left Sea View Lodge, I always passed by the Midland. But today an image of our outfits sneaked up on me: my ocean-blue dress and your peachy blouse; the silk underwear from Wood's; that brooch studded with mermaid-coloured gems.

The memory powered my stampede until I got waylaid by the chap from the Coffee Pot, who was pushing a twin buggy along the prom. 'Good morning, Miss Maloney,' he said. 'It's nice to see you getting out and about.'

Unlike some of our neighbours, he was a decent sort, but I would have to give him short shrift: I was almost within shouting distance of Vincent Roper now.

'I was going to pop in,' the chap said, detaining me, 'to introduce you to my granddaughters.'

He was beaming with such pride that I could hardly dash off without stopping for a moment to admire the babies. His daughter, so I'd heard, had been trying for years. Before I peered into the pram, I stole another glance up the promenade. Vincent Roper had paused by the Midland Hotel.

'This one here is Diza,' the chap told me. 'See that dimple on her right cheek? That's how I tell them apart.'

To me, the baby girls looked identical in every way: their wisps of dark hair, their large black eyes, their tiny lips, and the creases at their chins.

'And this one's Dorra,' he went on.

Vincent Roper was still ambling around by the Midland. He'd no doubt take shelter from the vicious wind in the Rotunda Bar, where he'd buy a criminally overpriced coffee. He'd be that type now – what with having gone to Cambridge, and having conducted that choir in Paris. His father had crowed about him from Blackpool to Barrow.

'In my wife's country,' the chap explained. 'Diza means gift and Dorra means joy.'

The babies' skin and hair and eyes all carried a hint of their grandmother's home – a land they would perhaps never see. I'm not one for cooing over children, but I found myself wishing that I could hold Diza and Dorra, feel their warmth and weight in my arms.

From the corner of my eye, I noticed that Vincent Roper had started walking again, so I made my apologies and then hurried up towards the Midland. 'Mr Roper!' I called out, but he continued to walk and the wind whipped my words out to sea.

As I crossed the road, he turned onto Pedder Street. I pursued him right into the red-light district – an area I hadn't visited for a good while. Frank, so I heard, cavorted with some of the women around here. Pictures of buxom girls used to litter these streets, but now it was riddled with craft shops and curio stores.

Vincent Roper was still marching ahead at quite a pace and, try as I might, I couldn't seem to reduce the distance between us.

'Vince!' I shouted, my hand springing to my mouth as if I could stuff the word back in. I could have sworn that he'd heard, but he continued to stride on ahead and I hadn't a clue what I would have said next. How dare he come back after all these years, calling himself an old friend? Above me a window screeched open, and a red-headed girl leant onto the ledge, her skin blue-white like skimmed milk. Although she looked straight down at me, her hair blowing around her face, she hardly seemed to notice I was there. She glanced back inside for a moment and said something I couldn't quite catch. Doubtless she had a man in her bed although it was just past noon.

Once darkness fell, cars would still inch along here, no doubt, and women like that redhead would emerge from the alleyways – all bones and stilettos and miniskirts. Nothing much would have changed, except they'd be from Romania and Latvia and God knows where. Zenka's get-up would be better suited to a brothel. Lord knows what Steph's dad saw in her. When she'd applied for the manager's post, I'd taken pity on this woman, down on her luck and far from home. She'd relied on me to translate many an episode of *Coronation Street* and I'd shared with her my recipes for shepherd's pie and Victoria sponge. But she was right as rain now, living with Dave and behaving as if she were Steph's mum.

That redhead brought back my own youth, when my own hair was as red and as full as hers, and she filled me with a lingering sense of unease – like the aftermath of a conversation that's trailed off too soon.

When I took my eyes off her, I caught sight of Vincent Roper heading down the alley in the direction of St Mary's.

I had to tell him that he couldn't stay in Sea View Lodge, that I'd meant it all those decades ago when I'd told him never to return. But I just stood there, deflated, incapable even now of following him into the church.

*

The priest who presents the Radio Mass waffles on about the 'mentally subnormal', and the 'Grace of God', while we stand in St Mary's choir stalls with Vince, waiting for the crew to signal that it's time for you to sing.

While the priest interviews Vince's father about the role of choirmaster and how he has trained your voice, you keep tugging at the sleeve of Vince's Scouting shirt: 'What noise does an Edie make?' you say over and over. And every single time you ask, Vince whispers in response: 'Edie Maloney sings like a star!'

Mum and Dad lean forwards in their pews, as if at any moment they might come up to fetch you.

'Come on, Edie, change the record,' I whisper, adopting one of Dad's favourite phrases.

Vince attempts to hush you by circling your palm in a silent 'round and round the garden'. But you pull your hand free. 'Bye bye, priest,' you call out, waving at him. 'Song now!'

One of the radio crew guffaws from the back of the church, but the choirmaster and the priest pretend not to have heard. Mum is giving you a hard stare, willing you to keep quiet, but Dad's shoulders are heaving. I have to look away or else he'll set me off too.

When it eventually comes to your duet, the whole congregation is silent in anticipation.

Vince sings the first verse. His voice, which broke some years ago now, is all hot buttered crumpets and Mirabelle jam. No one would have guessed that he had been called upon to step in just minutes before the start of the broadcast.

But when it is time for you to sing the chorus, you stand there, mute, your lips pursed.

The church is so quiet that it is as if no one dares breathe.

I try to elbow you into action, but your lips remain pursed.

I pray in my head to the Virgin Mary: please Our Lady, please make Edie sing.

But the organist reaches the end of the chorus and Vince has to launch into the next verse without you having sung a word.

Dad squeezes Mum's hand, and both of them stare at the floor. He will be swallowing back tears, and she will be blinking hard, determined not to let her make-up smear. *Que sera sera*, she'll say when we get out of Mass.

As Vince reaches the end of the second verse, the back door of the church cracks open: Frank Bryson stands there – his hair windswept, a cigarette raised to his lips – watching as if he couldn't care less.

I sense Vince willing you on. The church fills with the rustle of hymnals as he nudges you and clears his throat.

It's then that I feel your chest rise with a deep intake of breath, and your mouth opens in song:

> *Oh, hear us when we cry to Thee*
> *For those in peril on the sea*

Your eyes are fixed on Mum and Dad as Vince sings the next verse and, when it comes to your turn, you hit each note spot on, enunciating each word as clearly as your floppy tongue can manage:

> *Oh, hear us when we cry to Thee*
> *For those in peril on the sea*

Even the oldest and most fastidious of the congregation stand stock still, holding their breath, as if this will help you to complete your solo without faltering. Mum and Dad look like statues of Mary and Joseph. They don't even seem to blink.

> *Thus evermore shall rise to Thee*
> *Glad hymns of praise from land to sea*

As your last note fades into silence, your face lights up with the widest of smiles. 'Edie Maloney sings like a star!' you exclaim, and the congregation breaks into applause.

*

Edie Maloney sings like a star. Twinkle, twinkle, little star, how I wonder where you are. Where's your tummy? Down, down. That's right! Where are your toes? This little piggy went to market, this little piggy stayed at home. What noise does a pig make? Neigh! Stop teasing, Edie. You know. Oink, oink! That's right! We're very impressed with you. *Un*, *deux*, *trois*, *quatre*, *cinq*, *six*, *sept*, *huit*, *neuf*, *dix*. Congratulations! Hip, hip, hooray. Maeve and Edie, the cleverest twins in the seven seas.

*

Edith Maloney's parents report her abnormal floppiness and failure to reach developmental milestones. Mother suffered no illness during pregnancy but she was an elderly primigravida (at thirty-one years of age) and the twins were born slightly premature (at thirty-five weeks). Edith takes twice as long to feed as her twin sister, Maeve, and, unlike her sibling, has yet to crawl or walk. Although parents were cautioned against comparing their daughters, Edith's uncontrolled tongue movements, tightly furled fists and toes, and underdeveloped reflexes point towards spasticity. She will likely remain immobile, mute, and doubly incontinent.

Referred to orthopaedic department. Ophthalmologist and otolaryngologist referral for diagnosis of possible vision and auditory range deficiencies. Next appointment scheduled in six months' time for continued observation, in particular with relation to mental subnormality.

Parents were advised to institutionalise.

Signed: Doctor A. Rosenthal, February 3, 1935

*

Vincent Roper still hadn't returned although it was nigh on six o'clock. I tried to distract myself by emptying the dishwasher and then laying the tables for tomorrow's breakfasts, although these were usually Zenka's early morning chores. She wouldn't thank me for my efforts: I was all fingers and thumbs, chipping one of the side plates and spilling a vase of white roses.

The barbershop band was at a loose end so I roped them into helping Steph and me with the first of the decorations. The lead singer held the ladder steady as the bass pinned tinsel into the cornice. I made a start on our Christmas cards, although I kept making mistakes, and Steph and the other two singers sat around making paper chains with the care worker from Wirral Autistic Society, who always accompanied the band. All the while the blokes were singing 'I'll be Home for Christmas' and 'Jingle Bells' and 'Auld Lang Syne', and the rest of us hummed along.

I'd just be allowing myself to relax when the security light would switch on or a car would pull up outside. Then I'd remember all over again that Vincent Roper was coming. *Apologies for the confusion*, I braced myself to say. I wouldn't let him step across the threshold.

'Vincent Roper is a dear old friend, isn't he, Maeve?' announced Steph. 'A bit like me and Len.'

'I don't know where you got that idea from, my love,' I replied, aware of the care worker glancing up from her paper chain.

'That's what he said.'

'Well, he couldn't be more wrong.' But I found myself reaching into my pocket, as if my hand needed a reminder that Vincent Roper's note was still there.

'Is Vincent Roper a bad man?' asked Steph.

I had been surrounded by shards of sherry glasses and china teacups the last time Vince set foot in Sea View Lodge – my ocean-blue dress flung across my case.

'Is Vincent Roper your enemy?'

If the truth be known, Vince and I *had* once been a bit like Steph and Len: he'd shoulder my satchel on the walk from school; we'd guess what concoctions you and Mum would have cooling for us on the side: potato scones, beetroot puddings, carrots covered in toffee; we'd sit at the kitchen table doing our homework or playing with you until his father returned from the office.

'Let's not be melodramatic, my love,' I said, aware of the care worker and all the band members looking at me now. 'It's just that he caused a lot of breakages last time he was here.'

Oh, Edie, if Vince hadn't walked out of St Mary's, you and I could have grown old together. Our skin might have sagged at just the same rate, the backs of our hands becoming crêpey and veined. Our hair might have silvered over just the same years, its copper gradually giving way. We did share the same hair, the same eyes. Dad claimed that we would have been identical, all things being equal. But, of course, things never were.

Just then, the security light illuminated our front lawn. Vincent Roper stood at our gate, making no move to open it.

The thought of facing him made my stomach turn. His footsteps approached up our path until, eventually, a knock sounded.

I forced myself into the hall, and made myself open the door.

There he was: standing at the entrance of Sea View Lodge. Now that Frank lay cold in his coffin, Vincent Roper was the only man alive to have known me at both my best and my worst.

And yet I did not know this man: this man who wore brushed leather shoes, a cable-knit scarf, a hat that might pass for a beret; this old man still full of vigour, his gestures confident and purposeful.

'Maeve,' he said.

He sounded just like his father.

I remained there in the hallway, chill and numb as if I'd been swept up by a wave.

And Vincent Roper just stood there, battered by the wind, smiling and expecting me to invite him in.

'Mr Roper, I'm a—'

He leant down to kiss my cheek – his movement easy – the sandpaper rub of his face against mine. Anyone would think we were on the set of an old French film, not at a guest-house on the front in Morecambe. He smelled of cedar and bergamot. To think he'd become the kind of man to wear aftershave on a common-or-garden weekday. Dad owned one bottle of cologne that he eked out over nigh on a decade, wearing it only on special occasions: midnight Mass, their wedding anniversary, our birthday celebration.

Vincent Roper's scent made me wish that I'd put on my best blouse, or even my button-down dress – something that emphasised my bust a little more and drew attention from my waist. At least I'd touched up my make-up.

'Vince, please,' he replied, propping his cane beneath the coat hooks. Then he paused and smiled – a smile that failed to mask the strangeness of his reappearance after all these long years.

I refused to meet his eye.

'It's been a lifetime, I know, but do still call me Vince.'

'Mr Roper, I'm terribly sorry to disappoint you—'

He cocked his head slightly as if he might be a little deaf in one ear, the angle of his face making him look so vulnerable that I had to pull myself tall and inhale deeply: 'I'm afraid there's been some confusion,' I explained, trying to ignore his look of deflation. 'We don't have any vacancies.'

'Oh yes we do!' piped up Steph, who'd appeared in the doorway of the lounge along with the barbershop's bass. 'Welcome to Sea View Lodge,' she intoned, snapping back into work mode.

'And who are you?' asked the bass. 'I don't mean to be rude. You're supposed to introduce yourself first, aren't you? I'm a bass in Aspy Fella A Cappella.'

To his credit, Vincent Roper didn't bat an eyelid about being greeted by a singer with Asperger's and a receptionist with a floppy tongue and feline eyes. Steph could almost be mistaken for one of those poor Chinese cockle-pickers who perished on our sands. But, not long after her birth, her mum and dad had been on the verge of tears when I'd called Steph a Mongoloid. I'd taken care never again to say it out loud although I still found it a lovely word – full of horses journeying across the steppes. I couldn't think why the likes of Trish and Dave preferred to lumber their child with a syndrome; why they preferred to honour Doctor Down, who shut people away in an asylum.

The bass patted Vincent Roper on the back and welcomed him to Sea View Lodge. 'You'll have a bloody good time here,' he said. 'I don't mean to be rude. You shouldn't swear, should you?' He couldn't have been more different from the lead singer, that one, what with his swearing and his tendency to hug and shake hands and pat folk on the back.

'Pleased to meet you,' Steph put in, not to be outdone by the bass.

'Pleased to meet you again too,' laughed Vincent Roper.

'Let me show you to your room,' she continued, picking up his case. 'Len usually carries the bags, but he's only here in the day.'

And Vincent Roper just stood there, not knowing what to do.

'Steph, my dear,' I put in, 'you've made a mistake. We have no vacancies.'

'What about the Crocus Room?'

At this, the bass broke into song: 'She's made her way up through the frozen dark below, and there's a crocus in the snow.'

The carpet in the Crocus Room was wearing awfully thin. 'I appreciate that it's getting rather late,' I said above the hullabaloo. 'Shall I call the Balmoral? They're bound to have space.'

Vincent Roper cleared his throat. And that was all it took to bring you back again, raising yourself tall beside him, your chest rising, your mouth opening in song.

'Aunty Maeve?' said Steph, her hand waving in front of my face and her voice shouting above the bass's tune.

'What was that, my dear?'

'Shall I take Mr Roper to the Crocus Room?'

He continued to stand there, waiting for my reply, and the bass continued to sing.

'It's not at all suitable, I'm afraid, Mr Roper. There's not even an en-suite.'

'That sort of thing doesn't bother me one bit,' he said. Then, trying to catch my eye, he added: 'It's wonderful to find Sea View Lodge still full of song.'

'Some things never change,' I said, letting myself smile. We still gathered around the piano at every opportunity just like the old days with Dad and Vince and you. I made sure Zenka mopped the parquet each morning, cleaned the glass lampshades every Friday and laundered the chintz on the first Monday of the month – just like Mum used to do.

'I think I mentioned in my last Christmas card,' said Vincent Roper, leaning towards me, as if to catch my response with his good ear, 'that my son and his family have moved to the States?'

I had felt for him when I read that note in his card, but I failed to see what it had got to do with the price of fish. And yet I breathed in his cedar scent and waited for him to go on.

'And that I moved to a retirement complex.'

His kindnesses came back to me then: the way he'd cheered when you first learnt to walk, your body pitching from side to side as you made your way, all skew-whiff, along the church drive; the way he'd helped you in and out of the choir stalls each week; the way he'd poured your milk into a sherry glass so that you could join in the toast.

'We're neither of us getting any younger,' he said, fiddling with his hearing aid, his gaze pausing on Mum's old statue of the Madonna and child. He looked at me sadly then, as if he could tell that my life had stalled. 'Maeve Maloney,' he added, lowering his voice: 'it would mean so much to me to make our peace.'

CHAPTER TWO

Sounds from downstairs woke me before the sun had even begun to rise, so I crept from bed, listening out for more noise. I was beginning to think I'd dreamed it when I heard another thump, and then I was assaulted by the recollection that Vincent Roper had returned.

A tap was running, footsteps crossed from the kitchen to the dining room, a door opened and then closed. No doubt it was him, snooping around.

Just as I was heading down the stairs, I heard a great clatter of crockery, and then shushing sounds and laughter, and Steph telling Len to keep the noise down.

What an old fool I must have looked: seventy-nine years of age, my nightie wafting around my ankles, and preparing to give Vincent Roper a dressing-down. Thank goodness none of the singers were up.

I continued to the hall and called into the kitchen: 'What's this racket about?'

Steph darted out.

'What on earth is Len doing here at this ungodly hour? He's not due in till this afternoon.'

Steph clenched and flexed her fist, and then looked from me to the kitchen door. 'Len's not here,' Steph said, just as Len called out, 'Morning, Maeve!'

In the fifteen years that she'd worked here, I'd never once known Steph to tell a fib.

'You scared me witless.'

I barged towards the kitchen but, just before I reached the door, she blocked my way.

'This is not the kind of behaviour I expect from my goddaughter,' I began, but then, through the corner of my eye, I caught sight of a vase of snowdrops that had been set on one of the dining room tables. It must be some kind of occasion for Len to countenance fresh cuttings of the rare early-flowering variety.

Steph snapped into action: 'Please, take a seat,' she said, gesturing towards the table just as she did with our guests.

'What's all this in aid of?'

The expression on Steph's face could have turned just as easily into laughter or tears.

'Listen, love, I can't have you and Len messing around in the kitchen unsupervised. Anything could happen to you in there.'

Although Steph's top lip was trembling, and she was gesturing again for me to take a seat, I made my way into the kitchen. I wouldn't have been doing the right thing by them or their parents if I left them to it. Besides, we couldn't afford any more breakages: during the band's stay, we'd already suffered a smashed cafetière and a chipped side plate.

Just then, I caught Len pouring boiling water into the teapot. 'Stop that this instant! You might scald yourself.'

'Hello, my dear,' he called out. 'What are you doing in here?'

'I might ask you the same question, young man.'

The teaspoon clinked against the china rim of the teapot and, as he stirred, Len's tongue lolled from his mouth in concentration. Eventually, he replaced the lid and looked up at me. 'Breakfast will be served shortly, madam. Please take a seat in the dining room.' He gave an exaggerated bow, and I couldn't help but smile as he tried to shoo me away.

'What would your mum say if she knew I'd given you free rein of the kitchen?'

He looked at me as if I were a bit dim. 'It was Mum's idea,' he explained.

She didn't have any compunctions, it was true, about him traipsing across town on his own to get from their place to ours. In all likelihood, he did light their stove and fill their kettle.

I was clearly fighting a losing battle, so I let Steph lead me back into the dining room. Although I spent hours each day frying eggs, grilling mushrooms and filling little pots with thickly shredded marmalade, I couldn't remember ever having sat down at the breakfast table with any of our guests. The room looked quite different from this angle. I had a clear view through the French windows and down to the far end of the lawn. Len really had done a marvellous job: the fence looked miles better in that wild thyme colour; he'd planted the borders with ornamental heathers and scrubbed the lichen off the paving stones.

He was quite exceptional, was Len – although I'd had my doubts back when he and his mum called in out of the blue. I'd recognised him straight away as Len hadn't changed a bit since his schooldays with Steph. He'd still looked to be in rude health: his cheeks ruddy, his blond hair thick, his eyes bright and blue. But his mum had looked like a late autumn leaf that might fall apart in your palm. She'd sat on our garden bench, wrapping her coat tightly around her thin frame. 'Len's been bored out of his mind since we closed the caff,' she said. 'The day centre's understaffed so they just sit around half the time, twiddling their thumbs.' Her breath misted in the air as she continued to speak: 'He's ever so good at gardening – transformed my borders.'

I said nothing because I could tell where this was leading and I didn't much like the sound of it.

'He has a City and Guilds Certificate in Horticulture. The Lord Mayor presented it to him in the Town Hall.'

I could hardly be expected to employ all the town's waifs and strays.

'I'm sick, you see.'

Well, that was going on a year ago now.

'Penny for your thoughts,' said Len, who had appeared in the doorway, carrying a rack of charred toast on Mum's best silver tray, which I only used on high days and holidays, a tea towel draped across his right arm.

Steph busied herself with pouring my tea and dropping in sugar cubes, and then stirring it for longer than strictly necessary, all the while avoiding catching my eye.

I looked from one to the other but could tell that neither was about to speak.

I'd imagined in my youth that, once we married, Frank would make breakfast on celebratory mornings. On our birthday, he'd carry up a tray loaded with bacon and eggs, a pot of tea for me, bowls of porridge for the little ones and a mug of milk for you.

Steph set the toast in front of me, and then they both sat down opposite. I didn't like to mention that they'd forgotten the butter and marmalade.

Len leant on his elbows and Steph held her back ramrod straight, both looking at me with such anticipation that I felt obliged to take a bite of the burned bread. They were so quiet that I could hear every crunch.

'Come on then,' I said in the end. 'What's all this in aid of?'

Len opened and closed his mouth, and straightened that bow tie of his.

'I've not got all day. Zenka will be here any minute now and we'll have to get on with the band's breakfasts – not to mention getting ready for your blasted social worker.'

The sound of Vincent Roper clearing his throat gave me quite a start. God knows how long he'd been standing in the doorway. And me without make-up and in nothing but my nightgown. I tucked my feet beneath the table. Ordinarily, I wore dark stockings to disguise my swollen ankles.

'I am sorry. I've obviously intruded,' he said, blushing and looking down – more out of courtesy, I suspected, than nerves, although he'd been terribly nervous during our youth. 'When I smelled the toast,' he said. 'I thought perhaps it was only you up.'

'I did mention last night that the guest breakfast would be served unusually late.' As I spoke I noticed something peeking out of Vincent Roper's pocket: it looked to be metal, its red paint faded. 'Please feel free to come back at ten,' I continued, 'when the band members should have finally roused.'

Vincent Roper's face was a picture. No doubt his wife had been one of those lank-haired women who wouldn't say boo to a goose. Thank goodness I still had a fairly thick head of hair: folk told me that the silver suited my complexion, that my new cropped do emphasised the size of my eyes. I'd caught a glimpse of Cheryl last week as Frank's funeral procession passed Sea View Lodge. She'd gone in for jet-black dye – a terrible mistake at our age.

'I'm pleased to make your acquaintance,' Len announced, standing up and shaking Vincent Roper's hand.

My gaze strayed back to the metal object that poked from his pocket. There was something vaguely familiar about the shape of it, the colour of its paint.

'You've arrived just in time for a mug of tea,' offered Len. 'Mum says I'm an expert tea maker, as well as being a galanthophile, of course. That's my real area of expertise.'

I'd never come across the word *galanthophile* until that day, almost a year ago, when Len and his mum turned up. He'd got down on all fours at the edge of a patch of snowdrops, his face right up close to the flowers: 'I've only seen these once before.'

So much for his horticulture qualification. 'They're called snowdrops, my dear.'

I would always remember the way Len laughed at that – he could hardly catch his breath.

'But these are Galanthus the Groom!' he'd explained. 'Do you know how rare they are? I saw one at the 2009 Galanthus Gala in Hatfield.'

Dot had sat up straight and smoothed down her headscarf. 'Leonard is a founder member of the North West Branch of the Galanthophile Society.'

'We collect snowdrops,' Len had put in, sparing me the humiliation of having to ask. 'There are over one hundred and fifty kinds and you have some of the most rare. I didn't think these ones grew outside of Scotland.'

They made a right pair – Len and his mum, both of them proud as punch of his snowdrop society.

Vincent Roper was clearly familiar with the term *galanthophile* because he told Len that he was a keen gardener too.

'This is all very nice,' I said, as Steph loaded up a plate of charred toast for Vincent Roper. 'But I need to be getting on with the band's breakfast.'

As I pushed back my chair, Len took a deep breath and Steph gave him an encouraging nod: 'I love Steph!' he announced, throwing his arms around her.

'Of course you do, my dear. I do too.'

'Not like that,' he said, shaking his head at me as if I were a lost cause. 'Boyfriend-girlfriend love.'

Vincent Roper looked genuinely delighted, despite not knowing them from Adam. 'Congratulations!' he said, patting Len on the back.

I felt as if I'd been caught out laughing at an in-joke that I couldn't possibly understand.

'Len and me, we're a couple,' Steph told Vincent Roper.

'If you don't mind me saying,' he replied, 'a very good couple you make too.'

'Mr Roper, are you a couple?'

'My wife died about ten years ago,' he said, 'but we had a good innings, Hélène and me.'

As soon as he said it, his gaze flitted to me.

I felt my cheeks flush and I looked away. Vincent Roper had married, so had Frank. These well-worn facts still had the power to catch me out. If his annual Christmas cards were anything to go by, Vincent Roper and his wife had led a full life. Until I was in my twenties, it had never crossed my mind that I might fail to wed but, Edie, none of us thought to question your future spinsterhood.

'My mum's dying,' said Len. 'She sleeps in the living room now and I help the nurse to count out eleven pills for her to take in the morning and eight pills for her to take at night.' He paused then and bit his lip, and a fat tear rolled down his cheek. 'I'm the chief tea maker now.'

I gave him a hug. Vincent Roper should never have mentioned death when Len had just made a declaration of love.

'I'm so very sorry to hear that, Len,' Vincent Roper said, quite ignoring my glare.

Len loosened himself from my embrace and blew his nose. 'Mum says that Steph and me make the best couple to have ever walked on God's good earth.'

'And quite right she is too,' I said, the compliment unexpectedly pleasurable.

'I've saved up my wages,' went on Len, 'and now I have enough for the meal deal at Fayre and Square. We can have scampi or a small burger or gammon or something else that I can't remember, and for afters we can have ice cream sundae or jam roly-poly, and we can have lager shandies or squash. But Mum says it's better not to bother with starters because I'm not made of money and, in any case, it'll spoil our meal.'

Frank had asked me out on our first date just after your duet. While the rest of the congregation were milling around, congratulating you and Vince, Frank had pulled me into the Lady Chapel, saying nothing but pressing a torn page from his hymnal into my palm. My skin tingled with the awareness of his eyes fixed on mine, the heat of his hand. He'd smiled then and winked and turned on his heel. Alone in the Lady Chapel, I read the note he'd scrawled in the margins of 'For Those in Peril on the Sea': *Brucciani's, Friday. I'll pick you up at six.*

When Len stopped for breath, Steph nudged him. He looked puzzled for a moment but then something dawned on him: 'And Steph's dad doesn't mind, and neither does Zenka, but they said I should ask if you have any ob—'

Steph nodded eagerly.

'Ob-ject-ations?'

'Objectations,' Steph repeated, and then snuggled her head against Len's shoulder.

'Of course not, my dears,' I said – not that my opinion counted for much since I was clearly the last to know. 'How could I object to something as lovely as this?' Even as I gave them my blessing, I couldn't help but think of Dot and Dave and Zenka conferring behind my back about how best to break the news to me. Even Len and Steph, God love them, had found something that I'd long gone without.

*

My future as a wife collapses when I am just twenty-one, my destined spinsterhood slamming into me as I sit on the floor, my wedding trousseau strewn all around.

I stuff the new cotton bedding back into the corner of my suitcase, the material still smelling of the lavender water I had used to iron it. But one of the sheets is now torn where I'd ripped it from the bed that Frank and I had been due to share.

Dad tried to follow me when we got back from the church, but the nuns had told him to let me go, that I needed some time alone. 'You'll be more help in here,' they'd said, persuading him into the lounge. 'Edie needs calming down.'

A tear drops onto a pillowcase, darkening a spot on the unused bedding. It is the first tear I have shed today and it is such a relief to succumb. The sobs rise in deep gulps, wild and fierce, and I find myself grabbing one of the sherry glasses and throwing it across the room, then a saucer, a fork, a teacup, a plate. With each smash, I yell and cry and howl – sounds more often yours than mine.

But my rage subsides as quickly as it erupted, and I continue to sit there, sobbing, surrounded by shards of glass and china, my ocean-blue dress lying across the open case.

It is then that Vince appears at the doorway. I hadn't heard him arrive and can hardly believe that Dad let him through the front door.

'How could you?' I ask.

'I'm so sorry,' says Vince, picking his way through the broken glass.

I bat off his hand when he tries to hold me. 'How could you?'

'I couldn't not,' he says, hardly bringing himself to meet my eye. 'You wouldn't have thanked me for it.'

'Thanked you?' I ask, my voice steely. 'Frank and I were going to move back here tonight, we were going to look after Dad and Edie. We were going to make a go of things.'

At about this moment, Frank should have been holding me in his strong arms, leading me around the lounge in our first dance.

Vince sits down beside me and begins toying with the harmonica that you've brought back from the convent, along with the rest of your things: the China Red lipstick, the hymnal, the tin of beeswax.

Eventually Vince says: 'I care about you, Maeve.'

'You *care* about me?' The words spit from my tongue.

'I care about Edie too.'

'You should have thought about that earlier. How am I going to look after her and Dad and this place alone?'

Your whimpering is audible from the lounge. 'Neigh!' you keep crying, over and over: 'Neigh!' And I know that you are rocking back and forth, your fists clenched to your ears, and I suspect that you are lashing out at anyone who tries to calm you.

'I'll help you care for them,' says Vince.

His words make me pause. But he starts his national service tomorrow, conducting a military band. Much use he'll be to us.

'Marry me,' he says, still rubbing your harmonica between his forefinger and thumb.

I want him to look at me full in the face, to let me read his expression. But he continues to toy with your things, failing to meet my eye.

'Get out,' I say in the end, his pity igniting my anger. 'Never set foot in here again.'

*

Where's your foot? That's right! We're very impressed with you! Where's your mouth? What noise does a gob-tin make? What noise does a horse make? Neigh! It won't be a stylish marriage, I can't afford a carriage. Who do you love the best, Frank or Edie? What noise does an Edie make? Edie Maloney sings like a star. What noise does a Vince make? And applications for situations, and timid lovers' declarations. Bye, bye, Frank. Vince now. Never say goodbye because goodbye means going away and going away means forgetting. My name's Edith Mary Maloney, Sea View Lodge, 31 Marine Road West. Home, James, and don't spare the horses. What noise does a horse make?

*

April 23, 1947
Dear Mr and Mrs Maloney,

I hope you don't mind my mentioning that I have always admired your good cheer in the face of considerable adversity.

My son has noticed that your young and afflicted daughter has a surprisingly beautiful voice. I have been listening out for Edith during Mass of late, and it has brought me such joy, especially during these austere times, to savour her angelic song.

As choirmaster, I hope that I might nurture Edith's unschooled talent. Vincent has suggested that she might enjoy membership of St Mary's choir so I trust that you will forgive me for having already approached Father O'Reilly about this possibility.

Neither Father nor I find any reason to desist from this plan on the grounds of canonical legality, although we are in consultation with the Diocesan Curia. I have no doubt that the Most Reverend Bishop will take great personal interest in the circumstances of your unfortunate daughter. In the meantime, however, Edith would be welcome to join the choristers at their annual tea dance this Saturday and thereafter for our weekly practice on Wednesday evenings at 6pm. I suggest that Maeve accompany her to ensure Edith's well-being and that of the other choristers. As you know, Vincent is a very responsible young man and he will be only too glad to help Edith in and out of the stalls.

Please do not concern yourselves with any inconvenience or embarrassment that may be experienced by the choristers or congregation.

Yours in admiration,

Gerald Roper, Esq.

*

We are dressed in matching yellow twinsets and high-waisted slacks when Vince and his mother show up to escort us to the annual tea dance. Mum won't let me borrow her scarlet lipstick but she secures one of her tortoiseshell combs in my hair. Your auburn curls would also look neater pinned from your face but you bat away Mum's hands when she reaches towards you with a clip.

Mum keeps checking that I've not forgotten your flask and Dad keeps telling Vince to keep away from the Barbary Coast because the drunks all congregate in that part of town; to tell anyone who gives us any jip that they'll have Mr Maloney and his pals to contend with; to get us back before dark. He gets all tearful as we take our leave. 'Would you look at my girls,' he tells Vince and Vince's mother. 'My beautiful waifs and strays.'

'Waifs and strays,' Vince's mother repeats in her strong French accent, her tone uncomprehending. She twirls around and raises her arms above her head, each hand holding aloft a jar of Mirabelle jam.

A look passes between Mum and Dad – one that I can't quite read.

Vince's mother slows to a stop, and then bows so far forwards that her wild black hair almost touches the floor, and her green satin slip rises up her bare legs. It's the sort of thing that the mannequins wear in the shopfront at Wood's.

I'm sure Vince's mother would let me wear lipstick, she wouldn't pester me about wrapping up warm. I want to ask her about French food and what the women are wearing in Paris, so I'm a bit disappointed when Mum suggests that she stay for tea with them instead of accompanying us to the church.

We eventually get out of Sea View Lodge, the three adults waving at us from the front door: '*Au revoir, mes petits choux!*' calls out Vince's mother; 'Dance your socks off,' laughs Dad; 'You make us so proud,' shouts Mum.

The three of us head up the promenade, Vince and me either side of you, holding your hands.

'My name's Edith Mary Maloney, Sea View Lodge, 31 Marine Road West,' you tell him. 'What's your name?'

'You know his name, you ragamuffin!' I laugh. 'You see Vince every Sunday.'

By the time we reach Brucciani's, you're onto 'What noise does a wasp make? What noise does a snake make? What noise does a lion make?' And each time, Vince replies: 'I'm not sure Edie, what noise does it make?' And you delight in buzzing and hissing and roaring, and Vince and I pretend to be scared.

In between playing with you, I ask Vince questions about his mother: Is she from Paris? (I know already that she

37

grew up on the Île Saint-Louis but I want him to describe again the pleasure cruisers, the lights reflecting in the river, the cafés with tables outside.) What do they eat for dinner? (I am disappointed to learn that Vince too has spam and cauliflower cheese, although he also mentions a stew called *boeuf bourguignon*.) Has she taught him to speak French? (*Mais oui!*)

Vince slows down as we approach the fairground, and takes a glance at his watch. 'Would you like to look around, Edie?' he asks, as if you might actually respond.

You continue to practise your favourite phrases: 'Who do you love the best, moo-cow or ice cream?', 'Who do you love the best, ice cream or Edie?', 'Who do you love the best, Edie or Maeve?'

I avoid catching Vince's eye.

'Who do you love the best,' you continue undaunted, 'Maeve or Cheryl?'

Vince turns crimson.

I try to distract you by taking your face in my hands, and trying to capture your attention: 'Edie… Edie?'

Eventually you meet my gaze. 'Would you like to look around the fairground? Yes or no?'

'No.'

'Are you sure?'

'No.'

'Would you like to hear the organ grinder, Edie? No or yes?'

'Yes!'

The fairground is filled with the smells of roasted chestnuts and the sounds of honky-tonk and puppet shows. But it's not quite as busy as it used to be during the war when soldiers and WAAFs queued up for the rides, and nurses wheeled patients through the crowds.

Vince has done 'this little piggy' and 'round and round the garden' for you at least six times. Thinking he must be in need of a rest, I try to take over. But Vince and I both reach for your palm at exactly the same time, and his hand brushes against mine. 'Sorry,' we both say in unison, and immediately move apart.

As we approach the merry-go-round, Vince stops and begins fishing in the leather purse that's attached to his Scouting belt. He holds up a penny and blurts out in one stream: 'I've enough for a ride – I mean, only if you want to – I don't know if you two like that sort of thing.'

'We better not,' I tell him. 'It might make Edie sick.'

'Of course,' he says, nodding. 'I should have thought.'

The three of us continue to walk through the fairground, the squeals from the dodgems causing you to laugh, the shudder of the rollercoaster vibrating through the ground.

As we approach the exit, you halt, your fingernails digging into our palms. 'Gob-tin!' you shriek. 'Gob-tin!'

A boy tugs at his dad's sleeve and points at you. 'The Germans had the right idea about some things,' his father mutters.

Vince and I stare at the man long and hard. As ever with the folk who malign you, he is the first to look away.

Neither Vince nor I mention it, and I can't tell whether you've picked up on what's wrong. But you halt again, your fingernails digging harder into our palms. 'Gob-tin!' you shout. 'Gob-tin!' I have no idea what you mean by this or whether it relates somehow to that man and his son.

'What's the matter, Edie?' I ask, as you wrench yourself from our grip, and race towards one of the stalls.

It is Vince who spots the harmonica, its casing as red as a pillar box, its metal mouthpiece polished to a shine; Vince who empties out all the coins from his purse and bargains with the stall-keeper; Vince who understands just what you mean.

*

It was your gob-tin that I'd spotted, peeking out of Vincent Roper's pocket, its pillar-box paint now faded almost to brown. I'd always assumed that it was shut away in the shed, along with the rest of the stuff from our youth. When Vincent Roper saw my gaze stray to your harmonica, he slowly withdrew it, the rust on its metal mouthpiece causing me to feel quite unsteady on my feet.

'What's that?' Len asked Vincent Roper as I sat back down.

'Now you and Steph skedaddle,' I managed. 'If the kitchen's still in a state when Zenka arrives, she'll have your guts for garters.'

'I'm so sorry, Maeve,' tried Vincent Roper once Len and Steph had left. 'I came across it when I was clearing out my house, but I didn't mean for you to see it like that.'

I couldn't take my eyes off Vincent Roper's hand, knowing that it held something that had once been treasured by you. Your favourite word was *gob-tin*; you'd shriek it whenever you set eyes on your harmonica. *Come on, dribble-drawers*, Dad would joke, lifting it to your mouth, and you'd blow and blow until you managed a sound.

But your harmonica had become inseparable for me from Vince's proposal of marriage: the way he'd rubbed its metal casing between his forefinger and thumb while promising to help me at Sea View Lodge, promising to take care of you.

I was proud of Sea View Lodge and our annual visitors – Misfits Comedy, Mencap Musical, Manchester Young Carers – and yet, what a joy it would have been to have welcomed our guests with a man at my side.

'It's not right for it to be in my possession,' Vincent Roper continued. 'It rightfully belongs to you.'

I couldn't bring myself to touch it.

'I've gone about this all wrong, Maeve. I'm sorry.'

I continued to look at your harmonica, snug in Vincent Roper's large palm.

Throughout Frank's illness, I'd often imagined sitting by his bedside, cupping his hand in mine and stroking the scar at the base of his thumb; I'd imagined finally conjuring up the courage to ask why he'd abandoned us.

'I'll pack up the car and get off,' said Vincent Roper.

'That'd be just like you,' I said, 'to swan off.'

Last night I'd instructed him to check-out straight after breakfast; I'd once told him never to return. But I couldn't bear the thought that he might leave now.

CHAPTER THREE

Steph was safely out of the way by the time the social worker arrived. Although Len's mum and I had warned him to keep shtum about his romance, we couldn't trust him to resist throwing his arms around Steph or planting a kiss on her cheek. Social Services might not authorise Len's move into Sea View Lodge if it came out that he and Steph were courting. I'd rather have got Zenka out of the house too, but the social worker had insisted that our manager attend this meeting along with Dot and me.

'Aren't you looking well, Len!' exclaimed the social worker. 'And how are you today?' she asked Dot.

'Steph thinks I'm the most handsome man in the whole wide world!' exclaimed Len, straightening his orange bow tie.

'She's got good taste,' said Zenka, winking at him. She was lucky her eyelashes didn't stick together, the amount of mascara she wore. We used to trade beauty tips, back in the days when she still lived here: I used to paint her nails, persuading her to try some of my more natural shades, and she mixed face packs for me from rose water, honey and oats.

'Would you be a gent,' I asked Len, catching his mum's eye, 'and sprinkle some salt on the front path? We don't want Steph or her dad taking a fall when they get back from the sing-along *Sound of Music* – not to mention our guests.'

'Perhaps Len would like to show me around?' the social worker suggested.

'Do you want to stay in the parlour with us women,' I put in, 'or would you rather do some hard graft outside?'

'I like being outside!'

'Be off with you then!' I said, trying to hide my relief. 'Now, where were we?'

'Bear with me, Maeve, while I fill this in,' said the social worker, glancing up from her forms. 'Then perhaps you can give me the tour.' The impertinence of the woman, calling me *Maeve*. But *Miss Maloney* would have been even less appealing.

An image of Vincent Roper wheedled its way into my mind: his hand drawing your harmonica from his pocket. But he was out of the way, thank God. I couldn't afford to think about him when Len's future here hung in the balance.

'There's only one guest bedroom available to view,' I informed her. 'The other six are occupied.' At least she wouldn't see the damp patch in the corner of the Tulip Room, where I tended to stick the carers, or the single glazing in the bay windows. But I never put sickly types in the front rooms and the velvet curtains kept in the heat.

'This is the Snowdrop Room,' I told her. The towels and bedding all looked pristine as Zenka had bleached them in readiness for the social worker's visit. Zenka had been badgering me to change the name and colour scheme of this room for years.

'Wouldn't it make a lovely living room for Len?' she said. 'What fantastic views.'

'We reserve this room for our wheelchair users,' I told her, nipping that idea in the bud. But we were off to a good start: she'd noticed our tasteful décor and she appreciated the splendour of the bay. 'Take a look at the en-suite,' I encouraged her. 'You'll see it's all kitted out.'

During the inspection, the social worker kept writing things in her notebook. I dare say she was impressed by the parquet flooring, which Zenka had polished to a shine.

I led her up to the first floor, past the Honeysuckle Room, where I'd put the lead singer because he liked to be treated like a VIP and he did genuinely enjoy the view of the sands; past the Marigold Room, where I'd stuck the bass because he tended to snore and it didn't share a wall with our neighbours; past the Lilac Room, where I'd put the chubby chap because it had a partition door onto the Tulip and he often needed assistance from his carer during the night.

I was shepherding the social worker towards the staircase, when she noticed that the door of the Rose Room stood ajar. The tenor was a sensitive fellow, who wore his T-shirt two sizes too small and his cap at an angle that he spent some time perfecting, so he wasn't the sort to mind pink linens.

The social worker just walked straight over and peeped inside. 'Now this would be perfect,' she announced. 'Ideally, Len should have a private sitting room.'

'Our guest deserves some privacy too,' I reminded her.

She looked a bit sheepish at that and began to follow me up the last flight of stairs, which led up to our private quarters in the attic. I pointed out my room and Steph's room, relieved that the social worker was too busy jotting things down to ask to look inside. Back when Steph had moved in, no one had mentioned a personal sitting room.

I'd hazard a guess that the social worker was writing notes about our impeccable standards of cleanliness. She'd have a hard time finding even a speck of dust on our skirting boards. Few young folk like her could make such a claim about their own homes.

When I showed her Zenka's old room that I'd earmarked for Len, she began checking the upholstery for flame retardant labels, and she looked at each of the sockets and appliances for up-to-date PAT testing labels. Thankfully, Zenka had kept on top of all that, and Dave had recently fixed the door handle. Still, the social worker wasn't as complimentary as I'd hoped. No doubt the geometric wallpaper wasn't to her taste.

44

'It's a decent size,' she said in the end.

I just nodded. Least said soonest mended. On our way back down through the house, she asked me detailed questions about our routines. Dot and Zenka and I had already scripted our replies: Len worked on a volunteer basis (we'd agreed on a white lie since the last thing he needed was to get his meagre benefits cut); we'd conducted a risk assessment (I'd insisted that Zenka include a section on bathing); Len and Steph were absolutely, categorically, nothing more than dear old friends.

I kept the lounge until last because I felt sure that the social worker would be impressed by our music and film collection, neatly aligned on the shelves; the arts and craft box, stowed in the corner; the quilts I was working on for the chap from the Coffee Pot's granddaughters, folded across the back of the settee; our Christmas tree, festooned in paper chains and fairy lights and baubles.

It hadn't occurred to me that our guests would be in there because I hadn't heard a peep out of them for hours. But, sure enough, the four band members and their care worker were sitting with Vincent Roper, all of them scouring over some sheet music.

'And who are you?' asked the bass, just as he'd done when Vincent Roper arrived. 'I don't mean to be rude.'

'I'm Jennifer Tait,' said the social worker. 'I'm here to take a look around.'

The care worker beamed up at us: 'It's a treasure of a place,' she said. 'We wouldn't stay anywhere else.'

The lead singer looked a bit puzzled at that: 'We stay at Foxes Hotel in Somerset, and the Imperial in Blackpool.'

'I wasn't terribly impressed by that Travelodge where we stayed during the convention in Southport,' added the tenor.

The chubby chap was rocking back and forth, his hands clenched to his ears. But every now and then he would pick up the pencil and jot down a note on one of the staves.

'Do you enjoy your stays here at Sea View Lodge?'

The social worker's cheek knew no end.

'Oh yes,' the lead singer replied. 'I wasn't so sure about Maeve at first but she's been ever so good to me over the years.'

Vincent Roper caught my eye at that, and I couldn't help but smile.

'It was Maeve who taught me to take deep breaths when I get annoyed,' the tenor put in. 'And she's got a good collection of CDs.'

'I don't mean to interrupt,' said the bass, patting Vincent Roper on the back. 'But this chap here is a bloody good find. I don't mean to be rude.'

It turned out that Vincent Roper had been helping the band to transcribe a barbershop arrangement of 'Last Christmas'.

'This man was a baritone in the Minor Prophets.'

'That was a long time ago now,' said Vincent Roper. 'But it's coming back to me.'

Vince would spend hours in our youth picking out melodies on the piano. We listened to the same music, read the same books, watched the same movies. To think of the time we must have spent huddled over the wireless, tapping our feet to Ray Ellington; poring over his mother's copy of *Madame Bovary*; dangling our toes in the lido; and walking up and down the promenade, debating the relative merits of *Casablanca* and *Citizen Kane*.

Just then the chubby man stopped rocking, picked up the pencil and wrote a series of notes on the sheet music.

'Of course,' said Vincent Roper. 'That's exactly what it needed. We baritones have our uses.' His open face and the lines around his eyes spoke of a man who'd shown enthusiasm and generosity throughout his long life. Yet this same man had walked out of St Mary's without any regard for me.

The chubby band member was back to rocking, his eyes vacant, his hands pressed to his ears, so it was difficult to know whether he took in Vincent Roper's praise.

'You are helpful when it comes to chord progressions,' conceded the lead singer, 'but baritones can hardly claim to be indispensable.'

When the social worker and I closed the door of the lounge, she asked me about the kind of guests we host at Sea View Lodge. I explained about how we'd started to specialise in disabled holidaymakers fifteen years ago when Steph began working here.

We used to take all sorts: the Deaf Choir of Greater Manchester, a wheelchair basketball team, paraplegic windsurfers. But the deaf conductor had been terribly rude to Steph on one occasion and the sports teams never joined in our sing-alongs or attended my craft sessions. I steered clear of the physically disabled now. But I had more sense than to admit this to the likes of Jennifer Tait.

'The lady and elderly gentleman who were accompanying the barbershop band, did you make copies of their police checks?'

I just ushered her towards the parlour, allowing her to assume that Vincent Roper was a visiting carer. Whatever else I might think of the man, I'd trust him better than anyone with the likes of Steph and Len.

When we returned to the parlour, Zenka and Dot were deep in conversation. To her credit, Zenka immediately topped up the teapot and offered us a brew. I hoped that Jennifer Tait noticed the quality of our best china, which I'd got out in her honour.

Dot was looking increasingly drawn, and it didn't help that her new wig made her resemble one of the mannequins in the shopfront at Wood's.

I regretted having snapped at her when she'd phoned me about the social worker's visit: 'I can't have all and sundry popping in at a moment's notice,' I'd said.

But Dot insisted that the social worker had to return.

'Do you not think this is all a bit over the top? Len only potters around the garden.'

47

She went quiet for a moment. 'I thought you enjoyed having him around,' she said, her voice clipped. 'He's done a wonderful job.'

I recognised that tone. Mum had spoken like that to Vincent Roper's father. I'd heard her speak like that at the care committee hearing too, trying to keep both fear and frustration at bay.

Dot's breathing had been laboured and her voice had grown quiet by the time she finally admitted that Len's new flat had fallen through. 'The doctor says that I need to be taking it easier. And it's not really fair on Len.'

I wished then that I hadn't lost my rag.

'It's Len—'

'Of course he can, Dot,' I'd said, not wanting her to have to ask. 'Steph and I would love that.'

'That's why Jennifer Tait's scheduled the inspection tomorrow. It would just be until they've sorted a flat. She's arranged a place at Grove Hill but I can't bear the thought of him stuck in a place like that.'

'Of course.'

'I just need to know that he'll—' I could hear Dot take a deep breath and bring her voice under control. 'That he'll be loved.'

What a rigmarole: social worker's visits and meetings with Len's advocate and endless, endless forms. But there was no way I'd let Jennifer Tait send him to one of those terrible group homes.

As I handed her a cup of tea, I caught sight of a note about the lack of en-suite. How would she have liked a total stranger to intrude into her home, peering into the rooms, jotting things down and finding things wanting? And she couldn't have been more than about twenty-three years of age.

'I better not,' she said, gesturing to the mince pie I was placing on her side plate. 'They were delicious but two's my limit.'

Perhaps she objected to me using my bare hands. She looked like the hay fever, asthma-suffering type who's

48

terrified of germs. She could have been quite pretty with a smile on her face and a bit more flesh on her bones. She could have learnt a thing or two from Dot. Despite being at death's door, Dot still wore her yellow clogs, a multi-coloured smock, and that long string of lime-green beads. A little colour would have given Jennifer Tait quite a lift.

Neither Dot nor the social worker had eaten much, despite my addition of port and fresh cranberries. There had been a time when my baking was rather well-known around here. We used to do a roaring trade with morning coffees and afternoon teas. In the late fifties and early sixties, the promenade was always full of holidaymakers and locals: young men showing their sweethearts where they'd been billeted during the war; families taking a dip in the Super Swimming Stadium, or catching performances of the Black and White Minstrels or Morecambe and Wise; girls in bathing suits parading around the lido in the hope of being elected the next beauty queen.

Dad used to joke that all the single men in town had developed a hankering for afternoon tea. Our Welsh dresser was always piled high with French fancies and strawberry tarts – not to mention our famous coconut macaroons. But I'd called it a day back in the seventies. Hardly anyone sunbathed on the beach by then, even on the hottest of days. It just wasn't right to bake a tray of vanilla slices in the morning only to tip them into the bin at night.

'I'm going to have to go through a few things with you all,' said the social worker, eyeing up the last mince pie as if she might have regretted turning it down. 'I'm afraid some of them are a bit personal.'

'Let's get it over and done with.'

'Please don't take this the wrong way, but obviously this can't be a long-term solution, given your age.'

I'd have thought twice about taking in Len had I remembered it would involve all this. I'd been through it before with Steph. Dave had done his best to care for her after her mum died. But no man could be expected to plait

49

hair, buy sanitary towels and cook three meals per day – let alone a long-haul truck driver. When I'd heard that Social Services had him looking at group homes, I'd had to step in. No goddaughter of mine would move into an institution.

'I'll live to a hundred,' I told Jennifer Tait. 'Don't you worry about that.'

'I'm sure you're right there, but I wouldn't be doing my job if I didn't consider all contingencies.'

I shouldn't have allowed Steph to get so used to having Len around. It's just when life seems full of hope that the rug gets pulled from under your feet.

'You don't foresee any problems with Len and Steph living under one roof?'

'They get on like a house on the fire,' said Zenka.

She was trying to help, but we could have done without her practising her English idioms in front of Jennifer Tait.

'Been best friends since school,' said Dot, scratching at the edge of her wig.

The social worker looked Dot in the eye: 'They *are* just friends, are they?'

Dot hesitated and then glanced at me, so I put in: 'Oh yes, they're just pals.'

'Stranger things have happened,' the social worker laughed to herself, and then she looked back down at her notes and broached the subject of Dot's ill health: how wise she was to get Len sorted before it became too late. Zenka was welling up at the thought of Dot's demise, which threatened to set me off. God alone knows how Dot managed to listen to it all without breaking down. But she explained to the social worker about the provisions she planned to make in her will, and asked about the effects this might have on Len's benefits. I did try to take it all in but, God forgive me, the sound of poor Dot scratching her scalp was driving me round the bend.

'Why don't I let you look through some of these forms,' said the social worker, handing us some bumf about personalised care, 'while I go and chat with Len?'

I made to lead the way, but she said: 'Don't let me put you out.'

As she left the room, she glanced around our parlour. A reviewer from the *Visitor* once snootily referred to Sea View Lodge as *a shrine to yesteryear*, but no one in her right mind would replace Mum's brown goods with glass coffee tables and faux-leather armchairs.

Dot's wig, I couldn't help but notice, now sat somewhat askew. Perhaps she sensed me looking at her because she piped up: 'I can't thank you enough.'

I wanted to tell her about you, Edie, about how Len sometimes reminded me of you. He was made for show business, that boy – what with his announcements and his attempts at singing and his eccentric taste in fashion. Mum and Dad used to say that, all things being equal, you'd have likely set your sights on the stage. Remember when you first learnt to walk, Edie? It was just like you to put it off until there was an audience to watch, the whole congregation proclaiming it a miracle as you dragged one foot in front of the other down the length of St Mary's drive.

'You don't mind do you, love?' asked Dot, lifting her hand to her hair.

Before I had the chance to answer, she was removing her wig. 'That's better,' she said. 'We're all friends here.'

'Next time you come over,' said Zenka, 'I'll bring some chamomile lotion and give you a head massage if you like.'

Dot's poor scalp did look rather sore but I wouldn't let Zenka's shocking pink talons anywhere near me if I were her. I waited for Dot to pull a headscarf from her pocket, but she sat there bare-headed and – God forgive me – the sight of her quite turned me off my food.

'Let's hope that Len isn't making one of his proclamations out there,' she said.

He was probably confiding about his romance or about our cash-in-hand arrangement.

I was trying to keep up with Dot's explanations about executors and trusts and a letter spelling out her intentions, when Len bounded into the room. 'Jenny's getting married!'

The social worker did a double take as she saw Dot's bare scalp, and I quite enjoyed the sight of her caught off-guard.

'Don't mind me,' said Dot, gesturing towards her head and then struggling to stand. 'What wonderful news.'

Len began to thump out what I took to be a wedding march. If Jennifer Tait hadn't been here, I'd have given him a telling off for being so rough with Mum's piano. I could just about make out over the din that Jennifer Tait's fiancé had proposed in the Rotunda Bar at the Midland Hotel. The thought of it made me sick to the stomach.

Dot recounted her own proposal of marriage – apparently Len's late dad had got down on one knee on the top deck of the number 34. And Zenka told us that she and Dave had been sitting on the beach, eating fish and chips out of the packet, the day he professed his undying love.

They probably thought of me as a withered old virgin.

I did try to resist self-pity – it's an ugly affliction, I've always thought. And yet I couldn't help but find it unfair that some women dreaded the affections of their husbands, when I felt sure I'd have made such an accommodating wife. It would have been lovely to be disturbed from frying bacon by Frank's hand at my waist, to be woken by him in the night. But there are women who complain of such things – I've heard them in bus-shelters and tearooms – and marvelled that a woman could grow so familiar with the touch of her man that she might come to find it tiresome.

I sometimes half entertained the thought that I was disabled myself, and that everyone knew it but me. Perhaps this was why I'd ended up a spinster. Certainly folk used to whisper that our family must be degenerate. I never could tell if you knew you were different, Edie. I was never quite sure whether you noticed that people stole glances at you, whether you cared about staying at Sea View Lodge while I went off to school, whether you longed for a sweetheart of your own.

The social worker answered Dot's questions about her beloved (he worked in IT; they'd met through a friend; they'd already lived together for ten years or more; he wanted to honeymoon in the Lakes but she'd persuaded him into the Seychelles). No doubt he was one of those henpecked types who'd make her breakfast in bed at the drop of a hat, or turn down a night in the pub if she claimed to be feeling a bit out of sorts.

'I'll take this,' said Jennifer Tait, her diamond glinting as she picked up my Criminal Records Bureau certificate. I hoped she hadn't noticed my own lack of ring.

'Listen, I'll keep my eyes open for a suitable flat,' she promised, 'but it's wonderful that Len can move into Sea View Lodge for now. I'm really impressed with your set-up – he's clearly so happy here.'

Len straightened his bow tie and stood up from the piano stool. 'It's been a pleasure doing business with you,' he said, beaming and shaking the social worker's hand. But, in a flash, his expression darkened: 'I didn't like Grove Hill.'

I'd never known anyone to move so swiftly from one emotion to another, but he felt things deeply, did Len.

Dot opened her arms and gestured for Len to give her a hug. 'Look at my boy – the live-in gardener at Sea View Lodge. You never need to step inside Grove Hill again.'

'It's going to be fun,' laughed Zenka. 'I'll get to see your smiling face every time I come to work.'

'At Grove Hill,' said Len, blinking hard, 'one man was banging his head against the wall and lights out was at eight thirty. I don't go to bed until eleven.'

Dot had said that the carers stuck the residents in front of the telly and fed them chicken nuggets and frozen peas. When Dot told the manager that Len liked to keep busy, he'd said: *Well, don't send him here.*

'Under the circumstances,' the social worker told us, glancing at Dot sympathetically, 'I'll aim to get back to you by the end of today.'

Amazing what social services could do when there was money to be saved. It had taken over three months to get Steph's move confirmed, despite all the successful overnight trials, the updated police check, not to mention the reams of other paperwork that Dave and I had completed and returned on time.

'Over the next few weeks,' added the social worker, 'I'll sort out additional care. You should be entitled to an hour or so in the morning and evening, Maeve.'

'Over my dead body,' I said. 'I'm not having strangers traipsing in here.'

The social worker raised her eyebrows, and then continued as if I'd not said a word. 'And I'll look into getting you a Disabled Facilities Grant so that you can put up a partition to create a sitting room and install an en-suite. There are reams of forms, I'm afraid, but I'll see what else you're entitled to. We might be waiting some time before a suitable flat comes up.'

As far as I was concerned, Len could call Sea View Lodge home for evermore.

When I led the social worker to the door, she lowered her voice: 'The world needs more people like you.'

There was no one I despised more than do-gooders.

She took hold of my hand. Thank goodness I'd polished my nails this morning. Looking me in the eye, she said: 'Maeve, it really is a wonderful thing you're doing here at Sea View Lodge.'

*

December 5, 1947
Dear Mr and Mrs Maloney,
　　As a result of Beveridge's welfare reforms, my role as Voluntary Visitor will be replaced next year by an

official from the National Assistance Board. She will continue the regular inspections and inform you of any new state benefits to which you might be entitled.

It has been pleasing to see Edith in good spirits and well cared for, and I have always reported back to the Board of Control about your high levels of cleanliness, care and moral fibre. In my experience, it is almost unprecedented for a spastic born with such uncontrolled tongue movements, such tightly furled fists and toes, and such underdeveloped reflexes to develop any speech or mobility. The fact that Edith has learnt to walk and talk – albeit within limits – is testament to your indefatigable attention to her welfare. I could hardly believe my ears last time when she managed to make a sound on the harmonica, not to mention her recitation from 'Night Mail'. *Timid lovers' declarations* – what a wonderful line, and her pronunciation was better than I ever thought possible.

I'm sure that her severe subnormality must cause you daily distress, and that the recent increase in her rages must only add to your burden. One day you may need to consider her removal to the Royal Albert so that you can focus your love on your normal child. In the meantime, however, I will pass on all my reports to the National Assistance Board so that you can be advised accordingly.

I do hope that our paths might cross now and then.
With all good wishes,
Miss Strickland

*

And applications for situations, and timid lovers' declarations. Who do you love the best, Mum or Dad? Who do you love the best, Frank or Vince? Who do you love the best, dancing or singing? Who do you love the best, St Mary's or Sea View

Lodge? My name's Edith Mary Maloney, 31 Marine Road West. What's your name? For where there are two or three gathered together in my name, there am I in the midst of them. Home, James, and don't spare the horses! What noise does a horse make?

*

Dad and I are finally standing at the back of St Mary's, his hand squeezing mine, all eyes on us as we wait for the bridal march to begin. He's clipped his beard and his suit has been dry-cleaned; he smells of Pears soap and talc and Old Spice. In the past few weeks, he's mowed the lawn, repainted the Tulip Room and made a start on sanding the window frames – returning again to the Dad we know. Just this morning, he presented me with a cradle he'd carved himself and half-finished blankets that Mum had been knitting – gifts full of the hopes they continued to cherish despite everything life had thrown at them.

I have to swallow hard because the sight of you threatens to break me. Your hair looks darker, pared so close to the skull, your copper curls discarded. You turn your gaze from Frank and Vince, who are waiting at the altar, and you look me straight in the eye. A grimace furrows across your face, but when you open your mouth to speak your voice cuts through the stillness, each word so clear that you leave no room for doubt: 'What noise does a horse make?'

Dad grips my hand even tighter, and I know that he will be welling up just as I am. Our prayers have paid off: your voice has returned.

The nun beside you catches my eye, and she cannot contain her smile. It is just your style to hold off speaking clearly until you felt sure you could form a whole sentence.

I drag Dad towards you up the aisle – the organist struggling to keep up. We pass Frank's family, and bandmates, and fellow mechanics; girls from my college, and nuns, and parishioners of St Mary's; relatives over from Ireland, and regular guests at Sea View Lodge, and Dad's drinking pals.

When I reach you, I pause to kiss your cheek and whisper in your ear: 'Edith Mary Maloney is the cleverest girl in the seven seas!'

I am glad that you are wearing your peachy silk blouse but, despite the lovely outfit that Mum and I picked out for you all those months ago, you don't quite look like you. Your cropped hair emphasises the crookedness of your teeth, the slight squint in your eyes.

You grab me and ask: 'What noise does a horse make?'

I kiss your hand and then, finally, I coax myself from your grip and let myself take a proper look at Frank. He is wearing high-waisted slacks and patent leather shoes, and I try to push away the thought that he looks faintly ridiculous.

In my ocean-blue dress, I don't suppose that I look much of a bride. Mum was going to make me a gown with a high collar of lace and buttons of pearl. She should be sitting beside you right now, all decked out in her new pillbox hat.

I breathe in the church's smells of damp hymnals, molten wax and fortified wine. We'll all be back at Sea View Lodge tonight, your hair will grow again all copper curls, and I'll get you back to your old self.

'Neigh!' you shout out, grabbing at my dress as Dad and I try to proceed towards Frank. One of the nuns hushes you beneath her breath, whispers, 'Let go,' and tries to still your hands. 'Neigh!' you try again – a tinge of desperation in your voice. 'Let's go!'

As we approach the choir stalls, I see that Mr Roper is shaking his head. He couldn't understand why I insisted you came.

I wonder what Frank sees as he watches me approach in the dress that's hung in the wardrobe until now: the schoolgirl he first kissed on the doorstep of Sea View Lodge? The prospective student whose tummy rumbled as he proposed? The woman who stood in front of him in a bombed-out lot in Liverpool, opening up her heart?

I can't look Vince in the eye, and I don't want to glance over to you. I'll never manage to hold my emotions in check if I let myself dwell on your new-found voice, if I let myself look again at your dark, cropped hair.

As I recite the Penitential Rite, I squeeze shut my eyes and beg for God's forgiveness with greater conviction than I have ever done before. The sacrament of marriage will change everything: I will be Maeve Bryson, Frank will be my husband, we'll all live together in Sea View Lodge, and I will make amends.

Vince's hands shake as he makes the sign of the cross and an odd look passes between him and Frank. At least Vince will leave tomorrow for his conducting post with the military band. I won't have to keep facing him.

Just as Mr Roper makes his way to the lectern to give the first reading, you shout out again: 'Neigh! Horse!'

Vince and Frank both start. Vince holds Frank's gaze, until Frank eventually looks away.

'I can't do this,' Vince says in the end, handing him the rings. 'I can't be part of this.'

And then he turns on his heel, making his way down the aisle, walking slowly at first – his head bowed low as if he were an altar boy sent on an errand – but as he gets further from us his soles tap quicker and harder against the stone floor.

*

Once I'd emptied out this cupboard, everything would be ready for Len. Ever since Zenka had moved in with Steph's dad, I'd used this room for storage. It would be good to have some life in here again, to have Len's bow ties and Bermuda shorts in the wardrobe instead of the tortoiseshell shoes and sheepskin jackets that I hadn't worn for years.

The cupboard was mostly filled with bits and bobs that could go in the bin: half-used toiletries left by guests; out-of-date cough medicine; lavender bags that had lost their scent. But a shoebox full of old Christmas cards stood at the back, which I couldn't quite bring myself to chuck: messages from old friends with news of their marriages and their children, the number of cards dwindling as the years went by.

Strange to hold this box in my hands today, with Vincent Roper just downstairs. I had tied all of his cards with an orange ribbon, each year adding the new one. For the past few decades, he'd sent the official card from the cathedral: images of a stained-glass window; a baby in a manger; a dove holding an olive branch.

I couldn't fathom how he'd kept the faith. Dad and I had simply stopped attending Mass; we never so much as spoke of St Mary's.

I untied the ribbon and began to look back through the cards: as well as festive greetings, there were invitations and the odd note. Some of his words came back to me: his first job offer as an assistant conductor at the Notre Dame Cathedral in Paris (*Visit me. I miss you. I don't know what else to say*); his marriage (*Hélène will be so grateful for a friend over here who speaks French – you'll love each other, I'm sure*); his children's christenings (*We'd be honoured if you'd attend*); the death of his daughter (*Enclosed is a book we compiled of her life – we're sending a copy to all those we love*); the onset of his wife's illness (*I always assumed that I would go first*). But I had no recollection of others: an invitation to his fortieth birthday party; a notification about the death of his father; a message about joining one of his Cathedral coach tours. I would have felt bereft if his cards had stopped although I almost never replied and I hadn't wanted to see him these past fifty years. To think that he had continued to write.

There were letters here as far back as Vince's years in Cambridge: requests for my opinion on his compositions;

a back-and-forth about a libretto I'd written for him; a debate about the best translations of our favourite lines from *Madame Bovary*. I'd forgotten that we'd written to each other so regularly during those years.

I could just imagine you reciting 'Night Mail' at the sight of all these letters:

Clever, stupid, short and long, the typed and the printed and the spelt all wrong. The chatty, the catty, the boring, the adoring, the cold and official and the heart's outpouring.

Frank was never much of a writer. He sent me birthday cards when we were courting but he only ever wrote me one letter – a letter I've memorised word for word.

When a knock sounded at the bedroom door, I assumed that Zenka had come to mither me, or perhaps it was one of the singers wanting to show me his new costume.

'Come in,' I called out. 'It's not locked.'

But it was Vincent Roper who edged open the door. 'Apologies,' he said, 'for disturbing you. Perhaps now would be a good time to talk?'

Sitting there, surrounded by all his letters and cards, I felt as if I were in one of those dreams where everyone is fully clothed except me.

'It all seemed so clear back at home,' he went on, stepping towards me. 'But—'

He must have recognised his Christmas cards, spread out on my lap, because he was pulled up short.

Neither of us spoke for a moment. He caught my eye, and looked at me as if he'd asked a question and was waiting for my reply.

'It's too late to make amends,' I said in the end, thinking of the letter I'd tried again and again to compose to Frank: *Why did you leave?* I'd wanted to ask. *I've come up with so many theories over the years, but only one of them has stuck.*

Vincent Roper sat down beside me on the edge of Len's bed not saying anything for a while. 'I've never forgiven myself for walking out on you.'

The memory of Vince's footsteps echoed through me, the thud of the church door, the rattle of windows, the flicker of the candle flames.

'I still regret the way I behaved back then.'

'I need to get this room cleared before Len arrives with his things,' I said, sitting up straight and sorting the cards back into a pile.

He looked at me, his expression quizzical. 'Of course,' he said. 'Of course.' But he continued to sit beside me, his fingers drumming on the mattress, his body warm beside mine.

I wanted to ask him whether he had loved his wife, but the words stalled on my tongue. Of course he had. This truth would have winded me like a punch to the stomach. Vince would have been even less likely than me to have married someone he did not love. He'd begun his military service the day after my wedding, and then he'd been lauded as a conductor at the Notre Dame. Women would have swarmed around him, no doubt; it would have taken him no time at all to fall in love.

I breathed in deeply. 'I don't understand why you meddled in my affairs,' I managed, finding it easier than I had expected to release these words, these words I'd pent up for so long. 'Frank ended up unhappy.' A lump was forming in my throat so I didn't say out loud the words that had formed in my mind: *I have been so alone*.

'I thought I was protecting you,' he said. 'You could have had your pick of men.'

Frank couldn't have stayed, of course. How could he have trusted me to be a good mother when I'd failed to look after you?

'Did you really think I was that stupid?' I said, trying to read his response to see if it confirmed my suspicions that Frank had never been loyal. But I didn't feel any the wiser. 'You'd been trying to persuade him out of it for months.'

'It wasn't my place to decide, Maeve. I see that now.'

He looked so crestfallen that I fell silent. He too had known his fair share of loss: the untimely death of his little girl, his wife's long illness, his son and grandchildren so far away.

'I'll bet you were a good husband, Vincent,' I heard myself say, the words surprising me perhaps more than him. 'And I know you must have made a wonderful dad.'

He nodded slowly, looking down at his palms.

'Let me help you,' he said in the end.

While I folded my old clothes – which would be destined for Barnardo's if Zenka didn't want them – he filled a black bag with the half-used toiletries, out-of-date medications and the rest of the junk in the cupboard. I caught him glancing now and then at the stack of his cards and letters but we continued to work together in the stillness of Len's new room, neither of us acknowledging them.

CHAPTER FOUR

I resisted the urge to suggest the stair-lift for fear of insulting Dot. If I were ill, there's nothing I'd find worse than folk underestimating me.

Len did more harm than good, trying to steady his mum with one hand and holding his large wooden case in the other, and I made my way slowly behind them in case she lost her balance.

'What have you got there?' Vincent called to Len from the landing. 'Would you show me?'

Len hesitated so I added: 'Your mum's just fine with me.'

As Len headed towards Vincent, Dot gave a nod of appreciation.

The wooden case, it turned out, contained some rare snowdrop bulbs that Len had recently acquired: Heffalump and Wendy's Gold, he said – something odd like that. By the time he'd fumbled with the clasp (which I'm afraid I instructed Vincent to open for him in the end) and had then taken out each bulb to admire (they looked rather scrawny specimens from what I could see), Dot had eventually made it onto the landing.

'My room's on the top floor. It used to be Zenka's room but it's been empty for ages and it's better for it to be used and Steph and Maeve will be glad of a man around the house.' Len said all of this in one breath. He was getting a little over-zealous, trying to manoeuvre Dot onto the next flight of stairs.

'Hold your horses,' I said. 'Let your mum take her time.' The last thing we needed was for Dot to drop down dead, right here in Sea View Lodge.

Poor old Len did look crestfallen. He wasn't daft – he understood why the time had come to leave home.

Fortunately, Steph showed up at just that moment, peeping down over the banister. 'Maeve's going to bake your favourite quiche for dinner,' she told Len.

Good old Steph – that perked Len up.

'Maeve always was a great cook,' said Vincent. 'I still remember that *boeuf bourguignon* you made when I got back from my first term at college.'

We cut up the meat into tiny pieces for you, didn't we Edie, because you never did really learn to chew. Perhaps Vincent was also remembering the way you surprised us all by wolfing down the red wine gravy and mash, and then tucking into second helpings. Your unuttered name felt palpable here on the landing in the space between Vincent and me – Len and Dot and Steph unaware that Sea View Lodge had once been home to twins.

'You're going to have dinner with us, aren't you, Vince?' said Len.

Vincent caught my eye, and I found myself nodding, the stack of his cards and letters looming large in my mind. 'One extra won't be any trouble,' I heard myself say. 'I'm sure the band will appreciate your company.'

Judging by his smile, I could have just offered Vincent the moon.

'Wait till Steph shows you what we've done with your room,' I told Len.

'I'll get out of your way for now,' said Vincent, squeezing past Dot and me – his movements more confident than they had been in our youth.

'Steph's room,' Steph pointed out once we got to the top floor. 'Maeve's room. Bathroom. Len's room.'

They were like big kids, Steph covering Len's eyes with her hands, pecking him on the cheek, and guiding him into his newly decorated room. 'One. Two. Three,' she said before releasing her hands from his face.

'Wow!' He was trying his best to be brave, God love him. But there was a little wobble on his chin, and I could tell that Dot was also fighting back tears.

He did smile when he noticed the framed Blackpool FC poster that Dave had hung, and Mum's statue of the Madonna and child, which I'd placed on his chest of drawers. I knew Len would like it since he was such a stalwart of St Mary's and, this way, it could be out of sight most of the time.

The air still held a trace of Vincent's cologne, its scent of cedar strangely reassuring.

'Can I paint it tangerine like my bedroom at home?' asked Len.

Dad had put up that geometric-patterned wallpaper; I'd helped Mum to choose it. 'We'll see, Len.'

'Look at this, love,' said Dot, pointing to his bedside table where we'd placed a framed photograph of a snowdrop.

'Steph's idea,' announced Steph.

'A Galanthus Primrose Warburg,' said Len. 'See the yellow bit right there?'

Len placed his wooden case on the desk that Zenka had just polished, and he set about fumbling at the clasp. 'I've got something to show you,' and he gestured for Steph to join him. 'I'll keep my bulbs in the potting shed, once I've emptied it out.'

'How many times do I have to tell you?' I snapped. 'That shed is out of bounds.'

You reached into my mind – the length of your fingers, the paleness of your skin – your hands smoothing the embroidered pattern at the hem of your peachy silk blouse. I saw my hands – the veins less prominent then, the skin less freckled – placing your things into Mum's mint-green hatbox: Max Factor lipstick, a tin of beeswax, your hymnal and harmonica.

Dot looked at me as if she'd caught me kicking a puppy. Thank goodness Vincent wasn't around to hear me speak out of turn. He must have snapped at his wife and kids now and then, during all those decades of family life, but it was hard to imagine him losing his temper, this man who'd helped me give Len's room a new lease of life without ever once mentioning the stack of letters and cards from our past.

'I'm sorry, Len,' I said. 'It's just that I keep some very precious things in that shed, and I don't want them disturbed.'

'Remember what Jennifer Tait said about everybody needing their own space?' said Dot.

'We'll see about that!' replied Len, winking at Steph.

Dot hooted with laughter – you wouldn't have thought a woman so frail could make such a sound.

There was still no sign of the social worker and Dot said that there was no answer on her phone, just a message to say that she was either on another call or away from her desk at the moment. What kind of person would keep us waiting, today of all days?

Dot had kept soldiering on for far too long. I should have realised; I should have offered to take in Len months ago. With Christmas coming up, the timing couldn't have been worse.

'Here's your folder,' said Dot, passing it to Len. Then she turned to me: 'You know most of it already, and you can ask me for anything you need, but it might be helpful in the future.'

A future when Dot was dead. And my body wouldn't go on for ever. As Len showed Steph the pictures in his folder, the reality of this dawned. The silence between Dot and me was filled by Len reading the oversized captions: *On Fridays, I go to Funky Feet*; *Jennifer Tait is my social worker*; *I am a founder member of the North West Galanthophile Society*; *I like to eat gammon and chips at Fayre and Square*; *Stephanie Greene is my best friend*.

'They're so happy,' whispered Dot. 'I hope to God it lasts.'

Vincent's marriage had lasted. Even Frank was married till the end, although I'd heard he frequented those places on the Barbary Coast, that he carried on with a barmaid from the Tivoli.

'Steph's lucky to have you as a godmother. We don't see much of Len's,' said Dot. 'Is that what made you cater for the disabled? Being Steph's godmother, I mean.'

I should have told her that it was you who'd given me the idea. I'd pictured Frank and me running Sea View Lodge eventually, you and Dad entertaining the guests with your Irish folk songs and your ballads of the sea. I'd planned one day to take you on the ferry to France, to introduce you to jazz bars, and to feed you *tarte tatin*. But you never did get to take a holiday, did you, Edie? I, too, never made it to France.

Fortunately, Dot got distracted by a bleep from her phone. It was a text message from the social worker to say that she was dealing with an emergency and wouldn't be able to make it.

'Emergency, my foot. She's probably trying on wedding dresses or visiting a reception venue.'

Dot laughed: 'My husband,' she said, under her breath, 'he left not long after Len was born.'

What would Len's life have looked like, if it had been his mum who'd left? It was when something happened to the mother that things tended to go awry.

'Randy as a goat,' she continued. 'Went off with another woman.'

It struck me then that Dot may not have pitied me my spinsterhood, that there were some who'd say that my life had been rich and full.

'He died young,' she whispered. 'Good riddance.' And as she said it, there was something of her old sparkle in her eyes. 'Your husband,' she added. 'When did he pass?'

Her assumption gave me such unexpected pleasure that I half considered fabricating a husband who died a long while back. It was a miracle that Frank made it to seventy-nine, what with the weight he'd gained in middle age, those liquorice cigarettes he smoked till the end of his days.

'Actually, I never did wed,' I admitted.

Dot simply nodded and continued to look at me, and I knew that she was waiting for me to say more. It would have been a kindness to a dying woman to have opened up a little, to have told her about Frank. The words of his note muscled their way to the front of my mind: *Everything's broken and I'd kept kidding myself I could fix it.*

I knew I should share something more with this woman who was entrusting me with her son, but how could I explain about Frank leaving me without also confessing that I had abandoned you? 'Life had other plans for me, I suppose.'

'And what wonderful plans they were,' said Dot, just as Zenka and Dave came through the door with Vincent in tow. He was carrying a couple of bin liners, Zenka was holding a cardboard box and Dave was lugging a trunk.

'You got a lead weight in here, mate?' Dave asked Len.

'You joker,' laughed Len, punching Dave on the shoulder. 'You Shrimps are all the same!'

'You owe me big time, lad,' said Dave, pointing at the Blackpool FC poster. 'Do you know how hard it was for me to hang that bloody picture?'

Dave and Len always greeted each other with banter about their football teams. Vincent was laughing along. 'Isn't it fantastic, the way Morecambe FC's turning things around?'

He'd supported the Shrimps back in our youth, it came back to me now: Vince and Frank heading off to Christie Park on Boxing Day, their red-striped scarves flapping in the wind, the pair of them calling out their goodbyes – Frank all brawn and bravado, Vince all blushing and shy.

'I've got a football signed by every member of Blackpool FC's 2010 squad,' said Len. 'And I've got a home kit and an away one.'

It broke my heart to see Len's worldly belongings crammed into so few containers: not much to show for thirty-two years of life.

'In here, you'll find Len's lamotrigine,' said Dot, opening the trunk. 'He takes one in the morning and two at night.'

They used to prescribe barbiturates, but I heard recently that they didn't do much good, that they could actually make things worse. If only Mum and Dad had lived to learn that.

'And here's the baby monitor,' said Dot. 'He switches it on before he nods off.'

During all the time Len had worked for me, he'd never once had a fit. But I'd sit outside the bathroom when he took a shower, just as I did with Steph; I'd ban him from running a bath.

'You know all about the emergency procedures,' Dot continued. 'God forbid.'

*

We're here now, Edie. All's all right when Mum's here. Can you hear me? Oh, hear us when we cry to Thee, for those in peril on the sea. Can you see me? See Saw Margery Daw. Morning has broken, like the first morning. You're all right, Edie. You're all right now. I'm tired and shattered and exhausticated. We're here now, Edie. All's all right when Mum's here.

*

Edith Maloney's parents have confirmed that her health has not changed significantly since her last assessment, insisting that she does not need a neurology referral, although her tendency to grimace does appear to have increased.

She still wriggles frequently, grins inanely, and cries easily. She dribbles with excitement when spoken to (a source of pride if her exclamations of 'dribble-drawers!' and 'slobber-dobberer!' are anything to go by) and she sings uproariously. Her considerable repertoire consists of Irish rebel songs, Roman Catholic hymns, nursery rhymes and sea shanties. Peculiarly, her singing is far superior to her speech.

The patient's severe subnormality and continued ineducability and unemployability were confirmed by her failure to form a sentence from three given words (although she frequently párrots full sentences and even recites poems from beginning to end), her failure to calculate the number of half crowns in fifteen shillings (although she counts to ten in various languages), and her failure to state the similarities between an apple and a pear (she responded instead by singing 'Oranges and Lemons'). She fails to communicate her basic needs orally (hunger, thirst etc.), yet she chatters almost continuously (often expressing her feelings in an uninhibited manner).

She is, in short, an anomaly.

Parents still refuse to consider her removal.

Signed: Doctor A. Rosenthal, February 24, 1948

*

I am still haunted by that freezing morning when we were thirteen, unaware then that our lives were about to be split in two.

I still remember Dad rousing me from slumber by peeping his head through the door and whispering, 'Try not to wake her.' You'd had one of your funny turns the night before – your limbs like a rag doll, your lips worryingly pale – but if you got an undisturbed night's sleep, you always woke up fine.

My breath forms clouds and the cold air scorches my bare feet. Dad has left a pair of thick socks for me on the end of the bed, along with a padded lumberjack shirt to wear over my pyjamas. I know that in the kitchen I'll find my boots all scraped of mud and wiped clean. Dad is a great one for polishing shoes.

My memory of that particular morning has probably merged with my recollections of all the numerous mornings when Dad and I rose early to collect the eggs: the misting of our breath, the smell of straw, the chattering of my teeth, the warmth of the hens' bodies as they breathed in and out, the sensation of the eggshells solidifying in my palms.

I do remember the snow that day. It was so deep that it reached my knees and I had to hold onto Dad's hand. In my memory, the eggs we collected back then were white and perfectly smooth.

Although Dad tells me that we collect the eggs to give Mum a rare lie-in, she is already in the kitchen by the time we return – her face already made up with crimson lipstick and pencilled brows – stooping to slide a tin loaf into the range.

I couldn't understand why she refused to claim those gifted mornings. But now that I am far older than she was then, I appreciate the delight she took in those sleeping-waking hours. I now see that the weekend egg-collecting mission was more of a treat for Dad and me than it ever was for her.

Mum takes most of the eggs from us, but Dad keeps one aside. 'Let's show Edie,' he says, cupping the egg in my palms.

As we approach the bedroom, we hear a guttural noise inside. It sounds like you and unlike you all at once and, although you've never made this noise before, it instinctively fills me with fear.

As Dad shoves past me to the door, the egg smashes in my hand. Yolk and shell dribble through my fingers.

You lie splayed across the mattress, your limbs juddering, that sound coming from right down in the back of your throat.

As I stand there in the doorway, my hands slimy with egg, I want to reach out to you. I want Mum. I don't know what is happening but I know that I want it to stop.

'Lil!' Dad shouts, his fear heightening mine. 'Lil!'

He is kneeling now by the side of the bed, his hands hovering above your jerking limbs. 'Lil! For God's sake get in here!' His eyes are darting between the doorway and the bedclothes that are twisted around your body.

I stand there, rooted to the spot, egg yolk dripping from my hands to the floor and I realise with horrible clarity that Dad hasn't a clue how to help.

'I'll call for an ambulance,' I say.

'Remember that sermon,' Dad snaps. He is forever quoting from one of Father O'Reilly's homilies even though it was delivered years ago now. Lowering his voice, he adds: 'English doctors are just as bad.'

In the seconds it takes for Mum to reach us, your convulsions have slowed and dribble has seeped into your pillowcase. Dad's expression has softened and I am fighting back tears, hating myself for crying when you are the one who's in pain.

Mum sits on the edge of the bed, her arms enfolding your twitching limbs, her body sheltering yours. There's a part of me that wants to climb in beside you: two chicks, safe and warm.

Your eyelids blink and you grimace as if you have a bitter taste in your mouth.

I was too young to follow the sermon that made such an impression on Dad. But I do remember the tense quality of the hush during Mass that day, the way members of the congregation kept stealing glances at us but afterwards no one met our eyes.

'We're here now, Edie,' Mum whispers, stroking the clammy hair from your face.

You emerge from the seizure – your legs at awkward angles like those of a newborn foal; your knees bony and bruised.

'We're here now,' Mum repeats as your eyes open. 'All's all right when Mum's here.'

*

Excerpt from sermon delivered by Father O'Reilly on Sunday July 27, 1941 at St Mary's Church, Morecambe

My dear parishioners, it is with deep sorrow that I share with you today terrible news of great evil.

Trainloads of the mentally subnormal are being forcibly removed from their clinics on orders from Berlin, taken to a far off place and then brought to their deaths.

The Bishop of Westphalia has risked his own life to share evidence that the most defenceless of our German brethren are being treated like lame horses or cows whose milk has run dry. To tolerate such treatment of the mentally subnormal is to acknowledge that we too retain the right to live only so long as we are considered productive. No man will be safe if some doctor or some committee can declare him *unworthy to live*.

Do not kill, God the Father taught us in the Ten Commandments. If we follow these commandments then we, His children, shall be defended against death and destruction as a hen doth gather her brood beneath her wings.

Oh, most sacred heart of Jesus, grieved to tears at the blindness and iniquities of man, make us all know before it is too late that which belongs to our peace!

May Our Lord bless you and keep you, now and forever,

Amen.

*

Len had a defeated look about him as if he'd got out of bed for the first time after a debilitating disease. It had been awful, watching him say goodbye to his mum. We'd hardly had a word out of him for the rest of the day.

'Why don't you two look after Vincent and the musicians in the lounge?' I suggested.

I couldn't have Vincent thinking that I'd let Sea View Lodge go to the dogs. If only I'd checked that Zenka had plumped the cushions and emptied the wastepaper basket. At least she'd made up a bowl of lamb's lettuce salad and a jug of French dressing, and even baked a crusty baguette. Thank goodness that Dave had found the goat's cheese I'd requested with this week's groceries: Vincent would be surprised that I could still turn my hand to authentic French food.

'Aunty Maeve?' said Steph, and I realised that she was standing in the kitchen doorway. 'Vince has a camera.'

'Good for him.'

'He wants to give a slideshow.'

'Well, go on then. Make yourself comfortable on the sofa with Len.'

'Don't you want to see his slideshow?'

'I can't cook and watch a slideshow all at once now, can I?'

Steph continued to stand there as I layered slices of tomato onto the pastry. 'Vince is your dear old friend,' she said. 'I can cook. You relax.'

Well, this did make me laugh. 'He could be Worzel Gummidge for all I care. I'd still be asking you to stop mithering me.' Imagine the burned fingers and charred pastry that would result from letting Steph loose in the kitchen. 'Listen, it's a very sweet offer, my dear,' I added as I put on my oven gloves, 'but would you please shoo and leave me be?'

She looked so hurt that I added: 'Listen, love, you'll be a much bigger help to me if you'd keep our gentlemen entertained.'

As I said this, I opened the oven door to place the tart on the rack. I was only half concentrating because I was aware that Steph was still loitering. Didn't my oven glove go and catch on the tray, and the metal went and burnt my wrist.

To her credit, as soon as I yelped, Steph switched on the cold tap. Although I was itching to plate up the potato salad, she forced me to stand at the sink, my arm plunged in cold water for a full ten minutes. I had her to thank that the burn didn't scar.

As it happened there really was no need to rush because, when I eventually popped my head around the door to tell them that dinner was served, Len and Vincent were looking at a photograph and were deep in conversation. And the members of Aspy Fella A Cappella were decking themselves out in Father Christmas outfits and proudly donning the bronze medals they'd been awarded at the last convention.

'I'm going to take Steph to a ball,' Len was saying. 'And I'm going to take her on holiday to America – to Las Vegas or Florida or anywhere hot.'

He was a hoot. The ball was a non-starter, let alone a US holiday, for Pete's sake. I'd never attended a dinner dance or been on a trip abroad. Still, it was good he had his pipe dreams: we all needed them, after all.

'I asked Steph out at school but she turned me down. I asked her out again at Funky Feet and she said no. And I asked her again a month ago and this time she said yes!' Len jumped up and put his arm around Steph.

It had been going on all this time under my own nose.

'How many times did you ask Hélène out,' Len enquired of Vincent, 'before she said yes?'

Vincent caught my eye for a moment but I couldn't quite read his expression. 'Back then, I wouldn't have had the brass nerve to keep asking her out if she'd turned me down first time around.' He looked back down at his picture. 'I do admire your tenacity, Len.'

'Steph's your girlfriend, is she?' the bass asked Len. 'I don't mean to be rude. I'd like a girlfriend and all.'

'What about that woman who dances with you at the Thursday Club?' asked the care worker. 'You two seem to get on.'

'She's not really my type,' said the bass. 'I don't mean to be rude. It's just that I tend to go for blondes.'

'You shouldn't talk like that about women,' put in the lead singer, straightening his Santa hat. 'I fell for my girlfriend because we like doing the same kinds of things: every Friday we go up to the Legion and every Saturday we wander around the charity shops and then we have lunch at Wetherspoons. I always have noodles and she always has jacket potato and cheese.'

To think such a distinguished man had to resort to dining in Wetherspoons.

'I couldn't care less about the colour of her hair,' he continued.

'You've been with her for years now, haven't you?' said the care worker.

'I'm a lucky man,' he said, turning to me, his gaze sympathetic. 'You've not had such good fortune, have you, my dear?'

Thankfully, Len put in: 'You were with Hélène for years, weren't you, Vince?'

'Centuries!' piped up the chubby chap before rocking back and forth again.

Although the barbershop band had stayed with us numerous times before, I still marvelled at just how much that chubby lad understood.

'Do you tend to go for brunettes?' asked the bass, pointing at Vincent's picture of Hélène.

For an intelligent man, Vincent couldn't half be thoughtless. What could have possessed him to subject me to images of the perfect life he had led?

But nosiness finally got the better of me and I couldn't help but look at the photograph. Vince was wearing a tuxedo and Hélène wore a ball gown that was slit at the neck and had a bow at the waist. She was as tall as him and didn't look to be wearing heels. She was pretty too, with her pale cheeks, and her long hair loose around her shoulders. They were looking at each other and laughing, and the tips of their fingers touched.

I shouldn't have caved in to curiosity: nothing good ever came of it. The picture couldn't have been taken so very long after Vince walked out of St Mary's and then suggested marrying me himself. It hadn't taken him long to move on.

Life could have been so very different. Frank and I could have taken a trip to Paris; perhaps we would have had children to visit in America; or at least have attended the odd dinner dance.

'How about we make life easy and just have tea in here,' said Vincent.

I would have told him that he'd have to play by my rules if he wanted to stay in Sea View Lodge, but Len was already cheering and telling me that his mum sometimes let him eat tea in front of the telly if he'd been a good lad.

By the time Steph and I had fetched the plates and brought in the yule log for afters, Len was on his hands and knees, fiddling with the camera in an attempt to project photographs onto our television screen. He was doing more harm than good, pulling out leads and jabbing at buttons but Vincent managed to keep his cool and, by some minor miracle, they eventually got the blasted thing to work.

'Press that button would you, when I ask you to?' said Vincent, handing Len his camera, and I couldn't help but notice that he still wore a wedding band on his ring finger.

The first picture was of a middle-aged man. He was crouched on the ground, his arms around two small boys, and they all wore matching football outfits with preposterously large shoulder pads.

'That's Chris. He works in web optimisation and lives in Colorado now. Moved last year – his wife didn't much take to England.'

I stroked the tender skin on my wrist.

'And that's Tyler – he's fourteen. And the younger one is Jesse. He's quite a rascal.'

In between mouthfuls, Vincent instructed Len to scroll through the pictures. One was of a woman who could have been from no other country than America. She had perfectly bobbed blond hair, pearly pink lipstick, unnaturally white teeth and one of those necklaces with a heart hanging on the chain.

'This is absolutely delicious, Maeve,' said Vincent. 'Like a little taste of France.'

There was a touch of condescension in his voice, which brought to mind his father. No doubt Vincent and his family had stayed in chateaux, toured vineyards and picnicked beside fields of sunflowers. Vincent would have taken the kind of holidays that I'd only read about in my travel books. I'd almost learnt my Baedecker's Guide to France by heart during those early years when I still thought that Dad and I might take a holiday. To think that Vincent had now been reduced to a retirement complex, where they no doubt served watery gravy and overcooked joints.

I found myself asking him about his plans for Christmas, whether he'd be off to the States.

'Thought I'd let them spend their first Christmas there alone. Besides, I have to brace myself for long-haul flights these days.'

Aspy Fella A Cappella began singing 'I'm Leaving on a Jet Plane', and Len joined in a tad too raucously for my liking. Dot, no doubt, had introduced him to John Denver.

'They do a good roast turkey at my new place, so I'm told,' added Vincent, attempting to sound cheery.

Perhaps his daughter-in-law had made him feel unwelcome; perhaps he had no option but to eat Christmas dinner with a load of old fogies in a retirement home.

'And I'm off to Bruges in the new year on the cathedral coach tour.'

There'd been a time, not so very long ago, when I would flick through the travel supplements before delivering the newspapers to our guests. I'd dream of dining in canal-side restaurants, coaxing mussels from their shells, dipping frites into garlicky sauce. But surely Vincent didn't really want to tramp alone through frozen streets and sit in icy churches, listening to choral song.

Steph was glued to the screen as Vincent talked us through photograph after photograph of his grandchildren on sledges; his son barbecuing at a pool party; his daughter-in-law sunbathing on their deck. But poor old Len had stopped singing and was staring into space. We'd give Dot a call later on, check the nurse had popped by.

When we got to a picture of Vincent's son riding a motorised lawnmower, Steph said: 'You'd like one of them, wouldn't you, Len?'

Len nodded and began singing again.

Imagine Len on a motorised lawnmower: within a week, he'd have flattened his snowdrops or driven the damned thing into the garden wall.

'I can teach you to play that song, if you like,' Vincent told Len, heading to the keyboard without even asking my permission.

Sing-alongs had always been a weekly ritual at Sea View Lodge. Mum would play with those long fingers of hers, Dad would strum on the banjo, and you and Vince would sing in between blasts on the harmonica. You'd clasp your hands to your ears when I hit the wrong note, and then demand to continue alone.

If there were guests in, Mum would ration Dad to one beer and a whisky, and we'd sing something like 'Greensleeves' or 'Daisy, Daisy' or 'Scarborough Fair'. But if Sea View Lodge was empty, Dad would invite his friends over: red-nosed men with thick beards, men who smelled of pickled eggs and tobacco and ale. And then we'd sing songs like 'Kevin Barry' or 'Drunken Sailor' or 'Danny Boy'.

'God love you, my little Fenians,' Dad would say, and Mum would tut and shake her head: 'They're English roses through and through.' Then Dad would draw us all towards him, and he'd say: 'You're the pulse of my heart, my treasure, my love.'

Once we were courting, Frank joined in our sing-alongs – trying to keep pace with the ale drinking of Dad and his friends. Vince drank with them too but it always seemed to be Frank who became unsteady on his feet, Vince who helped him home.

Tonight Vincent had brought down a bottle of Burgundy, which went rather well with my goat's cheese tart. He'd bought it on his last coach tour, apparently. I could tell he was itching to tell me all about its vintage, that he assumed I knew nothing about wine myself.

Try as he might, Len kept hitting the wrong keys, and he was as tuneless as those deaf choristers who used to stay here. God alone knows what Vincent thought of it, but he always had been a patient soul and Len was a remarkably good showman. Thank goodness he was just bashing away at that old Casio keyboard, that we kept Mum's piano in the parlour. But the way he kept glancing back at Steph as he played, the way he moved his arms in flourishes and then crouched in close to the keys – you'd have sworn he was made for the stage.

'Tell me that you'll wait for me,' he crooned. It was unfortunate that Len had inherited his mother's terrible taste in music. When he got to 'So many times I let you down,' he lifted his head and looked at me, his eyes a little watery.

Frank used to sing beautifully, didn't he, Edie? I could still see the two of you now, practising your duet of 'For Those in Peril on the Sea', you sat on his lap although you were no longer small. 'Edith Mary Maloney,' Dad had said, 'you *are* a tease.'

I found myself joining in with Len's rendition of 'Leaving on a Jet Plane', although I'd always found it a most hideous song. As I sang, I reached into the craft box for some fabric. My conversation the other day with the chap from the Coffee Pot had given me an idea for decorating the quilts I'd sewn for his granddaughters: I would cut out letters and stitch the word *gift* into Diza's blanket and *joy* into Dorra's.

'Do you have Asperger's?' the bass asked. 'Do you want to be part of our band?'

'Steph and me, we have Down's syndrome,' explained Len. 'It means we have an extra chromosome.' Then he edged across the piano stool and patted the seat beside him. Steph hesitated, looking from Len to the tray in her lap and then to me.

'Go on, my love,' I said, looking up from my scissors and fabric.

Steph perched at the end of the stool, her back straight and her palms turned down on her knees.

Len nudged her in the ribs: 'You know the words,' he said.

I'd only ever heard Steph sing tunes from *The Sound of Music* so I was surprised when she joined in. Her mum used to sing this kind of thing when she was laundering our chintz or polishing our parquet – which she did rather better than Zenka. Steph must have picked it up back then. Her limbs relaxed and she seemed unaware of Len looking up from the piano, stealing glances at her. The fact that Len kept hitting the wrong notes didn't throw her off course. Then again, her voice wasn't much more tuneful than his.

Len thumped away at the keyboard in haphazard attempts at tunes, while the band members sang along and Vincent tried to conduct. Len's shade of blond was exactly the colour that Vince's used to be. I tried to imagine Len as an elderly gentleman with a cane, but I couldn't quite picture it. Len panted as he played – his poor heart might give out before he lost the colour from his hair.

'It's our turn now,' said the bass. 'I don't mean to interrupt.'

'We *are* the professionals,' said the tenor, nudging his cap to just the right angle. Had it been anyone else, I'd have spoken to him about wearing a hat indoors.

'Yes, Len,' I said. 'You come over here and help me thread this needle. I've been looking forward to the band all day.'

To my surprise, Vincent sat down beside me on the couch, his body just inches from mine. As the band members sorted themselves out, Vincent leant so close that I could smell the Burgundy on this breath. 'In all my years of conducting,' he whispered, 'it's Edie's voice I remember the best.'

And there it was: your name, which hadn't been uttered in years, here in the lounge of Sea View Lodge. It was such an unexpected relief to hear it that I almost took hold of Vincent's hand. I felt so glad that it had been him who'd said it; so glad that your name had been spoken in the warm voice of our dear old friend.

The lead singer announced that they would kick off with 'Jingle Bells'. I put the quilts aside and joined in with the hand clapping and feet stamping – your name still silently reverberating in the space between Vincent and me.

We were halfway through 'White Christmas' when the hammering started up. That burly chap from next door had chosen very unsociable hours to start on handiwork.

It stopped for a while and then started up again when we were onto 'Rudolph the Red-Nosed Reindeer'. I'd have to speak to our neighbours about this. We couldn't have them banging around at all hours – the band needed a good night's sleep before their performance tomorrow at the Winter Gardens.

CHAPTER FIVE

Len emerged onto the landing at the stroke of noon, wearing his Sunday best: a maroon corduroy suit complete with waistcoat and a new pink-striped dicky bow. Why his mother hadn't nipped his bow tie obsession in the bud, I'd never know.

But he didn't half have a sense of occasion. And quite right too. A first date really was a fine thing.

He was carrying a box wrapped in brown paper, which he'd decorated himself with felt-tipped pictures of what I took to be snowdrops.

The snowdrops in our garden had all looked the same to me, until Len pointed out that the inner petals of the rare ones were spotted yellow, whereas the common variety beneath the sycamores were spotted green. I'd never noticed before that some of our snowdrops had two flowers per stem while others had only one, or that some of their petals pointed outwards while others clasped in.

'You'd better wait in the lounge, young man,' I said. 'Your date will be down shortly.' God alone knows what beautification regimes Zenka was putting Steph through – they'd been ensconced upstairs for hours. Zenka could have made herself much more useful ironing the tablecloths and leaving me to help Steph get ready.

Len gave a little bow and handed me the gift.

'For me?'

He nodded vigorously: 'Well, go on then,' he said. 'Don't just look at it!'

He'd bought me a jigsaw of the West End Pier – couples waltzing in the outdoor dancehall, the sun setting behind the burnt-out shell of the pavilion. He'd left on the Oxfam sticker, which showed he'd forked out twenty-five pence.

Just then, the barbershop band gathered on the landing, all decked out in their Father Christmas stage-wear. Even the carer was wearing a Santa Claus hat and earrings made from baubles.

'Good luck!' I shouted as they piled down the stairs.

Len was grinning up at me. 'Do you like it?' he said, pointing at his gift. 'What do you think?'

'I think you're an absolute gent,' I replied as we followed the band members down through the house.

'It was Mum's idea. She said it would keep you occupied.'

The care worker turned and gave me a knowing smile. At least Vincent wasn't in earshot. The last thing I needed was for him to learn that I was now deemed worthy of pity by Len.

'Listen, love,' I said. 'Why don't you just take Steph to the Clarendon instead? It's much closer.' They'd have to pass Megazone Laser Quest on the way to Fayre and Square – a man was once stabbed there at four o'clock in the afternoon. Not to mention the boarded-up entrance to Frontierland, where lads with baseball caps congregated with girls who scraped their hair into ponytails. 'At the Clarendon, you can get two lots of fish, chips and peas for £10.'

'I don't like peas.'

'You don't have to eat them.'

'And there's a ball pool at Fayre and Square.'

To think they had to resort to a burger and a ball pool, when Morecambe used to offer such rich choice for youngsters. We'd had the Gaumont and the Alhambra and the Winter Gardens to choose from, not to mention the cinemas. The Winter Gardens was always my favourite dancehall: the band played on a stage and the walnut floor was polished to a shine. They even had cut-glass chandeliers.

You would have loved it there, Edie. Vince and I plotted to take you. But Mum and Dad never did let us, insisting that it wasn't worth the risk: perhaps you would have a seizure; perhaps some of the dancers would point and jeer; perhaps we'd get turned away at the door.

The dancehall was ripped out years ago now and replaced by Pleasureland Amusement Arcade. I hated to think of it now: video games and pinball machines and chewing gum stuck to the floor.

Steph appeared at the top of the staircase, all decked out in her usual leggings and baggy top. At least the jumper had some sparkly threads woven into it, but other than that you'd never have guessed she was off on a date. Zenka should have done better than that. Still, at least she hadn't smeared Steph's lips in that orange shade she went in for herself, or tried to load Steph's lashes with that garish blue mascara of hers. Steph's mum had always gone for a natural look, so it came as quite a shock when Dave got together with Zenka.

Like Mum, Trish had been a bathing beauty. Like us, Steph had grown up with stories of processions around the lido, the whole town cheering from the stands. Trish had won the local contest the first year she worked here, and her grandmother and great-grandmother had won it before that. Back in Mum's day, Sea View Lodge had been renowned for the beauty of its staff.

Trish contracted meningitis before she could teach Steph about moisturising and plucking and the like. It's not as if I'd failed to notice the thickness of Steph's eyebrows but I'd thought that the rigmarole would do her more harm than good.

I should have traipsed over to Blackpool to take her shopping in Debenhams, I could see that now; I should have booked her a makeover at a cosmetics counter, just as Mum had done for me.

Zenka peeked over the banister to watch Steph make her way downstairs. Steph brought both feet together on each step, her tongue peeping from her mouth in concentration.

'Oh, wow!' called out Len, hardly blinking as he watched her. 'Look at you!'

I hoped Zenka wouldn't use all this as an excuse to spend more and more time with her. Of course, now that Steph and Len were courting, she'd need some dressy outfits, a haircut, a makeover and cosmetics to boot. But there was no reason why *I* couldn't accompany Steph on a shopping trip. It's not as if Zenka had any cash going spare – she sent half of it to her relatives in Lithuania. Steph, on the other hand, had plenty of money in her piggy bank because her outgoings were so small: a bag of pick-and-mix each week (which Dave likely paid for); a new scrapbook each month; and Morecambe FC memorabilia for Father's Day and Christmas and Dave's birthday.

Zenka caught my eye and scrunched her nose as if to say, *We both love Steph – we are in agreement on this*. And I felt rather ashamed for having resented their time together.

Vincent emerged from the lounge, no doubt disturbed from his newspaper by the hullabaloo.

'We're going on a date,' Len told him.

'A date is a very fine thing,' said Vincent, smiling that expansive smile of his. 'A very fine thing indeed!'

'Steph's all dressed up nice,' said Len, as she continued to make her slow way down the stairs.

'She takes after her godmother,' said Vincent, daring to catch my eye.

I'd taken extra care with my hair today, and I'd dusted my cheeks with rouge. I was wearing my gold bangle and matching necklace.

When Steph reached the bottom of the staircase, Len leant towards her, kissed her and said, 'Hello, sexy!'

'That'll be enough of that, young man,' I couldn't help but chide.

Len asked Steph to give him a twirl and, although she blushed, she did turn around for him.

'You *are* smitten, my dear,' I told Len. It was all very well *oh wowing*, he'd just better not let her down.

*

July 2, 1955
Dear Maeve,

Everything's broken and I'd kept kidding myself I could fix it. I did want to do right by Edie and Mr Maloney too, but I'm not the man you want me to be. Things soured between us a good while back. You must have felt it too. You've changed so much that I no longer recognise you. I shouldn't have let things get this far. Vince was right. I should never have let his dad and Father O'Reilly talk me into the wedding. I just didn't know what to do.

I'm sorry,
Frank

*

Clever, stupid, short and long, the typed and the printed and the spelt all wrong. What's wrong, Edie? All's all right when Vince is here. T'wit-t'woo, I love you true. I like owls. Where's Frank? The chatty, the catty, the boring, the adoring, the cold and official and the heart's outpouring. Where's Frank? Oh, hear us when we cry to Thee, for those in peril on the sea. Edie Maloney sings like a star. Where's Frank? None can bear to think himself forgotten. Begotten son. Sun and moon and star. Edie Maloney sings like a star. Oh, hear us when we cry to Thee. Where's Frank?

*

You let go of mine and Vince's hands, as soon as we get into the church hall, racing straight into the middle of the dance floor, all leggy and knock-kneed, pitching from side to side in your orthopaedic boots as you push past anyone in your path.

The choristers are all dancing in couples – the girls wearing full skirts and capped sleeves, and I feel immediately self-conscious of our matching hand-knit twinsets.

Frank Bryson is at the piano. With his green cardigan and his hair trained into a cowlick, he looks like an American film star. He sings just as well as Vic Damone and he hardly seems to need the sheet music.

'Roar!' you keep shouting and you keep grabbing at people as we pass. Most of them know you so some of them laugh, others say *Roar to you too!*, and others still sheepishly turn away.

Vince and I trail behind you, trying unsuccessfully to prevent you from barging between couples. You elbow the girls out of the way, and then get the boys to dance with you. Everyone takes it in good humour – you are well-known around here and you always have been drawn to warm-spirited folk.

We eventually persuade you to join the queue for food. There are mounds of egg-and-cress sandwiches, and bottles of Vimto, and huge wedges of Victoria sponge.

'I spy with my little eye, something beginning with C,' I whisper.

'Curly hair, curly hair. I love a girl with curly hair!' you chant with just the intonation Mum uses when she rubs in your shampoo.

'Edie's the cleverest girl in the seven seas!' I tell you.

I haven't seen a spread like this since before the war. We all thought things would improve when the amnesty was announced, but you and Mum still pickle eggs, still make mock orange juice from turnips, still serve up trays of carrot fudge.

Cheryl is standing in front of us. She's wearing a polka-dotted dress and the boy she's chatting to can't take his eyes off her newly formed bust.

'What noise does a horse make?' you ask, grabbing Cheryl's hand and muscling in between her and the lad.

Cheryl tells the boy next to her that us girls need some time alone. 'So,' she asks once he's gone, 'who will you dance with?'

I admire her presumption that we can dance with whomever we choose. I can't even bring myself to admit that I have my eye on Frank.

I look out for him every Sunday – but he only shows up if he's singing the solo. On those days, I hardly follow Father O'Reilly's sermon or what we're supposed to be praying for during the bidding prayers. My concentration wanders to the darkness of his hair; the way he wears his shirt sleeves rolled up; his habit of digging Vince in the ribs during the 'Hail Mary'. They are unlikely friends; Frank risking the cane by reading his copy of *Melody Maker* beneath his desk, while Vince pores over sheets of classical music.

Vince has seemed on edge ever since we arrived at the church hall. He keeps glancing at Frank and then at the door. I have to ask him twice whether he'd like a glass of Vimto.

I'm in the middle of pouring you a beaker of milk from your flask, when the music halts and the dancers slowly come to a standstill.

As the choirmaster storms onto the stage, I understand why Vince is tense. Mr Roper claps his hands for silence but it takes a moment for the murmur of conversation to subside.

His face is very, very white and he stands there for an age, saying nothing. When he does finally speak, his voice is unnaturally quiet so that we have to strain to make out what he says: 'Your parents and I have gone to a great deal of trouble to treat you today. Who do you think decorated the hall? Who do you think saved up their coupons? Who carried these crates? And this is how you choose to repay us? By immoral dancing to this unholy racket? Boys from this very parish, boys not much older than you, were losing their lives out in France just a few years ago. You ought to be ashamed of yourselves.'

Frank simply stands and gestures towards the piano. 'It's all yours,' he laughs.

The choirmaster's eyes alight on us all of a sudden, and his expression changes. 'What a great shame,' he says, 'that our newcomers have been witness to such behaviour.' Mr Roper points towards us and everyone turns to look.

I wave in greeting but immediately feel that it's a childish gesture and let my hand fall to my waist.

'My name's Edith Mary Maloney, Sea View Lodge, 31 Marine Road West! Pleased to meet you!' you call out, and I feel thankful that I can stand behind you, holding you still, while all eyes rest on you.

Frank finally looks up, giving me a nod. There's something about his expression, as if he's secretly laughing, which makes me suspect that he's been aware of me watching him, that he's been aware of it for years.

Mr Roper has now taken on a more conciliatory tone. 'Edith Maloney is the newest member of our choir and, as you all know, her twin sister, Maeve, will be accompanying her.'

I am not an official member of the choir – Mr Roper has told me to mouth along because he says that I am the crow to your nightingale.

'Vincent has agreed to help,' says Mr Roper, 'so there's no need for the rest of you to be inconvenienced by Edith's afflictions.'

I want to tell him that you are a lovely singer, that the others should feel privileged to sing alongside you. But everyone's eyes are still on us.

Vince sighs but he also fails to speak up, and you appear oblivious – your attention now on your new harmonica, which you turn over and over in your palm.

'I will expect you all to extend a warm welcome to the twins and to demonstrate the kind of tolerance we've always instilled in you at St Mary's.'

Although they're still looking at us, at least I can avoid their stares by coaxing you to tear your gaze from your harmonica. But you clench onto it even more tightly and raise it to your mouth. You blow and blow, spittle flying, but you fail to make it sing.

Mr Roper turns away from us to take his seat at the piano, and he announces that we will now dance in a style befitting young Catholics. I wipe away your dribble with a hanky, and ready myself to dance with you in the corner while the others career into each other around the room. But Vince insists on dancing with you, thinking he's doing me a favour by letting me join in the ceilidh, and you are already cheering and grabbing his hands, and I can think of no excuse.

Despite myself, I quite enjoy the ceilidh. At least I don't have to speak to anyone and someone else is telling me where to move and who to dance with and what to do with my hands. And even Cheryl begins to look clammy, strands of her hair stuck to her face.

When it comes to my turn to dance with Frank, I notice that his sweat smells like sea salt and smoke, that his hands are large, that he seems to know all the moves.

The music stops and Mr Roper tells us that we'll take a refreshment break. And throughout the announcement, Frank keeps hold of my hands. If it had been Frank who'd suggested a fairground ride earlier, I know I'd have risked you getting dizzy. I couldn't have resisted squeezing beside Frank on the merry-go-round, his thighs pressed up against mine.

'It was good to dance with you,' says Frank, edging me away from the crowd. 'I thought you only spent time with swotty types now!'

He hands me a bottle of pop and tells me about the band he's formed. I pretend this is new to me although Vince has already told me that he's writing their music and has asked if I'll help with the lyrics. Just as I'm trying to think of something interesting to add, Frank's onto this milk bar he likes. I imagine sitting beside him in a booth at Brucciani's, sharing a Knickerbocker Glory and drinking shakes through straws.

Vince approaches, holding your hand, and Cheryl tags along beside you.

'I think Edie's getting a bit tired,' he says.

'Tired and shattered and exhausticated,' you say. You do look pale and your top lip has gone blue, the way it does when you desperately need a nap.

'You going to sing a duet with me one of these days, Edie?' says Frank, giving you a wink, but you just yawn and rub your eyes.

'You ready to head home?' asks Vince, and I know that we really must go because we don't want you having a funny turn.

'I was just about to say to Maeve,' puts in Frank, draping his arm around Cheryl's waist, 'that you and her should join Cheryl and me at the milk bar some time.'

*

I'd taken the opportunity while Len and Steph were out to bring over a batch of coconut macaroons as a housewarming gift for our new neighbours, and I planned to slip into conversation the disturbance caused by their late-night DIY. I stood on their doorstep, laden with the baked goods – not to mention the quilts for the newborn twins, which I'd drop off at the Coffee Pot on my way back.

When our neighbour opened the door, her face didn't show the slightest hint of recognition. And yet she'd waved to Steph and me across the garden fence a couple of times since she moved in. I should have been used to it by now – people were forever greeting us like long lost friends but didn't know me from Adam when they saw me alone.

It had been just the same with you: you befriended the man who drove the ice-cream van; the woman who walked her dog along the beach at sunset; the fishermen who hauled nets of mussels onto the old stone jetty. You had a sixth sense about who to approach and who to avoid. *Hello, Edie!* the warm-spirited folk would call out, *Up to mischief again?* I was just Edie's twin sister – they wouldn't have had a clue of my name.

'I'm from Sea View Lodge,' I told our neighbour. 'I thought it was about time I introduced myself properly.'

She sighed and kept me standing there as she scooped her hair into a clip. I always followed Mum's example, sorting out my hair and make-up as soon as I roused.

'The volume of your music was preventing my kids from getting to sleep last night.' She was one of those pre-Raphaelite types who looked down her nose at me as she talked. 'My husband's working away so I had to bang on the wall.'

'We have a very special band staying at Sea View Lodge this week,' I tried to explain.

'And we're looking forward to their concert,' she put in, 'but perhaps you could ask them to finish their rehearsals at a more appropriate hour?'

'They have Asperger's.'

'I'm aware of that,' she said.

And she begrudged them the occasional sing-along. I could see we'd have a fight on our hands with her. She'd be the type to petition to the council to get us shut down.

'We knew when we purchased the place that there was a B&B next door.'

I could just imagine her on one of those property programmes, throwing around phrases like *family time*, and marvelling at the affordability of Morecambe's large houses with gardens and views of the sea. She'd got rid of all their walls so that the front door opened straight onto an open-plan space that was vast and blindingly bright. I had never seen the like of it before – except on those property shows. All their floorboards were painted white, and all their cupboards and shelves – and even their Christmas decorations – were in a matching duck-egg blue. But, unlike on the telly, their couch was strewn with soft toys; their floor needed a good mop; and their dining table was covered with stacks of papers and books and not one laptop computer but two. Our lounge may not have been updated since Mum's day but everything had its place and we kept it spotlessly clean.

'We haven't complained about the heavy footfall of some of your guests or the snoring that's kept us awake,' our neighbour went on. 'We appreciate there's little you can do about that.'

'Indeed.'

'But the kids are so tired this morning that I've had to keep them off school.'

She was clearly a soft touch, letting her children stay home at the drop of a hat. 'Had you knocked on our door yesterday evening,' I told her, 'this could have been avoided.'

'I couldn't leave the kids,' she snapped.

Just then, her children emerged from the kitchen. The girl was decked out in a princess outfit, but the boy was a mess of curls and twisted dungarees and his face was smeared with baked beans.

The little girl eyed me up. I knew I should do something – not least because their mother's back was to them and she didn't appear to have heard them stir – but I could think of nothing to say: *Are you having a nice day off school?* (but that would get their mother on her hobby-horse again); *Aren't you a pretty girl and big, strong boy!* (but I prided myself on avoiding inanity). I'd just settled on: *And who do we have here?* when the little girl beat me to it. 'Mummy, who is that old lady?'

'Esmé, come and say hello to Mrs...'

I let her stew for a moment before I filled in 'Maloney'.

She didn't need to know about my marital status. Let her assume that I had grown-up children – perhaps that Steph was my granddaughter.

Vincent loved his wife – this knowledge elbowed itself into my mind.

'Is Mrs Maloney our new childminder?' asked the daughter.

My hand felt huge and somehow ridiculous as the little girl offered me her palm.

'I'm Miranda Philpotts, by the way,' explained our neighbour. 'And this is Esmé and Felix.'

I'd tell her that we all need to let our hair down now and again; I'd remind her that they had all been out in their matching Wellington boots throwing snowballs while Len was clearing our drive. It hadn't occurred to us to complain about that disturbance. And no doubt when summer came around, their kids would be splashing in their paddling pool while our guests would want to relax in the garden. I was sure Miranda Philpotts wouldn't want us banging on the fence about that.

'We're exhausted, that's all, what with both of us working full-time.'

I wondered whether Vincent's wife had gone in for women's lib, or whether she'd stayed at home and kept house.

'And the childcare's gone belly up.'

Esmé had snuggled right up to me now. I suspected she was taking it all in.

You used to cuddle me just like that during choir practice, your body plump, your palms cold, your skin smelling of milk and Pears soap.

'I'm just about at the end of my tether.'

She did look rather tired, but the likes of Dot soldiered on without expecting anyone else to dry their tears. And, despite living in a madhouse, I always found ten minutes each day to do my stretches, and another ten to put on my make-up and style my hair. If Miranda was looking for a shoulder to cry on, she'd chosen the wrong person. When life deals a terrible hand, it's best to keep busy. After Mum died, Dad pretty much gave up on household maintenance. One of the sons of Dad's ale-drinking friends was an odd-jobs man, and he was forever offering to help me out free of charge. But I took over the changing of fuses, the oiling of hinges, and the unblocking of drains. Whenever there was a noise in the night, it was always me who investigated.

'Felix, stop that, darling,' she said, as he tugged at her skirt. 'I've landed a big new project, Will's hardly here, and we've been back and forth to the doctor's with Felix's asthma. Sometimes I feel as if I live in that surgery.'

A line from your Certification Report repeated itself in my mind: *Parents did not seek medical intervention on the worsening of Edith Maloney's seizures.* Mum and Dad had lived with that guilt. I'd let them live with it.

Miranda was looking a bit tearful, so in the end I handed her the box of macaroons and said: 'You can feel that you've spread yourself a bit thin.'

She glanced up from her son and opened the box. 'I'm so sorry,' she said then, looking me straight in the eye. 'How selfish of me to moan with everything you have on your plate.'

'I was baking a batch anyway. It was no trouble.'

'We don't know how you do it,' she went on. 'You must have superhuman strength.'

Keeping busy had spared me from running to fat, and Steph had likely saved me from bankruptcy: ever since I'd employed her, disabled holidaymakers had flocked to Sea View Lodge.

And yet something about Miranda's comment, impertinent as it was; and something about the twins' quilts, folded over my arm; and something about the little girl, all soft and warm and holding me firm – something about all of this made me feel suddenly and extraordinarily sad.

CHAPTER SIX

Vincent was waiting for me on my return to Sea View Lodge, his shirtsleeves rolled a few inches higher than his wrists, his jumper draped across his shoulders – a style that no doubt went down well in France but was hardly suited to midwinter in Morecambe. Still, I was rather glad that I'd bothered to wear my button-down dress.

'I popped into the Midland earlier,' he mentioned. 'Isn't it wonderful to see it back to its glory days?'

It had stood derelict for decades and, although I was glad to see it restored, I very much doubted that it could be nearly as grand as it had been in our youth. I hadn't been tempted to take a look inside: trips down memory lane invariably cause more harm than good.

'Since Len and Steph are out on their date, I took the liberty of booking a table for two.'

He'd never been presumptuous in our youth. On our return from that awful ceilidh, Vince's pace had slowed and he'd paused for a moment, catching my eye. It happened so quickly that you probably didn't even notice it, Edie, but it's always remained in my mind. In that split second, as Vince leant towards me, I could almost taste his scents of Vimto and talcum powder and brine. But he just continued to gaze at me, blinking, until I eventually looked away. He turned then and took his leave, you shouting after him: 'Home, James, and don't spare the horses!' Part of me wished that he hadn't hesitated, hadn't tacitly asked me to decide. He took a glance back that night, just at the same time as I took a glance back at him.

Right now, I couldn't bring myself to look him in the eye because I knew he would be disappointed. 'That's kind of you,' I said, 'but I couldn't possibly.' If only he'd suggested the Clarendon or even the Coffee Pot. My button-down dress was quite suited to the Midland, but I hadn't stepped foot in there since before the night of our twenty-first birthday.

I'd seen it all so clearly, the life I was meant to lead: Frank watching as I headed across the lobby of the Midland Hotel; the gimlets we'd drink in the Rotunda Bar; the jazz band that would play as we taught you to jive. But we never did make it to the Midland that night.

'I see,' said Vincent sadly, studying me as if he were trying to read my mind.

'We have some leftover quiche,' I said, remembering the tenderness with which he'd mentioned your name last night, the scent of Burgundy on this breath. 'You could always join me for that.'

Vincent didn't need to be asked twice.

He called to cancel the booking and then followed me into the kitchen. Although I'd never before allowed a guest into the staff quarters, his presence felt strangely right. As I rooted around in the fridge, my mind was filled with the memory of your songs. Vincent got our gingham cloths and matching napkins from the linen cupboard, while I chopped the lettuce and tomatoes and onion, and all the while I knew that your voice lived on in him too. Then he popped into the garden, returning with a sprig of holly to decorate the table. Such presumption would usually have irked, but there was something that almost pleased me about Vincent taking it upon himself to set my kitchen table.

'The two of you sounded so beautiful on the Radio Mass,' I said. 'I can still hear you and Edie singing that duet.' I silently thanked Vincent for returning your name to my tongue. 'Nobody would have guessed that you'd stepped in at the eleventh hour.'

He beamed, looking almost like Len when I praised him for weeding the borders or potting the geraniums.

'Thank you,' he said, sounding rather formal all of a sudden.

The sensation in my stomach felt nauseatingly familiar: a man giving up on me, becoming cold. The son of one of Dad's drinking buddies had tried to court me for years, but he lost interest in the end; when the travelling salesman stopped booking into Sea View Lodge, I realised that I had begun to look forward to his visits although I'd never have admitted it to him; the retired headmaster from Sheffield stopped pursuing me as soon as he found a woman closer to home.

Tomorrow, Vincent would be back in his retirement complex, and I could pretend he'd never come back.

When I looked up from straightening the cutlery and smoothing out the wrinkles in the tablecloths, Vincent was holding out a rectangular-shaped gift.

'I hope you don't mind,' he said, offering me the Christmas present, and it dawned on me that it hadn't been formality but nervousness.

I found myself allowing him to place the gift in my palms and I didn't say *I couldn't possibly* or *It's too much*. What I did find myself saying was: 'Stay for Christmas, Vincent, and I'll open it then.'

And to my surprise, he didn't say *I couldn't possibly* or *It's too much*. What he did say, and without hesitation, was: 'I'd love to, Maeve. Thank you so much.'

*

We are waiting in the lounge for Frank Bryson to arrive.

I am in my Sunday best: a dress with capped sleeves and diagonal stripes and a belt fastened tight at my waist. I am also wearing my new patent leather Mary Janes, which contravene sixth-form regulations. Mum doesn't know that the teachers ban patent leather, whether we are in school or not, on account that it might reflect our knickers. She would never have allowed me to buy them if she'd known.

It is ten minutes past six and I am already beginning to worry that Frank might have forgotten or changed his mind, that I might have got it all wrong. Ever since he stopped courting Cheryl, I've plotted ways to attract his attention: setting my hair, stealing Mum's lipstick, and wandering past his house on my way to and from school.

'Poor Vince,' says Mum, and for a split-second I think that he has told her something, that he really had been about to kiss me that night of the choir social. And I wish she hadn't made me think of Vince – Vince with his moon – face and soft arms and sad blue eyes. But then she adds, 'Poor Gerald.'

Dad looks up from his *Manchester Guardian*. 'She'll just be visiting relatives in France,' he says. 'You know what this town's like for gossip.'

No one has seen Vince's mother for weeks. Some say she couldn't bear the English weather and has returned to her native Paris; others say she hated being a housewife and has rejoined her old opera company; others still swear a former lover's involved; and Vince just tells me, *She'll be back soon* – a questioning tremor in his tone.

You are sitting on Dad's knee, holding your legs out in front of you and distracting him from the newspaper by getting him to admire your new shoes. The doctor decided that you no longer need to wear the orthopaedic boots, so we chose you a pair of patent leather Mary Janes: sage-coloured and flat and a crossbar for added support.

'Don't you and Maeve both look snazzy,' Dad tells you. 'My beautiful waifs and strays.'

Mum re-clips my hair above my ears so that my curls fall around my shoulders, and I sneak glances at the clock, hoping beyond hope that Frank will show up soon.

'What noise does a chicken make?' you ask, bending your arms into wings. 'Ducky-lucky, cocky-locky, chicken-licken,' you call out, and then Mum and Dad and I all join in: 'The sky is falling in!'

Just then, a knock sounds at the door and Dad lifts you off his knee to open it.

'Good evening, young man,' I hear Dad say. 'I believe you'd like to step out with one of my beautiful twins.' He sounds so relieved that it makes me wonder if he too has worried that no one will court me, that mothers will warn their sons of our shoddy genes.

'Yes, sir,' Frank replies. 'That's something I'd like very much indeed.'

'The lad's brought you these,' Dad tells Mum, handing her a bunch of daffodils, as he leads Frank into the lounge.

Frank's tobacco-dark hair looks much more French than Vince's buttery blond, his olive pallor much more Mediterranean than Vince's ruddy cheeks.

Mum just nods in acknowledgement of Frank's gift. 'You'll have her back by nine,' she says. 'How's Vince bearing up?'

I feel myself blushing and I try to catch Frank's eye, but he just answers breezily: 'I'm not sure to be honest. He's been keeping himself to himself.'

You grab Frank's palm and get him to do 'round and round the garden' and then you hold your hands to his waist and push him in circles around the lounge, pretending to be a locomotive – a game you usually play with Dad.

Frank quickly gets the hang of it and he calls out 'choo-choo' and 'chug-chug', stealing glances at me and moving his hands as if they're the wheels.

Dad is laughing and you are beside yourself – all smiles and giggles and shrieks of 'choo-choo'. You drag me onto the back of your train and I find myself laughing and joining in, relieved that Frank likes you and that you like him.

As Frank and I eventually leave, you tug at his arm one last time: 'Edie's snazzy,' you tell him. 'Edie's snazzy. Edith Mary Maloney is the snazziest girl in the seven seas.'

Frank needs me to translate, which surprises me because I hardly ever have problems understanding you anymore. With his eyes on me, I feel aware of my stockings and garter and knickers that might be reflected in my patent leather shoes.

'There's no doubt about it,' Frank replies. 'You and Maeve are pretty snazzy girls.'

'Behave, Maeve!' you laugh, and then you pull tongues at me.

'I'm shocked and appalled!' I joke, as we always do when you are cheeky. Since Mum's not looking, I pull tongues too, which sends you into peals of laughter.

'Edith Maloney sings like a star!' you say, refusing to let go of Frank's arm. 'Edith Maloney sings like a star!'

Frank must have heard you make this same exclamation after your duet with Vince – a duet you should have sung with him. He had shown up late, cracking open the back door of the church just as you and Vince began. He held a cigarette up to his mouth, I remember, feigning the impression that he couldn't give a damn.

Perhaps Mum is also remembering this; perhaps this is why she is tapping her foot against her chair leg as she always does when she's anxious or annoyed.

Anyone could oversleep; Vince's father overreacted. Frank's own band will play gigs at the Gaumont and the Rotunda Bar and the Winter Gardens.

Dad prises your hand from Frank, and then opens the door: 'Be off with you, and remember to be having her back by nine. Her mother's not the kind of woman to cross.'

He is audacious, is Frank. No sooner has the front door closed behind us, and he's taking my face in his hands and drawing me towards him. 'You are a snazzy girl, Maeve Maloney,' he whispers, handing me a box decorated with a bow. Inside sit four chocolates dusted with sugar. He must have been saving up his rations for ages. He bites into one of them, and then places the rest of it into my mouth, the chocolate melting on my tongue. 'I've been meaning to take you out for quite some time.'

I am now a girl whose skin has been touched by a boy. And not just any old bloke, but Frank: this boy who likes tutti-frutti ice cream, who drinks Cumberland ale and wears two-toned leather shoes; this man who'll soon do his duty for our country.

Vince has never stroked my face, or told me I look snazzy, or even held my hand. Vince and I have never stepped out without you, so I don't suppose I've really been on a date before.

There's no doubt that Frank and I are on a date, however, because he's drawing my face even closer now, his chocolaty lips slipping across mine. And I'm not thinking about all the kissing lips we've traded at school because my body seems to know just what to do. Frank Bryson tastes of chocolate, and he smells of liquorice and tobacco and mint, and every inch of me is softening while every inch of him feels hard, and I'd never realised that a kiss could feel like this – this kiss with Frank Bryson on the front step of Sea View Lodge, Mum and Dad just the other side of the door.

As he releases me, I see you standing at the window, peeping through the curtains, and – although I cannot read your expression – when I let Frank take my hand and lead me down the path away from Sea View Lodge, I somehow feel that I have let you down.

*

October 17, 1948

Dear Mr and Mrs Maloney,

Congratulations on Edith's performance on the Radio Mass. She may still have a great deal to learn but you must certainly have already detected a distinct improvement. Her duet with Vincent was a triumph, despite her somewhat tremulous start, which can in no small measure be blamed on the absence of Frank Bryson. No one is irreplaceable, however, as Vincent's performance with Edith demonstrated. I am sure you will be relieved to hear that Frank Bryson's flagrant disregard for my rules and regulations has resulted in his dismissal from the choir.

Sincerely yours,

Gerald Roper, Esq.

PS. Thank you for your kind offer. Given our current difficulties, your hospitality would not go unappreciated. It will be a great relief to know that Vincent will have sustenance and company in the hours between the end of his school day and my return from the office.

*

Vince looks confused as his father hurries him into the drawing room. Mum and Cheryl jump up straightaway, as instructed, and I haul you to your feet. 'Congratulations!' we call out, and you whoop and holler and clap your hands, but you don't say *Congratulations!* although you've been practising all afternoon.

Dad pats Vince on the back. 'Well done, lad,' he says. 'You're a credit to St Mary's.'

Vince looks at me as if I can explain what's going on.

When we received the invitation, I'd imagined a room full of guests; trays of gin and tonic; bowls of trifle and fruit salad and blancmange. But the dining table is only set for seven. It'll feel a bit daft, just us and Cheryl. I hadn't heard that they were courting. Vince goes down in my estimations somehow, yet I had counted Cheryl as my closest friend just a few years ago, and I think no less of Frank for having stepped out with her back then.

'Get one of these down you,' whispers Dad to Mum, reaching for a glass of sherry.

'Joe, really,' says Mum. 'Behave yourself.'

'Behave, Maeve,' you say. 'I'm shocked and appalled!'

Cheryl looks awkward as you reach for her: 'My name's Edith Mary Maloney,' you say. 'Sea View Lodge, 31 Marine Road West. What's your name?'

'You know Cheryl!' I say, as she shakes your hand. 'We see her each week at choir.'

'Cheryl horse!' you exclaim.

Vince and I burst out laughing. You're right: she does look a bit like a horse with her thick chestnut hair, long neck and big brown eyes.

'Cheryl horse!' you say again, since it went down so well the first time.

But Cheryl isn't laughing, so it's a relief when you launch into all your favourite noises and phrases: 'Perfume! Gob-tin! Beeswax! Rub-a-dub-dub three men in a tub! T'wit-t'woo, I love you true! I love owls!'

Cheryl stopped bothering with me at around the same time that Frank asked me out, and then we drifted further apart when she started work and I carried on at school. It's a good job that you are monopolising the conversation because I don't want to pretend that we'll watch a movie at the Palladium some time, that I'll visit her in the market and take her advice on which shade of lipstick to buy from her stall.

'It's not every day a father gets to celebrate his son's offer of a place at Cambridge University,' announces Mr Roper, handing each of us a sherry glass but leaving you empty handed.

'The entrance exam means nothing,' warns Vince, 'unless I pass my A-levels.'

Although we were both presented with shields at prize-giving for the best School Certificate results, I'm also nervous about the A-level exams. I've been getting up before you wake to revise tables of irregular verbs; I've completed timed essays on the French Revolution with you sitting on my knee; I've even warned Frank that I won't be able to see him much during the month or so before my exams. I'm determined to get top marks, even though I don't suppose it matters much to anyone other than me.

'Congratulations!' you blurt out. 'Hip, hip, hooray!'

'Quite right, Edith,' says Mr Roper. 'These new A-levels are just a formality for someone who's already passed the University of Cambridge entrance examination.' Raising his glass, he adds: 'Most boys stay on an extra year to achieve what you've already managed. Now, I'd like to propose a toast.'

'Just a minute, Father. Edie, would you like a drink of milk?'

'Beer, please!' you call out.

Mr Roper does not look amused, but Dad laughs: 'That's my girl!'

'Stop teasing, Edie,' Mum puts in. 'Would you like a drink of milk? Yes or no?'

'Coca-cola and custard! Yuk!'

'Please do fetch her a glass of milk, Vince,' says Mum. 'That would be kind.'

While Vince is off in the kitchen, Mr Roper puts on a record. You plonk yourself down on the floor in your habitual position with your feet either side of your bottom, and you hold your ear up close to the gramophone. It is some kind of orchestral music and you are mesmerised. We never play classical music at Sea View Lodge but you seem to know the piece already because you are pretending to conduct and you're keeping perfect time. Mum seems as if she's half amazed at your skill and half embarrassed by your boisterousness.

Their house doesn't look as if it's seen many parties: the dining chairs are still in their protective covering, the couch bears no sign of ever having been sat on and there's a kind of chill that only sets into Sea View Lodge when a room's been vacant for weeks on end.

If Vince's mother were here, the air would be filled with the smells of shallots and garlic and wine.

I've overheard Dad saying that Vince's mother probably couldn't stand Mr Roper's pontificating; Mum chiding him: *You remember what she was like that time she called into Sea View Lodge.* I used to think that Vince's mother was probably on the stage in Paris, wearing green satin and bowing to encore after encore, but Vince tells me that she has never once called or written. Perhaps Mum is right. Perhaps Mr Roper really is an inspiration.

'Come along now, Edith,' Mr Roper says, as Vince brings in your milk: 'Stand up with the rest of us and calm down.'

Dad leans forwards and I can tell he's furious, but Mum places her hand on his arm and gives him a look that says, *Don't you dare*.

As Vince helps you up, he says, 'Let's not make too big a fuss about this. Anything could happen with the exams.'

'Nonsense!' says his father. 'Nothing will stop you now.' Raising his glass, he says, 'To Vincent!'

'To Vincent!' we all chorus, as Vince blushes and concentrates on clasping your hands to your glass. It was sweet of him to put your milk in a sherry glass, but you would have preferred a beaker.

Mr Roper ushers us all to the dining table, Mum helps him to bring out plates of mackerel and new potatoes and kale, and then Vince de-bones your fish and cuts up your vegetables into bite-size chunks before handing the cutlery to you.

'Tell us about the interview,' says Cheryl.

I feel like a child around her, aware that my hair isn't secured in a ponytail at my crown, my lips aren't painted scarlet, my dress isn't tied in a halter neck. I've always felt ungainly around her but it's worse now that she's working while I'm still at school.

As Vince tells us about having to write a fugue and having to sight-read a choral score, I see Frank and me eating ham sandwiches on the train; Vince meeting us at the platform and taking us to Trinity College; Frank and me wandering through the cloisters hand in hand; Vince playing a huge pipe organ and giving us a tour of high-ceilinged libraries. Best of all, we could attend one of those fairy-lit balls, Frank and me and Vince. Vince will have moved on from Cheryl by then: he'll be courting a gentle kind of girl, but one who knows her own mind; a pretty kind of girl, but one who wouldn't wear make-up or be overly keen on heels.

But I don't suppose Frank will want to spend his leave on lengthy excursions; he'll rather save his money for a deposit on a garage. And once he's finished his national service, our weekends will soon fill up. The band he's formed with his army pals are planning to play at the Alhambra and the Gaumont and the Winter Gardens. There won't be much point traipsing all the way down to Cambridge when we've got all this in our backyard.

The doorbell rings and Mr Roper excuses himself.

You continue to talk: 'What noise does a frog make? Who do you love the best, Peter Pan or the Lost Boys? Never say goodbye because goodbye means going away. Where's Frank? Where's Vince? Vince is right here. My name's Edith Mary Maloney, Sea View Lodge, 31 Marine Road West. What's your name?'

Above your chatter, I'm sure I can hear Frank's voice. But I must be wrong because he hasn't mentioned any upcoming leave from the barracks.

'I make a habit of turning up late,' he jokes, although he was never invited. Mr Roper has never liked Vince being friends with Frank.

'I'm afraid there's been some—'

But Frank doesn't let Mr Roper finish, because he's heading towards us down the hall and saying, 'Here are my snazzy girls!' And he's bending down to kiss both of us, his uniform stiff with the smells of smoke and oil.

'Where's Frank?' you ask.

'I'm right here!'

'Edith Mary Maloney is the snazziest girl in the seven seas!' you shriek.

'I couldn't have put it better myself,' laughs Frank.

Deep down I know I'm just ordinary-looking, that I'm no bathing beauty like Mum, but Frank does make me feel like a starlet when he calls me his snazzy girl.

Although you seem perfectly happy with your appearance, I wish I'd dressed you this evening – made you look your best. You are wearing a loose cotton blouse and slacks, and your hair could have done with a wash.

Vince stands awkwardly, as if he doesn't quite know how to respond to Frank's unexpected arrival, and he doesn't reply when Frank says that he hears congratulations are in order, that he always knew Vince was a first-class swot.

I feel both Frank's and Vince's eyes on me. And I become aware of my freshly washed hair, the ribbon at my waist, the freckles on my arms, and I too can think of nothing to say.

'Perhaps you'd like to sit on the couch while we finish our meal,' Mr Roper tells Frank.

'Don't worry,' laughs Frank, lifting you to your feet, taking your chair, and then sitting you on his knee.

You are beaming and repeating: 'Edith Mary Maloney is the snazziest girl in the seven seas!'; Dad's laughing and saying: 'What a treat, Edie, you weren't expecting to see Frank, were you, my love?'; and Mum's tapping her foot against the leg of her chair.

Mr Roper looks on aghast.

I have to work to avoid Frank's eyes because I know I'll laugh if I let myself look at him. But when I turn my attention to Vince, I detect something sad in his smile.

I feel pleased that Frank has shown up here unannounced, and yet his arrival has also made me feel out of sorts.

Mr Roper tuts and looks as if he's holding a private conversation with himself. But then he seems to remember his role as host. He clears his throat, places his cutlery across his plate, and then says: 'I'm afraid you've rather missed the main course, but I'm sure the ice cream will stretch to an additional bowl.'

'Looks like Edie's had her fill,' says Frank, tucking into the leftover food on your plate. 'I wouldn't like to see it go to waste.'

'Edith Mary Maloney is the snazziest girl in the seven seas!' you say again, grabbing at Mr Roper's sleeve.

'Let go, Edith,' he says, before turning to me. 'Maeve, I hear from Vincent that you are not lacking in intelligence yourself.'

'Let's go!' you interrupt. 'My name's Edith Mary Maloney, Sea View Lodge, 31 Marine Road West. What's your name?'

'What do you intend to do once you've finished school?'

I want to tell him that it wouldn't kill him to acknowledge you. But instead I say that I'll help Mum in the kitchen at Sea View Lodge, that I'll introduce a nightly cocktail hour, and open up the lounge for afternoon teas.

'You shut up!' you squeal. 'Let's go!'

Mum catches Dad's eye, but they follow Mr Roper's lead and pretend not to have heard you.

'You stink!'

You say this with such glee that it is hard not to laugh.

'Maeve listens to the wireless in French,' Dad says. 'She understands every word.'

Mr Roper realises that Dad's finished his drink, so he reaches for the decanter of sherry. But Dad holds up his hand and says, 'Would you be having a whisky over there?' and Mr Roper gets flustered and says, 'Of course, of course. I should have asked.'

'Fifty-fifty whisky and water. Plenty of water,' Dad says, ignoring Mum's disapproving stare. 'The teachers say Maeve's bound to come top of the class,' Dad continues. He has a mischievous look on his face as he says this. I've noticed that he only mentions my achievements to the more pompous guests at Sea View Lodge. He'll drop in the fact that I'm head girl or that I got ninety-eight per cent in my Latin test, and then he'll chuckle to himself as if to say, *There, you see. It hadn't occurred to you that a daughter of mine might be such a clever girl.*

'Have you considered teaching?' Mr Roper hands Dad the glass of whisky, and he's apparently directing this question at him.

I picture myself at the front of a classroom, sticks of chalk in my hand; I imagine leading the prayers at assembly; I see myself on the top deck of a ferry, taking a group of sixth-formers on a trip to France.

I try not to look at Mum and Dad because I don't want them to think that I'd rather be a French teacher than help to run Sea View Lodge; that I'd rather go to college than take you to choir and keep you away from our less friendly guests.

'As it happens,' Mr Roper says, 'I have a few contacts in the profession.' And then he holds forth about a teacher training college in Liverpool, about a friend of Father O'Reilly, about marvellous Sister So-and-So who writes for the *Tablet*, about Catholic education and scholarships, about how he could make a few enquiries on our behalf.

'You've shown us a great deal of kindness over the years,' Mum says and I brace myself for what might come next: *But we'd appreciate it if you'd refrain from planting silly ideas in our daughter's head* or *Please don't meddle in our private affairs.* Mum rarely puts her foot down in public, but when she does she's a sight to behold. 'Of course, it's up to Maeve,' she adds, 'but I suspect she'd appreciate that.'

Dad drains his glass in one swig. He'll be as taken aback by Mum's response as I am.

'You're drunk!' you joke, repeating it to anyone who'll listen.

I hardly say a word as Mr Roper fetches our desserts. Mum would let me go to college in Liverpool; I could make friends with other girls who want to read Georges Sand and watch films by Jacqueline Audry; I might even get to take a ferry to France.

'What do you think of Father's idea?' whispers Vince.

While everyone else is entranced by your chatter, I tell him about trying to get my hands on some novels by Flaubert.

'I found a copy of *Madame Bovary* upstairs,' says Vince, leaning towards me. His shoulders have broadened of late, as if his puppy fat has hardened into muscle. 'Mother had written her name on the inside cover.'

Vince hardly ever mentions his mother these days. Something about the quietness of his voice, or perhaps it's the way he runs his fingers through his thick, blond hair – something makes me feel as if we've just shared a secret, as if he wouldn't speak of his mother to anyone else.

I ask him whether he's heard from her and he tells me that he's none the wiser, that his father now refuses to mention her name. 'We could go to France,' I suggest, 'find your relatives. Maybe they know some more.' I realise then that I am being watched. The intensity of Frank's gaze makes me turn from Vince.

When the others are deep in conversation, Frank whispers in my ear: 'Don't let Mr Roper bully you.'

It surprises me that he doesn't realise how much I've dreamed of large lecture theatres, library ladders and dormitories.

Vince catches droplets of your ice cream with his napkin so that you do not stain your slacks. A doctor once told Mum and Dad that you'd never learn to feed yourself; the Health Visitor told them that it is ten times harder for you to lift a spoon to your mouth.

Once you finally finish, proclaiming the meal *scrumdiddlyumptious!*, Vince wipes your chin clean and you take your time placing your spoon back into the bowl – always so keen to get everything right. I think that's why you waited so long before walking, that's why you tottered at the top of the stairs for months before tackling them from bottom to top – some kindly guests cheering you on from the hall.

'The Maloney twins are rather special, Frank Bryson,' Mr ·
Roper continues, which starts me on a coughing fit. 'Edith is
the finest singer in the choir.'

'I happen to agree with you there,' Frank says.

'And Maeve would do very well at teacher training
college.'

As I'm telling Mr Roper that it'll all depend on my exam
results, I become aware of your breathing. Your hand is
nestled down your slacks; your eyes are closed and you are
sighing contentedly.

I sense that Mum and Dad have noticed too, but they do
not catch my eye.

'What kind of marks do you think I'll need?' I ask to try
to keep Mr Roper from noticing.

Cheryl and Frank share awkward glances.

As Mr Roper talks about percentiles and curves and
educational standards, I coax your hand from your slacks
and then Vince encourages you to sing along to the music as
though nothing untoward has occurred.

Mr Roper continues to speak about the bright future
that lies ahead of me, never letting his gaze stray from
mine.

*

Behave, Maeve! I'm shocked and appalled! Where's your
front bottom? Down, down. That's it! Rub-a-dub-dub three
men in a tub, and who do you think they be? Where's your
front bottom? Hello Maeve! Up to mischief again? What
noise does a pigeon make? Coo-coo-coo-coo-coo-coo.
Down, down, down. Rub-a-dub-dub. Breathe in through
your nose and out through your mouth. That's it. What noise
does a pigeon make? A jug in a bedroom gently shakes.
Warm, warm, warmer. Rub-a-dub-dub. T'wit-t'woo, I
love you true. Rub-a-dub-dub. Coo-coo-coo-coo-coo-coo.
Behave, Maeve!

When the phone rang, Vincent and I were still sitting at the kitchen table although we'd long since finished the last of the quiche. The letters I'd tried to compose to Frank careened through my mind with such force that I almost wondered if Vincent could make out the questions I'd held inside for so long: *Did Frank blame me? Did it start on the night of our birthday? Did he ever have any regrets?*

The phone call released me from the pressure I was putting on myself to ask Vincent the things I now could never ask Frank.

'Sea View Lodge, how may I help you?' I asked – my pen in readiness to jot down a booking.

'Maeve, it's me.'

The sound of Dot's voice startled me. My attention had been so much on Vincent and Frank that I'd let myself forget about Steph and Len. 'What's happened?' I asked, my hand already flicking through my address book for the number of our local police station.

'What's wrong?' I asked. How could I have let them out of my sight? 'Has Len had a fit?'

I was assaulted by an image of your limbs flailing against the bath, your mouth contorted, your face half submerged, your head tapping against the side of the tub.

'Mum!' I'd called out, trying to quell the panic in my voice. 'Dad!'

My arms had felt weak as I pulled your head from the water, your body convulsing and heavy all at once. You fell back beneath the surface for a moment as your head jerked from my grasp. I tried to drag your torso up onto the rim of the tub, but you kept slipping from me.

'It's nothing like that,' she said, but my relief couldn't erase the memory of you fitting in my arms. 'They've popped in here on their way home,' she explained, 'so they won't be back for another hour.'

'We shouldn't take our eyes off them,' I said, the phone cord tightly wound around my finger. 'Mongoloids are too trusting for their own good.'

Before I realised what I'd done, Dot was in hoots of laughter. 'Maeve, love,' she said, 'you can't say that nowadays!'

My cheeks were burning. 'I didn't mean anything by it, Dot,' I said. 'I was just so worried, that's all.' I hoped to God that Vincent hadn't overheard.

Dot was still laughing when she said, 'Just don't go saying it in front of Jenny.'

It took me a moment to realise that she was referring to the social worker. We both went a bit quiet then and I pictured her hand drifting to her bald head.

'You must be finding it a bit quiet this afternoon, without Steph and Len.'

I wanted to tell her that I'd been entertaining a gentleman as it happened, but Vincent was in earshot. In any case, it wouldn't have been right to let on that I had company when her own home must have been feeling so empty over the past few days.

CHAPTER SEVEN

Although there was no answer, I sensed life in Len's room: the whisper of bed linen, the slightest creak of a floorboard, the click of a switch. He's not had a seizure or heart failure; the lad has every right to take forty winks in the afternoon. The social worker had quite thrown me off-guard, calling in on spec at the weekend.

'Len,' I tried. The poor thing had looked so pale when he got back from his mum's. Steph was also exhausted – I'd sent her off for a nap too, just until our new guests checked in. 'Len, my love, the social worker's here to see you.'

'Wait a second!' he called out.

He must have been napping because I could hear him opening his chest of drawers and rifling through his clothes. 'Just a second!' he called out again.

'She can wait, my love. Don't you rush. I'll pop back in ten minutes.'

I headed down to the first floor, rehearsing the responses I'd scripted with Dot: Len did not earn a salary (what was the world coming to, when we had to pretend to be employing slave labour); we never left Len with a guest unattended; we did not enter his room uninvited; he could still attend Funky Feet discotheque, and Mass at St Mary's, and we'd even host the North West Galanthophile's annual meeting. Jennifer Tait wouldn't trip me up.

Classical music was playing in Vincent's room. It felt unfamiliar and yet pleasing for Sea View Lodge to thrum with orchestral song. Perhaps Vincent was sitting in the armchair, his eyes closed, remembering the days when he conducted in Paris; or perhaps he was lying on his back, taking a snooze, his mouth slightly open in sleep. I'd put many a bachelor and widower in the Crocus Room over the years. It didn't have an en-suite but it benefited from the warmth of the fire that we kept stoked in the parlour below, and the yellow cushions and bedding brought some cheer. Even the loneliest of chaps brightened up after a day or two in there. Vincent wouldn't go in for primary colours at home but his place would likely have an air of peace about it: walls lined with alphabetised records; a music stand by the fireplace; an old-fashioned gramophone instead of a flat-screen TV. Lord knows how he coped with the chaos around here.

I knocked on Vincent's door, surprising myself with my own audacity.

He opened it immediately. 'Shall I turn it down?' he asked.

'Not at all. I've been enjoying it.'

He invited me in, gesturing for me to take the armchair, which held his imprint in its seat, while he lowered himself onto the edge of the bed. The carpet in here really was wearing thin and the window frames were a disgrace.

'It's Josquin des Prez,' Vincent explained, 'the great experimenter of the Flemish School.'

Soeur Blandine popped into my mind – the scent of her miniature cigars, the taste of the Pineau that she brought back from her Belgian convent: iced honey and marzipan, its last-minute burn.

'I'm getting in the mood for my trip to Bruges,' he explained.

'There was a time,' I admitted, 'when I dreamed of travelling around Europe: Bruges, Paris, Luxembourg. There was even talk at one time of me teaching for a month or two at a school in the Congo.'

Vincent looked as if there were something that he wanted to say, but he waited for me to go on.

117

'That all went by the wayside, of course, what with Dad and Sea View Lodge. I've barely left Morecambe in years.'

'There's a spare place on the coach, I believe.' He spoke nonchalantly, smiling as if it were easy to extend such an invitation.

I felt almost certain that this *was* an invitation, but perhaps he was just making a statement of fact. For all I knew, he might have a lady friend. He'd no doubt be popular among the widows in his retirement complex and the women who arranged the cathedral flowers.

'These days, I have Len and Steph to think about.' I couldn't quite bring myself to look him in the eye.

'You'd love Bruges,' he said, his tone sympathetic and perhaps also disappointed. 'The canals, the restaurants, the market squares.'

'I was on my way upstairs to fetch Len,' I said, suddenly regretful of having admitted to dreams long dead.

By the time I returned to Len's door, I'd given him at least ten minutes. But he still kept me waiting on the landing until he eventually cracked open his door. 'Jenny's here?' he asked, blinking as if stung by the light.

'I'm afraid so.'

He did make me smile, the way he squeezed out, pulling the door tight shut behind him as if he had the crown jewels in there.

He seemed to wake up a little as we made our way down the stairs. 'Jenny's come to see me?' he asked as if he couldn't quite believe his luck.

'She's decided to grace us with her presence, yes.'

The classical music was still playing. On previous days, Vincent had left for his stroll around now.

Len beamed: 'Jenny's my friend. She's beautiful and kind.'

'She could be Cinderella's ugly sister for all I care.'

The lead singer opened his bedroom door. 'What beautiful music,' he said, his voice all soapy-vowelled as if the accent

118

had been rinsed away. 'Josquin des Prez's "Ave Maria", if I'm not mistaken?'

To think that the highlight of such a man's week was a bowl of noodles in Wetherspoons.

'The Hilliard Ensemble? I must admit, I prefer the Tallis Scholar's recording myself.'

'We're on our way to see Jenny,' said Len. 'Jenny helped me get on the horticulture course.'

'I see.' The lead singer nodded gravely.

'I'm sure Vincent would be delighted to talk with a fellow aficionado,' I told him. 'You'll find him in the Crocus Room.'

As we headed down the last flight of stairs, Len chatted on about Jenny's many virtues. 'She'll understand,' he proclaimed, 'why I need a potting shed.'

'You're not going anywhere near that shed.'

'Gardeners need potting sheds. Mr Hutchinson taught us about it at college and he's a professional horticulturaler.'

'If I hear you mention that shed one more time, you'll be out on your ear—'

Your tin of beeswax, and lipstick, and hymnal strewn across the floor; my teacups, and sherry glasses, and unused bedding. Your hands again, reaching; my fists scrunched to my eyes.

'And don't think I don't mean it,' I added, storming into the kitchen, the echo of my outburst pounding in my mind.

The sight of our shed through our kitchen window brought me up short. Rain was thrashing against its felt roof, which was stained from years and years of sea winds, snow and storms. No doubt everything in the old blue suitcase would now be blistered by damp. The Max Factor lipstick would have melted, the tin of beeswax would be jammed shut and the pages of the hymnal would have warped.

The suitcase was tucked away at the back of the shed behind decades of junk: Dad's banjo with the broken strings; heaps of tarnished tools; hardened paintbrushes; an old fish kettle; lengths of corroded copper piping; sacks and sacks of sand.

'Everything okay?' called out Zenka, popping her head through the door of the utility room.

I inhaled deeply, filling my nostrils with the smell of mince pies: butter and sugar and cranberries. And then I forced myself to focus on the task in hand. 'Nothing for you to worry about,' I told her. As manager, she was only responsible for the day-to-day chores. The last thing we needed was for her to let on to the social worker about Len's date with Steph or, God forbid, the banknotes I gave him each week.

What a thing to have said to Len. Please God, don't let Jennifer Tait have overheard.

I loaded up the tray with Mum's silver coffee pot and her sea-blue cups and saucers, my mince pies as warm as sun-baked sand. Jennifer Tait would think it was the only thing I could bake. I'd have saved a few coconut macaroons, if I'd known she was coming; I'd have given Zenka the afternoon off. I should report Jennifer Tait to her manager for showing up like this at the weekend with her fiancé in tow, ordering tea as if this were an ordinary visit.

Just as I was about to take the tray through to the lounge, the social worker barged into the kitchen. So much for her privacy policies.

'This is a working kitchen,' I said, picking up the tray. 'I'd thank you for stepping back outside.'

'I need to have a word in private, Maeve. Perhaps there's somewhere else we could go?'

'I thought that was you,' said Zenka, emerging from the utility room. 'Good to see you again, Jenny.'

'If you'd like another meeting,' I put in, 'you'll have to write to me well in advance so that we can find a mutually convenient time.' I caught sight of the shed again. Its contents flapped around my mind like a seagull trapped inside: mismatched crockery, unused bedding, ivory-handled cutlery, rose-coloured sherry glasses, black-and-white photographs, my ocean-blue dress, your peachy silk blouse. 'You can't stop by and expect to have a meeting at the drop of a hat.'

Jennifer shot a conspiratorial glance at Zenka as if to say, *What's got into her?* And they both just stood there, staring at me.

'What?' I said in the end.

'Len's just told me something a bit worrying,' explained Jennifer.

Me and my big mouth. I should never have let myself get drawn on the subject of that shed. 'You're a great one to criticise. Where were you on Thursday when Len moved in?'

'That's why I popped in now. I feel awful about not having been here.'

'So you should,' I said. 'I was appalled.'

Although Zenka didn't move from the doorway of the utility room and didn't say a word, I could sense her disapproval: we'd agreed to butter up anyone from social services.

'I agree, Maeve,' said Jennifer Tait. 'We're criminally short-staffed.'

My wrists were aching so I put down the tray. 'Let's get this over and done with.'

'Len just claimed that he's going out with Steph.'

He'd gone and blown it now. 'It's a bit of fun, that's all,' I said, willing Zenka to keep her mouth shut. 'They're just like big kids.'

'You don't think they're—' She hesitated, glancing towards Zenka as if she could help her out. 'Sexually active?'

So she did think that I was a withered old virgin, that Zenka would be better equipped to discuss such things than me. If only Jennifer Tait had seen them return from their date, Len helping Steph to remove her coat, the two of them brimming with stories: the chocolates the waitress gave them for free; the way she let them play in the ball pool after the kiddies had left; the mistletoe that hung in the porch.

121

'Have they been going into each other's rooms?' she persisted.

'The thought wouldn't cross their minds,' I said, aware of Zenka looking at me.

Jennifer Tait stared into the middle distance, sighing and frowning. 'Do you know if Len is fertile?'

'You're barking up the wrong tree.'

'I don't suppose Steph's on the pill?'

I gestured for her to keep her voice down.

'I know Len won't be too keen on this,' she said, almost as if she were talking to herself, 'but we might have to move him to Grove Hill – at least until we've worked out what's going on.'

Zenka gasped. 'You can't!' she said, and I felt grateful that she had spoken up. 'You can't do that.'

Just then, our doorbell rang.

'That'll be our new guests,' I told them, my voice shallow. 'This will have to wait.'

I kept thinking of that poor bloke at Grove Hill who'd been banging his head against the wall while the staff looked on; I kept imagining Len, lying in bed at 8.30pm, unable to sleep while the night-shift carer watched evening TV. My nerves were so jangled that it took me some time to open the front door.

Angela stood behind Caroline's wheelchair in readiness to manoeuvre her sister into the hall.

'Welcome back,' I said, my attempt at cheer coming out as shrill.

Caroline nodded her head, the tendons in her neck straining with effort, drool hanging from her mouth as her face lit up with a smile.

'We made good time,' said Angela, a little out of puff.

I wondered how much longer she'd be able to manage alone.

'We'd expected to hit traffic so near to Christmas.'

They'd come here each year from Liverpool ever since Dad's day. They always followed the same routine: a visit to the Antiques Emporium, a movie at the picture house, Brucciani's for ices and coffee with cream. When Caroline took her afternoon nap, Angela and I would spend an hour or so sewing patches onto a quilt.

Zenka threw her arms around Angela and kissed Caroline on the cheek as if she were greeting long lost friends although she'd only known them for a couple of years. The sisters had grown more alike since they hit middle age. Angela had lost weight and was now almost as thin as Caroline, and they both wore glasses these days, their oversized lenses making them resemble wise old owls. When folk took the time to really look at Caroline, they saw an elegant woman sat in that chair. They were a refined pair, tall and slim, their hair beginning to silver, pashmina shawls arranged around their shoulders. Just the kind of people to appreciate the Snowdrop Room. Lord knows what they thought of Zenka although they seemed genuinely pleased to see her again.

I hoped that Jennifer Tait might shrink off to her fiancé but she just stood there in the kitchen, waiting for us to finish. While Zenka and I were chatting to Angela and Caroline, I kept remembering the crumpled expression on Len's face when he'd told us about Grove Hill; I kept imagining how we'd break it to Dot. She'd no doubt try to put a brave face on it but her fear would show in her eyes and the grip of her hand.

Although Zenka often dealt with check-ins, I felt bereft as she led Angela and Caroline into the Snowdrop Room. Jennifer Tait and I stood in silence for a moment, neither of us knowing where to start. 'It would break Dot's heart,' I said in the end. 'Len would be miserable there.'

It was difficult to tell whether Jennifer Tait was listening. She clearly didn't have a clue what to do for the best.

'It's going to be tough to sort out anything much,' she said in the end, 'with it being Christmas next week.'

So we might get a reprieve, not because she gave two hoots about Len or Dot but because she didn't want to do a scrap of work during her blessed holiday.

'I'm going to have a more detailed chat with Len,' she went on. 'Is Steph around too?'

'You want me to wake her from her afternoon nap?'

'You better had, I'm afraid.'

'What a fuss about nothing.'

'I hope you're right. It's going to be a nightmare to get an appointment at the clinic over Christmas.' She paused again as if she were having second thoughts. 'I've booked annual leave on Monday but maybe I'll pop into the office to consult my manager and file a report.'

All those reams and reams of documents crammed inside that old blue suitcase. 'What is it with you people and reports?'

'I'll call Dot,' she said, keeping her voice calm, 'and you'll have to speak to Steph's dad.'

'What!' My voice ricocheted around the kitchen and my hand slammed against the work surface. If Dave gets a whiff of this, he'll throw Len out of Sea View Lodge himself. 'Mark my words,' I said. 'If you chuck Len into that dump at Grove Hill you'll never forgive yourself.'

*

You are sitting on my lap entertaining yourself by singing 'Morning Has Broken' while I am ensconced in translating a *Le Monde* article on the victory of the Allies, and Vince is concentrating on transposing a piece by Debussy.

'Shall I get the door?' asks Vince, looking up from his sheet music, and it's only then that I register the knock.

'Knock and the door will be opened,' you say as I lift you from my lap.

'Seek and ye shall find,' Vince and I chime.

Mum is in the back garden, airing the Welsh blankets, and Dad is harvesting our plums. The Honeysuckle Room is free so I could always put guests in there.

I'm surprised to find a young woman standing on our doorstep since most of our guests are couples or men travelling alone. The Crocus Room is also free. It's a single but it doesn't have an en-suite. 'Welcome to Sea View Lodge,' I say, stepping aside to let her in. 'How may I help you?'

'You must be Maeve,' she says. 'I'm here to see your mother.'

Mum would never have put on her overalls and tied a handkerchief around her head if she'd remembered she had a visitor – especially one who wears pearls in her ears and a pencil skirt cinched tight at her waist. Perhaps she has something to do with the Bathing Beauty Contest.

As I make my way to the back garden, I let myself imagine that the lady will ask Mum to enter me for Miss Morecambe. I am rather proud of my bust but the girls who parade around the lido have much slimmer thighs than mine. Surely the lady didn't seriously think that I could inherit Mum's title.

'Who is it, my love?' asks Mum, and I realise that I forgot to ask our visitor's name. 'I'll find out soon enough,' she says, lowering her voice so that Dad can't hear. He's very particular about who we let through the front door.

'Vince is with Edie,' I tell her because I know that this is what she's about to ask.

As we make our way inside, Mum removes her headscarf and fixes her hair. Instead of sitting back down at the kitchen table with you and Vince, out of curiosity, I follow Mum all the way into the hall.

'Miss Beechwood,' says the lady, extending her hand, 'from the National Assistance Board.'

'Mrs Maloney,' replies Mum, her voice clipped.

'We've been trying to contact you for some time.'

Mum moves ever so slightly, her body blocking the kitchen door. Perhaps the brown envelopes in the bureau contain correspondence from the National Assistance Board. A few times recently, I've wandered into the parlour to find Mum staring at official-looking letters, Dad telling her to throw them away.

'Please excuse me,' Mum says, gesturing to her overalls. 'You've caught us at rather an inconvenient time.'

'The Voluntary Visitor passed on your notes,' says Miss Beechwood, then she lowers her voice: 'I understand that your daughter is *severely subnormal*.'

I hardly dare breathe, aware that Mum will send me away the moment she remembers I'm here.

'I just need to meet her to make an assessment. I won't take much of your time.'

Mum says nothing, and I can tell that she's battling between her instinctual politeness and a desire to get rid of Miss Beechwood.

'You might be entitled to welfare payments.'

'I see,' says Mum, her arms remaining folded across her chest.

Since the war ended, I've often overheard Mum and Dad worrying over bills and complaining that we have fewer guests now that the civil servants have moved back from Morecambe to Whitehall.

'Mrs Maloney,' laughs Miss Beechwood, breaking into a smile. 'I'm here to help.'

It is me who steps aside, me who says, 'Edie's just through here.'

In the kitchen, we find Vince cutting up your potato scone into bite-sized pieces while you drink from your beaker, a droplet of milk dribbling down your chin.

The sound of Miss Beechwood's sigh tells me that I should have trusted Mum; I should never have stepped aside. 'How miserable,' Miss Beechwood whispers.

Vince catches my eye and frowns.

You put down your beaker and reach for her hand. 'My name's Edith Mary Maloney,' you say, ignoring Miss Beechwood's hesitation and grabbing her palm, 'Sea View Lodge, 31 Marine Road West. What's your name?'

Miss Beechwood looks panic-stricken as you continue to shake her hand.

'Let go, Edie,' says Mum, working your grip loose, 'there's a good girl.'

'Let's go!' you exclaim. 'Let's go!'

'You are clearly worthy of our assistance,' Miss Beechwood tells Mum. 'You don't have to shoulder this burden alone.'

'A pot of tea please, Maeve,' says Mum, a steely quality to her voice. 'We'll be in the parlour.'

I get out the tea tray, keeping my back to you and Vince as if you might tell from my eyes that it was me who'd led Miss Beechwood into the kitchen.

As I pour the boiling water into the pot, Vince says: 'I'd be tempted to chuck it over her.'

The shock of his words almost causes me to spill the hot water, and he looks rather surprised at his own aggression. But when Dad comes in from the garden, he doesn't seem to register the atmosphere in here. His basket full of bruise-coloured plums, and I wonder whether Vince is imagining his mother at a stove in France, stirring a pan full of sugar and fruit.

'I could murder a cuppa,' Dad says. 'Pour one for me, would you?' He passes me a ripe plum. 'You're the pulse of my heart, so you are, my treasure, my love.'

I fetch another of Mum's best cups and saucers, adding them to the tray.

'What's the occasion?'

When I tell him that we've received a visit from the National Assistance Board, he storms out of the kitchen.

I follow him, the tea tray heavy in my arms. When we get to the closed door of the parlour, we overhear Miss Beechwood asking Mum whether you are menstruating yet.

I've used rags for a few years now but your breasts are only just beginning to swell, your armpits have only recently become covered in down.

'When the time comes,' says Miss Beechwood, 'I can help you get everything arranged.'

Perhaps Mum won't be so cross with me if the welfare state provides us with a lifetime's supply of rags; perhaps you'll be eligible for benefits once you're no longer considered a child.

'It's miraculous really. It prevents so much harm and they're in and out overnight.'

'I'll tell you what's miraculous,' says Dad, slamming open the door, 'that my wife is giving you the time of day.'

'I beg your pardon,' says Miss Beechwood.

'Joe,' warns Mum. 'Miss Beechwood is from the National Assistance Board.'

'And she can bleeding well feck off back there.'

I stifle a laugh and I expect to see Mum fight off a smile as she usually does when Dad says the things that she's too polite to utter. But she looks as though she might burst into tears.

'I'm here to help,' says Miss Beechwood. 'I was just telling your wife that you might be entitled to one of Beveridge's welfare payments.'

'Do you think we don't read the newspapers?' says Dad. 'Do you think we don't know about Beveridge and his eugenics meetings? First you'll have your state registers and your operations—'

'I understand that you are Roman Catholic,' puts in Miss Beechwood, lowering her voice just as she'd done to say *severely subnormal*. 'I appreciate the Irish have different views on such matters.'

'You'd be as bad as the Germans,' yells Dad, 'given half the chance. You should be ashamed of yourself, treating human beings like lame horses.'

*

Edith Maloney's late onset of puberty has not significantly affected her health. Her parents have confirmed that her seizures have increased in neither frequency nor duration.

She has now started to menstruate, and is beginning to display inappropriately sexual behaviour, but her Roman Catholic parents vehemently oppose any suggestion of sterilisation.

Signed: Doctor P. R. Samuel, September 19, 1951

*

There, there, Edie. Be a good girl. We don't want you having another of your funny turns. Turn around, Edie. Wave bye-bye. Shave his belly with a rusty razor. What noise does a razor make? Put him in the bilge and make him drink it. Vimto and custard! Yuk! Deep breaths now, Edie. Hush now, baby. When the bough breaks, the cradle will fall. All's all right, Edie. You'll be right as rain. It's raining, it's pouring, the old man is snoring, he went to bed and cracked his head and couldn't get up in the morning. Morning has broken. You've woken now, Edie. We're here. You're coming round.

*

Vincent dropped his newspaper as I crashed into his room. 'They're gone,' I managed, grabbing onto the dressing table and knocking over his shaving brush. 'Len and Steph – they're gone.'

'What?' he asked, placing his hands on my arms.

'They've taken their suitcases and most of their clothes,' I said, meeting his eye. 'Steph's scrapbooks have gone, and Len's case of bulbs.'

My trembling gradually stilled beneath Vincent's touch like wrinkles smoothed from bed linen.

'That damned social worker's to blame,' I told him. 'She found out about Len and Steph.' Even as I spoke, part of me knew that *I* must take some responsibility for driving them away. I had lost my temper with Len, told him he'd be out on his ear if he mentioned the potting shed one more time. But I didn't share this with Vincent because a memory niggled at the edges of my mind: standing with Frank in a bombed-out lot in Liverpool, my blouse in need of rearranging, a football deflating in the gutter, my confession resounding in the silence between us.

'My God, the sinking sands.' My skin crawled with the sensation of my recurring nightmare: the quicksand sucking me under, filling my mouth and nose and eyes.

'Len and Steph have more sense than to venture out onto the sands.'

'I need to call the coast guard.'

'Let's think this through. Could they have gone to Steph's dad's?'

'A woman had to be rescued just a few days ago.' My voice sounded thin, as if I were short of air. 'She was only out by the clock tower.' I batted off Vincent's hands and searched the room, frantic, banging into the chest of drawers and upturning the jar of coffee. 'Your phone, Vincent. Give me your phone.'

He took his mobile from the inside pocket of his sports jacket. 'Think about it,' he said as he handed it to me.

The firmness of his tone pulled me up short.

'They wouldn't have taken their suitcases to go out onto the sands.' And then something dawned on him: 'Anyway, the tide's been in for hours.'

Through the rain-smeared window, I could see that the tide was high and there wasn't a soul on the promenade for as far as the eye could see.

'Perhaps you should give Steph's dad a call in case they've shown up there?'

I couldn't face the idea of admitting to Dave that I'd neglected to keep an eye on Steph; that the social worker was insisting on an appointment at the sexual health clinic; that I'd gone and upset poor Len. 'Dave's on one of his long-haul deliveries. There's no point worrying him.' How could I ever have countenanced taking in Len and Steph, after my neglect of you?

They couldn't have got far in this weather. Someone would have spotted two Mongoloids hauling suitcases along the prom. There'd be a perfectly reasonable explanation. Later on, we'd all gather around the piano, laughing about our scare. 'They might have ducked into the Coffee Pot to shelter from the rain. Would you stay here in case the singers return?'

'They're perfectly capable of looking after themselves,' said Vincent, pulling on his jacket. 'And isn't Zenka downstairs?'

'Whatever you do, don't go mentioning this to her.'

Neither of us spoke as he followed me out of his room and down through Sea View Lodge.

As I opened the front door, I found myself gripping onto Vincent's arm to brace myself against the wind.

'You stay here,' he said. 'And I'll bring my car to your front gate.'

Not so very long ago, I would have argued that we could just as well go in mine. But I almost crashed into a van, six months or so back, when I was trying to reverse onto Marine Road West. To my shame, I hadn't been behind the wheel again since.

As Vincent ploughed his way down our front path, his head bowed to the rain, I forced myself to think systematically about the places where Len and Steph might be: perhaps we'd find them in the Coffee Pot, tucking into large plates of steak-and-kidney pie or bowls of chicken korma; or maybe they were playing in the ball pool at Fayre and Square; or they might have gone to the market to see some of Dot's friends. Len wasn't the type to hold grudges. He'd have forgotten what he'd been upset about by now. I'd give him my word, as soon as we found them, that he could go off to B&Q with Dave and choose a brand-new potting shed.

As I battled down the front path, Vincent got out of the car to hold open the passenger door.

'The Coffee Pot is just up there,' I said, as soon as he got behind the wheel.

Hardly any other fools were venturing out in this storm so Vincent had no problem pulling out onto Marine Road West. Please God let them have taken shelter.

'That's it, just here,' I said, opening the door before he had quite drawn the car to a halt.

'Careful,' he cautioned, but I was already clambering onto the kerb.

I had to grip onto the railing as I hobbled down the steps into the Coffee Pot. My knees had been aching ever since I chased Vincent halfway across town.

As I opened the door to the café, the smells of onion gravy and mash made me feel confident that I'd find the pair of them here.

'What brings you out on a day like today?' asked the owner, who was standing behind the counter, rocking his granddaughters in their twin buggy.

'You'll catch the death of cold out there,' added his wife, tucking my quilts around the babies' tiny limbs.

Although I only popped in once or twice a year, the owners always treated me like a long lost friend.

'Let me get you a nice cup of tea,' she said.

'You're not to leave until that rain packs in,' he added.

'Have you seen Len and Steph?' I asked, before he got onto the lack of visitors down this end of town, and the effect of the weather on trade. We had the same conversation each time and yet the Coffee Pot was always full of builders eating full English breakfasts, and elderly couples taking advantage of the OAP deal. I already knew that Len and Steph weren't here but I scoured the room as if they might just appear.

'Len was in a week or so ago, visiting the babies and chatting up the wife. He's an awful charmer, that one.'

'If they come in later, can you give me a call?' I asked, grabbing a pen from the counter and writing my number on a napkin. My handwriting looked so wobbly that it could have been written by Len or Steph themselves.

I tried not to betray my panic – we didn't want all and sundry nosing into our affairs – but I clearly failed because he was all for joining me on my search. 'My daughter's in the kitchen and the wife can cover here.'

'There's nothing to worry about,' I insisted, turning on my heel, the lack of conviction clear in my tone.

As I got back outside, I found Vincent making his way down the steps to the Coffee Pot, and offering me his hand.

'You'll be more use to me if you stay in your car and keep the engine running,' I said, although the firmness of his grip was reassuring.

He continued to stand there, getting drenched: 'Dare I say it, Maeve, but you will be more useful to Steph and Len if you avoid breaking your leg on these steps.'

Talk about the blind leading the blind: Vincent with his stick and me with my sore knees. But I let him continue to take me by the hand. The roughness of his palm surprised me – this kind of hand had lopped off overhanging branches, changed tyres, and sanded window frames.

'Do you think they might have gone to visit Dot?' he asked as he helped me up the stairs.

The last thing Dot needed was for Len and Steph to show up at her sickbed, announcing that they'd run away from Sea View Lodge. Surely she would have called. 'Let's try some of their favourite spots on the seafront before we venture further afield.'

I had Vincent pull up to the kerb every few hundred yards, and he insisted on getting out with me each time: the waitress at Fayre and Square was overcome with emotion about Len's first date; some of the market stall-keepers welled up at mention of Dot's lad; the Hell's Angels in the Tivoli, who helped to run Funky Feet, offered to ride around town; and that pipsqueak of a manager at Gala Bingo just smirked and shook his head.

At every stop, I could feel Vincent's disapproval growing. We were sitting in Gala Bingo's deserted car park when he eventually said: 'Dot and Dave are their parents. They have a right to know.'

'Just let me think.' I closed my eyes and pressed my hands to my forehead as if I could work out their whereabouts by sheer force of will. 'It'll come to me.' I couldn't begin to imagine how I could possibly broach any of this with Dot or Dave.

We sat there in silence for several moments, the rain lashing against the windscreen, the wind battering at Vincent's car.

The Gala Bingo stood where the Gaumont used to be. Frank and I used to dance there now and then to make a change from the Winter Gardens. You would have loved the old dancehalls; I should have fought harder to bring you along.

I pressed my hands more firmly into my temples. They could have checked into a guest house. Steph had a full piggy bank and Len kept a stash of money under his bed. Between them they could probably come up with enough for a night or two in one of Morecambe's cheaper boarding houses. Lord knows where to start.

Vincent was drumming his fingers against the walnut dashboard and he was looking into the middle distance at the twilight that was creeping towards us across the bay. 'I don't mean to be alarmist, Maeve. But it might not hurt to inform the police.'

'The police!' My voice cut through the hum of the heater, its force causing Vincent to start. 'It's all very well for the likes of you to show up here, suggesting I call the police. Next you'll want me to get that social worker involved.' My words came to an abrupt halt, but I could still feel the pounding of my heart.

Vincent cleared his throat. 'Would that be such a terrible idea?'

'If you're going to make stupid remarks, you might as well leave me to look for them alone.'

Your certification report flooded into the silence that followed: *Parents did not seek medical intervention on the advent of Edith Maloney's seizures.*

'That social worker wants to throw Len out of Sea View Lodge,' I explained.

I could still see the young doctor examining you, registering your crooked teeth but failing to notice the length of your lashes.

'Wants to stick him in some place that sounds worse than a kennel.'

'Throw him out?' Vincent looked confused.

The well-to-do had no idea about the battles fought by the likes of our family just to stay together. No wonder Mum and Dad had tried to keep you away from medics.

'She's gone and booked them an appointment at the family planning clinic and she's insisting I tell Steph's dad.'

'I've got it!' exclaimed Vincent, immediately shunting his car into gear. 'They'll definitely be at Dot's house,' he claimed, as he swung out onto Lord Street. 'You'll have to direct me.'

I was still reluctant to risk upsetting Dot, but he sounded so confident that it had to be worth a try. As I instructed him to turn left at the police station, and then guided him through the back streets, he told me that Len had forgotten something at his mum's place, something that he needed before Christmas Eve.

Most of the houses in this area went to town on decorations: illuminated reindeer, plastic icicles and artificial trees. If it weren't for Steph and Len and our guests, I wouldn't get out the tinsel until Christmas Eve. Yet I felt surprisingly moved by the effort made by the families around here. Do you remember, Edie, how Mum and Dad used to fill Sea View Lodge with garlands of holly? They always had a pan of hot whiskey on the stove; they always stuffed our stockings with chestnuts and clementines.

Although it had only been a few days since Len had moved into Sea View Lodge, Dot's house had already changed:

her balcony was bare since Len had brought his potted snowdrops to Sea View Lodge; the curtains were drawn; and a carrier bag was trapped on her railings, thrashing about in the wind. I should have thought to send Dave over to put up some Christmas lights.

'The social worker's right about one thing,' said Vincent, turning off the engine. 'Dave does have the right to know.'

The man would not let it drop.

I got out of the car without replying, my confidence in Vincent faltering. If Len and Steph weren't here, we'd scare poor Dot witless with news of their disappearance. But he strode ahead, his stick arcing through the rain. By the time I caught up with him, he'd already knocked. He raised his fingers to his lips and cocked his head to one side. 'You'll hear better than I can,' he said, fiddling with his hearing aid. 'But I think that's Len.'

I couldn't make out much over the drumming of the downpour on the metal balcony.

The curtain twitched, and I was convinced that it was probably just Dot. But then, Len cracked open the door. 'It's a secret,' he whispered, raising his fingers to his lips. 'Nobody knows we're here.'

'You're not wrong there,' laughed Vincent as he followed me into the dark hall.

'We were out of our minds,' I said, as Len opened the door to the living room.

'Sorry, Aunty Maeve,' said Steph, her eyes already welling up. 'I'm sorry.'

Dot was propped up in a recliner chair, a half-eaten package of fish and chips on her lap. 'I did call,' she said, 'but I just got through to voicemail and then we got somewhat distracted.'

'Shh!' said Steph, raising her finger to her lips. 'It's a secret!'

The smells of batter and vinegar made me hungry, but I couldn't fathom how Dot could stomach such food in her condition. 'I'm so sorry, Dot,' I said. 'This is the last thing you need.'

Len's and Steph's suitcases stood at the end of Dot's metal-framed bed, further cluttering her overfilled living room. All the side tables were covered with pill boxes and audio books and bouquets of poinsettia and chrysanthemum.

'Oh, I don't know. There are worse things than a surprise visit from your son – especially when he comes bearing fish and chips and good news.'

'Mum!' warned Len.

I said nothing, waiting for them to explain.

'I hope there's been some kind of misunderstanding,' said Dot. 'Len's under the impression that he'll get kicked out of Sea View Lodge.'

'We'll get a new shed in the January sale,' I promised Len, praying that he hadn't overheard the social worker and her talk of Grove Hill. And I just hoped that Dot wouldn't enquire too much more.

Len popped another chip into his mouth, and looked as if he didn't understand.

'Dave can take you to B&Q, and help you choose one that's just the right size.'

'I want to stay in Sea View Lodge,' he said, a little wobble on his chin.

'Aunty Maeve,' piped up Steph. 'Len and me, we're a couple.'

'Of course you are, my dear, and Sea View Lodge is your home. But that doesn't give you the right to run away at the drop of a hat.'

'We will not be separated,' said Len, offering Steph the last chip. 'Not ever.'

'Of course you won't.'

'But Jenny told you that I had to move out.'

That bloody social worker had a lot to answer for. As if Len didn't already have enough on his plate. 'Over my dead body,' I assured them.

'Are you going to die, Aunty Maeve?' said Steph.

'My mum's dying, aren't you, Mum?'

Dot sighed. 'It happens to the best of us, I'm afraid.'

'It's just a silly phrase,' I put in, throwing an apologetic glance at Dot. 'I just meant that I give you my word.'

'Mum needs me to count out eleven pills in the morning and eight pills at night.'

'You did a tremendous job, love,' said Dot. Her voice didn't even threaten to break, but I had a lump in my throat just listening. 'You don't need to worry,' she went on, 'the nurse pops in twice a day.'

'And *you* don't need to worry about being separated,' I added. 'I won't allow a soul to keep you apart.'

'Do you promise?' asked Len.

I nodded.

'Do you promise you promise?'

I nodded again, and Vincent said, 'And I can promise a sing-along this evening if that appeals.'

If only some of his energy would rub off on me: I'd need a nap as soon as we got home. 'So long as Vincent's not too tired,' I warned them. 'He's been kind enough to drive me around town all afternoon.'

'It was the least I could do,' said Vincent, smiling in acknowledgement of my half-spoken thanks.

'It's made me terribly dependent,' I admitted, 'no longer driving.'

As Vincent chatted with Steph and Len, I took the opportunity to warn Dot to expect a call from Jennifer Tait.

A concertina file stood open beside the sofa, and various financial documents were stacked around the floor.

'Oh God,' she said, taking my hand. 'Tell me Len's not got it right about Grove Hill?'

'It won't come to that,' I told her, conjuring all the confidence I could muster. 'Len told her about him and Steph, that's all, and she jumped in at the deep end, convinced they're getting up to mischief.' It was sacrilegious, the way social services and the NHS were encroaching on their romance. 'She's booked them an appointment at the clinic, and instructed me to tell Dave. Fuss about nothing.'

'I wouldn't be so sure,' whispered Dot. Then she lowered her voice even further, so that I could hardly make out what she was trying to say.

I had to ask her to repeat herself at least three times until I worked out that she was asking me to protect Len. 'You don't need to worry about protection. They'll be safe as houses with me.'

Dot's body was rocking and it took me some time to work out that the breathy sound was laughter. It was clearly causing her pain, but she couldn't get it under control. Although there was hardly much humour in our situation, laughter began to rise up in me too. What must Vincent think – the two of us giggling like girls?

'No, Maeve,' said Dot, a tear trailing down her cheek. She held out a bony hand, gripping mine with surprising force: 'I've always taught Len to use protection.'

CHAPTER EIGHT

Len and Steph returned from St Mary's with Dave and Zenka in tow. It was a good job I'd made a huge pan of beef bourguignon. Perhaps Sunday lunch together could become a ritual – so long as Zenka didn't insist on cooking her Lithuanian food.

Len tugged up his Bermuda shorts – the sky was cloudless but it was hardly an appropriate outfit for December 23rd – and he bounced his beach ball up our hall. Ordinarily, I would tell him off for such behaviour, but I wanted to get through today with as little drama as possible. God alone knows how I'd break it to Dave that his daughter had an appointment at the sexual health clinic.

I ushered them all to the parlour, only to find Vincent winding fairy lights around a small Christmas tree.

'Surprise!' he laughed. 'No one had bought this one because of its wonky trunk. I couldn't leave it to languish in front of the Alhambra all over Christmas.'

This would give Zenka something to gossip about: Vincent had entered the parlour, which was normally strictly out of bound to guests. Just wait until she heard that he'd be spending Christmas with us.

'I'll give you a hand with that later,' I said, although I would have dearly loved him to stay: he would have helped me feel a little less spinsterish, a little less outnumbered by couples.

'Of course.' Vincent blushed that crimson blush of his, and he just missed treading on one of the fairy lights as he headed to the door.

'Where are you off to, Vince?' asked Len. 'I insist you stay.' He straightened his fluorescent green dicky bow, and then cleared his throat: 'Steph and me, we have something important to say.'

Dear Lord, what on earth could they have up their sleeves now?

Vincent looked from Len to me and then back to Len. 'Perhaps I'd better just—'

'I won't hear of it,' said Len.

'You are our friend,' said Steph.

Zenka patted the couch, encouraging Vincent to sit down beside her.

Steph positioned herself and Len in front of the Christmas tree, which stood all skew-whiff behind them. She tucked the label into the collar of Len's shirt, then straightened her skirt and took a deep breath. 'Len propositioned me for marriage and I accepted his proposition,' she announced, holding out her hand to show us her engagement ring.

They were a hoot – they'd only been courting for five minutes. I caught Vincent's eye and we shared a smile.

'She said yes!' Len exclaimed.

'Len and me will be a married couple.'

I'd bought Len a remote-control car for Christmas, and I'd found a yodelling CD for Steph. God love the pair of them – they were like children playing at being grown up.

'Oh yeah!' shouted Len, clapping his hands in the air as if he were an American preacher. 'Father Pete will marry us at St Mary's.'

'And we will be Mr and Mrs Shepherd.'

Len put his arms around Steph, and they held each other's gaze although tears were welling in Len's eyes.

The poor loves were in for some terrible disappointments – no one in their right mind would marry the pair of them.

'He propositioned me on the bus yesterday,' said Steph.

Like father like son. I seemed to remember that Dot's late husband had got down on one knee on the number 34.

'And then Dot gave us her ring.'

'Mum says that Steph will be the best daughter-in-law on God's good earth!'

So that's what they'd been so secretive about yesterday. Dot may be at death's door but she could still cause mischief. If she honestly thought that all this could end happily ever after, then her illness had affected her worse than I'd thought.

Steph held out her plump little hand for her dad to admire. 'Now Jennifer Tait and me both have engagement rings.'

Dave played for time, keeping hold of her hand, his eyes fixed on the ring.

'You dark horse!' laughed Zenka, throwing her arms around Steph. Then she drew Len into a group hug. 'Congratulations to you both. I'm on top of the moon.'

She was probably delighted at the thought of playing mother of the bride, but you had to give it to her: Zenka had responded much better than Dave. He was still slumped in his armchair. How on earth could I tell him about Steph's appointment at the sexual health clinic now? Typical Jennifer Tait – lumbering all of this onto me.

I caught Vincent's eye and it was clear that he had also clocked Dave's lack of cheer.

Poor old Len and Steph. I'd do my damnedest to persuade the parish priest to give them an informal blessing. That should put an end to all of this.

'Isn't it tradition to ask the father's permission first?' said Dave in the end.

'What if you'd said no?' asked Len.

'My point precisely, mate.'

'All you need is love, love, love,' sang Len into the microphone he'd made of his fist.

Dave sighed. 'I hate to break it to you, Len, but you need rather more than that.'

'We're not stu–pid.'

'We've made a list of everything we'll need,' said Steph, holding her back especially straight and then showing us all her scrapbook: 'Here's the kind of wedding dress I'd like,' she said, pointing to a picture of Kate Middleton.

'Beautiful,' agreed Vincent.

'And I'd like snowdrops in my bouquet,' she said, turning the page.

Dave was swallowing hard.

'And Len will need a ring.'

'Don't get carried away just yet,' I put in. 'Best to take things slowly.'

'Invitations, a suit, a best man,' added Len, racing through the pages of Steph's scrapbook.

There was that Mongoloid couple in St Anne's, who'd married a while back. The *Visitor* ran a feature on them. They'd also known each other since they were kids. Surely Jennifer Tait couldn't stick Len in Grove Hill if he and Steph were man and wife.

'A buffet,' Len continued.

Sea View Lodge had seen more than one wake and it was about time it witnessed a wedding. I could just see their big day: our plum trees festooned with ribbons; legs of lamb with rosemary, perhaps, or roast chicken with tarragon sauce; meringues with strawberries and cream. But I mustn't let myself get carried away with their nonsense.

'And a disco,' Len added.

We could have a party and an informal blessing. In the long term, nothing would have to change.

'We'll need our own home,' piped up Steph as if she'd read my mind.

Her words brought a gasp from deep inside of me.

'Great,' muttered Dave.

'It's far too early to be planning ahead,' I tried. 'Most people wait for years before even thinking about that.'

Steph took hold of my left hand and studied it for a moment before looking sadly into my eyes: 'I love Len and Len loves me,' she explained.

'Of course you do, so why not enjoy things just as they are?'

'Aunty Maeve, married couples live in a home of their own.'

*

It is the night before our A-level results and I am sitting beside Vince on the stone jetty, our legs dangling over the edge. Mum and Dad are sure I'll pass with flying colours, Frank's more interested in his army pals, and it's hard to know if you understand about exams. Vince is the only one who shares my nerves.

The sun has just begun to set over the sea, when Vince says, 'I've brought something to show you.' He pulls a book out of his satchel, its hard cover seaweed green.

'*Madame Bovary*! Your mother's?'

He opens it and shows me her flamboyant purple signature.

'Does your father still refuse to talk about her?'

Vince's finger traces the letters of his mother's name. 'If I try to bring her up, he changes the subject. I can't even tell if he knows where she is.'

I can't imagine a world without Mum, Dad closing in on himself. If only I could read Mr Roper's mind, and then tell Vince what I found. 'What do you think happened?'

Vince and I continue to sit there, watching the sun sink a little lower, as he confides that his mother had been out of sorts in the months before she left. 'I don't think she was very well,' he says in the end – the tautness of his posture bringing to mind that phrase of Flaubert's: *I itch with sentences that never appear*. There's a finality to Vince's tone that prevents me from asking more.

'Shall I read to you?' I suggest, not yet ready to leave.

His hands brush against mine as he places his mother's book in my palms and we lean in close so that we can both see the page. I read in the best French accent I can muster, the foreign lure of the words enough to make my recitation feel illicit – not to mention that Mr Roper and Mum and Dad would surely disapprove of *Madame Bovary*.

Vince takes the book from me as soon as my voice begins to tire, as if he knows just what I need. He reads on, his tone as smooth as sea-worn glass, his accent sounding just like his mother's. I think of what Vince has said, about his mother not being well. Perhaps she went back to Paris to be nursed by her family until she died, or perhaps she committed suicide and his father couldn't bear to tell him.

We sit on the stone jetty for a long time, the book passing between our hands, our bodies so close that the words vibrate between him and me, one voice picking up where the other left off.

'*La parole humaine est comme un chaudron fêlé*,' he reads, '*où nous battons des mélodies à faire danser les ours—*'

The strange images jolt through me while the rhythm of Vince's voice continues to lull: '*quand on voudrait attendrir les étoiles.*'

'It's beautiful,' we both say at once, my hand reaching for his arm, his flesh giving a little beneath my touch in a way that Frank's does not. We look into each other's eyes for a moment and, at the same time, we both look away. 'I'm not quite sure what it means,' I admit, 'but I know somehow that it's true.'

Vince underlines the phrase and we bat words between us, translating Flaubert's world into our own:

– *Language*
– Or how about *human speech*?
– *Tin kettle*
– Or maybe *kettle* would do?
– *Beat*?
– *Hammer*?
– Or what about *tap*?

Human speech is like a cracked kettle, we come up with, *on which we tap rhythms for bears to dance to*. And then we spend ages playing with the last phrase: *stars, pity, move*. But between us we make it ours: *music that will melt the stars*.

The sea breeze has picked up, causing my eyes to water, so the stars really do look as if they might melt.

'We should sit here every year on this day,' I tell him, 'sharing news of the countries we've travelled to and the books we've read, news of our work and our children. And every year you should bring your mother's copy of *Madame Bovary*.'

'We're going to be fine tomorrow,' he says as if he's responding to my suggestion. 'You and me, we're going to pass with flying colours.'

The truth of his words makes me smile. Vince and me, we will be fine; we've worked so hard for this. And as Vince folds down the corner of the page, I feel sure that he'll be at Cambridge University when he next picks up his mother's copy of *Madame Bovary*. He will think of me at Notre Dame College and he will remember this night when we sat side by side at the end of the stone jetty, the sea beneath our dangling feet, the stars above our heads melting in the sky.

*

Subject: Relationship between Leonard Shepherd and Stephanie Greene
From: jennifer.tait@lancashire.gov.uk
To: seaviewlodge@seaviewlodge.co.uk;
dorothy.shepherd@btinternet.com
Cc: safeguardingadults@lancashire.gov.uk

Dear Maeve and Dot,

It was good to see you earlier today, Maeve, and helpful to speak with you, Dot. I just wanted to let you know that I have called the Genito Urinary Medicine Clinic on Thornton Road and, although they have no appointments until 3.00pm on December 28, I've asked them to prioritise Len and Steph should any cancellations occur. The receptionist will call you directly, Maeve. During the appointment, Len will have a fertility test, and both Len and Steph will be offered sexual health tests. Appropriate contraceptive methods will be discussed.

Since Steph no longer has an assigned social worker, it is your responsibility, Maeve, to protect her from harm. I strongly urge you therefore to inform Steph's father about this situation as a matter of urgency. I will look into returning Steph to our books asap.

I know that you do not believe Len and Steph are sexually active, Maeve, but we must take precautionary measures. When I spoke to them, they refused to discuss the precise nature of their relationship. Respect for their right to privacy must be balanced against their need for protection as vulnerable adults who require high levels of support to retain, use and communicate relevant information as part of their decision-making processes.

Having now spoken to my manager, and having taken Dot's and Len's feelings into account, we have decided that it will be unnecessary to move Len to Grove Hill at this time. I reiterate, Maeve, that it is therefore your responsibility to protect Len and Steph from possible harm.

Once I am back from annual leave, I will arrange an evaluation to assess Len's and Steph's understanding of possible practical, medical and emotional effects of intercourse to work out whether they have the mental capacity to make independent choices about their sexual lives.

I will follow up with you both on January 2, when we can also touch base about Len's long-term housing options.

Kind regards,
Jennifer

*

Frank and I are leaning against his new Ford Anglia, which he's driven around here to surprise me.

'You're to keep it parked at Sea View Lodge,' Mum tells Frank.

I'm about to remind her that it's up to Frank where he parks his own car, that we are not children now – but Dad stops me by winking at us behind Mum's back, and raising his fingers to his lips. He's right, of course: I don't want to sour our goodbyes.

'You're only to use it to visit Maeve,' she continues.

Frank just laughs this off and Dad concentrates on stowing my suitcase and box of books in the boot. He is at least as taken by the car as Frank: they've had the bonnet up and Frank's been pointing out the carburettor and pistons and braking pads, and Dad's tried out the driving seat and talked about horsepower and costs per gallon – Mum tutting and shaking her head.

Vince has been reading *Peter Pan* to you in the parlour to keep your mind off my departure until it's time for us to leave.

Frank and I plan to stop for a picnic, so we really must get off. But Frank insists that Dad takes a photograph of us first. He puts his arm around me, and Dad makes a joke about it being a brave man who'll dare keep a Maloney girl waiting, while Mum goes to fetch you and Vince.

'You'll thank us for this photograph later, Maeve,' Dad assures me.

Mum and Vince lead you down the path from Sea View Lodge, but you keep jerking and screeching and forcing them to stop after every few steps.

'You go on ahead,' Vince tells Mum. 'We'll take our time, won't we, Edie?'

Dad hugs me long and tight and I can tell that he's holding back tears. 'We're so proud of you, my love,' he says. 'You deserve to have the time of your life.'

I am rather pleased with myself. All those months of hard work have paid off: creeping out of bed so as not to wake you; memorising quotations in the parlour even before Mum and Dad got up; turning down nights with Frank at the Winter Gardens during his leave so that I'd get a good night's sleep before my exams.

Once Mum has coaxed her hand from yours, she kisses me and reminds me to find a telephone so that I can let them know when we've arrived. 'Introduce yourself to the other girls in your dormitory. They might end up friends for life.'

When I try to kiss you goodbye, you push me. 'Will you miss me, Edie?'

'All friends together!' you say, and you stamp your foot and shout, 'Maeve and Edie and the Lost Boys!'

'I'll come home again soon,' I promise but you burrow your face into Vince's chest and refuse to wave goodbye.

You have clasped your hands around Vince's neck, and Dad is soothing you and telling you not to worry as he works your grip loose.

Vince and Frank barely acknowledge one another, and it's difficult for any of us to concentrate on goodbyes because you have thrown yourself onto the pavement, and you're screaming out the lyrics to 'For Those in Peril on the Sea': Vince barely meets my eye as he hands me an envelope and wishes me luck; Dad is crouched over you saying, *There, there, Edie. Be a good girl*; and you are kicking and bawling and red-faced with tears.

Mum is standing a good arm's length away, saying, 'Hush now, baby. Don't spoil things for Maeve.' But Dad is bent right over you, trying to pick you up. You tug at his hair and scratch his face.

'Come on, Edie,' says Mum. 'Let go. What will Vince think?'

'Deep breaths now, Edie,' Vince says.

As Dad looks up, you kick him hard in the face – the metal buckle of your shoe cracking across his jaw.

He bellows, his hands leaping to his chin and tears springing to his eyes. 'Feck!' he shouts. 'That fecking hurt.'

You are stunned into silence. Vince scoops you from the pavement, comforting you, as Mum takes Dad's face in her hands and whispers something to him. He bows his head towards her, kissing her on the crown.

'Edie, how about you and I go back inside to finish off *Peter Pan*?' asks Vince. 'Or how about *letter of thanks, letters from banks, letters of joy from girl and boy*?'

You turn from me, still dementedly singing 'For Those in Peril on the Sea' and dragging Vince in your wake. I wonder how you'll cope when Vince goes up to Cambridge in a couple of weeks. I wonder if he's told you he'll be leaving, whether you understand that you'll no longer go to choir rehearsals or sing solos during Mass.

'Keep in touch,' Vince calls over his shoulder as he reaches our front door.

Mum gives me one more kiss and says, 'I couldn't be more proud.' Then she turns to Frank and adds: 'No racing, you hear.'

'If you're not happy there,' Dad tells me, 'we'll drive straight over and bring you home.'

'You'll have a whale of a time,' Mum says. 'I'll go and help Vince with Edie. You stay out here, Joe, and wave them off.'

Just then two of our guests dash down the path – they are from Liverpool and they're honeymooning at Sea View Lodge. Thankfully they aren't the sort to be put out by your rage.

'So glad we caught you,' says the woman. 'Call us when you're settled in. We'll take you to the Locarno.'

But I can hardly concentrate on their invitation because I am taut with the possibility that you are having one of your seizures, that any moment now we'll hear cries from within.

The couple stand here next to Dad, all three of them waving: the honeymooners calling out 'Bye!' and 'Good luck!' and Dad sniffing and blinking back tears.

Just as Frank pulls away from the kerb, the window of the Honeysuckle Room opens and Mum leans out, waving with one hand and raising her cigarette holder to her mouth with the other. I keep looking back, hoping that you and Vince will appear beside her. But she remains alone, blowing long spirals of smoke into the autumnal air.

As we drive past the Alhambra and the Midland and the Super Swimming Stadium, past the Winter Gardens and Brucciani's and Central Pier, Frank puts his hand on my leg. I want this, I remind myself: I want to read new books and watch French films and go dancing at the Locarno; I want to live in halls of residence and make new friends and take notes in large lecture theatres. But the reality has only just hit: to do all this, I have to move to Liverpool, away from Sea View Lodge and Frank and Mum and Dad and you.

I remember then Vince's envelope in my pocket. *To Maeve*, he's written in his neat hand, *who loves all things French*. Inside, is a recipe for *boeuf bourguignon*, which he's copied from his mother's folder. When Vince and I are back for Christmas, I could persuade Mum to spend her rations on shin beef and bacon. But I don't suppose we could get our hands on garlic or wine.

Neither Frank nor I speak as he heads down the coast road and drives out of town. He doesn't ask about Vince's envelope, so I replace it in my pocket without saying a word. I stare out of the window and watch the fishing boats flung about on the waves, all the while holding back tears and hoping that Frank hasn't noticed.

'You don't have to do it,' Frank says eventually. 'We could just turn back.'

'I wish you were coming too,' I say.

Frank laughs at this. 'Flunked my Leaving Cert, got chucked out of choir. Don't think I'm cut out for college.'

'You're a great mechanic,' I say, dabbing my eyes with my polka-dotted skirt. 'And you're the best singer in the regiment.'

'I won't argue with you there.'

Something has been playing on my mind all morning and I can't work out whether or not I'm being reasonable. I am wondering why Frank has spent all his money on this new Ford Anglia when he was supposed to be saving towards a deposit on a garage.

'So long as you're sure you want this,' he says.

I breathe deeply and sigh and take him in: his green cardigan, his dark hair and olive skin, his chestnut-brown eyes; the smell of carbolic on his hands, the birthmark behind his left ear, the speckles of ginger in his dark stubble, the hardness of his stomach. 'I love you, Frank Bryson,' I say.

'I should bloody well hope so,' he laughs, and then pulls off the main road and takes the car up a steep country lane.

'Shortcut?'

'You could call it that.'

Frank brings the car to a stop in a glade right up high above town. He leans his elbow on my headrest, and stares into my eyes for so long that I have to look away. But I resist the urge to speak first.

'I love you too, Maeve Maloney,' he says eventually, and I am intensely aware of our bodies and our breath and the smallness of the car.

My stomach begins to rumble and Frank presses his ear to my tummy. I find the warm weight of his head in my lap reassuring but he holds it there for so long that I half wonder if he's fallen asleep.

'How did you save up enough to buy this?' I ask, the words stumbling over each other as they leave my mouth.

'Didn't he tell you? Your father lent me the money,' he says, his ear still pressed to my stomach, his words vibrating in my lap. 'We're sharing it.'

Dad had always dreamt of owning his own car. He spent hours scouring classified ads in the *Visitor*, and admiring the Morris Minors and Austin Ascots that sometimes drove along the promenade.

'Or that's the idea,' Frank adds, as his fingers trace the hemline of my skirt. His hand inches up my thigh and my body is edging down the seat and I'm thinking to myself: *This is it.*

I'd heard of girls at school who'd given themselves to boys behind the boulders beneath the pier or in abandoned beach huts, but I'd always assumed that Frank and I would wait until our wedding night, that we would marry when I was through with college.

And yet here I am in Frank's new Ford Anglia, the feel of his tongue and his hands and the sound of his breath so good that I fear nothing on God's earth could persuade me to stop.

But I make myself think of college and babies and mortal sin, and I am sitting up all of a sudden and straightening my skirt and tucking my hair behind my ears. 'This isn't right,' I say.

Frank looks into my eyes again for what feels like an age. 'Sometimes,' he whispers, 'the wrong thing is the right thing.'

'But we have all the time in the world.'

'There's no need to wait anymore,' he tries, his breath still a bit raggedy. 'I'll be out of the army in a few months.'

I just shake my head and Frank sighs.

I hardly dare breathe, worried that any more movement or word from me might ruin everything.

He unwinds the window and then lights a cigarette. There's something about the way he holds the tip to the flame, the slow way he inhales, that tells me he's plucking up the courage to speak. But he says nothing and just sits there, smoking and counting the polka dots on my skirt.

'It was awful, wasn't it,' I say in the end, 'to see Edie so distressed?'

I can't tell whether you know how long I'll be away, that I'll be coming back; whether you know that none of the choristers have offered to take over from Vince and me; I can't tell whether you'll miss me, or whether you'll soon forget.

'She'll be fine by now – playing choo-choo trains or singing hymns with Vince.'

'I don't think she has any idea that he's leaving too.'

'I didn't bring you up here to talk about Vince – or Edie, for that matter.' Frank takes both my hands in his, and looks at me for so long that I begin to feel uneasy as if he might see right inside me and not like what he finds. But then he laughs and shakes his head and he's kissing my neck and he becomes my Frank again. 'I meant to wait until we stopped for our picnic,' he whispers, taking a little box from his pocket. As he opens it, a diamond glints in the light. 'My grandmother's,' he adds.

I hold out my hand but, as he edges the ring up my finger, I hear myself say: 'We won't marry until I'm done with college, will we? There's no need for me to give up.'

*

Speed bonny boat like a bird on the wing. Edith Maloney sings like a nightingale. Maeve Maloney sings like a crow. Maeve is the cleverest girl in the seven seas. *Un, deux, trois, quatre, cinq, six, sept, huit, neuf, dix.* Where's Maeve? Maeve and Edie and the Lost Boys. All friends together. For ever and ever, amen. Where's Maeve? Behave, Maeve. I'm shocked and appalled! Who do you love the best, apples or oranges? Oranges and lemons, say the bells of St Clement's. Who do you love the best, St Clement's or St Mary's? Who do you love the best, Vince or Frank? Oh, hear us when we cry to Thee. Shave his belly with a rusty razor, early in the morning. Morning, Father O'Reilly! Morning, Mr Roper! Morning has broken, like the first morning. Morning, Maeve. Where's Maeve gone?

*

August 31, 1951
Dear Joseph and Lillian (if I may be so familiar),

I hear that we all have cause for celebration. You will be unsurprised to hear that my dinner party for Vincent was not premature. I was also glad to learn that the good word I put in for Maeve at Notre Dame College did not go unheeded. At the very least, it should offer her a reprieve from the simmering resentment she must naturally feel towards Edith, not to mention the great effort it must take to so charmingly conceal.

I am speaking on behalf of our whole congregation when I tell you that poor Edith, despite her afflictions, has been the source of our most profound admiration and joy. Her first awe-inspiring rendition of 'For Those in Peril on the Sea' forms one of my most prized memories. As you know, her voice has gone from strength to strength and I hope that it is not immodest of me to take some small credit for this improvement.

It is therefore with deep sadness and regret that I must inform you of the painful decision arrived at by Father O'Reilly and myself. I am afraid we have had to reconsider Edith's membership of the choir. Of late, the regularity and extent of Edith's seizures and inappropriate behaviour have disrupted choir rehearsals and caused unfeasible distress. None of the other singers feel able to take over from Maeve and Vincent the responsibility of caring for Edith. I hope you understand that her health and moral welfare have been at the forefront of our considerations.

I do hope that this most difficult decision will not cause any undue sorrow. Would it be impertinent of me to tell you that I have always admired from afar your stoicism in the face of considerable adversity?

Perhaps you would do Vincent and me the honour of joining my dear friends Jim Mullen (an organist of some distinction) and his wife, Eileen (a keen amateur pianist), for a game of bridge on Friday evening?

Please know that you are all most valued members of our community at St Mary's and that you are in our thoughts and prayers.

With the deepest regret,

Gerald Roper

*

Dave held his head in his hands, and Zenka just stared at him as if she couldn't understand why he wasn't cracking open the champagne.

'I'll check on the neepies and tatties,' said Zenka. Ever since she'd got together with Dave she'd been trying out phrases, which I was forever having to correct. She'd have been better off practising her accent.

Vincent leant towards me and whispered, 'Shall I get out of your way?'

'Stay,' I said, surprising myself with the force of my feeling. 'Do stay.'

Dave just continued to sit there, so to break the silence, I said: 'They were looking at Steph's scrapbook in bed this morning.'

His head jerked up as if he'd been woken by a loud noise. 'What?'

'I wondered what they were scouring over,' I said, realising my mistake.

There'd been no harm in it: Steph was in her pinstriped pyjamas and Len was wearing a T-shirt that read *Flame Pilgrimage to Lourdes*. Len had looked for the life of him like an oversized scarecrow, his straw-coloured hair all over his eyes; and Steph looked more than ever like a chubby Mongolian girl. They were big kids, that was all – my very own waifs and strays.

'You've been letting my daughter share a bed with that lad?'

Dave thumped the occasional table, causing the coaster to rattle.

'Oh dear,' said Vincent, flinching as if Dave's outburst were causing him anguish on my behalf.

'Let's not make a mountain out of a molehill,' I tried.

'Don't you tell me how to feel about this,' Dave said, rubbing the ball of his hand.

'Angela and Caroline are in the Snowdrop Room,' I told him. 'Would you keep your voice down?' Thank goodness the barbershop band weren't around.

'This is a fucking disaster.'

Vincent leant forwards as if shielding me from the force of Dave's words.

'They'll forget about it in a week or two,' I said.

'That's it. Steph's moving back home.'

'Don't let's get carried away. They'll no more marry than they'll holiday in Las Vegas or Uzbekistan or Timbuktu or wherever the heck they're dreaming about this week.'

'I should never have let you persuade me that I couldn't manage on my own,' said Dave, looking at me as if he no longer recognised my face. 'Why the hell did you keep this from me?'

I could hear the breath moving through Vincent's body, the springs of the sofa creaking as he shifted his weight. Vincent had advised me to tell Dave, claiming that her dad had a right to know. I could see now that Vincent's advice had been sound and, for the first time, I let myself question my motives for taking in Steph and Len.

CHAPTER NINE

My nap had been riddled with my usual nightmare – and there was no point just lying there, staring at the ceiling – so I'd got back up again and taken Len's baby monitor downstairs, intending to bake some stollen.

But I heard voices on our front path and, when I opened the front door, I caught sight of a gang of youths running away from Sea View Lodge.

I breathed in the ice-scented air, trying to get the stink of the nightmare out of my nose. So it took me a moment to notice the graffiti. At first it was simply the intrusion that sickened me: their paint sprayed across our front wall; their cigarette stubs in our flowerbed; their footprints on our lawn. It took a moment for me to realise that the word they'd smeared read *SPAZZER*.

The sight of it made me unsteady on my feet, old injustices veering up: names whispered behind hands – degenerate, inbred, imbecile; your lack of schooling; your exclusion from the choir.

But the thought of Len and Steph caused me to pull myself tall. This mess needed covering up before the pair of them roused from their nap.

It took me a good ten minutes to find the whitewash and brushes among the rest of Len's tools, which he stored in the cupboard under the stairs. And then I had an awful job lifting the tin and carrying it through the hall. Lord knows how I'd manage to open the lid.

My poor arm was so sore that I had to put the tin down as I opened the front door. It was then that I noticed Vincent standing at our garden wall deep in conversation with Miranda Philpotts and the Aspy Fella's tenor – the two younger folk all decked out in running gear.

'Having a mother's meeting?' I called out, before realising what was going on.

A bucket of whitewash stood at Miranda's feet and her training shoes were splattered with paint. She had already covered the graffiti with one coat but the letters were still showing through.

She hid the paintbrush behind her back, just as Vincent and the tenor positioned themselves in front of the wall. Their clumsy attempts to shield me from the abuse caught me between laughter and tears.

I was on the verge of apologising to the tenor, telling him that the person who did this must lead a very unhappy life. As if the poor man didn't have enough to contend with at home. He'd once told me that some louts in his neighbourhood posted all sorts of horrors through his letterbox. His resilience had quite broken my heart. I'd wanted to take him in my arms, but his limbs tensed if anyone touched him; my embrace would have felt like an assault. I'd taken him for a carer when the band first arrived at Sea View Lodge, so I wouldn't have had him down as the target of bullies. Perhaps the yobs had noticed his tight T-shirts and fondness for a cappella.

Instead of showing them my brush and taking over from Miranda, I found my foot nudging my own tin of whitewash out of sight.

The arctic breeze carried the pine scent of our tall fir, and I silently thanked God for His bounty. Len's churchy mumbo-jumbo must have been rubbing off on me. I felt in my bones that all would finally be well: Dave would realise that there was no harm in the romance between Steph and Len; they'd forget all about a home of their own; Jennifer Tait would leave us alone; life would return to an even keel. Len would hang up his forks and shovels in his brand new potting shed, nurturing our garden throughout the winter and coaxing it back to life in spring; Zenka would hoover and polish and mop; Dave would change burnt-out fuses and oil stiff hinges and deliver our groceries; I would fry eggs and knead dough and peel potatoes; and Steph would serve breakfast, just as we'd done for years.

'Would you care to join me on my morning stroll?' asked Vincent.

A brisk walk might rid me of my nightmare – a way to face my fears: during my nap, the quicksands had sucked me under, and I was reaching out for Frank but he just stood there, watching me struggle, and my palms looked paler than usual, my fingers slimmer, and I realised that my hands were yours.

I wished I could make myself scarce to let them finish their act of kindness undisturbed. But I held up the baby monitor to show Vincent that I couldn't possibly leave Len and Steph unattended. Just then a noise crackled through the device: the whisper of draught protector against thick pile carpet, perhaps.

I braced myself for the padding of Len's feet towards Steph's room, but the door simply clicked shut again and I heard Len make his way back to bed. After that, the only other sound was that of the pigeons cooing in the eves.

Vincent took the monitor from me, a glance passing between him and Miranda. 'You take a stroll alone, in that case,' he said. 'I'll call straightaway if there's a problem.'

'And you get off on your run,' Miranda told the tenor. 'I might catch up with you.'

'Last one before we leave,' he explained. 'Such a beautiful spot you've got here.'

I didn't make enough of it these days, focusing instead on the way the salty air had scoured the paint from our window frames and the ocean winds had caused that fir tree to keel or blown off another tile. We really did need double glazing and the roof really was on its last legs – jobs that I could ill afford. Someone else would no doubt gut the place once I was dead and gone.

Perhaps I *would* take a stroll – just so far as the Eric Morecambe statue, get some sea air in my lungs.

The promenade was almost empty, the silence broken only by the distant lap of the sea and the cawing of gulls. The ambers and pinks of dusk cut through the sky, and silver water slashed through the swathes of slate-coloured flats.

In my nightmare, the quicksands weren't quicksands but eggs – some white, some speckled, others the palest of blues; their shells cracking, their rotten yolks filling my mouth and nose and eyes.

But this part of the beach was perfectly safe. No harm could come to me here. I picked my way around rock pools, the sand breaking damply beneath my soles, the wintry sun stroking my skin. I felt a sudden impulse to unlace my shoes and peel off my socks. I wanted, more than anything, to feel the sand beneath my feet.

Your feet thrashed into my mind: your toes wonky and overlapping, flinching if anyone touched them.

You were laughing in that photograph of me dangling you over the sea – your cheeks dimpled, your mouth open wide. You loved letting the water creep up to your ankles, you'd squeal and giggle as a wave crashed into the backs of your knees.

The picture would be black-and-white, of course, but my memory was in full colour: the greens and greys of the sea; the lavender of your wide-collared dress; the bright blue of your eyes and the copper of your hair. A stranger could pick up that photo and mistake you for any happy child. But if he looked a tad closer, he'd spot your lopsided posture and your orthopaedic boots waiting on the shore.

By the time I sat my A-levels, you'd lost your love of paddling. On those afternoons when we needed to keep you from getting in the way at Sea View Lodge, you'd look at

Vince and me – your face full of anticipation – if we suggested a walk along the promenade. You'd sing to the honky-tonk music of the barrel organ, and you'd skip between us, holding our hands. But by then you'd no longer countenance dipping your feet into the waves.

As I stood there, the winter sun sliding towards the sea, a crab crawled out of a nearby rock pool. Did Vincent feel his visit had been a success, I found myself wondering while I watched the crab edge closer. Did he think we'd made our peace? Perhaps we had. I could certainly imagine sending him a Christmas card next year; I might even consider allowing him to holiday annually at Sea View Lodge. And yet, we had hardly spoken of you. During this whole week, your name had only been uttered twice. When Sea View Lodge was empty of guests, perhaps Vincent and I would find a way to talk about you again. By the end of today, the barbershop band would have checked out and Caroline and Angela were leaving at half past five. Perhaps then we could edge a little closer to the real peace Vincent had come here hoping to find.

I must have sat there contemplating the tide for quite a while because the sky was a dark indigo by the time I heard the sound of a dog barking in the distance, ignoring its owner's limp commands. The crab scuttled back into the rock pool as the dog bounded towards me, its paws thudding on the sand – and, as I turned, I saw that it was followed by a man in late middle age.

'I'm sorry,' he said as he approached.

He had chestnut eyes, and olive skin, and flecks of ginger in his facial hair, and I could just tell that he was one of Frank's brood.

'He doesn't mean any harm.'

I'd spotted them several times over the years: Cheryl looking harried, the kids jostling for the buckets and spades, Frank lagging behind; years later, I saw him and his sons cheering outside the Sports Bar after England had beaten France; once, a decade or so ago, I'd spotted him with his daughter on the opposite pavement when I was on my way into town. Later, I'd imagined pulling him aside, asking him to explain what had happened between us. But, in reality, on each and every occasion, I had simply bowed my head and pretended not to have seen him.

'No harm done,' I managed, already turning on my heel as Frank's son put his dog back on the lead.

*

The whole church falls silent after the door slams behind Vince. Even you don't make a sound.

I stand facing Frank at the altar, not daring to meet his gaze, the look that had passed between him and Vince replaying in my mind. *I can't do this*, Vince had said. *I can't be part of this*.

I am willing Father O'Reilly to launch into our vows but he just stands there, frozen, his arms still open in prayer.

I half expect Frank to make some kind of quip. *Vince was a brilliant organ scholar*, he might say, *but he's not up to the task of best man*. The congregation would burst into relieved laughter, and Father O'Reilly would get on with our nuptial Mass. But Frank just clenches his fist and then opens it again, staring down at our rings as if he's surprised to find them there.

I'm vaguely aware that I'm rocking, the motion fending off Vince's words: *I can't do this*; *I can't be part of this*. His voice reverberates through me like my own conscience, and I realise that my hands have gravitated towards my stomach as if I can hold in the ache that's swelling from its pit, as if I can hold back the knowledge of why Vince left.

I bring myself to look at the congregation: Frank's army pals whispering behind their hands; the heads of the nuns bowed low in prayer; my college friends shifting in their pews. Mr Roper, who's white with rage, is staring at the door as if he can force Vince to return. Dad's eyes are on me, and he's nodding with a naivety that breaks my heart, a nod that says: *You can do it, my love. Go on.* As my gaze lands on you – your hair cropped, your teeth wonky, your eyes so big and blue – I realise that it's Mum I'm hoping to find in the congregation, Mum who'd know just what to do.

I look back at Frank, willing him to take me in his arms despite Vince's footsteps still shuddering through me, the pressure of his words: *I can't do this*; *I can't be part of this.*

'Neigh!' you call out again from your pew, the nun trying to hush you. 'Horse!'

Your cry startles Frank into action. He reaches towards me then, and I let myself hope that all will be well even though everything tells me that this cannot be so.

'I'm sorry,' he says, handing me our rings and failing to look me in the eye. 'I'm so sorry.' Then he walks away, leaving me alone at the front of the church, the whole congregation staring up at me from their pews, the bands of gold still warm in my palm.

A howl ricochets around St Mary's, a howl that bends me double, while Frank breaks into a run.

*

What noise does a horse make? Home, James, and don't spare the horses. Edith Mary Maloney, Sea View Lodge, 31 Marine Road West. Dribble-drawers, slobber-dobberer, gob-tin player extraordinaire, my little Fenian, my grown-up girleen, my English rose, my twinny-win-win. In the bleak midwinter, frosty wind made moan. Oh, hear us when we cry to Thee, for those in peril on the sea. Sea View Lodge, 31 Marine Road West. Rest in peace. Who do you love the best, Peter Pan or the Lost Boys? Never say goodbye because goodbye means going away. Will you miss me, Maeve? The pulse of my heart, my treasure, my love. Edith Mary Maloney, Sea View Lodge, 31 Marine Road West.

August 10, 1954
Dear Doctor Dawson,

I am writing on behalf of Mr and Mrs Joseph Maloney to inform you of their desire to continue caring for their daughter, Edith Maloney, in their family home. Please know that I will act as their legal representative at the County Borough of Lancashire's Care Committee hearing, which will consider her removal under the Mental Deficiency Act of 1913. As such, I request copies of the aforementioned patient's medical records.

Mr and Mrs Joseph Maloney have asked me to convey their love for their severely subnormal daughter. It is imperative that the Care Committee understands that Mr and Mrs Joseph Maloney have put a great deal of thought and prayer into this matter, and that they are unanimous and unwavering in their belief that Edith's needs continue to be best served by them.

Should the Care Committee ignore their parental wishes, Oglethorpe, Mullen and Roper will press for an appeal and represent the Maloneys at such a hearing.

Yours sincerely,
Gerald Roper, Esq.
(Senior Partner of Oglethorpe, Mullen and Roper)

*

I couldn't seem to conjure any enthusiasm from Len and Steph about our Christmas cards from the young carers, so we all fell into silence. We finished our crumpets just as the clock on the mantle chimed nine, the tick of the minute hand marking my growing frustration with Vincent, who was late back from his last-minute Christmas shopping. Admittedly, I hadn't invited him to join us for dinner but I would have thought that it went without saying. Perhaps he didn't think I would serve him an evening meal now that all our guests had checked out, but poor old Len and Steph could have done with some distraction.

They looked so deflated, having sensed that Dave hadn't quite shared their joy. I could hardly look at Steph after her announcement that she wanted a home of her own. She might as well have said that Sea View Lodge was not home enough, that her love for Len left less love for me. She might as well have said that I didn't have a clue, never having myself been loved by a man.

'Time for bed, you two,' I said: 'You've a long day tomorrow if you plan on going to midnight Mass.'

I'd end up awake half the night, one ear open for footsteps between Len's and Steph's rooms. At least I'd persuaded Dave not to drag Steph back to his place. But I still hadn't told him about the clinic.

'I'll be up in a few minutes to check that you're in your own beds,' I said, not quite meeting their eyes. 'Be off with you.'

Vincent had a front door key, so there was no real need for me to wait up. I'd just load the dishwasher, and then check the cash register. If he wasn't back by then, I'd keep the hall light on and leave him to sort himself out.

We all just needed a good night's sleep. Len and Steph would forget all about their plans for a home of their own. By tomorrow, they'd be onto dreams of Disneyland or parachuting or joining the circus.

As I placed the tray of dirty crockery onto the sideboard, the security light lit up our back lawn. I nearly jumped out of my skin. I'd quite forgotten about the graffiti until now. All we needed was a gang of vandals trespassing into the garden of Sea View Lodge. They'd better not trample on Len's snowdrops.

I peered out of the window, my heart thumping, but I couldn't make out an intruder. The tall fir tree was silhouetted dark against dark, the last sea storm having caused its trunk to keel towards Sea View Lodge. It was just a branch falling in front of the sensor; the wind had been strong again tonight.

It was only then that I noticed what had triggered the security light: the door of the shed was swinging back and forth on its hinges, the shed's contents piled up outside.

I made my way into the garden, treading between bags of sand and copper piping and Dad's broken banjo, halting at the sight of the cradle stood in the middle of the lawn, all made up with half-finished blankets, a teddy lying on its back.

Dad had carved that wooden cradle as my wedding present, just as his father had carved one for him, and his father before that. The lemon coverlets and the mint green bear were the last things Mum had knitted before she died. The ball of yellow wool sat in the cradle, Mum's needles still crossed through its heart.

The rain plastered my hair to my face and the sopping wool of my jumper clung to my chest and back and arms. But I continued to stand there, the shed door banging back and forth, the cradle creaking, the security light periodically illuminating Dad's leather camera case; piles of tarnished tools, hardened paintbrushes and broken plant pots.

My gaze kept flitting between the unused cradle and the old blue suitcase, which lay a few metres away from the rest of the stuff as if it had been cast aside.

Whenever the security light clicked off, the contents of the suitcase invaded the darkness. In my mind's eye, I could see each and every object trapped inside: all those family photographs; the ivory-handled cutlery; the rose-coloured sherry glasses; plates and cups and saucers, some of them plain white, others patterned with rosebuds, and others still edged with a single green stripe; unused bedding; a tin of beeswax; China Red lipstick; a hymnal; my ocean-blue dress; and your peachy silk blouse. Those reams of letters and reports would be in there too: some penned by the Voluntary Visitor, others by the GP, the Medical Inspector, Mr Roper, and the nuns.

God alone knows how long I'd been standing there, unable to touch the wood that Dad had carved, the wool that Mum had knitted; unable to return my old suitcase to the shed where it had been stowed ever since I'd stuffed it full of your documents, and my wedding trousseau, and all the things returned by the nuns. God alone knows how long I'd been standing there, equally unable to turn away.

The rain kettle-drummed against lengths of old copper pipe so I didn't hear when Vincent approached, his arms laden with gift bags.

'What's going on?' he asked, panic flavouring his voice, his hand gentle on my arm as if he thought I might break.

His touch brought back all the long years of humiliation and shame.

'What's happened out here?' he asked, his eyes fixed on the cradle that stood in the middle of the lawn.

The security light clicked off again and darkness dropped around us.

He kept his hand on my arm and I didn't have the energy to shrug it off. 'Let's just get inside,' he said. 'It's deathly cold out here.'

'It's all been destroyed.'

'What was that, my dear?' he asked, waving to trigger the security light.

But I couldn't answer because sobs surged through me, racking my body so that I could do nothing more than allow him to guide me back indoors.

'That's it,' he whispered, putting down the gift bags and leaning in so close that I could feel his breath warm on my skin. 'Here we go.'

He immediately headed back outside, and I sat there, alone, at the kitchen table, my teeth chattering and my body afflicted by shivers.

Rain would have seeped through the hinges of the suitcase, bleeding into the papers and spoiling the ink. It would stink inside of damp cotton and rust.

When Vincent returned, nudging the kitchen door closed behind him, he was holding the blue suitcase in one hand and Dad's broken banjo in the other. The old camera hung around his neck.

'Don't,' I said, a tremor muscling into my voice.

But he wiped down the suitcase, failing to understand. I said nothing, unable to ask him to return it to the shed.

Once he'd removed his coat, he sat down beside me, breathed deeply, and finally looked me in the eye: 'What's going on?' he asked.

'This'll be Len's doing,' I said, startling myself with the volume of my voice. 'I'm in half a mind to wake him up right now —'

Vincent's hand felt warm and heavy on mine, but I raged on: 'He can get down here and put everything back into the shed.'

The old cradle would still be standing in the middle of the lawn, its hinges creaking in the breeze, the woollen blankets becoming sodden with rain.

I shrugged off Vincent's hand.

Even to Mum and Dad, my life had seemed so clear. We'd all taken it for granted that my marriage to Frank would be blessed with children; that I would make them grandparents.

'Hush now, my dear,' Vincent said. 'Don't wake them.'

'How dare you hush me in my own home?' I whispered under my breath, water pooling beneath my elbows.

'We need to get you out of those clothes,' he said, ineffectually dabbing my sleeves with the wet tea towel. 'What happened out there?'

'You're no help, coming back here at all hours, treating Sea View Lodge like a hotel.'

He chuckled at that and there was a split second when I could have caught his eye, laughed along and asked him to fetch a fresh towel from the airing cupboard. But I let myself look at the old suitcase, the sky-blue leather darkened to twilight by the rain. And I let myself remember my ocean-blue dress and your peachy silk blouse, the terrible sounds that came out of you on the night of our twenty-first.

'My mother had a suitcase similar to that,' said Vincent. 'Though hers was pale green. I thought of it at the convent, only today. I remembered Father folding nylons and lace handkerchiefs into its satin pockets. I hadn't thought of that case in years.'

To me, Vincent's father would always be putting on cream leather driving gloves, pulling on each finger one by one; he'd forever be leading us out of the convent, his hard soles tapping against the stone floor.

'The convent?'

'I visit every year. But today I realised something about my father, something I wished I'd realised long ago.'

I continued to study the grain of the table but I hardly let myself breathe.

'He was deeply misguided,' Vincent said softly, trying to meet my eye. 'But he wasn't a bad man.'

I startled myself with the slam of my palm against the table. 'How dare you tell me how to judge your father after everything he—' My voice cracked and I couldn't continue to speak.

'I'm sorry,' he said. 'I'm sorry that my father intervened, that I allowed him to persuade us.' He paused then, and I couldn't read what was going on behind his eyes. 'And I'm sorry about my behaviour on the day of your wedding. I made such a mess of things.'

If he hadn't walked out of the church, Frank would never have left. After our wedding party had dispersed, we'd have sat around the piano – you and Dad, Frank and me – and we'd have sung 'Daisy, Daisy' and 'Danny Boy', and somehow or other we'd have made our way.

If Vince hadn't returned that night and proposed, I might

have regained control of myself; I might not have let them take you away.

Vincent stared down at his hands, then closed his eyes and breathed deeply, chewing on his lip as he thought. 'We've neither of us got long left,' he said. 'Perhaps it is time to forgive?'

Many years ago, I'd told Vince that it was his fault you had died, that if it weren't for him you'd still be alive. I'd told him to get out of my life, although he'd persisted in writing from time to time.

'Get out,' I told Vincent, just as I had done half a century ago, my voice now eerily calm.

He blinked and, as he did so, he reminded me of the young Vince standing at the front of St Mary's, singing the duet with you.

'It was selfish of me to return,' he said, shoving back his seat. 'Just because I was lonely and fancied a trip down memory lane.'

The anger that had flared in his voice died just as quickly. But it was too late. He'd admitted it now: he'd come here on a hopeless mission to find the girl I once was; he wasn't the least bit interested in the woman I was now.

I watched him leave the kitchen, his shoulders hunched, aware all the while of the water dripping from my cuffs.

A memory reared up, a memory that I couldn't quite place: Vince's soapy hands brushing against mine as he passed me the crockery to dry, the size of them surprising me; Vince drawing me into a hug, my sense of his shoulders' broad span, the weight of his arms, the whispered kiss on my crown.

Tonight I sat in this very same kitchen, listening to Vincent's footsteps move up through the house. A tap turned on and then off again, the wardrobe door creaked open and later I heard it click shut, and then a suitcase thudded against the floor.

I could have stayed in the kitchen but I found myself walking into the hallway and watching as he made his way to the door. He hesitated for a moment, and then pressed your harmonica into my palm.

Even then, I knew that he would stay if only I asked him; even then I knew that life was offering me one last chance and that I was throwing it away.

But I didn't say, *You're right, Vincent, it is time to forgive* or *I'm sorry, Vincent, I was wrong*. What I did say, my words coming out so quietly that I couldn't be sure whether he heard, was: 'It's too late, Vincent. It's far too late.'

He bowed his head and then pressed on down the front path, his shoulders slumped in defeat.

I continued to stand there, shivering in my doorway, your harmonica small in my hand.

I watched as he placed his suitcase into his boot, watched as he gazed out across the night-blotted bay, watched as he took a glance back at Sea View Lodge, watched as he started up his car – the sound erupting into the night. I watched as he drove up the empty marine road – past the Alhambra, and the old funfair, and the Winter Gardens, and up towards the Midland Hotel. I watched as his car followed the curve of the coast and then disappeared out of sight.

PART
TWO

CHAPTER TEN

I am drowning in mud. Frank turns his back on me, his body silhouetted against the red light of dawn as he makes his way towards the clock tower across the firm sand.

The mud turns into cracked eggs, their yolks sucking me under, slipping between my toes and thighs and armpits, and the more I flail the more the yolks slurp between my fingers until I can no longer raise my hands.

Rain is drumming on my head, my sopping hair sticks to my face, and the water runs into my eyes. My hair and eyes, identical to yours.

Frank has reached out for the handrail; he's raised his foot towards the steps that lead up to the prom.

A distant owl hoots, and there's a tiny voice whispering: *open your eyes, rouse yourself, towel yourself dry.*

But the rain continues to stream down my face and I let myself sink a little more.

*

I see you, Edie, standing bare, your hands clasping my wrists, your face and breasts and hips in line with mine. You let me take your weight as you lift one leg over the rim of the tub and then you stumble slightly, and I move my hand to your armpit to steady you.

'Nothing to worry about,' you say.

You watch as I sprinkle baking soda into the water to

soothe your nappy rash, as I work up a lather, as I rub a soapy cloth from your ears to your toes.

Your body has changed during my years at college: your breasts rounder, your legs stronger, your tummy – which you never did learn to pull in – a little plumper, perhaps. It's hard to imagine that as a child you'd been matchstick thin. I take more notice of your body on this particular night, it being our twenty-first birthday. Later, I will run my new Max Factor lipstick across your fulsome lips. With your lovely bust and bright blue eyes, you would have been a real bombshell – all things being equal.

I still don't know what caused your marionette limbs and wonky teeth and scarcity of words. Perhaps the town gossips were right and there was a deficiency in our genes; or perhaps it was down to Mum's age; or our slightly premature birth; or perhaps the doctors didn't notice that you lacked oxygen during our delivery; or perhaps I deprived you of nutrients or damaged you in the womb.

Even now, I see your eyelids crinkle shut as I massage your head with shampoo, as the water darkens your coppery hair, as it streams down your spine. I see you straining with concentration as I place the flannel in your palm.

Although I've asked you to scrub your armpits, you touch your elbow. 'Up, up,' I instruct, guiding your hand. 'You can do it, I can help you.'

'On my own!' you call out, delight spreading across your face as the flannel touches your armpit, so I clap and cheer and call out, 'Edith Mary Maloney is the cleverest girl in the seven seas!'

You keep repeating it over and over: 'The cleverest girl in the seven seas!' you exclaim, splashing foam high into the air. 'The cleverest girl in the seven seas!' A bubble lands on your nose, and you turn cross-eyed from staring at it so long.

But I also see the tufts of hair in your armpits, and I know that I should shave them: they will look unsightly with your new cap sleeve blouse. But I do not pick up the razor; I do not take the time to remove that hair.

I see you wriggling in the bathtub, water spraying across the room as you scissor kick your stiff legs just like Frank has shown you. I love to see Frank's broad back bent low as he teaches you to dance. I love the way his large hands cup your tiny palms, lifting them up and down like an expert puppeteer.

I resume my bathing instructions (Where are your armpits? Where's your front bottom? Where are your knees? Where are your feet?), but my mind is still on Frank. I imagine him watching me as I head down the staircase in my ocean-blue dress. I imagine the gimlets we'll drink in the Rotunda Bar at the Midland Hotel, the jazz band that'll play as we teach you to jive. You'll quickly get exhausted and will want to sit on Dad's knee. Then Frank will move me slowly round the dance floor, his legs pressed up against mine.

Little do I know that I will never again dance with a man; that you will never wear lipstick; that your legs and armpits will never be smooth. Little do I know that I will soon lose Mum and Dad and Frank and you. But I cannot lose the images of what happened that night.

It is something as small as a brooch that leads me to leave you alone. Mum and I had bought it from the costume jewellery stand at the Co-operative Emporium and, as I stand there in the bathroom, it strikes me that I can't remember where I've put it. My outfit won't be complete without that brooch. I plan to pin it to the bow at the small of my back so that Frank will see the mermaid-coloured gems when he twirls me around the dance floor.

As I leave the bathroom, you are giggling and splashing and singing: 'Thus evermore shall rise to Thee, glad hymns of praise from land to sea.'

I can't be sure how long I stay in our bedroom, searching for the brooch, which I eventually find beneath a stack of underwear. I can't be sure how long I stand there, admiring my jewellery and my underwear and my dress that hangs in the wardrobe beside the outfit that Mum and I have chosen for you.

We had taken a special trip to the Co-operative Emporium, leaving you and Dad at home so that we could purchase the glad rags without worrying about you grabbing a shop assistant, or breaking some cut-glass crystal or lying on the floor and pulling Mum's hair. But perhaps that's not quite fair because you rarely have rages any more. Mum and I had simply seized the opportunity to spend an afternoon alone.

For you, we settled on a peachy silk blouse, embroidered with flowers. I chose a raw silk in ocean blue. The shop assistant wrapped a tape measure around my breasts and hips and waist while I stood in the changing room in my white cotton knickers and brassiere. It was then that Mum suggested we should pop into Wood's Lingerie Store on the way home, that it was high time I owned a decent set of underwear, that a birthday celebration at the Rotunda Bar deserved the best outfit that money could buy. Mum, I'm certain, hadn't purchased any underwear from Wood's since her beauty queen days, had never treated herself to silk.

I can't be sure how long I spend imagining the champagne on my tongue, the ribbon round my waist, the string of rhinestones – which I'm hoping Frank has bought for me – encircling my wrist.

I am tracing my fingers across the lace of my new brassiere and dreaming about Frank's hands on our wedding night when I hear the noise from the bathroom.

It's only then that I race back across the landing, my legs tangling and causing me to stumble, sweat springing at my palms, my heart pounding.

Your limbs are flailing against the bath, your mouth is contorted, your face half submerged.

To this day, I can still hear the tapping of your head against the side of the tub.

'Mum!' I call out, trying to quell the panic in my voice. 'Dad!'

My arms feel weak as I pull your head from the water,

your body convulsing and heavy all at once. You fall back beneath the surface for a moment as your head jerks from my grasp. I try to drag your torso up onto the rim of the tub, but you keep slipping from me.

I am screaming now.

My mind has not moved quickly enough: it is only now that I clamber into the bathtub, that I hold your head above the water by sitting behind you and gripping you beneath the armpits, the hair I've failed to shave against my palms.

You are still fitting by the time Mum and Dad reach us. It is Mum who pulls the bathplug; it is Dad who thwacks your back, causing water to spurt from your mouth. They both kneel on the tiles, their hands clammy as they stroke your juddering limbs and peel your drenched hair from your eyes and nose and mouth.

'Mum's here,' she keeps whispering. 'There's nothing to worry about when Mum's here.'

And slowly your eyes stop rolling, your movements slow and you begin coughing up more water and vomit.

I see your eyes blinking open and I feel your limbs calm and I taste the baking soda on your skin. I hear you too. I'll never rid myself of the sounds that come out of you then; those terrible phlegm-filled cries.

*

By the time the ambulance men arrive, you are deeply asleep, your breaths long and guttural, your limbs heavy. I am towelling you dry, stroking gently because after a seizure even the lightest of touches can cause you to flinch.

To this day, I am haunted by the fear in your eyes as the ambulance men try to lift you. I am still woken in the dark of the night by an image of your towel slipping from your body, the ambulance men looking away. I still see your plump little tummy, your pianist fingers, the plum-coloured stretch marks across your bust.

Dad scoops you from the stretcher and bears your fully grown body as if you are a tiny child. Your head lolls on his shoulder and your dribble seeps into his shirt. 'Dad's here,' he keeps whispering, using Mum's expression. 'All's all right when Dad's here.'

Your bare legs are wrapped around his waist, your bottom supported by the crook of his arm. I notice your nappy rash and I know that the ambulance men have seen it too, and I feel it is wrong for you to be so exposed.

I drape the towel around you and then Dad carries you downstairs, Mum and me and the ambulance crew processing behind.

The paramedic fires questions at Mum:

– How long?

– How often?

– Is she taking barbiturates?

Dad lifts you onto the bench in the back of the ambulance. He's hardly uttered a word.

There isn't enough room for us all, so Mum tells me to wait for Frank and to follow on with him. Lowing sounds come out of you as the motor starts up and you clench your fists to your ears.

The doors are slammed shut, and then you are taken away from me. I watch as the ambulance drives along the length of the promenade, past the Alhambra, and up towards the Midland and the Super Swimming Stadium. I continue to watch until long after the ambulance has disappeared from view, long after it would have passed the Winter Gardens and the Gaumont and the golf club.

It is only then that I realise how cold it's become. Without warning, I am shivering and my teeth are chattering and I am sobbing, deep and childlike. My limbs feel suddenly weak and my skin is clammy with sweat. The shrieks from the rollercoaster and the smells of popcorn seem to come from a whole other world.

I close my eyes and inhale and tell myself you'll be fine.

Once I've eventually regained control of my breath, I head back inside to call Frank.

I manage to prevent my voice from cracking as I ask the operator to put me through. The telephone rings on and on and I'm acutely aware of the Bakelite against my skin. I let it continue to ring although I know by now that Frank must already be on his way and I will be transferred back to the operator soon.

I find myself climbing upstairs until I'm standing in the doorway of our attic room. Your candlewick bedspread, tangled across your mattress, is stained with sick and dribble and specks of your blood. The pillow dips with the shape of your head. My own bed – standing beside yours – wears matching linen: my bedspread, perfectly white, is tucked neatly into my mattress and my pillows are plump and smooth. My new silk underwear lies just as I left it, spread out for me to admire.

The sight turns my stomach. I replace the knickers and brassiere into the chest of drawers as if I'd never removed them.

I strip your bed, trying as I do so not to imagine where you are now. I have never been to a hospital. Mum and Dad have always tried to avoid them, and – other than your seizures – none of us has ever fallen seriously ill. We've been blessed, Mum says. I pray that you are sleeping because I know that the glare of the hospital lights and the weight of the gas mask would make you sick with fear.

I open the window in the hope that the sea air will replace the poorly smell of your seizure. A breeze moves through our attic room, rippling across the fabric of our new outfits, which still hang side by side in our wardrobe. Your peach blouse rubs up against my blue silk dress and then they swing apart. I stare at them for a moment – the way they sway together and then drift apart – but then I close the wardrobe doors.

Mum had told us to be in the drawing room all dressed and ready for a toast and exchange of presents by half past six.

But it is almost a quarter to seven by the time Frank arrives, all dressed up for a dinner dance at the Midland Hotel.

*

Edith Maloney, admitted at 18:24 on August 7, 1954

The patient, who suffers from convulsions associated with severe spasticity and mental subnormality, sustained a grand mal seizure (duration of approximately seven minutes). This was complicated by inhalation of water due to occurrence of the convulsion while bathing. Direct physical injury sustained during the seizure resulted in lacerations to the face and forehead, requiring eleven sutures, and minor bruising to the ankles, knees and upper torso. It is possible that cranial trauma resulted in contusions to the frontal and/or temporal lobes of the brain – albeit difficult to verify given the severe mental subnormality.

*

By the time Frank and I arrive at the hospital, you have fallen into an exhausted sleep. I thank God that you're not awake to the ranting of the tramp in the waiting room, to the hospital's smells of Dettol and bedpans and sweat.

As Frank leans over you, your eyelids flicker and your limbs twitch. Mum strokes you and whispers a prayer, and Dad hums 'Danny Boy', and I just stand there at the end of your bed, fearful even to touch you.

The doctor who eventually approaches looks little older than us. He speaks gently, directing his words at me more than at Mum or Dad. Frank always says that my accent has changed, that ever since I went off to college I've become all well-to-do. Maybe he's right; maybe that's why the doctor is speaking to me. He whispers, I suspect, more through fear of having to deal with you if you wake than from concern that you need to rest.

As he examines you, I see him register your crooked teeth, your wonky toes and unshaven armpits. He does not seem to notice the length of your coppery eyelashes; your perfect earlobes, soft as rabbit-down; the arch of your eyebrows; your fulsome lips. He does not see my twin. The girl who laughs and jokes and sings; a girl who is stubborn and fearsome and strong.

'You'll understand that I must ask some questions,' he says.

I see myself turning from you; I hear the sound of your giggles, your hands splashing the bathwater, your voice repeating, *The cleverest twins in the seven seas!*

'Of course,' Mum says, and the doctor glances over at her.

Dad says nothing, his hands tense around the metal bars of your bed. He didn't think we should have called the ambulance. He's always mistrusted medics.

'Who was bathing her?'

There is silence for a moment until I speak up: 'It was me.'

'What happened?'

I see my fingers tracing the lace of my new brassiere; I see that brooch, its glass catching in the light. And I hear again that noise from the bathroom: the tapping of your head against the tub.

'She fitted,' I say. 'It all happened so fast.'

Frank puts his arms around me and I let him draw me towards him – away from the doctor's gaze. Frank's smell is strangely musky – as if he's taken to wearing aftershave.

'How often does she suffer from convulsions?'

Mum's hand rests on Dad's. She glances at him before giving the doctor a reply. 'Every week or so of late.'

The doctor writes something in his notepad, and then sighs before looking up. 'Have you told your GP?'

Mum looks down at her hands and slowly shakes her head. It's so quiet I can hear her swallow.

'She should have been on medication,' the doctor tells me, as if I'm the only one who'll understand. 'If she'd been removed to the Royal Albert, the doctors there would have put her on barbiturates.'

I know I should tell him that *I* left you in the bathroom; that Mum and Dad have never neglected you; that they didn't tell the GP because they were scared he'd send you away. But I just stand there, nodding to the doctor, and letting Mum and Dad take the blame.

*

Edith Maloney: Case referred to Care Committee, August 7, 1954

Parents did not inform their GP, Doctor Samuel, of the increase in frequency and duration of their daughter's seizures. Despite medical advice, they have repeatedly refused their daughter's removal to the Royal Albert. She would be better suited to full nursing care, where barbiturates could be administered and she could receive bed baths.

Additional note: as Roman Catholics, they are vehemently opposed to her sterilisation.

*

Frank drops us off in the new Ford Anglia. He sees us to the top step of Sea View Lodge, but he does not come inside.

Once the door thuds shut, the three of us cling to each other in the hallway, the smells of iodine and gravy on our clothes, whisky on Dad's breath and cigarettes on Mum's. Dad's chest moves as he swallows hard, and then Mum begins to shiver. I run my hand up and down her back, realising for the first time that she is terribly small.

'At least she's fast asleep,' Mum says – her skin so pale that she looks as if she's taken a kick to the stomach.

Dad is red-faced, his eyes bloodshot and wet. 'They sedated her,' he replies.

'We'll be back tomorrow before she wakes.'

'The bastards – we should have refused to leave.'

'She'll be home again tomorrow, sitting beside us at tea.'

'Do you not remember what Father O'Reilly said in that sermon?' Dad asks, loosening his hold on us. 'About being at the mercy of our doctors? About certifying patients and receiving the command to—'

I only remember its aftermath: the quiet of St Mary's, all heads turned towards us. Perhaps I had been circling your palm with 'round and round the garden' while Father O'Reilly spoke, or perhaps I was daydreaming, or simply too young to understand.

Dad breaks down, turning away from us and hiding his face in his hands.

I have never seen Dad weep before. I want to reach out to him and yet I cannot. Mum too seems rooted to the spot. After a moment or two, she creeps towards him, and then strokes him right from his nape to the small of his back. 'That was an awfully long time ago,' she whispers, pulling him towards her. 'And England isn't Germany, Joe.'

Dad rears away from her. 'Don't kid yourself,' he shouts.

'The nurses are—'

'They'll be trying again to take her away.' He storms into the lounge and, as soon as I hear him banging around in the drinks cabinet, I know instinctively that Mum is mistaken. Something is terribly wrong.

Mum and I say nothing as we go into the parlour, collapsing into the armchairs by the unlit fire.

'The nurses are taking good care of her,' she says in the end. 'Dad's just overwrought.'

A memory barges into my mind, or perhaps it's just an imagined scene: a tremor in Father O'Reilly's voice; lame horses; a hen sheltering her brood beneath her wings;

trainloads of Germans with stiff limbs and squints and crooked teeth.

We shouldn't have let the nurse usher us out of the ward; we should have held onto the bars of your bed; we should have refused to leave.

'The doctor was right,' Mum says, wincing at the sound of Dad's footsteps stomping up the stairs. 'We should have told the GP how often she was fitting. Maybe barbiturates would have helped.'

And still I sit there, saying nothing.

Mum looks torn, as if she doesn't know whether to stay with me in the parlour or whether to follow Dad upstairs. But she takes a deep breath, reaches over to me and begins stroking my hair. 'What happened, sweetheart?' she whispers.

I cannot meet her gaze. My fingers toy with the tapestry on the arms of the chair, the bracelet Frank gave me at the hospital catching on the threads. I'd coveted every one of its rhinestones, every one of its links shaped into figures of eight. But I know I'll never wear it again.

'How long did it last?'

I shake my head, and still I can't look up. 'I'm not sure,' I say in the end. 'I'm sorry, I can't be sure.'

'Try to remember, my love,' she says. 'Please try.'

CHAPTER ELEVEN

I lay in bed for a long time, staring at the damp patch on the ceiling, your rusted harmonica still in my palm. I listened to the tick-tock of the rotating seconds and minutes and hours, your hands still floundering, the fear still fresh in your eyes, those sounds still coming out of you, those terrible phlegm-filled cries.

I could swear an owl continued to call from the branches of the fir outside even as dawn broke across the sky. But I just lay there, submerged in memories of you: your fulsome lips, your plump tummy, the bubble that landed on your nose. Although I shivered beneath the damp sheets, I couldn't bring myself to rise.

The sounds of Sea View Lodge merged with the sounds in my mind: floorboards creaking; a kettle howling; your head tapping against the side of the tub; the back door opening; footfall back and forth across the garden; Len huffing and puffing; the lowing sounds that came out of you.

A key turned in the lock. That would be Zenka. She'd never once arrived to find me still in bed, even on days like today when we had no guests.

My recurring nightmare curdled with my memories: bathwater and foam and quicksands that turned into eggs – their whites cold and viscous and creeping right up to my mouth.

I heard Zenka making her way to the parlour, opening and closing the door; I heard her continue into the kitchen. 'Maeve?' she called out. 'Maeve?'

Perhaps she thought I'd died in the night. Zenka would no doubt relish the opportunity to paint our furniture in garish colours and replace our sing-alongs with hair and make-up demonstrations. Folk would no doubt assume that she was Steph's mum.

I knew I should get up and put on my housecoat; I knew I should let Zenka see that I was fine. But I was floored by memories of you: I couldn't have moved if I'd tried.

Zenka had made her way right up to the attic now, and I braced myself for a knock on the door. But her footsteps stopped at Len's room. I could hear Zenka's voice and Steph's, but I couldn't make out what they said.

Your voice always sounded a little like music even when you were just speaking. You always said each of your phrases with exactly the same stresses and pauses, exactly the same high tones and low: *Edith Maloney sings like a star! The cleverest twins in the seven seas!*

When Zenka's knock eventually came, it startled me even though I'd been waiting for it. 'I'm fine,' I tried, but my voice came out like a whisper.

'Are you okay?' asked Zenka, peeping her head round my door. She approached my bedside, and then lowered her face to mine, the toothpaste still minty on her breath, shock registering momentarily in her eyes.

'You will be more comfortable if we change these,' she said, as if it were nothing out of the ordinary to find me in bed fully clothed. I felt so exhausticated, as you would have said, that I allowed her to lever me up, to prop pillows behind my head, to place your harmonica on my bedside table, to peel the cardigan from my arms. I couldn't remember climbing the stairs last night; I couldn't remember lifting my quilt.

I let her help me out of bed and into the armchair; I even let her unbutton my shirt, unclasp my bra, rub me down with a towel and pull my nightie over my head.

'That's good,' she murmured as she peeled off my socks. Thank goodness I scrubbed my heels with a pumice stone each week; thank goodness I'd recently painted my nails. 'That's better,' she said as she dried my toes.

I felt too weak to resist.

'You will feel more comfortable now,' she said, as she replaced my damp sheets with fresh bedding. 'You must rest and let me take care of everything else.'

As she helped me back into bed, I sank a little lower into the quicksands, letting the stinking egg whites creep right into my ears. Yet still I could not rid myself of the Medical Inspector's conclusion: *She can no longer walk and has lost even the minimal levels of speech she previously had. She is, in effect, vegetal.*

*

Dad leans over the bars of your hospital bed, trying to prop you up on the pillows, but you flinch when he lifts you and a tear trails down your cheek.

He holds his face close to yours and whispers, 'You're the pulse of my heart, my treasure, my love.' And he strokes your hair, which is heavy with grease. 'Mum and Dad and Maeve will be meeting with the doctors tomorrow, my love, to get you out of here.' He stands up from your bed, swallowing hard before turning away.

I can see his silhouette through the curtain, his hands screwed to his eyes. I hope you don't realise that he's crying; you hate to see any of us sad. Your eyelids keep drooping and your gaze is glassy. God knows what they're injecting into your veins.

While Dad waits at the other side of the curtain, Mum and I sponge you down, using towels and Pears soap that we've brought from home. We take care to use lukewarm water and to stroke your skin with the lightest of touches. But you keep whimpering.

'Mr Maloney,' we hear the ward sister say at the other side of the curtain, 'visiting hour is drawing to a close.'

'Sure now, we'll be out of your way as soon as my wife's finished bathing our girl.'

'You're saints the pair of you,' she says.

'Saints we are not,' he replies. 'We're lucky to have two wonderful girls.'

Mum catches my eye and gives a sad smile, but I look away, concentrating on drying you gently with a soft towel, blotting the dampness from your skin. As I lean down to kiss you, I swear that you try to kiss me back. Neither Mum nor Dad have levelled any blame at me but, a few times over the past weeks – as I packed your towels or made sandwiches or leant in to kiss them – I've felt them looking at me with an expression that says: *You've let us down.*

'We've got the certification hearing tomorrow,' Dad confides to the nurse, 'so we'll be missing visiting hour.'

'I'll get one of the nurses to give Edith a bed bath,' she offers. 'So long as we're not too rushed off our feet.'

Mum puts on your nappy while I button up your nightshirt, both of us bracing ourselves for what Dad will say next.

'We'll pop in on our way to the hearing,' he tells her. 'We can't have her thinking we've abandoned her.'

'That's one thing you don't have to worry about,' she says, her tone gentle. 'Edith doesn't *think* anything. She's pretty much vegetative, I'm afraid.'

It's difficult to know whether or not you take anything in, but your eyes seem briefly more alert, and your limbs tense as if every inch of you is concentrating on her words.

'Until tomorrow,' Dad says, his fury barely contained, his footsteps pounding out through the ward.

You are already clammy again and I am also breaking into a sweat.

'That won't be possible,' she calls after him before whipping open your curtain. 'If you're finished in here, Mrs Maloney?'

Mum pulls the bedding back over you before meeting the ward sister's eye. 'We know you're all extremely busy,' Mum tries. 'If we popped in tomorrow morning, we could bathe Edie ourselves.'

'You heard what I told your husband,' she snaps. 'There's nothing more to say.'

*

Who do you love the best, cabbage or sprouts? Pork pie and custard. Yuk! Ducky-lucky, cocky-locky, chicken-licken. The sky is falling in. All fall down. Down, down. Where's your head? Up, up. There it is! That's good, that's better. What are the similarities between an apple and a pear? What noise does a horse make? Home, James, and don't spare the horses. Edith Mary Maloney's the cleverest girl in the seven seas. Where's your tongue? Where's Maeve? Where's Mum and Dad? Who do you love the best, carrots or Vince? Scrumdiddlyumptious! Tweedledum and Tweedledee. For those in peril on the sea and beeswax and gob-tin and lipstick. Where's your mouth? What noise does a dog make? Bow-wow, bow-wow, bow-wow.

*

Mum follows Mr Roper's advice and gives the judge and Certification Committee a little bow. Dad gazes into the middle distance and I stare each of the officials in the eye. Our GP, Doctor Samuel, is the first to turn away but none of them hold my gaze for long – they check their paperwork or clean their glasses or consult with one of their colleagues. There's something familiar about the way Mr Roper nods to the judge, as if they play golf or chess or drink sherry together.

I assumed that the courtroom would be oak-panelled, the floors marble, the curtains velvet. I expected the judge to wear a wig and hold a gavel. But the court looks more like a makeshift office or a classroom with its Formica tables and carpet tiles and plastic stacking chairs. Although the window is open, the room is stuffy and smells of fresh paint – as if the walls might still be sticky to the touch.

The judge clears his throat, puts on his spectacles and spends what feels like an age reading the documents on his desk, sometimes frowning, sometimes nodding and – on one occasion – letting out a long sigh.

Shouldn't he have already acquainted himself with your file? Shouldn't he have met you?

When the judge eventually looks up, he rubs his bearded chin and says, 'This case need not detain any of us for long.'

We'd assumed that the hearing would last all day, that we would miss visiting hour. I had offered to sit with you in the hospital instead of coming to the hearing, but Mr Roper told us that Vince would visit you, that it was more important for me to be here. The attendance of an educated and devoted sibling – a twin no less – might help your case. Little does he know that it's my fault you are stuck in hospital too weak to move or talk, so weak that it's a struggle for you to smile. He just sees me as the twin who got the best exam results in town, the twin who was awarded the Diocesan Scholarship to study French at Notre Dame.

I watch Mr Roper, trying to gauge whether the judge's words should fill us with hope or dismay. He continues to sit with his legs aligned from the ankle to the knee, his back held straight, his eyes on the judge. As he concentrates, he gives the slightest of nods. This gesture reminds me that he speaks the same language as the doctors and administrators and judge – a language that Mum and Dad and I are only just beginning to learn.

Mum and Dad are property owners and pillars of the community – this will work in their favour, Mr Roper has told us. *Thank goodness for Miss Wilkinson*, Mum has said more than once over the past few weeks, *Thank goodness she died an old maid*. Mum inherited Sea View Lodge from her employer – although it had been a private residence then. Miss Wilkinson was elderly and childless, rattling around in such a large house, a spinster with only Mum to cook and clean and accompany her to concerts at the Winter Gardens.

My thighs are sticking to the plastic chair and I feel sure that, when I stand, my skirt will be stained with sweat.

The judge looks down at his notes again: 'Is it still the express wish of the parents to have their severely subnormal daughter returned to the family home?'

'It is, Your Honour,' says Mum, standing tall. I can tell from her pinched tone that she is trying with all her might to keep both fear and frustration at bay.

'Please address the court through your elected legal representative,' replies the judge, glancing down at his notes. 'A Mr Gerald Roper, Esquire?'

Mr Roper is on his feet now, but as Mum sinks to her seat she adds: 'We love her, Your Honour.'

'As the court has heard, it is the heartfelt wish of the Maloney family that Edith remains in their care.' Mr Roper's voice wavers and, for this, I almost let myself like him.

'I take heed of this request,' replies the judge without meeting Mr Roper's eye. For a split second, I think that this is his verdict, but he continues to speak: 'I also note the GP's assessment of the patient's infantile and inappropriately sexualised behaviour.'

Dad's fingers drum against the chair leg and Mum's fist is so clenched that her nails must be pressing half moons into her palms.

'I acknowledge too the Superintendent's recent assessment of the patient, post the grand mal seizure and resultant inhalation of water, in which he outlines the benefits of long-term hospitalisation.'

I look at the Care Committee, trying to work out which of them is the Superintendent. There is a handsome young man, with hair as dark as Frank's, and I feel ashamed to have noticed this at such a time. But he's too young to be the

Superintendent; surely someone his age couldn't hold your fate in his hands.

'I have weighed the psychological needs of the patient against her medical requirements, and any potential threat she may pose to the community at large.'

I see Dad take hold of Mum's hand and I wish that Frank were here to take hold of mine. But he couldn't have taken a day off – not when he's saving up for the deposit on a garage.

The judge pauses to wipe his forehead with a handkerchief, then he removes his glasses and looks at Mum with an expression that may be pity or sympathy or bewilderment.

I realise at that moment that I have never hated before. I thought I hated Mr Roper for excluding you from choir, but my feeling now is as hot as oil spitting in the pan, as loud as the Orange marchers who beat their drums outside Notre Dame. I hate this pompous judge for making us wait a moment longer than necessary; I hate the good-looking doctor and the way he keeps nodding and running his fingers through his hair; I hate the prim secretary, who's holding her pen in readiness to complete her minutes.

*

Case of Edith Maloney August 23, 1954

Circumstances which render the defective liable to be dealt with, upon petition, under the Mental Deficiency Act, 1913:
Prolonged grand mal seizure of severely subnormal patient whilst bathing.
County Borough of Lancashire Statement of Particulars to accompany Petition:
NAME: Edith Mary Maloney
ADDRESS: Sea View Lodge, 31 Marine Road West
DATE OF BIRTH: August 7, 1933

CONDITION: Spasticity and severe mental sub-normality, combined with related grand mal epilepsy
WEIGHT: 8st 6lb
HEIGHT: 5'1"

Medical report certifying that the individual is a fit person to be removed:

Edith Maloney's medical records testify that she has never been able to wash, dress or feed herself and that she is doubly incontinent.

Since her grand mal seizure and resultant inhalation of water of August 7, 1954, she can no longer walk and has lost even the minimal levels of speech she previously had. She is, in effect, vegetal, and no longer displays even the infantile qualities noted in the GP's most recent assessment.

Parents did not seek medical intervention on the worsening of Edith Maloney's seizures.

As devout Roman Catholics, they are also vehemently opposed to sterilisation.

The effects of the grand mal seizure and resultant inhalation of water on August 7, 1954, make her less of a social liability but increase her vulnerability. She would benefit from full nursing care, where she could receive continuous supervision, regular sedation, daily dosage of barbiturates and weekly enemas to inhibit seizures.

Signed:

Doctor F. Dawson

(Medical Inspector of County Borough of Lancashire)

Judgement of Certification Hearing, August 23, 1954:

Edith Maloney's parents have petitioned strongly for her to remain in their family home. It is therefore considered inadvisable to force her removal. Although she is to be returned to her parents, it should be recorded that the County Borough of Lancashire's Care Committee considers that the welfare of the severely subnormal patient would have been better provided through institutional care.

Signed:

Judge Peter Bines

*

We arrive at the tail end of visiting hour to find Vince sitting on the stool beside your bed, one arm around your shoulders and the other holding your hand. His back must be aching but he's reciting 'Night Mail' to you, his mellow voice and placid expression betraying no hint of pain. 'Letters for the rich,' he's saying, glancing up as Dad bounds into your bay, 'letters for the poor, the shop at the corner and the girl next—'

'Home, James, and don't spare the horses!' calls out Dad.

Vince breaks into a smile. 'You've done it,' he says. 'Thank God.'

I could swear that you too are trying to smile.

And we all seem to sigh then as if we've been holding our breath until now.

Dad is scooping you out of the bed and wrapping you in a blanket; Mum is nudging your hair out of your eyes and kissing your brow; and Vince and I stand facing each other, off to one side. I am biting my lip and trying to hold myself tall. But when Vince throws his arms around me, I collapse into tears. It's only now that I truly let myself feel how close you were to being taken from us, the extent of the harm that I have caused.

'Good on you,' says the elderly lady opposite, the sweet peas that Mum had brought her standing in a vase at the end of her bed. 'She brings out such love in us all.'

The ward sister approaches from the nurses' station, her stride slow and even, her face blank. 'Our patients would appreciate some quiet,' she says when she reaches us.

'Quite the reverse,' pipes up the elderly lady. 'It's good to have a bit of life in here.'

A flicker of amusement plays across the nurse's eyes but she continues as if she's not heard a word. 'Edith will be more comfortable back in bed.'

Your head is lolling at an awkward angle and one of your arms is hanging out of the blanket.

'We're taking her home,' says Dad. 'The judge found in our favour.'

It's difficult to tell from the nurse's expression whether or not she's been informed. 'That may well be the case,' she replies, 'but that doesn't mean you can just take her home.' Her tone remains hushed.

'I think you'll find it does,' says Dad, holding your floppy body tight to his chest.

The nurse's eyes rest on Dad's tie, which hangs loose around his neck, and then she turns to Mum. She must notice Mum's mascara-smudged eyes. I cannot imagine the nurse ever having a hair out of place; I can't imagine her wearing anything other than her uniform. 'Here we can administer sedation and barbiturates and enemas. Her condition might deteriorate if you take her home.'

Mum tucks your arm back beneath the blanket. 'Oh, holy St Jude, apostle and martyr,' she prays beneath her breath.

'Let's be getting out of here,' says Dad, angling you away from the nurse. But Mum hesitates.

'Come on now, Lillian,' he says. 'Let's be getting our girleen home.'

I take Mum by the elbow, hoping to nudge her into action, but she stands firm. 'Do you really think we'll be doing her harm,' she asks, 'if we take her home?'

The ward sister nods gravely. 'That *is* my opinion, I'm a—'

'It's love that she needs,' puts in the elderly lady, who's never received a visitor in all the weeks you've been here. 'Drugging her up to the eyeballs is doing her no good at all.'

'I'm giving you my medical opinion,' the nurse continues.

'Give her your opinion as a mother. What would you want for your own girl?'

For the first time, the ward sister acknowledges that the patient has spoken. Then she rubs her eyes with the balls of her hands, causing her starched cap to sit askew. 'Make sure she drinks plenty of milk,' she says in the end. 'Mash up potato and carrots, puree apples and pears. She might manage a soft-boiled egg in a couple of days.'

'Thank you,' says Mum, her knees almost giving way.

The nurse glances around the ward, and then she whispers: 'If you need anything, please don't hesitate to get in touch.'

CHAPTER TWELVE

I am still thrashing in the quicksands, my limbs heavy with exhaustion, when I see you standing at the edge of the mud pool, looking just as you did before getting into the tub on the night of our birthday: your tummy plump, your shoulders tiny, your auburn curls shining in the sun. 'The cleverest twins in the seven seas,' you say, just as you always did. 'Who do you love the best, Frank or Vince?' You reach out your hand to me for 'round and round the garden', and I grasp at your palm. But you cannot haul me out of the quicksands and you are beginning to topple.

'Edie!' I shout, the word exploding from my mouth.

'Aunty Maeve?'

The mud disappeared then and I found myself swaddled in bedclothes, a weight at the bottom of the mattress.

It was you, sitting on the end of my bed in the room we used to share, the wintry light catching in your auburn curls, your peachy silk blouse falling across your lovely bust, your pale palm small in mine.

'Let's go,' you said, stroking my hand as you slipped away.

The weight shifted at the bottom of the mattress, and Steph said, 'Who's Edie, Aunty Maeve?'

'Sleep talk,' I managed, the words crawling from my furred tongue.

'You don't have meningitis, do you, Aunty Maeve?'

Poor love – this fear would never leave her. I propped

myself up although the exertion weakened me. 'I'm right as rain, my love,' I said, drawing her towards me.

As she snuggled her head onto my shoulder, her body plump, her palms cold, I remembered that she wanted to leave Sea View Lodge, that she and Len wanted to set up alone. I closed my eyes and breathed in deeply, and I could almost inhale your scents of milk and Pears soap.

I only realised I was crying when I felt sobs move through Steph. 'I miss Mum,' she said.

'Oh, my love,' I said, 'of course you do.'

Just then, Len edged open the door. He was trying so hard to be quiet that he brought to mind a cartoon thief.

'Do you have something you want to say to me?' I asked, trying to rekindle some of the fury I'd felt last night.

'Yes!' said Len. He held out a tray loaded with cured meats, sliced tomato and cucumber, a bowl of cottage cheese and a jug of coffee. 'This is what people eat for breakfast in Lithuania, and this is what they drink in the great US of A.'

'What time is it?' I asked, remembering that the goose needed picking up from A. J. Baker's, that I'd planned to get Dave to drive me over to Blackpool to see if we could surprise Zenka with poppy seeds and herring for her twelve-course Christmas Eve supper.

'Time for breakfast in bed,' laughed Len.

It was only then that I registered his stars-and-stripes hat and matching dicky bow. No doubt we had that slideshow of Vincent's to thank for this new-found interest in the USA.

Vincent had left. The recollection caused me to sink back down on my pillow. Frank had died and now Vincent had gone. I had sent him packing. He had glanced back at Sea View Lodge before starting his car; he had driven up the empty marine road; he had disappeared into the emptiness that stretched out ahead.

*

When the knock eventually sounds, I jump and spill brandy all over my hands. I dash into the hallway, wiping my palms on my pinny, and praying that it will be Frank at the door.

It is such a relief to see him standing right here, right now on our front step: the motor oil that stains his knuckles however much he scrubs his hands; the vein on his bicep that looks like a flash of lightning and that I know lies just beneath his rolled up shirt sleeve; the hardness of his arms and chest as I draw him into a hug.

'How's little Edie?' he whispers, his breath warm and smoky, his sweat musky and sweet. He never usually wears aftershave just to call in here.

'She hasn't fitted,' I tell him, 'and she enjoyed *Listen with Mother* this afternoon.' In the few weeks since you've been home, you've become so much healthier and these glimpses of happiness fill me with hope. 'Mum's feeding her in the parlour and I'm in the middle of serving nightcaps. Give me a hand, would you?'

Frank pulls up a chair and sits beside the Londoners, who are taking a trip down memory lane. He chats away with them while I concentrate on all the things Mum would usually do: offer cigars to the man and cigarettes to the lady; draw the curtains; place chocolates on the occasional table; pour whiskys or brandies; take orders for coffee or Horlicks or tea.

I always thought that I supported Mum and Dad a great deal, helping in the kitchen and keeping you out of sight of our less friendly guests. But now, I realise, I only ever did bits and bobs at Sea View Lodge. Until we received the Certification Report, I didn't even know that the medics wanted to sterilise you.

'Whitehall-on-Sea, we used to call it,' the man says – as if Frank wouldn't already know – throwing back his head and guffawing. 'It was full of civil servants during the war.'

Frank asks about where the man was billeted; whether he remembers the airmen shooting their rifles on White Lund or the WAAFs practising their drills along the promenade; did

201

he get to see Arthur Askey, Tommy Trinder or Ivor Novello? He can talk to anyone, can Frank. Once we're married, he'll entertain our guests of an evening while I mix dry martinis and gin sours.

I am trying to relax into this image of Frank living with us all at Sea View Lodge but my whole body is tense with the prospect of you fitting or crying or being sick, the expectation that Mum might at any moment call out for help.

'Ring the bell,' I tell our guests, gesturing to Frank that we're finished in here, 'if there's anything more you need.'

We find you in the parlour, sitting on the armchair all propped up with cushions, while Mum lifts spoonfuls of jelly to your lips and catches drips from your chin with a flannel.

'Let me take over there,' says Frank, lifting you onto his knee.

'How's my snazzy girl bearing up?' he asks.

Mum switches off the shipping forecast, which was playing in the background. 'It's so good to see you,' she tells Frank. 'Edie's been looking forward to it, haven't you, love?' Mum would usually be running around after us all: brewing tea; serving up a bowl of leftover trifle for Frank; popping in and out to check on our guests; calling Dad to come and join us. But she stands there, rubbing the small of her back and rolling her shoulders. Her hair is clipped to her nape in a bun because she hasn't had time to wash and style it; her face is nude of lipstick and blush. She is too tired to be lifting you in and out of bed; she is too old to be getting up several times each night. I must do more to help.

Dad follows us into the parlour, two bottles of beer in his hands, his overalls stained with dust and grease. 'I thought I heard your voice,' he says. 'Be getting one of these down you.' Dad has become red and fleshy over the past month, whereas Mum has become bony and pale.

You tug at Frank's shirt and gesture towards the piano – the effort causing dribble to trickle down your chin and your arm to flop at your side.

'Piano?' Frank asks and you smile and make a deep sound that doesn't form into a word. But you will speak again and we will get you back on your feet – even if it means having to wear those orthopaedic boots once more.

'That's got to be a sure sign she's getting better, Lil,' Dad tells Mum, looking at you in wonder.

Frank lifts you like a groom carrying a bride over the threshold, the muscles in his arms flexing but no strain showing on his face.

'There's a girl,' he says, and you snuggle into his shoulder as he sits you on his lap. He plays 'Morning Has Broken' – his arms reaching the keys from around your waist – and you even moan along to the hymn.

When Dad picks up your harmonica and suggests a rendition of 'Danny Boy', I expect Mum to remind him that our guests are trying to relax next door, but she just continues to sit there, her eyes closed, and she even hums along to the tune.

By the time Frank's finished playing, Mum looks as if she's about to nod off. But she raises her hands to her face and begins to massage her temples. Without opening her eyes, she says: 'Say night, night to Frank now, Edie. Bedtime for my girl.'

'I'll take her,' I say. 'You have a rest.'

You begin to grumble and I'm not sure if it's because you don't like your routine tampered with, or whether you're not yet ready for bed.

Mum sighs as she stands. 'You two haven't had a moment to yourselves in weeks, and you'll be back at college soon. Why don't you head out to Brucciani's for an hour?'

I've been thinking about college for a while. I wonder if I should tell them that I won't return to Notre Dame, that I'll stay and help at home. But something stops me from saying it: an image of my lecturer and his wife sitting around a dining table with friends from France and Belgium and Switzerland, all of them drinking red wine and eating baguettes and Camembert cheese, classical music playing on the gramophone, the children asleep upstairs. Besides, if I quit I'd have put Frank through this long engagement for nothing. 'Perhaps I could postpone going back for a couple more weeks?'

Dad looks relieved but Mum shakes her head: 'You just concentrate on your studies. Thank goodness we have your graduation to look forward to.'

'Not to mention your wedding,' says Dad. 'It's been keeping us going, so it has.'

Frank gives me a little wink. 'You're quite right, Mrs Maloney. Maeve's worked so hard.' But he's standing up as he says this and he's carrying you towards me. 'I just popped in to see this snazzy girl of mine,' he's saying and he's kissing you on the forehead. 'I've got an early start tomorrow so I better get off.'

And there's that drained-out feeling that I've been getting recently, every time Frank leaves, like bed sheets wrung out to dry.

I am glad that Frank lowers you onto my lap, your body soft and warm. I bury my face in your curls – the colour and shape and texture of them identical to mine – so I don't have to smile breezily at Frank as if I don't mind; I don't have to breathe in his musky scent; I don't have to meet Mum's eye.

You let out an almighty howl, repeating the same noise over and over – a clammy, screeching sound. I can't tell if you are trying to say something, or whether this is a cry of frustration or tiredness or pain.

Frank leans over to calm you. 'What's all this nonsense?' he says. 'What's got into my snazzy girl?'

You sniff at his cardigan, wrinkling your nose at the unfamiliar scent of his aftershave, and then you lash out, still repeating this same broken sound. You scratch his face right from his temple to his chin with those lethal fingernails of yours that we've not yet managed to trim.

*

204

For those in peril. Cheryl. Frank stinks! For those in peril. Perfume. Morning has broken, like the first morning. Blackbird has spoken, like the first bird. What noise does a crow make? What noise does a horse make? Cheryl horse. Neigh! You stink! You're drunk! Bottle of beer, Dad's here! Never fear, Mum's here! Exhausticated and tired and shattered. The summer's gone, and all the flow'rs are dying, 'tis you, 'tis you must go and I must bide.

*

LANCASHIRE HEALTH BOARD
PRESCRIPTION

Mr
Mrs Lillian Maloncy
Miss

Address: Sea View Lodge, 31 Marine Road West
Age and diagnosis of patient: 53 yrs, menopausal fatigue and migraines
For use only by dispensing officer:

* Amylobarbitone sodium (30 tablets): 1 per day, before bed

Signature of Doctor:
Doctor P. R. Samuel
Date: October 14, 1954

*

I sneak my hand into Frank's pocket and snuggle my palm against his. I am glad that he has suggested a stroll around the city, that he isn't dashing straight back home. We are wandering aimlessly through a part of Liverpool I've never ventured into before. I am grateful for the balmy September evening, for the smells of fried chicken and egg curry, for the sounds of guitars and kettledrums and tambourines. I am grateful, finally, to have some time alone with Frank.

Deep down, part of me is also grateful, in a way, to be back at college. I won't have to lie awake, starting at every noise in the night, getting up and leaning over you to check that you're breathing. Vince has been visiting each day but he'll be returning to Cambridge soon, and Frank has been coming whenever he can but he's busy doing overtime at the garage. I'll return to Sea View Lodge every weekend and I promise myself that I'll get up early to sort out the guest breakfasts; I'll change your nappy; and I'll hold you still so that Mum can trim your nails. The hardest part is watching your hand shakily lifting the spoon – a skill you've just relearnt; the way you gaze at me adoringly; your wobbly attempts to smile.

Frank and I snake through street upon street of terraces, winding our way through alleyways. And all this time, I am trying to find a way to explain to Frank about what really happened that night with you.

Frank has a bottle of ale and, although I don't much like beer, I take a swig when he offers it to me. We walk like this as night slowly falls, the bottle passing between Frank's hand and mine. All the while I'm hoping that we're not spotted by any of the nuns from Notre Dame. My scholarship is reliant on good moral standing as well as top marks.

I suggest that we go into one of the social clubs for a bite to eat, but Frank simply shakes his head and we continue to walk. It's always been down to me to comfort Frank – when he flunked his exams, when his band failed to get gigs, when the bank manager refused him a loan. I don't know how to tell him that *he* now needs to comfort *me*.

He looks as if he's on the verge of saying something and I half hope that he will come straight out with it, that he'll ask what really happened.

There's an abrupt gap between the terraces where a house was bombed, and a group of boys are playing football in the empty lot. The ball comes bouncing towards us. Frank stops it with his foot, kicks it right back and then runs over to join their game. I lean against the wall, which bears the marks of what used to be floors and ceilings and staircases – its innards exposed.

Frank cheers as one of the boys dribbles the ball past the others and then kicks it into the makeshift goal. I imagine us, some years from now, enjoying a summer's evening in our own backyard, a baby feeding at my breast, a little one tugging at my skirt, Frank teaching our eldest to catch.

A woman opens her front door, and calls for her son to return inside. Over the next half hour, other women call out from their doorsteps or from opened windows until each of the boys has returned home.

Frank makes his way back to me – he's out of breath and his floppy hair has stuck to his forehead with sweat.

'Guess what I was thinking about?' I ask, standing on tiptoes and then pulling his forehead towards mine. We haven't played this game in years but I feel sure he'll know that I was picturing him playing with children of our own.

We stand there for a moment or two, our foreheads pressed together, and then he gently pulls away and stares into my eyes for a long, long time. 'I'm not sure,' he says in the end, sighing and shaking his head. 'Do you know, I've no idea.'

The football, which has rolled into the gutter, is slowly deflating.

I look back at Frank. 'Try harder,' I tell him.

His breath is warm with exertion and beer, and his skin is hot with sweat. My body knows now that sometimes the wrong thing *is* the right thing, my arms instinctively drawing his chest towards mine, my heels lifting from the ground as Frank presses my back to the wall.

The sensation of him, hard beneath his jeans, makes me feel somehow powerful and something inside me gives way.

Everything else is blocked out: I just know that if I succumb to Frank, everything else will be okay.

I raise my face to his but when our lips touch he blinks as if he's just woken. He holds his face away and steps back, and I am left standing there against the wall, my skirt rucked up and my blouse in need of rearranging.

He says nothing, just sighs deeply and runs his fingers through his hair.

I find myself blurting out everything: I don't miss a single detail of what happened on the night of our birthday.

I tell him about sprinkling baking soda into the water, about working up a lather, about rubbing a soapy cloth from your ears to your toes. I tell him about shampooing your curls, about my plan to paint your lips with my new Max Factor lipstick, about the tufts of hair in your armpits that I never took the time to shave.

I tell him about the brooch that I'd intended to pin to the bow at the back of my dress, about not being sure where I'd left it. I tell him about turning from you and leaving the bathroom, while you continued to giggle and splash.

I admit that I can't be sure how long I stayed in our bedroom, searching for the brooch.

I even tell him about spreading my new brassiere on my bed, about tracing my fingers across its lace, imagining his hands on our wedding night.

I tell him about the noise from the bathroom, about racing across the landing, about your limbs flailing, your mouth contorted, your face half submerged.

I tell him that I can't get rid of the sounds that came out of you then: those terrible phlegm-filled cries.

And Frank just stands there as I tell him all this.

I want him to take me in his arms, to say he still loves me, that it was all a terrible accident. But the silence between us is filled with the distant sounds of tambourines and kettledrums and guitars.

CHAPTER THIRTEEN

It was gone 3pm and Zenka would be itching to serve up her twelve-course supper as soon as the first star appeared in the sky. I felt too weak to rise, but I could hardly excuse myself on the grounds of illness when poor old Dot was making the effort to get here.

I'd spent all day up in this room, listening to Dave and Len hauling my things across the lawn, Zenka calling out to them with instructions on what to dry out in the utility room and what to replace in the shed. But the noise from outside had faded over the past hour or so.

I was counting to ten in French, preparing to shrug off my quilt at *dix*, when a knock sounded at my door.

Dave called out: 'Are you decent?'

'Just one moment!' I called back, throwing off my covers. No doubt Zenka would have told him that I'd spent the whole day in bed. There was no such thing as privacy around here.

My feet felt a little unsteady and I had to balance myself on my bedside table. My hand brushed against your harmonica: the same metal that you used to raise to your mouth, blowing and dribbling until a note blasted out; the same metal from which Dad used to form those happy-sad sounds.

'You okay?' called Dave.

I could have done without the prospect of Zenka's pickled herring, smoked eel and sauerkraut. And I could have done without another scene with Dave.

'Come in,' I called, before remembering that my hair was unbrushed, my face unwashed.

Dave loitered at the threshold of my room. 'Sorry to disturb you,' he said, 'when you're trying to get some rest.'

'My first day off since 1955.'

'Zenka thinks you might be upset about yesterday,' he said. 'I'm sorry for losing my temper.'

'You do know that Len and Steph are just like friends really?'

'Can I come in?'

I sat in my armchair, averting my gaze from the damp patch at the corner of the ceiling. Dave perched on the end of my bed – the only man ever to have done so, discounting that retired headmaster who claimed to have been walking in his sleep.

'I don't know what to think,' said Dave. 'He makes her happy, doesn't he?'

'Jennifer Tait has booked them into the clinic,' I blurted out. 'She said to err on the side of caution.'

Dave sat there, staring at the carpet, his hand rubbing up and down his arm, the slightest hint of a tan line revealed and then hidden as his T-shirt sleeve lifted and fell. 'Yeah,' he said in the end, still staring at the carpet, 'Dot mentioned it, and the mental capacity test.'

I had imagined many possible responses to this news, but I had never expected Dave to react like this. Eventually he looked up and said, 'Trish used to say that it was a good thing in a way, when Steph had tantrums as a toddler, or when she was embarrassed to hold our hands in her early teens.'

I thought of that cradle, its hinges creaking, its lemony blankets sodden from the rain. Zenka and Dave and Steph and Len, they would all have seen it standing exposed on our back lawn.

For the first time, I let myself imagine that Len and Steph might really share their nights as well as their days: that she might sidestep the creaky floorboards; he might make room beneath the duvet, lifting up the bedclothes to invite her in; they might share ticklish secrets just the two of them. And then I saw a vision of my own life made up of night after night of a bed unfilled.

I sat here in the attic room we used to share, a room I never expected to sleep in alone. Sometimes I used to will myself to fall asleep before you did else your little snores would keep me awake for hours; sometimes I'd wait until I heard you nod off before I'd dream of Frank's lips and his hands.

'I do appreciate everything you've done for Steph,' said Dave. 'It's meant the world to me to know how well she's been loved.'

*

I stand with my friends outside Notre Dame, worrying at my engagement ring. They're throwing glances at each other – concerned on my behalf that Frank is running so late. These girls, in many ways, are just like me: Anny from Birkenhead who loves Baudelaire; Mary who wants to teach history back at her old school in Southport; Sarah who'd really like to be an actress but has been persuaded to give teaching a go. We borrow each other's dancing shoes and books and rosary beads. But my engagement ring makes me different: a man has proposed and I have accepted and this is only just the start of things.

It won't be long, though, before they each follow suit. But marriage will take me along a path that you can never share.

Every time I hear the sound of an engine, I convince myself that it'll be Frank. I try not to look up too eagerly. Mum and Dad have persuaded me not to return to Morecambe for once, insisting that you are doing just fine: walking with assistance, singing more cheerfully, eating huge mounds of sausage and mash. You'll be talking again soon enough, they're sure. It's the first weekend that Frank and I will have spent alone together in months, so I have it all planned: tea in the refectory with the girls from my dormitory, and then drinks in the Philharmonic Dining Rooms with my film society friends before the screening of *Les Enfants du Paradis* at Liverpool University's cinema. We'll give the movie a miss because it's not Frank's sort of thing. In any case, it'll be a good excuse to sneak off, just the two of us, to try out one of the coffee houses in town. Frank and I will have a good time. Everything will work out fine.

But the refectory will close in twenty minutes and we're supposed to be meeting in the pub in half an hour.

This time when an engine sounds, Frank's Ford Anglia races down Mount Pleasant. He screeches to a halt right flush to the kerb, despite having pulled in at such speed.

The girls all cheer, their eyes on Frank as he jumps out of the car and sweeps me up in his embrace. His exuberance fills me with relief, his touch reminding me of the way things used to be. I feel proud to have him as my fiancé – this man who I've admired since we were kids; this man whose band will soon play gigs; this man who's going to run his own garage.

He holds my face in his hands and looks into my eyes.

The scarf I bought in Lee's with some of my scholarship cheque is tied in a bow at my neck – I thought it looked rather fine, but it feels a bit silly now.

'How's my swotty fiancée?' he asks, and I know he won't notice my scarf or my skirt or the way I've styled my hair. 'Nice of your swotty friends to give me a welcome reception!' he adds, winking at Sarah.

The girls look at each other, not quite sure what to make of his comment, but when I start to laugh they realise he's joking and look relieved.

'The refectory closes any minute,' I tell him. 'There's liver and onion, and for afters there's syrup sponge. And we're supposed to be at the Philharmonic Rooms soon.'

Frank frowns. 'I thought we'd grab dinner at a place in town. Glen and Audrey mentioned somewhere they like. It was supposed to be a surprise.'

I feel sure I'd mentioned on the telephone about drinks in the Philharmonic Rooms with the film society folk, about the screening that we could skip if he preferred.

'The honeymooners who were staying the day before you first came here,' says Frank. 'Don't tell me you've forgotten them.'

I hesitate. I am looking forward to introducing Frank to Doctor Pascal, who's married to a woman from Liverpool. Their little boy speaks both English and French. They are friends of Soeur Blandine, who is unlike any of the nuns at St Mary's: she does not cover her corkscrew curls; she smokes miniature cigars and drinks Pineau from her convent in Belgium. She's even set up a school in the Congo.

Frank nudges me and says: 'Bet I can read your mind.'

'Try me.'

Then he presses his forehead against mine and pretends to draw my thoughts: his tacit way of telling me that all will be well, that he knows me through and through, that he does not cast blame.

'You're worried you'll starve,' he announces, moving his head from mine, and I'm aware that my friends are watching us and laughing.

'I do love that about you,' Frank says, as if we're not being observed. 'The way you like your food.'

Frank loves me, I'm thinking. *Thank God that's not changed.*

'You still playing in your band?' puts in Sarah, running her hand through her long black hair.

Frank gives her a rendition of 'Bewitched, Bothered and Bewildered', right there on the kerbside. He tells her that it's hard to rehearse now that they've all moved out of the barracks. But they're sure to start getting bookings soon.

'Ronnie Scott's playing at the Locarno tonight.' She leans forwards as if she's telling us a secret. There's something in her tone that tells me I've gone up in her opinion.

'We could just eat in the refectory,' says Frank, taking

hold of my hand. 'If you've got your heart set on this swotty film society.'

There'll surely be another opportunity later this year to introduce Frank to my film society friends, to take him to the Philharmonic Rooms. He doesn't have to meet Doctor Pascal and Soeur Blandine tonight. We might end up chatting in French and then I'd have to translate. It'd be easier to sit alone in a café, talking about Frank's garage and his band, about Sea View Lodge and Mum and Dad and you. Later, perhaps, he'll lead me into the Locarno, holding my hand and introducing me as his girl. I can't risk spoiling things now.

The girls gather around Frank's car, taking it in turns to sit in the passenger seat, stretching their legs and stroking the camel-coloured leather and polished walnut.

As we drive off, Mary shouts, 'Don't do anything we wouldn't do!' and Sarah says, 'Might see you in there later.' And they wave and wave – and I do feel lucky to be driving in a Ford Anglia to a night on the town with my fiancé.

I wind up the window as Frank speeds down the hill, and we are alone again – all snug and close in his car, separated only by the handbrake and the gearstick. I'll never tire of him: the line ironed down the front of his trousers, the thread that's begun to unravel at the left-hand cuff of his cardigan. Late tonight, perhaps his hand will be at the small of my back, his stomach and chest against mine, and he'll be leading me around the dance floor to Ronnie Scott and his band.

When Frank pulls to a stop at the junction, he takes hold of my hand and toys with my engagement ring. 'It's good to see Edie back on her feet,' he says. 'She's a marvel that sister of yours.'

Part of me is tempted to marry him tomorrow, to let him have his way with me every night, to fall pregnant again and again until Frank and I have a whole brood.

'Once we're married, I was thinking that we could host groups from local asylums on their annual holidays. Mum and I could serve afternoon teas and you and Dad and Edie could entertain them of an evening with your songs.'

Frank doesn't answer. I stroke his arm but his body is rigid. He keeps his eyes on the road and releases the handbrake.

'I don't mean instead of your garage,' I say.

I wait for him to answer but he focuses intently on his driving and I can see his Adam's apple move each time he swallows. 'I thought you wanted to spread your wings,' he says in the end.

There had been a time when I'd tried to persuade Frank that we could move to Paris. But deep down I'd always known that this could never happen. After Frank finished his national service, we'd talked of making our home in Liverpool: we'd imagined dancing all night in underground bars; I'd take him to coffee houses where we'd set the world to rights; Frank's band could play in the Casanova and the Kinkajou. Back then I'd assumed that there would be plenty of time before we'd need to move back to Morecambe; plenty of time before Mum and Dad would need me to take care of you.

'Everything has changed,' I say.

I reach to him across the handbrake, kissing the birthmark on his neck.

'It *has* changed,' Frank replies quietly. 'You're not wrong there.'

*

Dear Frank,

I've tried to write to you umpteen times since I heard about your illness. In my heart of hearts I know that I won't get as far as addressing the envelope, let alone sticking it in the post.

I wish I'd asked years ago whether you blamed me for what happened to Edie, whether you thought I'd end up a negligent mother.

I wish I'd asked whether you couldn't bear the prospect of moving into Sea View Lodge, whether you weren't up to the task of caring for us.

I wish I'd asked what first caused you to have second thoughts and when you first felt that things had broken?

But it's far too late for all of this now, so I'll leave you to spend your last days in peace.

*

My memory of those moments before the phone call are as crisp as morning frost. I see my young self sitting cross-legged on my dormitory bed, trying to read Flaubert's descriptions of the servant girl and her selfless devotion to her mistress's children. But part of me is aware of one of the other students applying nail polish and singing along to the wireless.

I remember, sharp as anything, reaching the bit where the servant girl has a seizure, and feeling as if I could not bear to reread it – my mind flitting between Flaubert's own convulsions, the other student, Frank and you.

I really should file and polish my own nails before I return home next weekend, and I am trying to recall when we last clipped yours. I must help Mum to do them as soon as I get back to Sea View Lodge.

I am only dimly aware of the phone ringing down the hallway, of the other student's singing petering out. I can't get your favourite line from *Chicken Licken* out of my head: 'The sky is falling in.'

'It's for you,' she says, approaching my bed. 'Gerald Roper, I think he said.'

I tear down the corridor and am out of breath when I reach the phone: 'What's happened?' I ask. 'Has she fitted?'

'Your mother's had a funny turn, my dear. It's nothing to worry about.'

'Mum?'

'She's just rather faint and disorientated, that's all.'

'What has Doctor Samuel said?'

Aneurisms bleed into the pause that follows; tumours swell; infections rage.

'I'm sure it's nothing that a long rest won't cure. But you'd be a great help to your father if you could get home.'

I remember walking back into the dormitory, the smell of nail polish turning my stomach. I know that I didn't say a word to the other student, just headed straight to my wardrobe and picked out my nightgown and some underwear, a commentary running through my head the whole time: *I am folding my clothes with excessive care; I am putting my toothbrush into my wash-bag; I am fastening the clasp on my blue leather case.*

But I can't remember getting to Lime Street Station, or whether I had to wait long for a train. I simply remember sitting in the carriage, looking at the other passengers, and wondering whether they could sense my fear.

I tell myself our story, beginning at the moment I wandered out of the bathroom: your seizure, the certification hearing, Mum's exhaustion, Dad and Frank withdrawing into themselves. The terraces give way to new suburban bungalows and the railway platforms widen and eventually grey gives way to green. But everything has been looking up: you can walk if one of us links our arms with yours; Dad has been entertaining our guests with tunes on your harmonica; Mum has got some colour in her cheeks; Frank still loves me.

A lady of about Mum's age passes me a handkerchief and pours a cup of tea from her flask. As I sip it, I close my eyes: Mum may be little but she's strong; no family suffers such misfortune; this cannot be happening to us. Mr Roper is probably overreacting, as usual: I'll get back to find everything's fine.

But as soon as I reach Sea View Lodge, I know that everything is far from fine. I recognise Mr Roper's car outside and Father O'Reilly's bicycle. All of our curtains are drawn and only the lounge lights are on. As I head up the front path, the house seems deadly quiet. And that line from *Chicken Licken* resurfaces: 'The sky is falling in.'

Mr Roper opens the door, and leads me straight into the lounge. 'Your mother's still rather poorly, I'm afraid.'

You are kneeling on the floor in your habitual position, legs askew, and you are rocking back and forth with your fists clenched to your ears.

'Your father's adamant that he won't let Doctor Samuel set foot in here,' Mr Roper tells me, his voice hushed.

One of Mum's friends from the church looks up from her ineffectual attempts to console you. 'You can hardly blame him,' she says, gesturing towards you with her eyes.

I remember Doctor Samuel at the certification hearing, averting his gaze from mine.

'I suggest it only as a precautionary measure,' adds Mr Roper. 'He'd just prescribe bed rest, I'm sure.'

I step towards you but Mr Roper puts in: 'I suggest you go straight up to see your mother.'

Their bedroom is so dark that I can hardly see a thing. But I can hear Mum's breath, rattling and foreign, the sound each time Dad swallows, the mutter of Father O'Reilly's prayer. He nods at me as I sit down beside him, and then he crosses himself and takes his leave.

'All's all right, Mum,' I say, holding her hand. The tightness of her grip reassures me. 'You're going to pull through.'

As my eyes adjust to the dark, I see that Dad is staring into space, not seeming to see Mum or me.

I should never have gone back to college; I should never have put myself first.

Mum's face is twisted at an awkward angle and it's difficult to understand what she's trying to say.

'What happened?' I make out in the end, her grip on my hand tightening.

'You've just had a funny turn,' I explain. 'You're exhausted, that's all.'

She shakes her head, her movements almost imperceptible, her eyes beseeching.

She had looked at me like this once before. *Try to remember, my love*, she'd said then, her hand stroking my hair. *Please try*.

I should have admitted at the time that I had wandered off in search of my brooch, that I couldn't be sure how long I'd left you alone in the bath while I stood in our bedroom, admiring our new outfits and dreaming of the night ahead.

Despite the pleading look in her eyes, I continue to stroke her hand and I persuade myself that I cannot be sure what she means. Frank has been so distant since I told him what happened. It would be selfish to burden Mum with my confession now.

Mum begins to speak again, her voice so weak that I have to hold my ear right up to her mouth. 'Edie,' she keeps saying. 'Edie.' And then eventually I make out: 'Take care of her.' The effort causes her head to fall back on the pillow.

'Dad and I will keep on top of things until you're fully recovered and I'll never let you get so exhausted again.'

Mum squeezes my hand even harder and there's a desperate look in her eyes. Part of me wants to call Doctor Samuel, and yet this was the man who would have forced your removal to the Royal Albert, the man who would have sterilised you. I lean right up close to Mum again but, although I can feel the heat from her skin and I can smell the sourness of her breath, I can barely hear her words. 'Maeve,' she tries.

'I'm here, Mum,' I keep saying. 'I'm right here.'

'Maeve,' she tries again.

And in the end I think I decipher what she's trying to say: 'Maeve, take care of yourself.'

*

Breathe in through your nose and out through your mouth. That's it. Where's Mum? Mum's in her bedroom. This is the night mail crossing the border, bringing the cheque and the postal order. Night, night. Sleep tight. And I shall sleep in peace until you come to me.

*

Dad and I spend all evening alternating between sitting at Mum's bedside and sitting downstairs with you. All night, I pray: *God save her, God save her. I'll do anything if you'll just grant us this.*

Every time I enter her room, she tries to tell me something, repeating the same phrase over and over. But it's difficult to make out what she wants. I try holding a glass of water to her lips but she shakes her head; I offer her a cold compress but she doesn't want this either; I switch the lights on but this makes her wince. And all the time, I'm thinking: *This cannot be happening to us.*

As the night draws in, Mum is becoming paler and paler, and desperate moaning sounds come from her lopsided mouth. I try to prop her head up with pillows; I make sure that the blanket isn't tucked too tightly into the mattress; I offer her the water once more.

I feel guilty for being aware of the ache in my back from leaning over her bed; guilty for nipping to the toilet; guilty for the relief I feel when Dad takes over at her bedside; guilty for having returned to college; guilty for wanting to call Doctor Samuel; guilty for failing to contact him; guilty for having left you in the bath.

Just before midnight, I enter Mum and Dad's bedroom to find it silent. I hold my breath and lean right close to her mouth.

I stay there for several moments although I know in my heart that her breath has stopped. She looks like Mum and, at the same time, not quite Mum – as if her lips have never smiled at one of Dad's jokes, as if her arms have never drawn me into a hug, as if her eyes have never brightened at the sight of you stepping towards her.

I'll never know whether she died with Dad at her bedside or whether she went as Dad and I crossed on the stairs. I'll never know whether she died in her sleep or whether her last moments were filled with pain and fear. But what I did know suddenly, and with startling clarity, was that all night she had been asking for you and we had kept you apart.

CHAPTER FOURTEEN

Sea View Lodge was filled with the smell of Zenka's ham roasting, making me long for my Dad's fried breakfasts: bacon and eggs, soda farl and white pudding, mushrooms and fried potatoes and heaps of baked beans. It was the one meal he continued to cook well into his nineties, and afterwards he'd sit on that bench at the bottom of the garden, smoke his pipe, and then snooze. He must have thought of you and Mum sometimes when he sat there, staring into the distance. But we never uttered your names.

I would do things differently with Len: we'd talk of Dot after she died, just as I talked with Steph about Trish. It did no good to put a stopper on grief – if only Dad could have taught me this.

I closed my eyes and tried to conjure up Mum and you: your chin in her hand as she painted your lips; or singing 'For Those in Peril on the Sea' as you helped her rub beeswax into our furniture; or your occasional blasts from the gob-tin as she insisted that you were not your daddy's Fenian, you were your mother's English rose.

But another memory kept elbowing these soft-focused versions of you out of the way: a fraught trip to the market; stamping of feet; the scent of perfume; a tube of lipstick in China Red.

And then Vincent's words slipped into my mind – the things he'd said when he returned: *We're neither of us getting any younger. It would mean so much to me to make our peace.*

How would he be spending Christmas Eve, down at his retirement complex? I could see him, sitting in an armchair, his newspaper unread in his lap, a cup of tea growing cold by his side. But he wasn't the type to mope, was Vincent. He'd have called in at a neighbour's, bearing mince pies; he'd have arranged to meet old friends at the pub before heading to midnight Mass.

I could just see him winding his cable-knit scarf around his neck, looking every bit the Frenchman, shielding himself against the cold. I could just see him pulling his sheepskin gloves onto those large hands of his: hands that had dared many years ago to reach out to the woman who would become his wife, the breadth of his palm against hers; hands that Hélène would have clutched both times she went into labour; hands that he'd have pressed to his eyes when their little girl died; hands that would later have held cold compresses to Hélène's forehead as he sat by her bedside during her long demise. These hands of his – their skin the colour of sand, their downy hair like sunlight, their nails always clean and pared – these hands I could have known and loved all my days.

I reached into my bedside cabinet for the stack of Vincent's Christmas cards, all fingers and thumbs as I tried to untie the orange ribbon. His address and phone number at the retirement complex were written in chestnut ink inside last year's card, his script so elegant that it rivalled my own.

My mouth was dry as I picked up the receiver but I had to dial his number immediately, lest cowardice overtake.

*

It is our twenty-first birthday and we are walking along the promenade with Frank. He's holding your hand and I wish he would take hold of mine. We will marry at St Mary's next summer after my last exam. By then, Frank might even have saved up enough to put down the deposit on a garage. Dad has said that he can postpone paying him back for his share of the car.

I would usually reach out to Frank if I wanted to walk hand in hand. But it doesn't seem like a good idea today. Besides, it is muggy so the last thing I need is to press my clammy palm against his.

'How old are you, Edie?' I ask.

'Eighteen!'

'You fibber. Try again.'

'Nineteen!' Your shout is fraught with frustration.

'Higher, higher.'

You smack your head with the ball of your hand and I have to coax your stiff arm back to your side. 'Don't hurt yourself, Edie. That's not nice. We're twenty-one today. You know that.'

The sky is grey, the air is close, and the sea is ominously still as if holding its breath before a storm. The Ferris wheel is not rotating and the bumper cars are all parked up. Although a guard sits in the cabin, no one queues at the entrance. Everyone has decided that today is a day for drinking lemonade and eating ice cream and congregating around a wireless, waiting for the storm to break. Frank is in a bit of a huff because he doesn't want to go to the market. But I can't miss the bedding stall, which only comes to town once a month.

If I'm honest, I would rather you hadn't come with us, because you don't much like shopping and you'll only get in the way. I've been looking forward to dressing together later on, but I would also have liked some time alone with Frank.

We've both been eagerly anticipating this dinner dance at the Midland Hotel but things seem to be going awry. You are fractious – perhaps because we're not following your usual routine – and Frank's moods sometimes last for days.

All the awnings are out, the shop shutters are open and

the tables are laden with potatoes and beans and lettuces and even bananas and pineapples.

Gilbert's is up ahead – the jewellers where I hope Frank has bought my birthday present. The bracelet I've been coveting is studded with rhinestones, its links shaped in figures of eight. I imagine Frank's hands brushing against my wrist as he fixes the clasp at my pulse; I imagine the barely there feel of it against my skin, how the rhinestones will be set off by the ocean-blue of my new silk dress; I imagine it glinting on our wedding day, the choristers singing as Frank lifts my hand and eases my ring right up the length of my finger. You will join the choir again. As soon as I'm back from college, I'll insist that Mr Roper lets you return.

But on my wedding day, my attention won't be on the choir or the congregation. I will only focus on the scar at the base of Frank's left thumb from an accident he had at the garage, and the burn mark on the inside of his arm; on my manicured fingernails, and on my writer's bump; on the rings we will exchange.

As we approach Gilbert's, I slow down to peek through the window. I want to see whether the bracelet is still there or whether Frank has picked up on my hints.

Through the shop front, I see boxes and boxes of rings and necklaces, bangles and brooches; gold and silver, diamonds and rubies, sapphires and pearls. I don't see the rhinestone bracelet that I've set my heart on. Frank has hurried you ahead and is gesturing for me to catch up. Despite his black moods and unpredictability, I love this man.

I catch up with you and Frank, and he nods in acknowledgement but neither of us speaks. Instead, I breathe in his familiar smells of motor oil and tobacco and, as we approach the sweet stall at the entrance to the market, I notice the female stall-keeper do a double take when she sees you, and then steal a second glance at Frank – my olive-skinned fiancé – and I glow with the knowledge that he has chosen me.

You are unusually quiet – perhaps you have sensed the stall-keeper's discomfort, or perhaps you have picked up on Frank's bad mood.

A clap of thunder explodes overhead and rain tips from the sky like a washerwoman emptying dirty water from an upstairs window. We duck under the tarpaulin cover of the sweet stall, the rain drumming against it. Just as I am paying for a liquorice stick for you, the corner of the tarpaulin collapses and a shock of water drenches us – streaming through our hair and plastering our clothes to our skin. Instinctively, we have grabbed each other: you are crying, and I am laughing, and Frank is peeling the hair from our eyes, a droplet of water sliding down the bridge of his nose.

'There's the butcher's,' Frank points out. 'Have you got the ration book?'

I want to get to the bedding stall before all the best bargains sell out. I squeeze the rainwater from my hair and gesture towards the linens, but he is already leading you towards the butcher's. At least I can look at the bedding without getting distracted by you.

The floor of the market is mucky where the rain comes down between the tarpaulin covers. I wish I hadn't worn my new navy shoes as their tortoiseshell leather is now splattered with mud. I should have kept them wrapped in their tissue until this evening, but I couldn't resist trying them on.

When I reach the bedding section, the stall-keeper won't let me touch any of her fabrics because I'm so drenched. I point at the ones I like and she lifts the protective covers and lets me take a peek. There are piles of sky-blue candlewick bedspreads, pink Welsh blankets edged with satin, Lancashire cotton pillowcases with flowers embroidered at the edges and matching sheets and quilts. These are the ones I want; I know that straightaway. The embroidery almost matches the stitching I've done myself on the muslin I've already bought for our bedroom curtains. I can just imagine slipping under these covers in our very own bed: the cool satin of my nightie; the warmth of Frank's limbs.

I have boxes of goodies stowed in a suitcase under my bed at college – things I've been collecting ever since Frank proposed: bone-handled cutlery, rose-coloured sherry glasses, plates and cups and saucers, some of them plain white, others patterned with rosebuds, and others still edged with a single green stripe. Each and every one of these things I've chosen with care and bought with money I put aside each week from my scholarship cheque – money I would have spent on cigarettes had I smoked. I love every single thing I've bought and I'm looking forward to showing them all to Frank. There are quite a few things he hasn't yet seen because he hasn't made it up to Liverpool much this year; he's been doing lots of overtime to save up for a deposit, and it makes more sense for me to come home so that I can also see you.

'I'll go ahead and get them,' I tell the stall-keeper. 'I don't think my fiancé minds what I buy.'

'I never have met a man who likes to shop,' she says as she wraps our new pillowcases and sheets and quilt in brown paper and ties it up with string.

Just as I'm paying for the bedding, I spot you and Frank chatting to Cheryl at the make-up stand. Although I am training to be a teacher at Notre Dame College and I am here buying bedding with Frank Bryson, the sight of Cheryl still makes me feel like an awkward thirteen-year-old. She's wearing a cream mackintosh that's belted tight at the waist and her hair is held in place by a red silk scarf.

I pluck up the courage to make my way over. You are stamping your feet by the time I reach you. 'Hush now, Edie,' I say. 'What's the matter?'

'Behave!' you shriek. 'I'm shocked and appalled!'

'It's okay now, Edie. Nothing to worry about when Maeve's here.'

From the corner of my eye, I see Cheryl raise her eyebrows at Frank. But when she notices me looking, she concentrates on rearranging her stock – lining bottles of nail varnish in order of shade, opening up compacts and arranging blusher brushes.

I try to make conversation but you are still stamping and crying out. Cheryl's gaze lingers on the new bedding in my arms. I am a woman who is engaged to be married. I have just bought Lancashire cotton sheets for my marital bed. Cheryl does not yet wear a diamond on her ring finger. And yet I feel somehow as if she has the upper hand.

You squeeze me so tightly that your nails dig into my palm.

'I'll just take that China Red lipstick,' I end up saying, 'and then we'd best get Edie home.'

As I lean towards her with my coins, I catch the overpowering scent of her perfume.

'Yes,' replies Cheryl, looking at Frank. 'You'd best make the most of the gap in the rain.'

*

It's raining, it's pouring, the old man is snoring. What noise does an old man make? Snore! See Saw Margery Daw. Knock and the door will be opened. Seek and ye shall find. Where's Frank? I'm the finder, you're the seeker. Warm, warm, warmer. Where's Cheryl? You can do it, I can help you. Warm, warm, warmer.

CHAPTER FIFTEEN

Perhaps Vincent would be in the kitchen of his retirement bungalow when his phone rang out, slicing cured sausage for his dinner, along with strips of fig jelly and wedges of ripe cheese. Perhaps his shirtsleeves would be rolled to the elbow, revealing arms still muscular from gardening and piano playing and daily walks. Or perhaps he would just be slumped on his couch.

'Hello,' said his voice in my ear – faint but unmistakably his.

'It's Maeve,' I said.

His breath whispered through the receiver and then he fell quiet before he slowly said: 'Maeve.'

I wouldn't have blamed him for raising his voice or slamming down the phone, but there was something about the way he let out his breath and repeated my name that showed me he was pleased to hear my voice.

'I'm sorry,' I said.

I could still hear his breath but he didn't reply.

'It was wrong of me to throw you out into the night.'

My need to know for sure the truth about Frank grew in the silence that followed, my readiness to hear it battling against my desire to make amends with Vincent. 'Somewhere deeply buried, I think I've always known that Frank was having an affair with Cheryl,' I said, the sound of their names tawdry when passed from me to Vincent. 'Even on the day of our wedding, I think I knew deep down,' I went on, aware that I was blathering. 'But I need to hear you say it. I want to cast out any doubt.'

The sound of Vincent swallowing merged with the drumming of my pulse in my ear.

'I didn't realise he'd left any room for doubt,' he said in the end, his voice clipped.

'It must have been hard for you too,' I tried.

'For me?'

'Weren't you courting Cheryl for a while?'

Vincent laughed at that but the sound was joyless. 'I don't know where you got that idea from.'

'She was at that dinner party, the one your father threw when you got offered your place at Cambridge.'

'I don't honestly remember her being there, Maeve, although I remember you and Edie quite clearly.'

'When did it start?' I asked, ridding myself of the question I'd stored up for so long. 'I mean between Cheryl and Frank.'

'Oh, Maeve,' he said, his tone frustrated and yet not quite unkind. 'It was all so long ago.'

Vincent was a man who had fallen asleep beside his wife each night for several decades; a man who'd lost a daughter; and seen his son marry and leave. No doubt he regarded me as a tired old spinster, raking over old times.

'I need to know.'

'It had been going on for a long time.'

I wondered if he was toying with his wedding ring.

'They kept putting off telling you – after your birthday, after your mother's funeral, after your last exam.' I couldn't tell whether his anger was directed at Frank or at me. 'She kept giving him ultimatums, and he kept thinking that the two of you might work things out. But then he kept picking up with her again, and she kept on taking him back.'

It had started before our birthday. Frank had broken things between us long before I'd confessed to him that I'd left you alone in the bath. I had chosen to believe that I pushed him into Cheryl's arms, and I continued to cling to this story even though it had threatened to drown me. 'I've spent years thinking that he wasn't up to the task,' I explained, half aware of Len and Steph singing down in the kitchen, 'that he was too weak to help me care for Dad and Edie and Sea View Lodge.'

'Well, that might also be true,' Vincent said abruptly. And then: 'Goodbye, Maeve,' his tone a little more gentle. 'I really must go.'

*

Dad refuses to leave the parlour when Mr Roper arrives. 'I can't face it, treasure,' he says. 'Would you tell him to go?' Your head is nestled on Dad's shoulder, the two of you rocking back and forth.

'He's brought a pan of beef and dumplings. Father O'Reilly's housekeeper must have made it.'

'He really must go,' Dad says, taking a swig from his bottle of beer. 'I wish he'd just leave us be.'

'He needs to know what hymns we want at the funeral,' I tell him, unable to believe that I'm saying such words. 'He needs to tell Father O'Reilly whether you'll give a culogy.'

You begin to hum 'For Those in Peril on the Sea' and Dad just repeats, 'Would you be a treasure, and ask him to leave us be?'

As I head back to Mr Roper, Dad joins in with your quiet song – the sound filling me with both anger and sadness. This should not be down to me, I'm thinking, even as I'm telling Mr Roper that Dad is seeing to you. I want also to tell him that we need some time; that we need to sit in the parlour, just the three of us; that we need to stare out of the window for hours on end. But Mr Roper is sitting there, the pan of beef and dumplings on the occasional table, his notepad open at the list of guests he's managed to inform of our bereavement.

'It's hit your father very badly,' he says. 'Your mother was such a pillar of strength.'

I long to talk about Mum: her skill at balancing all of her tasks without ever seeming rushed off her feet; her knack of knowing just what to say; her way of behaving as if life couldn't have been better – although things can't have turned out as she'd expected during her beauty queen days.

'You have very large shoes to fill, my dear,' Mr Roper goes on. 'You may as well start here and now by helping me with this.'

His formal tone and taut posture couldn't be more different from Vince's full vowels and hesitant movements. I want Vince to sit with us in the parlour; I want him to sing along with your tunes; I want him to help me cut your toast into shoulders to dip into soft-boiled eggs. More than anyone, it's Vince that I want right here, right now – Vince with his moon-face so unlike his father's pinched expression.

Mr Roper lists bidding prayers and Gospel readings, the names of Eucharistic ministers and people he's lined up to carry the offertory gifts.

'I thought it might be apt?' he asks.

'I'm sorry?' My mind has shielded itself from this conversation and I have no idea how my body has responded to Mr Roper's words: I could have been rocking or staring blankly or even humming one of your songs.

'I wondered about the choir singing "For Those in Peril on the Sea"?'

I agree that this would be apt, part of me realising that I should have offered him tea, part of me knowing that Mum would have taken the pan of beef and dumplings into the kitchen as soon as Mr Roper arrived, that she might have invited him to join us for dinner. But I do not interrupt him by offering tea or suggesting he stay because it is all I can manage not to break down.

'I've arranged for Vincent to come up from Cambridge so he can look after Edie.'

It takes me a moment to understand what he's said.

'Father O'Reilly's housekeeper would have done it,' he

continues, 'but she'll be preparing the refreshments for the wake.'

I want to tell him that I need you to sit beside me in the pew, your head resting on my shoulder, the scent of Pears soap on your skin.

I want to tell him that you are Mum's daughter, that you have far more reason to be there than him.

I want to tell him that you are a human being, that we all share the need to grieve.

My anger with him shrieks through my mind yet I remain silent; it races around my body yet somehow I remain still. 'That won't be necessary,' I tell him. 'Edie will be attending Mum's funeral with Dad and me.'

Mr Roper looks at me with open-mouthed amazement.

'Do you have everything you need?' I ask, knowing that my fury won't be contained for much longer.

As he gathers up his things, he tells me to heat through the stew on a low heat for at least twenty minutes. 'I cooked it extremely slowly,' he says, 'to make sure that the beef would be tender. There's carrots and dumplings in there too, so you don't need to worry about accompaniments.'

I am so shocked by the news that Mr Roper cooked the stew himself that I begin to wonder whether Mum was right all along. Maybe this greyhound of a man really is marvellous. Maybe we can rely on him.

'I'll tell Vincent to purchase his train ticket in any case,' says Mr Roper on his way out. 'You might find that you change your mind.'

*

My name's Edith Mary Maloney, 31 Marine Road West. What's your name? For where there are two or three gathered together in my name, there am I in the midst of them. This is the night mail crossing the border. Beeswax. Rub-a-dub-dub three men in a tub. Where's Mum? The summer's gone, and all the roses falling. Where's Mum gone? Oh, hear us when we cry to Thee.

*

I stand beside Cheryl in the kitchen, passing her every vase and jug and bottle we own. The air is heavy with the scent of lilies and our hands are stained with pollen. I try to focus on the rhythm of our work: the clink of glass on the sideboard, the rush of water from the tap, the snip of scissors on stalks.

I do not want to think about Dad at the lectern, his gaze fixed on the stained-glass window as if he didn't quite know how he'd found himself there. 'Lillian,' he'd said, his voice cracking and then his whole body crumpling. 'Lillian,' he'd said again, as if he were crying out to her for help.

As Cheryl and I continue to arrange the floral tributes, Mum's friends from St Mary's carry in trays of dirty cups and saucers and leftover vanilla slices and coconut macaroons.

I place one vase of lilies onto the kitchen table, nudging it until it sits right at the centre and trying not to think about the way I'd stayed in the pew, letting Mr Roper take over from Dad. I should have held Dad's hand and told the congregation about the pride Mum would take in a tray of perfectly baked meringues; about the hours she'd spend rubbing beeswax into the furniture, and running up tablecloths from fabrics she'd pick up at the haberdashery stall; about the precision with which she filed her nails and applied her red, red lipstick; about the way we always felt that everything was all right just because she was there.

Vince leads you through the kitchen, his movements grown more confident during his years at Cambridge, the bike riding and punting and rowing having lent his skin a wholesome shade of brown.

You walk slowly in the orthopaedic boots that Mum had ordered just before she died. Your gait is more lopsided than ever, you need to link arms to keep your balance, and your free hand is now permanently twisted out to the side. But, with help, you are walking again. And I'll get you speaking again if it's the last thing I do.

At least I'd stood up to Mr Roper about your right to attend Mum's funeral; at least you'd been sitting by my side, continuing to sing 'For Those in Peril on the Sea' when my voice cracked and gave way to tears.

'We thought we might leave them to it, didn't we, Edie?' says Vince as he sits you beside him on the back step, his arms around your shoulders. There's a low murmur of male voices coming from the drawing room where Mr Roper is sitting with Dad and Frank.

You are rocking back and forth and Vince is gently hushing in your ear and lifting your curls from your eyes.

I want his breath in my ear too, his hands on my hair. I want him to tell me that I was right to return to college, that it was what Mum wanted. But even as I'm thinking this, I leave you and Vince and I take another of the vases through to the drawing room.

Dad is staring out of the window, a line of drool trickling into his glass of whisky. He has not shaven since Mum died and his beard has begun to stray up his cheeks.

Mr Roper is talking to Frank in hushed tones, but they fall silent when they notice me. 'Take a seat,' says Mr Roper.

Frank joins me on the couch and holds my hand as he has not done in quite some time.

Mr Roper clears his throat: 'Perhaps your father has spoken to you about my proposal?'

Dad is still staring out of the window but I can't tell whether he notices the geese that fly in formation against the bank of pink clouds.

Don't abandon me, Dad, I'm thinking. *Keep going for me*. I need him to photograph my graduation, to walk me down the aisle, to hold my first child. I need him to help me with you. I want to take him to France, to introduce him to

235

wine and baguettes and Camembert cheese. I need him to see what we will become.

'Father O'Reilly and I have been putting our heads together,' continues Mr Roper, 'about how best to support your father, especially while you finish your exams and prepare for your wedding.'

There's something about the way Frank stares intently at Mr Roper that makes me think of a boy play-acting at being a man, something about the way his hand lies still and tense on mine.

I find it hard to like Mr Roper but Mum used to say that he was marvellous for soldiering on after Mrs Roper disappeared. He did represent us at the certification hearing; he did fight to get copies of all your medical records. And it is Mr Roper who has cancelled the guest bookings this week; Mr Roper who's arranged a rota with some of the women from St Mary's so there'll always be someone to lend a hand when we reopen.

'It need only be for a few months,' Mr Roper is saying: 'Just until you've graduated. Your father's in need of a break.'

I say nothing. The reports that Mum used to write for you pop into my mind. Do you remember how Mum and Dad would treat us to buck rarebit in the café on West End Pier after my last day of term?

– *Maeve has a vocabulary well beyond her years*, Mum would read out to Dad in between sips of fresh leaf tea.

– You're a clever girl, so you are, Dad would say.

– *She has already devoured half of the books in the library.*

– You take after your mammy.

– *And yet she is kind to those less gifted than her.*

– What did I tell you?

– *Although she is a creative soul, she must make sure that her imagination does not get the better of her.*

– You're your daddy's daughter, all right.

And then Mum would move on to the report she'd written for you:

– Edie has worked extremely hard this year.

– There's no denying it.

– She can recite the Hail Mary and the Our Father.

– And very devout she is too.

– She can even sing 'Danny Boy' from start to finish.

– Edith Mary Maloney, you're a real colleen. You sing like a star, so you do.

– and Maeve has even taught her to count to ten in both Latin and French.

– We must have done something right, Lillian.

– She brings a smile to the faces of even the most cantankerous folk.

– Our waifs and strays are the cleverest and most beautiful twins in the seven seas.

I must start up those reports again: *Edie is back on her feet.* Soon, please God, soon: *Edie is speaking again.*

'Father O'Reilly has kindly agreed to marry you the day after your graduation. Vincent will take on the duties of best man. And then after the wedding, Frank can move straight in here.'

I will never again feel Mum's hand on mine, painting my nails, or dressing a burn, or taking the whisk when my arm begins to tire.

She had been full of advice of late: *Your happiness should never depend solely on your man – you need friends as well, and interests of your own; plant ideas in his mind and let him think they're his.* And she'd begun to confide in me too: *I can forgive your dad's shortcomings because his jokes never fail to bring a smile to my face; I knew I'd chosen the best of men the day your dad stood up to the doctor who told us to send Edie to an asylum, pretend she'd never been born.*

But I had so much more to ask her about how to be a good wife and how to get the best from your man.

'Frank is in agreement about the nuptial arrangements,' says Mr Roper. 'It's all taken care of, isn't it, young man?'

I hear each time Frank swallows. He nods but says nothing, his hand still on mine.

*

April 16, 1955

Dear Joseph,

Please accept my profound sympathy for the untimely loss of your wonderful wife. I always found Lillian a most remarkable woman. She managed the care of Edith (which must have been exhausting much of the time) and the running of your charming guest house with the utmost finesse. She was a woman who endured life's not insignificant burdens with admirable calm.

I trust you agree that a friendship has developed between us over the years, Joseph, and it is therefore not untoward of me to admit that I have always admired the compatibility of your union and the deep love that the two of you clearly shared.

As a man who has also been forced to cope without the support of his wife, perhaps I might be so forward as to proffer some advice? Keep looking ahead, day by day. Eventually, you will find that weeks and months have passed and, one day, you'll realise that it has been years since you lost your love and – although the pain only changes, never leaves – you know that you've been tested and you've survived.

You will, I trust, forgive me if I express myself bluntly: do not succumb to drink and depression, Joseph. You have your daughters and your business to take care of and – although the parishioners of St Mary's will do all we can to support you – you'll have to rise to the challenge.

Strong words, I appreciate, Joseph, but we are not the kind of men to go in for platitudes.

Having said this, there's only so much a man can bear and it's important that you don't attempt to take on more than you can stand. The death of dear Lillian has taught us all the danger of that.

As such, I have taken the liberty of approaching Father O'Reilly. He has suggested the possibility of the Sisters of Nazareth housing our dear Edith and attending to her needs, at least until such a time as Maeve has completed her final examinations and her marriage to Frank Bryson has taken place. It would be a great shame for Maeve's studies to be abandoned now, just a few months before her graduation. I have it on good authority that Maeve has lived up to her initial promise and that Notre Dame made a sound decision in awarding her the scholarship.

The Sisters of Nazareth have a rich history of housing God's unfortunate children. Please take it on my personal assurance that Edith will be in good hands until such a time as you are ready – with the help of Frank and Maeve – to look after her yourself.

Know that you can turn to me, Joseph, during these most trying times.

With the greatest of sympathy,
Your friend Gerald

*

The sun has sunk low in the sky and Dad has sunk into a whiskyed slumber – his mouth slack, his hand hanging limply from the arm of the chair, his snores threatening to wake him.

All the mourners have gone home now, except for Vince. He'll have to return to Cambridge early tomorrow, so he will also take leave of us soon. Part of me dreads him going, as if this will mark the end of something, and another part of me longs to be alone with Frank.

You are sitting between Frank and me, your head on my shoulder, your hands stroking mine. You have pale pianist's fingers, whereas mine are mottled and stubby. Perhaps we wouldn't have been identical, all things being equal. Perhaps Dad is wrong about that.

Your fingernails need trimming. I should have done them before the funeral but I couldn't bear one of your rages, and I never did find the right time.

Frank stares down at his hands, which are joined as if in prayer. And yet something about him brings to mind a jazzman about to take his last set – his tobacco-stained fingernails, the scar at the base of his thumb, the way he squeezes his hands to a private rhythm. Once Vince has left, we'll get you and Dad off to bed, and Frank will know what to do.

But right at that moment, Frank claps his hands to his knees and stands – the speed of his movements out of tempo with the mournful mood of the room. 'Right,' he says, as if he's following instructions in his head. 'I'll have to head off now.'

You begin to rock back and forth, that keening sound coming from deep inside of you. As Frank crouches down to your level, your arm thrashes out to the side and you bat him away.

'I'll be back again tomorrow, my snazzy girl.' Dry skin has flared up on his eyelids and it looks as if each blink is sore. Mum would have told me that he's exhausted, that I've been expecting too much of him. And yet, I cannot help but feel that he's letting us down.

I follow him into the hallway, still half hoping that he'll change his mind or say something that will somehow make everything right. When I reach for him, he holds me but his body never slackens into the embrace. 'I'll be back tomorrow,' he says. 'Give Edie a kiss from me.'

I watch as he walks up Marine Road, away from Sea View Lodge. He meets someone in front of the Alhambra, and they both light cigarettes and stand there staring out to sea.

So it is Vince who drapes Dad's arms around his shoulders and supports him up the stairs; it is Vince who removes Dad's shoes, loosens his collar and sets a glass of water beside his bed.

It takes a long time to settle you: we say the Our Father and the Hail Mary; I read to you from *Peter Pan*; I count to ten in Latin and French over and over again. You know that something is wrong but I cannot tell whether you understand that Mum is dead, that we will never see her again.

By the time I get downstairs, Vince is at the kitchen sink, swilling damp tea leaves from china cups, scrubbing salad cream and custard and icing from plates. The scent of lilies cloys in the steamy air. I pick up one of the tea towels that Mum must have laundered just a week or so ago, and then I stand beside Vince at the sink. He passes me the plates to dry, soapsuds moving from his hands to mine, the only sounds those of water and cloth, crockery and cutlery, the opening and closing of cupboard doors. The same thought keeps running through my mind: *Vince and I are both motherless now.*

As we work our way through the stack of dirty plates, I dread Vince clapping his hands together and telling me he must get back.

'What do you think of your father's plan?' I say eventually.

He presses his hands against the bottom of the washing-up bowl, and I can hear the sound of breath moving through his nose. 'I'm not sure,' he says in the end, looking at me as if to gauge a response: 'I'm not sure this is the right time to make that kind of choice.'

'Dad's broken and Frank's exhausted,' I say. 'I'm dreading Edie's next fit.' For the first time since Mum died, I let myself cry – the sobs rising through my body like a wave breaking in a swell across the shore.

Vince draws me towards him, his damp hands cradling my head to his chest. His shoulders have broadened during his years at college; my body feels small in his firm embrace.

'I'll be here for you, Maeve – if you want me, that is.' The span of his chest and the weight of his arms feel surprisingly like a homecoming. 'Just think about what's best for you. Think about what's best for Edie. Everything else will fall into place.' As he whispers a kiss on my crown, I feel no pressure to move.

I don't know which of us empties the basin, which of us hangs up the tea towel, or who opens the parlour door. I don't know which of us arranges the cushions, which of us lies down first, or who spreads the Welsh blanket across our limbs.

I know that we lie together for a long while, still clothed in our funeral garb; Vince behind me, our legs almost touching; our breath rising and falling in time. His body is so close that I can hardly tell whether I hear or feel his chest move as he swallows, whether my nape tickles with his whispered words or in anticipation of his touch. I cannot even tell whether he has spoken or sighed although each sound and movement is amplified by the night. He might be telling me that he itches with sentences that never appear. He *might* be itching with words.

When the cushions beneath us shift, I fear that he will edge his body from mine or turn his back to me. In that moment, I see Mum's face twisted at an awkward angle; Frank clapping his hands to his knees; Dad's stray tufts of beard. And I just know that Vince is about to get up, that now he will take his leave.

But he levers himself onto his elbow, and I can feel him looking at me – my neck and lips and brows all tingling beneath his gaze. So slowly that it takes me a moment to feel convinced that he's moving, he lowers his face towards mine. This same Vince had leant towards me once on the promenade, so close that I could almost taste his scents of Vimto and talc and brine; this same Vince read to me at the end of the stone jetty, the sea beneath our dangling feet, the stars shining bright up high.

Gradually, I turn to face him full on, my skin itching with words: *Sometimes the wrong thing is the right thing.*

And just like that, Frank appears in the sliver of space between Vince and me, his ear pressed against my rumbling stomach; his hands edging a ring onto mine.

And just like that, my body rolls over and I turn away from Vince.

During the quiet that follows, our breathing returns to an even keel and neither of us moves. Surely the wrong thing could never be the right thing, and yet I will Vince to remain at my side.

'You shouldn't rely on Frank,' he says in the end, as if he's been reading my mind.

CHAPTER SIXTEEN

There had been finality in the way Vincent had ended the call. The ache in my stomach was like hunger pangs after a Lenten fast – all the stronger for my suspicion that he had been ready to forgive me, that I'd blown it by bringing up Frank. The full weight of mortality bore down on me, now that I would never again hear my name on his tongue, never again feel his large hands on my shoulders, his arms drawing me towards him.

Len and Steph were still singing in the kitchen, and Zenka's voice now joined in, reaching the high notes with ease. I felt a sudden relief that they were here with me in Sea View Lodge, that the cavernous feeling in the pit of my stomach was not matched by empty rooms. To think I'd subjected Vincent to a Christmas alone in his retirement bungalow – no one to help him measure the ingredients for the cake, no one to share the stirring of the stiff mixture, no one to enjoy the spiced scent as it baked.

I made my way down all thirty-three stairs, each and every one of them a trial to my poor knees. I had to be with Steph and Len, and I had an inexplicable urge to see Zenka too.

'Len has something to say,' said Zenka, as soon as I entered the kitchen, the three of them working together to decorate our cake with the plastic reindeer and sprigs of holly.

'I'm sorry,' he said, chewing his lip. 'I wanted to make a start on my potting shed but I ran out of time.'

'You've put everything back now, haven't you, Len?'

added Zenka. 'Except for a few bits and pieces that are drying out in the utility room. And you've promised not to mess with Maeve's things again.'

Len nodded, unable to meet my eye. 'Sorry, Maeve,' he managed, and I couldn't help but give him a hug.

The blue leather suitcase still stood next to Dad's broken banjo in the corner, just where Vincent had left them. None of this seemed so important now, although my gaze still strayed to the window. The lawn had been cleared of the cradle that Dad had carved, the blankets and teddy that Mum had knitted.

'Steph helped me to launder the fabrics, didn't you, Steph?' said Zenka. 'They're drying out in there.'

I peeped through the door: the lemon blankets hung from the washing line and the teddy was pegged by its ears. In the warm fug of the utility room, your things crept back into my mind: the tin of beeswax, the hymnal, the Max Factor lipstick, the red harmonica. I never did work out why you wanted to take them.

*

Breathe in through your nose and out through your mouth. That's it. Where's your mouth? Gob-tin! Dad! Where are your lips? Lipstick! Maeve! The most beautiful twins in the seven seas. Where's your beeswax? Mind your own beeswax. Mum! The butcher, the baker, the candlestick maker, all put out to sea. For those in peril on the sea. Vince! T'wit-t'woo, I love you true. I like owls. I like Sea View Lodge, 31 Marine Road West. West or north-west, four or five, occasionally six later. Lundy, Fastnet, Irish Sea. But come ye back when summer's in the meadow, or when the valley's hushed and white with snow, 'tis I'll be here in sunshine or in shadow, oh, Danny boy, oh, Danny boy, I love you so.

*

I keep taking rests on my walk back from the market, my string bags heavy with the groceries that Mum's friends will need during the week ahead. I've written out her recipes for chicken soup and shepherd's pie and honey-roasted ham.

Although I've baked batch upon batch of Victoria sponge for all the visitors who've called in to pay their respects, I've only picked at food since Mum's death. It's the first time I've left the house since the funeral and it's not just my body that feels weak: the outside world now seems flimsy too. The clock tower and the stone jetty and the Midland Hotel all look as if they're about to collapse into the sea.

I keep trudging along the promenade, promising myself another rest once I reach Brucciani's. Mr Brucciani has offered us a free batch of ice cream so that Mum's friends don't need to worry about making desserts; Dad's drinking buddies have offered to do check-in and check-out; Mr Roper will pop in on his way to and from work. Dad just needs to take care of you. I'll be back again each weekend. It'll only be for a couple of months, just until my exams are through.

I am panting with exhaustion by the time I put down my bags on the bench opposite the Balmoral. You and Dad will be all right for another few minutes. Mum told me to remember to take care of myself. When I left an hour or so ago, Dad was playing 'Drunken Sailor' on the harmonica and you were singing along.

The water laps at the shore, the waves a deep shade of turquoise; the gulls are honking, raucous as ever; the fishermen still cast their nets out to sea, just as they did the day that Mum died and every day before and since.

I feel unexpectedly ravenous, a longing rearing up in me for salty chips and battered cod, thick slabs of buttered bread, jam roly-poly and custard, mug after mug of milky sweet tea. And after I've had my fill, I want to wrap myself up in blankets and lie beside you, burying my face into your coppery curls, and sleeping for hour upon hour until day finally breaks and we're eventually ready to rise.

Just as I'm about to gather up the grocery bags, a howl rips through the stillness of the bay, the sound droning on and on, drawing my gaze. It's Dad I see further along the promenade, clutching to the railings and baying out to sea.

I grab my bags and race along the front, my heart thumping, my eyes searching for you. And I am thinking – as I have done so many times this year – *This cannot be happening to us*.

When I reach Dad, his howl gradually fades to a whimper, and he slowly turns to look at me as if he's just woken from a deep sleep. His eyes are bloodshot; his hair thick with grease; a bead of saliva is trapped in his beard. As I lean towards him, I catch the whisky on his breath.

My hand slams across his face and I am shouting: 'Where is she? Where is she? You couldn't take care of her for even an hour.'

But he continues to stare at me, and it's hard to tell if he even knows I'm here.

I should be with you. You could have a fit or take a tumble or get locked in.

That's when I see you, back by the Balmoral, loitering on the pavement, your foot trembling above the kerb. 'All's all right, Edie,' I call out, reaching you just in time. 'All's all right when Maeve's here,' I say, stopping you from stepping out onto the road. And then, finally, I take in what I've just witnessed: your first unaided steps since the night of your seizure.

*

April 28, 1955

Dear Mr Joseph Maloney,

Please accept my sympathy for the loss of your dear wife, whom Father O'Reilly informs me was a God-fearing woman and a pinnacle of St Mary's congregation. I understand that her loss is putting considerable strain on your family, which has already endured a great deal.

Although it is unusual for us to take in someone as incapacitated as your poor daughter, we have included your family in our prayers and feel that God is calling us to welcome Edith into our community of Sisters and feeble-minded girls. Here at Mary Mount we strive to follow Our Lady's example of selfless care and prayerful devotion. Father O'Reilly suggested that Edith might particularly benefit from our sung matins since she is enthusiastic in her choral worship of Our Lord.

We are making preparations for Edith's arrival, as I am sure you are too. Due to limitations of space, we ask that you pack no more than four personal items that Edith can store in her private locker. Please be assured that Mary Mount will provide all necessities such as linens, clothing and toiletries.

May our Lord bless you and keep you,

Sister Winifred Aloysius

(Mother Superior of Mary Mount Convent, Sisters of Nazareth)

*

You are ever so patient, Edie, letting me lift and lower each of your limbs, allowing me to roll you over on the towel I've laid on your bed, lying still as I sponge soapy water across your shoulder blades, along your spine and down between your legs. I can't bring myself to chant *rub-a-dub-dub three men in a tub* and you, too, are unusually quiet. Perhaps you've also had a permanent stomach ache since the day Mum died, perhaps you too feel always on the verge of being sick.

I lever you up from the bed, the thick hair beneath your armpits damp against my hands. Shaving them would take an age and I've never found the right time. Trimming your fingernails has been enough of an ordeal – even though Frank held you still and said *Edie's manicure* as I tried to avoid cutting your skin. Frank is a man to rely on.

You are shivering as I towel you dry but you smile as I puff talcum powder across your breasts and stomach. Dad often used to dress you and I'd hear your squeals of laughter from downstairs as he blew raspberries onto your tummy. But since Mum died, he's only cleaned himself when I've drawn a bath for him and led him upstairs, let alone lifted a finger to help wash you.

I could change my mind even now. Instead of fetching your slacks and peachy silk blouse, which still hang in our wardrobe unworn beside my ocean-blue dress, I could dress you in your usual twinset. During the time I spend staring out of the window – my back to you, swallowing hard, and counting to ten – I could make the decision to drop out of college.

Dad has been pottering around the garden all morning, waiting for Frank to arrive – even though I told him that he wouldn't be here until ten.

As I turn back to you, you try to say something. At first I think you're just moaning but you repeat the same noise as I hoist your slacks over the mound of your nappy. It begins to sound like you're saying *porridge*. 'You don't even like porridge,' I remind you. 'And you've already had two rounds of toast. Do you want another one, my little greedy-guts?'

I manoeuvre your arms into your cap-sleeved blouse, wishing now that I had taken the trouble to shave your armpits.

You keep repeating the same sound as I run a wide-toothed comb through your curls. When we were children, you used to squawk and lash out as we tried to untangle your hair, but toenail cutting is now the only problematic part of your toilette.

'Knowledge,' you say, your tongue thrashing, or at least that's what the noise has begun to sound like.

I could change my mind even now as I watch you admire yourself in the mirror – running your hands across the embroidered pattern at the hem of your blouse. I could pause before putting my Max Factor lipstick, the tin of beeswax, your hymnal and harmonica into the mint green hatbox that Mum had bought for my wedding.

Mum would have been mortified that we were sending you off to Mary Mount with a load of old tat. She did tell me to return to college, to concentrate on my studies. But she did tell me to take care of myself. It's only for a few months – just until Frank and I are married and he's moved in here.

I force myself to smile and talk breezily as I lead you out of the bedroom and down through Sea View Lodge. 'Frank will be here soon,' I tell you. 'Frank loves Edie very much indeed.'

And as we reach the front door, I spot him speeding towards Sea View Lodge – he never did abide by Mum's instructions to park the car here. Dad jolts upright just as Frank screeches the Ford Anglia to a halt.

He knows without me telling him that Dad needs help to get into the car. I thank God that Frank really is a man to rely on, that he will make a good husband, that he'll allow me to make a good wife.

As he helps Dad onto the back seat, he calls out: 'How's my snazzy girl?' And he lifts you into the air, your legs dangling from side to side. 'Don't you look stunningly beautiful today?' he adds as he lowers you beside Dad.

I could still change my mind. I don't have to get into the car, place the hatbox on my lap, let Frank pull away from the kerb. But I do all of this, and then I glance back – half expecting to find Mum leaning out of the window, waving us off, her cigarette smoke spiralling into the air.

Frank keeps both hands on the wheel, his eyes fixed firmly ahead. We drive past the Alhambra and the Midland and the Winter Gardens – none of us saying a word. Frank does not so much as glance at me as we speed past the turning to the glade above town. It is almost three years now since he proposed.

By the time we pull into the long drive of Mary Mount Convent, you are tugging at the hem of your blouse and repeating that same sound you'd been making earlier. 'Knowledge... knowledge,' you keep saying.

We drive past lines of crops. Nuns in their habits stand beside women in blue pinafores – some of them digging, some of them tilling the soil, and others throwing weeds into a barrow.

As we draw closer to the convent, the farmland gives way to rose gardens and medicinal plant collections and long stretches of lawn, the wheels of Frank's car moving from tarmac to gravel with a stately crunch. The convent itself looks like a Georgian mansion, bright white against the blue of the sky, all columns and verandas and casement windows – nothing like the grey stone and iron bars I had dreaded.

When the engine cuts out, we all sit still for some moments, and I could change my mind, even now.

But eventually I open the car door. The scent of rosemary fills the warm air, the sandstone gravel gives way beneath my sandals, and the memory sets like the shutter falling on Dad's camera.

You are still trying to say this word that sounds like *knowledge*, but it has taken on a questioning tone. I help you out of the car, holding the hatbox in one hand and using the other to guide you towards the veranda, your steps uncertain on the gravel. Sometimes you clench my hand and jerk to a stop. Instead of leading you back to the car and telling Frank to take us home, I hush in your ear and stroke you and persuade you to take another few steps. Frank follows behind us, helping Dad out of the car. I cannot bear to turn around.

Two nuns stand waiting for us at the top of the steps – one about our age and one about the same age as Mum. I feel a pang of resentment towards the older nun simply for being alive.

The nuns smile at us but then keep turning back to the young woman who stands between them, trying to calm her as she jumps up and down. This girl is overweight – her waist at least twice the size of yours, her hair is shorn close to her head, and I can't help but notice that her eyebrows meet in the middle.

'You must be Edith,' says the older nun, reaching for you and helping you up the stairs. Her slim hips and dry hands give the impression of a woman who thrives on hard work. Mum would have liked her.

'I'm Sister Winifred, this is Sister Anthony and this is...' She waits, her eyebrows raised in expectation.

The young woman's face breaks into a grin and she shouts, 'Bernie!' She clambers towards you and cheers, before grabbing your hand and shaking it and saying, 'Welcome to Mary Mount! It's my job to look after you.'

I would look like Bernie if I couldn't keep active, if I couldn't pluck my eyebrows and style my hair. You are fortunate to have fine brows that are naturally arched.

You stamp your foot and grimace. I remember how you used to say, 'Pleased to meet you. My name's Edith Mary Maloney, Sea View Lodge, 31 Marine Road West. What's your name?' Now you make inarticulate sounds and saliva foams at your lips.

It isn't too late, even now, to change my mind and take you home. But I have made my decision and I am focusing only on the younger nun, who's shaking my hand and saying, 'We are so sorry to hear of your loss.' Her eyes are a softer blue than ours, her lips more cushioned, her creamy skin unmarked by freckles. I suspect her hair is white-blond although it's hidden beneath her veil.

Bernie's skin is also creamy, but her eyes are large and as brown as a conker.

As Dad and Frank approach, even now I wonder whether Sister Anthony envies me my handsome fiancé.

Bernie snatches the hatbox from my hands and begins to make off with it. I want to demand it back but I just stand there, stunned, watching her run down the corridor with your things.

Sister Anthony calls after her: 'Good girl, Bernie. Slow down now, there's a good girl.'

'Forgive Bernadette,' Sister Winifred says as I prise your fists from your ears. 'She's excited about Edith's arrival, and we'd said she could be helpful by carrying her things.' Her eyes stray to Dad who is being propped up by Frank, but she does not betray a reaction.

As we step from the veranda into the parlour, it takes a moment for my eyes to adjust to the lack of light although outside the sun is at its height.

Mr Roper and Vince sit in armchairs at the far corner of the room. They have no right to be here. Has Mr Roper told them that Dad just needs a break? That I am an exemplary twin? That he chucked you out of choir?

'Why aren't you in Cambridge?' I ask Vince. 'Don't you have exams?'

Vince can hardly bring himself to look at me, but I cannot tell whether he averts his eyes from shame at telling me not to rely on Frank or from disgust that I am abandoning you.

'It's just a flying visit,' puts in Mr Roper. 'We have a few things to attend to here.'

Vince just nods, his gaze set on the ground. He caught the train back up to Cambridge the day after Mum's funeral. It was all very well, telling me not to rely on Frank, but at least Frank was here with us in Morecambe while Vince was poring over books in Cambridge.

Mum entrusted me with your care but she also told me to take care of myself. I'm following her advice; this is what she would have wanted me to do.

I reach for the letter in my bag. I've written instructions on your care, adding to it as yet another thing came to mind:

– *Lie Edie on a towel and chant 'rub-a-dub-dub three men in a tub' as you wash her with a soapy sponge. Do not run her a bath under any circumstances.*

– I will trim her nails each week. Please do not distress her by attempting this yourselves.

– Edie prefers her toast sliced into soldiers.

– Please don't assume Edie's not following if she doesn't sing during Mass. Once she knows the melody, she'll sing it solo from beginning to end.

'Knowledge?' you ask again, and Vince eventually says: 'Aren't you clever, Edie? Getting into college!'

I notice his hesitancy. But this has got nothing to do with him.

The parlour has the same institutional feel as the common room at Notre Dame: something about the largeness of the space; the donated look of the mismatched furniture; the smells of liver and onion, candlewax and stiffly starched cotton.

'College,' you try again, squeezing my hand.

Sister Anthony smiles and says: 'Both the Maloney twins are going to college.'

Frank sneaks a glance at Sister Anthony and I wonder if he finds her more attractive than me. I could see her wearing a sparkle of eyeshadow and a baby-blue Alice band, a creamy twinset and pencil skirt; I could see her dancing all night at the Locarno but still showing up on time to the next morning's lecture. Even in her habit, I can tell that she is prettier than me.

Sister Winifred clears her throat and raises her eyebrows. I have a horrible feeling that she can read my thoughts and I wish Sister Anthony's looks hadn't slipped into my mind. I am about to sit down and focus all my attention on you, when Sister Winifred says, 'It will be best for all concerned, not least for little Edith, if we keep the goodbyes short and dry-eyed.'

Frank catches my eye and I can tell that, like me, he had imagined we'd spend several hours together, showing the nuns how to pour your milk to an inch beneath the rim of the beaker, how to count to ten in French to help you to nod off, how to hush gently in your ear.

But Mr Roper seems to know the routine because he's already leading Dad towards you. Dad wraps his arms around your shoulders and squeezes you so tight that you begin to struggle.

The colour has drained from Vince's usually ruddy cheeks. This is all so much harder with him looking on.

'Let Edith say goodbye to Maeve now,' says Sister Winifred but Dad continues to hold you, sobbing into your hair.

'Don't frighten her,' she says, and Mr Roper tries, unsuccessfully, to prise Dad from you.

Sister Winifred taps Dad on the shoulder, and then whispers something in his ear. I can't hear what she says but Dad snaps into action, wiping the tears from his eyes, stroking your arms and – once you are still – guiding you towards me.

As I kiss you and tuck your curls behind your ears, I see that Dad has creased your new blouse.

'Sister Anthony will show Edith her new living quarters.'

'I'm happy to help,' I say, taking your hand.

A look passes between Sister Winifred and Sister Anthony. 'I'm afraid family members are not allowed beyond the parlour,' Sister Winifred says. 'These rules come from very many years of experience, my dear.'

Sister Winifred nods at Sister Anthony. As the young nun takes hold of you, a look of panic flashes across your eyes.

I could have saved you from this but instead I say, 'All's all right, Edie. All's all right when...' – immediately regretting it because, of course, neither Mum nor I would be here. Instead of leading you back onto the veranda and out of the convent, I kiss you on the forehead. 'Have a lovely first week at college and I'll see you at the weekend.' I try to persuade myself that you will soon feel fine.

As Sister Anthony leads you onto the corridor, your fingers toy with the embroidery on your silk blouse. Your footsteps become quieter and quieter, and your body becomes more and more hidden in shadow until you and

Sister Anthony disappear behind the curtain that hides the living quarters from view.

The rest of us sit in silence for a few moments, Dad still staring down the corridor.

'What time shall I bring Maeve and Mr Maloney to visit on Saturday?' Frank pipes up.

Sister Winifred doesn't answer straightaway, as if she's finishing a private prayer. 'I'm afraid we don't accept visitors during the first four weeks,' she says eventually. Turning to me, she adds: 'Visiting hour is on the last Saturday of each month thereafter.' She must see the look on my face because her own expression softens. 'I know it may be difficult, my dear, but Edith needs time to settle in – just as you did, I'm sure, when you enrolled at college.'

'She doesn't need to settle in. She's only going to be here until I finish my exams.'

Mr Roper gasps. 'Maeve!' he says and, despite myself, I keep quiet.

'Sister Winifred?' Vince asks, clearing his throat. 'Perhaps an exception can be made?'

Mr Roper leans forwards, and I expect him to launch into one of his lectures. But he whispers to Sister Winifred: 'Given the circumstances?'

She shakes her head sadly and worries at the wooden cross around her neck. 'It *is* for the best,' she says. 'She'll never feel at home here otherwise.'

'She doesn't need to feel at home here. She'll be back at home in less than two months.' My voice is louder than I had intended.

Sister Winifred continues to speak quietly, 'It would be best for Edith to have a peaceful time for the duration of her stay, however long that might be.'

'We know exactly how long it will be: seven weeks and six days.'

Mr Roper shakes his head at me. 'Thank you, Mother Superior,' he says. 'We quite understand.' Then he stands and puts on his cream leather driving gloves, pulling on each finger one by one, before gripping my hand and leading me out of the convent, his hard soles tapping against the stone flags.

Even now I could wrench myself free; I could race after you down the corridor. But I let Mr Roper march me outside, Frank and Dad and Vince in our wake. In the distance, you are crying and Bernie is shouting and Sister Anthony is trying to calm you both.

Just as Mr Roper bundles me into Frank's car, Sister Winifred approaches. 'My dear,' she says, 'we are all God's children and none of us ever quite know what plans He has in store.'

*

Subject: Confidential message for Maeve
From: vinceroper1933@gmail.com
To: seaviewlodge@seaviewlodge.co.uk

Dear Maeve,

Apologies if I seemed rather offhand when you called, but all of us have our limits. It was foolish of me to expect that age would act as a shield. Even now, it is difficult for me to feel composed in your company.

Regretfully and respectfully, I ask you never to contact me again.

And yet, with love,
Vince x

*

I was sitting at the dining table, picking at my Christmas Eve meal, although my mind had crawled beneath an eiderdown, trying to hide itself from the festive cheer. Still, I had to put on an act for Dot who, despite her frailty, had made the effort to get to our twelve-course meal.

'There's hay under the tablecloth,' Zenka announced. She had introduced us to numerous Lithuanian Christmas Eve traditions over the years – sweep and mop and change the linens; bathe and get into clean clothes before supper; prepare a chair, plate and candle for family members who have died during the year; seek forgiveness from anyone you've hurt – but the hay was new to us.

'You must reach under and take one stalk,' Zenka instructed Steph. 'No peeping!'

Len covered Steph's eyes and Dave saved an unfinished bowl of borscht from spilling as she tugged beneath the tablecloth. I smiled at their antics, and even enjoyed them, but all the while I was containing the knowledge that Vincent had asked me never to contact him again. He'd sent that email a few hours after our call. I could just see him at his desk, fountain pen in hand, staring down at the words he'd composed and then crossed out, until he eventually came up with the message that he'd typed out for me.

Steph held up a long thin stalk, and Zenka told us that this meant Steph would marry a tall thin man before next Christmas Eve.

Vincent admitted that he felt something for me; he had signed off *with love*; he had opened himself up to me at the very same moment that he kept me at bay.

'That's you out the picture,' joked Dave, nudging Len.

And even Dot managed to laugh, which made me realise that she had likely been following the conversation all night, although her eyes looked dazed, and she was so drowsy that I'd had to spoon the mushrooms and sauerkraut onto her plate, and then spread her rye bread with honey.

The sight of her made me feel guilty for the physical ache of my grief. Vincent's email confirmed something I'd never quite let myself believe: he hadn't simply cared for me, he hadn't simply pitied me, he hadn't just wanted to get one over on Frank. Vincent had loved me. He had loved you too. He had taught himself to adapt: he'd taken that job at the

Notre Dame, and there he'd met Hélène and chosen to let himself love again.

'You joker!' laughed Len. 'Next year we can have Christmas in our new place, if we're back from our honeymoon by then. We're going to Disneyland or New York or maybe Las Vegas.'

Dave stole a glance at Dot. No doubt they were worried about how to break it to Len and Steph that they never would marry, let alone cope in a place of their own. The social worker's mental capacity test would scupper all their plans.

Only fools expect gratitude, I'd always known that, and yet I couldn't help but feel let down by Steph. I heard myself say: 'What would I do if the pair of you went off and left?'

Although I'd meant it to sound light-hearted, I could feel everyone's eyes on me. 'What have we got here?' I asked Len in an attempt to change the pitying mood.

'Zenka couldn't find poppy seeds and I don't like those biscuits anyway, so it was my idea to have an American pudding, and Zenka said that doughnuts are popular in America, and I wanted to make them myself but Zenka said it would be easier to get them from the Co-op.'

Lord knows what would have happened if Len had been let loose with a vat of boiling oil. No one in their right mind would let the pair of them live alone. And even as I was thinking this, I was also feeling the gnawing loss of Vincent. The only trace of him at Sea View Lodge was the gift bags he'd left for Steph and Len.

'Well, they look delicious, my dears,' I managed, and I even attempted to smile.

I cut Dot's doughnut into bite-sized pieces, trying not to think of Vincent's attempts to make his peace, of his request that I keep away from him during whatever years remain.

Before Dot took a mouthful, she reached for her glass of champagne. 'A toast,' she said, and all of us leant towards her because her voice had become terribly faint. 'To fresh starts!'

We all clinked glasses, Dot spilling half her champagne before it reached her mouth, and I tried not to think of her chair empty next Christmas Eve, a candle lit in her memory.

At least I had put a brave face on things, at least my dark mood hadn't seeped into the room.

Just as I was thinking this, Zenka reached for my hand beneath the table, the gentleness of her touch telling me that she had read my pain. I turned to face her, my hand still in hers. Although my eyes began to well up, I did not turn away, and it was then that I knew what I must do.

PART
THREE

CHAPTER SEVENTEEN

I should have known that Dot's health had deteriorated since she was about to move into the hospice, but it was quite a shock when the nurse helped her out of the cab. She was skeletal – all collarbone and elbow and knee – and her stomach was now distended like those starving Ethiopians that used to be on TV.

The nurse who pushed Dot's wheelchair was probably in her sixties like Dot, but she looked hearty as if she'd see her grandchildren marry and perhaps have kids of their own. As they inched their way up the path, they paused to admire Len's rare snowdrops. That's when I noticed the roof tile on the grass. Thank goodness nobody had been in the garden when it blew off. Lord knows how much a roofer would cost, what with scaffolding for a place this tall.

'It'll be spring before we know it,' said Dot, just as Tilly Brannigan sped past them, a surfboard strapped to the back of her high-performance wheelchair – her father jogging to keep up.

Dot stared at our young guest, mesmerised by her agility, but she allowed us to lever her from her own chair without a hint of self-pity.

As soon as we guided her into the parlour – which looked terribly drab now that we'd taken down the Christmas decorations – the nurse excused herself, asking directions to the bathroom.

Once we were alone together, waiting for Len, I didn't know what to say. I had planned to tell her that I'd love and care for him as if he were my own. But it would be an acknowledgement that she wasn't long for this world and, although she was on her way to the hospice, she might not thank me for the reminder.

I found myself staring at the dents in the carpet where Vincent had placed the stand for the wonky Christmas tree that he'd picked up outside the Alhambra. And I wondered whether there had been any men in Dot's life during the thirty years since Len's dad upped and left.

I wanted to open up to her a little. I could hear the words in my mind but it was so difficult to say them. 'Taking in Steph and Len,' I began, knowing now that I'd have to finish what I started, 'has been the best opportunity life ever offered me.' And it was such a relief to hear those words, to know that I had spoken them.

Her lips were cracked and dry and she had to keep licking them but she was nodding and listening intently.

'I always assumed I'd have kids of my own,' I admitted, wondering if I should offer to hold Dot's glass to her mouth. 'I had a fiancé once and a very dear friend – dearer to me than I acknowledged at the time. Both married other women, became dads. I misread them both it turns out. Thought too highly of one; not highly enough of the other.'

'We've all made mistakes,' she whispered. 'Trick is not to repeat them.'

I wanted to help Dot take a sip of water but I was worried about humiliating her. We always had to cut up your food, bathe you and help you to put on your clothes: I'd never considered any of this cause for shame. Perhaps it would have been different, if injury or illness had disabled you later in life. But you were just you – my twin who preferred her toast sliced into soldiers, who loved us to dust her with talcum powder when we changed her nappy, to blow raspberries onto her stomach.

'I repeated the same old mistakes time and again,' I admitted, thinking of Vincent when he first returned: the way his scarf had been wound around his neck in the style of a Frenchman;

the way he'd cocked his head to one side; the way he'd lowered his voice and told me that he would like to make his peace.

I'd rehearsed what I wanted to say to Dot for fear that I'd lack the courage in the moment to find the right words: 'You and Dave both gave me such gifts, such unexpected gifts, when you made me an honorary grandma.'

She looked suddenly exhausted, her body slumped in her chair, as if she had been using all her reserves just to sit up straight and take in my words. She tried to say something in response but her voice was so weak that I could only make out: *Len*, *Grove Hill*, *Steph*.

The social worker had conducted that mental capacity test weeks ago now, but we were still none the wiser because her manager hadn't signed off on it yet.

'I'll fight for them tooth and nail,' I said, wondering if I should promise her more.

Before I could decide what to say for the best, Len came into the room. 'Mum,' he whispered, spreading open his arms.

'My boy,' Dot managed, as he hugged her with a gentleness that I had rarely seen in Len.

'He's one in a million,' I said, before I slipped out to leave them some time alone: 'You've done a good job with him.'

*

Subject: Mental Capacity: Leonard Shepherd and Stephanie Greene
From: jennifer.tait@lancashire.gov.uk
To: dave.greene20@yahoo.co.uk;
dorothy.shepherd@btinternet.com
Cc:seaviewlodge@seaviewlodge.co.uk;
safeguardingadults@lancashire.gov.uk

Dear Maeve and Dave,

Apologies for the delay in getting back to you on this. The management team has now reviewed my mental capacity assessment, copies of which I'll put in the post. We have reached the conclusion that both Stephanie and Leonard understand the practical, medical and emotional effects of intercourse, and therefore have the mental capacity to make independent choices about their sexual lives. Given that the GUM Clinic gave both Len and Steph a clean bill of health, and that Steph was fitted with a contraceptive implant, there's no longer any reason to prevent them from sharing a room.

Can we schedule a meeting to discuss this with them? I will also explain my concerns about their capacity to understand the legal and financial implications of marriage – a concern I believe we share, Dave. I am aware that Dot would dearly love for them to marry and have agreed with her to revisit the idea of marriage at a later date.

Kind regards,

Jennifer

PS. I'm sorry to hear that you didn't get the go-ahead for Len's en-suite after filling in all those forms.

*

I should have relished the idea of a whole afternoon alone: the chance to paint my nails, pore over the road atlas and do my stretching exercises undisturbed. But I sat in my bedroom, my fingers outspread as I waited for the varnish to dry – the whip of the wind around the chimney and the hammer of the hail against the dormer windows slowly threatening to drive me round the bend. Sea View Lodge was so lonely, what with Len and Steph at the hospice; the Brannigans on their annual trip to Morecambe's Super Bowl; and Zenka in town, buying purple dye and getting a sign engraved with the words *Bluebell Room*. She was right, of course, the white towels and bedding were such a faff, but it would always be the Snowdrop Room to me.

I'd asked Zenka whether she needed a hand with the shopping; I'd offered to teach the Brannigans to quilt. For decades, it hadn't occurred to me that I would see Vincent again, but now his absence left such a gap: the sound of classical music streaming from the Crocus Room; the way his daily constitutional was timed like clockwork; his hand brushing against mine as he helped me to clear up the plates. How I'd love to sit beside him on the couch, reading *Madame Bovary*, drinking large glasses of Burgundy and wrangling over translations.

I should have watched one of those old French films, which I'd treated myself to on DVD and never found the time to watch. But I would only end up longing to compare notes with Vincent as we had done in our youth.

My mind kept drifting back to the social worker's email. *It won't be a stylish marriage*, I kept hearing you sing, *I can't afford a carriage*. And I kept remembering the closeness of Vincent's body on the night of Mum's funeral, the warmth of his breath.

As I tested whether my nail polish had finally dried, I thought of what Vincent might be eating in Bruges: sole meunière, perhaps, or endives braised and then wrapped with ham and baked in gruyère cheese.

I was pretty sure that he *had* invited me to join him on the coach tour. What I would do to be with Vince in a beer cellar now, drinking a blond ale from the bottle; or perhaps we'd be wandering through cobbled streets, trying white chocolate filled with raspberry cream or dark chocolate studded with candied peel.

Dot had been right when she said that we all make mistakes, that the trick is not to repeat them. Vincent was right that we're neither of us getting any younger.

Once my nail polish finally dried, I lifted the atlas from my bedside table. It fell open at exactly the right page, and I traced my finger across the highlighted line – a route I'd now committed to memory.

If you had been here, in this room we used to share, you would have asked me to read you the story, clasping your hand to my chin, and listening intently while I read out the names of the towns en route: Preston, Wigan, Sandbach, Stoke-on-Trent. Perhaps you would have said: *Home, James, and don't spare the horses*, or perhaps you would have got bored and wandered off.

Usually it was impossible to know how much you'd taken in. But sometimes the look in your eyes, or the clutch of your hand made me feel that you had understood: when I went off to college, you left a picture of me on my bed, and you ignored me during my first trip home; when Mum died, you knew, I think, that our sky had fallen in.

My hand came to a rest at the fold between the pages of the atlas. The last part of the journey might prove tricky but I would get Len to help me look it up on the computer. I just needed the weather to improve: I couldn't even drive around the corner, let alone halfway across the country, in the kind of hail that was beating over Morecambe today.

I was bracing myself to get up from the armchair to make a start on my stretches – if my back gave out on me, it would scupper all my plans. But a loud creaking sound rooted me to the seat. My gaze darted from the damp patch in the corner to the draughty window frame.

When an almighty crash shook through the room, my body curled into itself: my eyes closing, my knees drawing up to my face, my arms shielding my crown. The after-effects juddered through my skull and teeth and spine.

I'm not sure how long I sat there, foetal, the thud of things falling all around. But, when I eventually dared to raise my head, the dust was beginning to settle. The carpet was strewn with glass and slabs of plaster; pine needles and twigs and melting bullets of ice. A branch of our fir tree had smashed through the window, just a foot from where I sat, the gaping hole in the glass exposing my attic room to the wide Morecambe sky.

And yet a feeling of deep calm warmed my chill limbs and a shaft of sunlight broke through the dark clouds.

*

Abuna UK
Homeserve
Worcestor
West Midlands
WR5 8CS

Customer Address:
Maeve Maloney
Sea View Lodge
31 Marine Road West
Morecambe
Lancashire
LA3 1BY

CLAIM FOR WORKS TO BE CARRIED OUT AT THE ABOVE PROPERTY

Dear Miss Maloney,

The results of our survey show that the rafters, window frames, and fir tree at the above property were already in poor condition prior to the storm of January 10, 2013.

The wind speed was not sufficient to have caused a healthy tree to fall, and the section of roof was only damaged because wet rot had already affected the wood.

As a gesture of goodwill, Abuna UK will pay out on the removal of the fir tree and we will protect the affected areas to ensure no further damage to the property.

Clause 73b of your policy excludes deterioration caused by gradually operating causes. Abuna UK therefore rejects all claims for damage to the roof and window.

Yours sincerely,
Paula Kelly
(Chief Loss Adjustor)

*

Dave handed Jennifer Tait the opened packet of Jaffa Cakes and Zenka placed our mugs on the arms of our chairs. She hadn't bothered to get out our cake stands or silver strainers or sugar tongs. I could have insisted on baking some macaroons for the social worker's visit, of course, or making a pot of fresh leaf tea. But during the past few days, I'd just sat and watched while Zenka rehoused the Brannigans in the Balmoral, and Dave called the insurance company and spoke with the builders. Perhaps they were right and I was still in shock.

'Dave and I spoke with Dot at St John's,' said Jennifer, stealing a glance at him.

I suppose Dot had a right to know that her son's bedroom had been blocked off; that he was camping out downstairs, wearing Dave's tracksuit bottoms and jumpers. She would hoot with laughter at the sight of me in Zenka's red Lycra.

'She made a suggestion,' Jennifer went on, 'which I think might solve some of your more pressing problems.'

It wasn't right to go begging from Dot on her deathbed: anything she'd managed to squirrel away over the years must remain in that trust. 'It's just like her to be so generous,' I said, 'but we must think about what's best for Len.'

Jennifer's mouth was full of Jaffa Cake, so I took the opportunity to tell them my plan: 'We can only reopen to visitors once all the timbers have been treated or replaced and all the tiles and leading's made good. I checked my building society book and I have just enough to cover the costs of erecting the scaffolding.'

'The insurance company's refusing to pay,' put in Dave.

Jennifer was wearing that sympathetic expression of hers.

'Only a fool would rely on loss adjusters and surveyors,' I went on. 'But we've got a whole community of people who'd hate to see us close down.' Perhaps things would have panned out differently if Mum had asked for help instead of exhausting herself with nursing you and cooking for our guests and keeping Dad on the straight and narrow.

Zenka moved to sit beside me on the sofa, taking my hand in hers. 'Mencap,' she said, 'and the Autistic Society and the Young Carers' Association.'

I squeezed her hand and tried not to think of the roof of my bedroom shrouded in tarpaulin; a *Danger No Entry* sign taped across the top flight of stairs.

'The folk who run Funky Feet would put on a fundraiser,' added Dave, 'and I'll bet Len could sort out a collection at St Mary's.'

I resisted the urge to ban interference from the church: I'd accept help from anyone willing to save Sea View Lodge. Poor old Len and Steph couldn't sit around an empty guest house all day twiddling their thumbs.

'It's a relief to hear that we're all on the same page,' said Jennifer. 'We're all thinking about what's best for Len and Steph.'

One way or another, we'd get through this. I'd been right to swallow my pride.

'You know I've always been a great admirer of all you do at Sea View Lodge,' she said, catching Dave's eye again in a manner I found disconcerting. 'And I'm sure all of us here will do everything in our power to ensure that your good work continues.'

I could see Sea View Lodge standing derelict, just as the Midland had done for years, her windows smashed, graffiti scrawled all over her walls; I saw myself cooped up in an old folks' home.

'But, best-case scenario,' warned Jennifer, 'it will still take weeks to get the place back up and running. And it's not really viable for Len and Steph to be camping out in a building site.'

I'd keep Len out of Grove Hill if it was the last thing I did. No honorary grandson of mine would live in a place where he was fed fish fingers and frozen peas and shunted off to bed at 8pm. God alone knows what else went on behind those closed doors. I switched off the telly whenever they aired clips from Winterbourne View: staff shoving fully clothed residents into cold showers, punching them in the face and pouring mouthwash into their eyes.

'Dot's leaving her house to Len,' explained Dave, as if I hadn't been party to all the discussions about setting up the trust. 'And now that she's in the hospice, there's no reason why the pair of them can't move in.'

Damn Jennifer Tait for raking over all this. 'They haven't talked about living together in weeks,' I tried. 'It was just a passing phase.'

The three of them sat there quietly, each waiting for the other to break the silence. Eventually Zenka spoke up: 'They don't want to upset you, Maeve.'

I almost felt grateful to Jennifer for rabbiting on – at least all eyes were no longer on me: 'Ordinarily it takes months to sort out funding and care provision but, given the urgency of the situation, I've been given the green light to arrange a temporary team of carers,' she announced. 'All being well, we should be ready for Len and Steph to move in next week.'

CHAPTER EIGHTEEN

The Philpotts stood waving from their front door – he fully clothed and she shivering in a Japanese dressing gown, their children in their pyjamas. A photograph capturing this scene would betray no hint of the mayhem next door. I tried to avert my gaze from the felled fir tree and the log-splitting machine, from the *No Vacancies* sign that was still on display. Every time I caught sight of that sign, I felt less and less optimistic about our prospects of ever raising enough money to treat the roof timbers; of ever again welcoming paying guests to Sea View Lodge.

At least the builders had retrieved our stuff from the blocked-off attic rooms. Grateful as I was to Zenka for letting me share her wardrobe, I'd never been so pleased to pull on my button-down dress. And it would have been a crying shame for Len and Steph to be forced to move into Dot's place without their *Sound of Music* DVDs, their scrapbooks, Blackpool FC memorabilia and snowdrop bulbs.

'Are you sure you don't want me to drive?' asked Zenka.

I shook my head although I was sorely tempted. Last week, I had finally plucked up the courage to get behind the wheel but I'd been a nervous wreck by the time I'd reached the solicitor's office, my gearstick and pedals feeling alien and beyond my control. I hadn't dared drive again since. How was I going to manage the M6? It had been years since I'd tackled a motorway.

Len wound down his window, letting in a gust of wintry air.

'Good luck!' shouted Miranda.

'Keep in touch!' shouted Mr Philpotts – whose first name I still didn't know, despite all his kindnesses of late: passing on the details of a roofer who'd done some work for him; telling us about a scaffolding firm that might give us a good rate. Still, I could have done without them watching me try to back onto Marine Road West. Truth be known, I would have rather Zenka had gone on ahead with Dave in his truck, left me to drive Len and Steph over to Dot's house alone.

'We'll be back again tomorrow,' laughed Len.

'Thursday,' corrected Steph.

She was right, of course. Jennifer Tait had arranged a placement for Len at a horticultural social enterprise – God knows what that meant – and she'd booked Steph onto a hospitality course. She'd wanted them to go there three days a week but she'd only got funding for one. I could find plenty for them to be getting on with at Sea View Lodge, guests or no guests, but, with the place closed, I didn't have any money to pay them. Whatever social services might say, I hated employing them as slave labour.

Miranda called out: 'We'll expect an invitation to the housewarming!'

'House blessing,' Len corrected her.

I couldn't quite bring myself to pull out into the line of traffic that roared along Marine Road West, so I took a glance at Sea View Lodge. With the gable window hooded in tarpaulin, it hardly looked like home.

Len and Steph said that although they were moving out, they wanted to continue to work here. But I was no fool: the era of the waifs and strays was drawing to a close. Sea View Lodge would feel so empty without *The Sound of Music* playing in the background, and Len's wireless permanently tuned to Radio Two. There'd be no joy in the early mornings without hearing Steph potter around upstairs.

I kept hesitating and missing the brief gaps in the traffic; no one would guess that I'd been the designated driver throughout most of my adult life. By the time Dad and I had saved up for a car of our own, he was riddled with diabetes and his eyesight had begun to fail. Frank kept that Ford Anglia, just as Mum had feared, and he never did pay Dad back.

The Misfits Comedy Troupe, who stayed with us every winter, had congregated outside the Balmoral to wave us off. They'd promised to donate their show's profits to our building fund: last night they'd made a loss of £42.55. Mencap Musical and Aspy Fella A Cappella had done rather better at their gala performances but our building fund still totalled only £394.

'Father Pete will bring holy water and candles,' piped up Len, as I eventually pulled into the stream of traffic. 'And we'll have communion in our front room, won't we, Steph?'

'We're going to sing "Do Not Be Afraid" and "Ave Maria" and "In My Father's House", aren't we, Len?'

Hopefully, this blessing would appease them since the social worker's boss had apparently scuppered their plans to wed. Something about the Mental Capacity Act. Dave had tried to explain but I don't think he'd understood himself.

'At our wedding,' added Len as if on cue, 'we'll sing "Love is Flowing Like a River" and "My Favourite Things". Father Pete says it's a jolly good idea, Steph and me living together before we get married, doesn't he, Maeve?'

'So you said.'

The coastal wind was buffeting the car this way and that. I had to keep adjusting the wheel just to stay on course.

'But we're not to tell the bishop that, are we?'

'Probably best you keep it under your hat.'

We headed towards the Festival Market, where Steph had picked out some synthetic sheets – Zenka should have warned her about static – and Len had chosen some tangerine-coloured towels. Len stared at the market, turning to look through the back window. Perhaps, like me, he was remembering the time when he'd written a thought for the day on each of Dot's paper napkins, and customers had queued to get his pearls of wisdom along with their fried egg baps and sugar-steeped tea.

'Isn't that where you bought your plant pots?' I asked Len as we approached Northern Relics Antiques. It felt reckless to have spoken although, in years gone by, I happily chatted as I drove.

Len began to talk about the snowdrop bulbs he intended to plant on their balcony. Dave and Zenka had spent the last week getting Dot's place sorted for them to move in, spring-cleaning and painting and clearing out her clothes – which seemed rather distasteful with Dot still clinging to life in the hospice. Zenka had planted red cyclamen in the window boxes; made up their bed with my orange patchwork quilt that had originally been destined for the Marigold Room; hung their new curtains; and even decorated the living room with prints of rare snowdrops, Blackpool FC memorabilia and *The Sound of Music* stills. Ingeniously, she'd used my old cradle as a storage basket for Steph's scrapbooks in the hope that the pair of them would forget about using it for anything else.

The right turn at the Gala Bingo required me to hold the clutch at the biting point as cars whizzed past us in the opposite direction, each one causing the windows to rattle, and I lost sight of Dave who had sped on ahead.

I tried not to think of turning up this road on that terrible drive to the convent, Frank silent, Dad dribbling, you tugging at the hem of your peachy silk blouse.

What on earth were we thinking, letting Len and Steph move out here? There wasn't a thing to do in this part of town: no cinema, no discotheque, no ice cream parlours or tearooms. Just street upon street of matching houses, blocks of flats, and cars lined along both sides of the road.

'The abode of Leonard Shepherd and Stephanie Greene-soon-to-be-Shepherd,' announced Len as I turned onto Dot's street. He did a marvellous job, did Len, of looking on the bright side. He knew as well as the rest of us that social services had vetoed their plan to marry, that they could only move in here because his bedroom at Sea View Lodge was out of bounds and his mum was dying in St John's.

The metal balcony that Len wanted to line with pot plants was so rusted that it couldn't be trusted to bear much of a load.

This was a terrible idea. We couldn't possibly abandon them here with a team of new carers. We'd employed the only ones available – school dropouts, the lot of them. And total strangers to boot.

I stalled the car as I tried to pull up at the kerbside.

We should never have opened up the poor loves to the kind of horrors endured by people like them: staff stealing money from their benefits, louts calling them names, cabbies refusing to pick them up.

I didn't restart the engine: I had to find a way to put a stop to this.

But Zenka's palm was already on the door handle; Len and Steph were already scrambling to get out.

I froze. I could not just sit there and let them be led away.

By the time Zenka had opened my door and offered to park the car herself, there was some kind of kerfuffle going on between Dave and the new carer.

I looked up to see what they must have noticed a split second before: someone had sprayed the word *MONG* in big red letters across the front wall of Dot's home.

What were we all thinking, exposing the pair of them to the cruelty of the world? At least at Sea View Lodge, the Philpotts and I had been there to shield Len and Steph from local bullies.

Len was pointing at the spray paint and sounding it out: 'M-O-N-G,' he said.

'That decides it,' I blurted out, sick at the realisation that Sea View Lodge's vandals may have been spying on Len and

Steph. 'They can't possibly move in here. Let's turn straight back around.'

'Mong,' whispered Steph.

I couldn't console myself with images of horses and dumplings and yurts. Len and Steph looked so despondent: it was enough to break the hardest of hearts.

Zenka's hand squeezed mine, but it was your voice that spoke up in my head. *Behave, Maeve!* you whispered.

Len and Steph were still staring up at the graffiti.

Part of me wanted to pull away from Zenka, to usher them back into the car. I wanted to drive straight back to Sea View Lodge, where we could care for each other as if nothing had changed. But I knew that you were right. If Vincent were here, he would have agreed. He would have told me not to make things worse. I could just imagine him suggesting that we're an adaptable species, we humans. We can find all sorts of ways to love and be loved. And I missed him then with a ferocity that quite caught me off-guard.

'Anyone who calls you that,' I said eventually, 'leads a very unhappy existence.'

'Yeah,' said Len, his face brightening as he rounded us all into a group hug. 'I'm not a mong. I'm a galanthophile.'

*

May 24, 1955
Dear Joseph and Maeve,

I suspect you might appreciate some news of little Edith, whom all of us have grown rather fond of since she joined our family here at Mary Mount. She particularly enjoys the company of Sister Anthony, who sits beside her during matins, and it is a real joy to hear them sing together as they complete their daily chores. Bernadette, the feeble-minded girl whom you met briefly, is keen – in her own boisterous manner – to attend to Edith's every need. When Bernadette is not working in the laundry, we are almost certain to find her at Edith's side. Indeed, they are so joined at the hip that we have dubbed them 'the twins'.

We are looking forward to receiving you in the parlour from two o'clock to four o'clock on the fifth of June and we believe that you will find Edith much improved even after such a short period here at Mary Mount. The frequency of her seizures has lessened considerably in the past weeks – the regularity of the routine here and our early lights out policy may well have helped in this regard. On that note, Edith has become used to sleeping without the night light that you mentioned in your instructive letter. It did take her some time to get used to the darkness of the dormitory and the whole family here at Mary Mount suffered several sleepless nights as a consequence.

You also mentioned that Edith drinks only milk. Sister Anthony is under instructions to give her a glass at the weekend if she has behaved herself during the week, and on Sunday mornings she has hot buttered toast as you requested. During the rest of the week, she eats porridge and drinks tea for breakfast, as do the rest of the family here at Mary Mount. Once Edith is returned to your care, I'm sure you will appreciate our efforts to curb her more demanding habits.

It is with great sadness that I must inform you of poor Edith's continuing inability to articulate any words with an acceptable level of comprehensibility. Her unstinting efforts to communicate do offer some hope, however, and are testament to her indefatigable spirit.

You are both in our thoughts and prayers. I trust that you are able to concentrate on your studies now that the burden of tending to Edith has temporarily been removed, Maeve, and that life is regaining an even keel, Joseph. Trust in the Lord your God with all your hearts and minds and souls.

Yours in prayer,
Sister Winifred Aloysius

*

I return to the lounge after throwing Vince out of Sea View Lodge to find you rocking gently back and forth, your hands on your ears, Sister Winifred beside you praying beneath her breath. When Dad rests his palm between my shoulder blades, I realise that I am rocking too. His hand trembles and he keeps repeating, 'My poor girl. My poor, poor girl.'

I stare at the cradle that stands in the middle of the room, at the tiered wedding cake on the mantle, at the *Just Married* banner strung across the mirror. Vince just proposed to me: I know this has happened but I cannot feel it, my whole being wrung out by Frank's abandonment. I slide my diamond ring up towards my knuckle and then back down, wishing that Dad had got rid of the cake and the cradle, that he'd thought to take down the banner.

I try not to think about the look that passed between Frank and Vince, about the bands of gold warm in my palms. I try not to think about Mum, about the way she would have held me and rocked with me and reassured me that all's all right when Mum's here. I try not to think about Vince's proposal, your harmonica in his hand.

'I'll kill the bastard,' shouts Dad, his fist thumping on the arm of the chair, his voice whisky-tinged again after weeks off booze. 'Just wait till I get my hands on him.'

You are whimpering now.

'Hush please, Edith,' says Sister Winifred. 'There's a good girl.'

I continue to stare at the tiered wedding cake and the *Just Married* banner, and I continue to slide the diamond ring towards my knuckle and then back down.

Dad punches the arm of the chair again and lets out an almighty roar.

Sister Winifred starts and then collects herself. 'Little Edith's getting frightened,' she says. 'I think it's best if we return to Mary Mount – just until you're in a fit state for her to return.'

I nod and continue to rock, my fists scrunched to my eyes. I do not hold you or kiss you or whisper in your ear. I do not look you in the eye or comfort you or try to explain that I'll collect you from the convent tomorrow. I just let Sister Winifred lead you away because I cannot bear to raise my head to watch you leave.

*

My name's Edith Mary Maloney, Sea View Lodge, 31 Marine Road West. What's your name? Home, James, and don't spare the horses. What noise does a horse make? Neigh! What noise does a Maeve make? Roar. What noise does an Edie make? T'wit-t'woo, I love you true. My name's Edith Mary Maloney, Sea View Lodge, 31 Marine Road West. Sea View Lodge, 31 Marine Road West. Sea View Lodge, 31 Marine Road West.

*

Initial Inspection of Sunnyfield Support Services care provision for Stephanie Greene and Leonard Shepherd

Description of care provided:
The service supports a couple who have learning disabilities in their own home. Support provided is person centred and consists of full-time care throughout the day and night. A range of audits and systems are in place to monitor the quality of the service provided.

<u>**Summary of inspection:**</u>

We visited the home, met the service users, and observed care and support being delivered. We also talked with the unit business manager, team leader, members of the staff team, family and friends. We could see that the service users (for whom this is their first experience of living independently) were being cared for by enthusiastic and empathetic staff.

One service user told us that one staff member: 'supports Morecambe FC, but he's all right really. He took me to Bloomfield Road last week. We won 4–2. And he lets me go and see my mum every few days. And we built a potting shed too.' The other service user was equally happy with the care provision: 'They help me and my fiancé to cook curry and lasagne. We enjoy living in a home of our own.' Her father told us that his daughter's new-found independence has increased her confidence, and a close family friend mentioned her relief that the house was always kept clean.

However, they also expressed concern about the lack of meaningful daily activities. They feel that the local authority's decision to gradually reduce staffing levels will exacerbate this problem and also result in substandard care.

There has been a recent safeguarding incident when a member of the public used abusive language to the service users during an unaccompanied trip by public bus. An account has since been set up with a local taxi firm.

Sunnyfield Support Services should monitor the needs and desires of people who use their services, and any issues should be raised with the commissioning bodies.

*

I could tell something was wrong as soon as the nurse looked up from the reception desk: something about the way she replaced the telephone onto its cradle, something about the way she inhaled and then rubbed her hands against her trousers.

'Mrs Maloney?' she asked.

Even at such a moment, I enjoyed her assumption that I must have married.

'I'm glad you're here,' she said. 'It was you I was trying to call.'

Len and Steph must also have sensed something awry because they looked at me as if I could make everything better.

An image of Mum came into my mind. I saw her sitting on the edge of the bed in our attic room, stroking the clammy hair from your face and whispering, 'We're here now, Edie. All's all right when Mum's here.' And I remember how your limbs had stilled and you blinked and it seemed as if everything really was all right when Mum was there.

'You must be Len,' said the nurse. 'I've heard all about you from Mum.' She may as well have worn a uniform since she'd clipped her nurse's watch to one of the large pockets that covered her bust. I've never had much time for all this *let's pretend we're not really in a hospital* malarkey.

'And this is?'

Steph fiddled with the hem of her new top.

'Tell the lady your name, love,' I prompted.

'My name is Stephanie Greene,' she said, trotting out the phrase as if she'd studied it in a foreign language textbook.

'Steph's my fiancée.'

The nurse raised her eyebrows and then immediately tried to disguise her surprise.

'We're getting married, me and Steph,' he said, doffing his boater. He was also wearing his pink-and-peppermint-striped blazer because Dot had asked him to come in something colourful. At least his eccentric fashion tastes hadn't rubbed off on Steph. She was in her habitual leggings and tunic top. We were all glad to have our own wardrobes back. 'We're here to visit my mum,' Len continued, looking down at his feet and swallowing hard.

'Your mum's asleep at the moment, Len, so perhaps you and Steph would like to have a drink in the lounge first? We've got a great collection of DVDs and lots of games.'

And before Len had the chance to answer, she was herding us into the lounge.

I'd never visited a hospice before Dot moved in here – you and Mum both died so suddenly and I'd nursed Dad myself in Sea View Lodge, his last illness mercifully swift. Hospices pride themselves on being homely, on not being like a hospital, but St John's was very thinly disguised. I hated to think of Vincent visiting Hélène in such a desolate place as this. The dining table was covered with a wipe-clean cloth, and cheap-looking armchairs stood around the edge of the room – all facing one of those big flat tellies. There was a vase of imitation roses on the dining table, but that was the only splash of colour in the room: the floor was covered in that terrible laminate that's supposed to pass for wood, the walls were painted off-white and the curtains were an insipid shade of what you could call green. If anything, it resembled an old folks' home.

I couldn't face the idea of selling up as Vincent had done, moving to a retirement place, being forced to get rid of my French film collection; Mum's piano and her statue of the Madonna and child; Dad's bench at the bottom of the garden; the mirror at which you used to sit, practising new words. But if our fundraising efforts continued at this rate, I'd soon be forced to mothball all of the upper stories of Sea View Lodge. On the state pension, I could only afford to heat one or two rooms on the ground floor.

'We have orange squash,' the nurse said, 'hot chocolate, tea, coffee. What do you fancy?'

Len's cheeks had become ruddy again and he was no longer looking at me as if I had all the answers. 'We prefer Belgian hot chocolates,' he said, 'but we'll drink anything going.'

The gift bags that Vincent had left for Steph and Len contained sticks of Belgian chocolates, glass mugs that he mentioned were popular in Bruges and instructions on how to stir the chocolate into hot milk.

Steph cleared her throat and shook her head.

'Oh,' said Len. 'I'm most sorry. I almost forgot. Steph hates coffee – black, white, cappuccino. Doesn't matter which, she doesn't drink any of them. And she's not a big fan of alcohol. But I'm working on that!' He nudged Steph and they caught each other's eyes and giggled. 'She's promised to try champagne at our wedding.'

'We don't have any champagne but I'm pretty sure I could rustle up a couple of hot chocolates,' said the nurse. 'They might not be up to Belgian standards, I'm afraid.'

'I'll be off then,' I put in. I'd promised to help Mencap Musical check in at the Balmoral. There couldn't have been a problem with Dot else the nurse wouldn't have been wasting our time with hot chocolates and DVDs. I would speak to Dot when I came to pick them up. 'I'll be back at six. If you have any problems you can give me a call. Steph knows my number.' One of their care workers had set up an account for them with a local taxi firm but Len and Steph could hardly afford to splash out on that sort of thing. Besides, I was taking any opportunity to drive these days. I'd managed to get here without stalling and hadn't even felt nervous, although I'd felt rather sickened by the roar of the traffic as we crossed the M6.

'0.7.7.3.5.4.4.1.1.6.7,' piped up Steph.

'We'd appreciate it if you'd stay,' said the nurse, glancing up at me from the DVDs. Her tone told me that my initial impression had been correct: something was terribly wrong.

The nurse didn't object to Steph's choice of *Popeye*. At least she didn't spout any of that 'age appropriate' nonsense that Jennifer Tait went in for.

I felt like a bit of a spare part as the nurse fiddled with the television, and Len and Steph made themselves comfortable on the sofa.

'We're just going to make your hot chocolates. We won't be a minute.' The nurse spoke loudly to make herself heard over the *Popeye* theme tune.

As I followed her into the adjoining kitchen, I caught a whiff of fish fingers, baked beans and mash.

'Dot's taken a turn for the worse, I'm afraid,' she said as soon as she closed the door.

'I gathered.'

'We don't think she'll last long.'

As I watched the nurse fill the kettle, it felt wrong to be making hot drinks while poor old Dot lay dying just a corridor away.

The nurse cleared her throat. 'We thought you might want to explain the situation to Leonard.' She dropped a sodden teabag into the commercial waste bin. 'We thought it might be better for Len if it came from you.'

She was right, of course. But what a thing to have to explain. I could hardly bear the idea of returning to the lounge: would we switch the television off (which would signal to Len and Steph that something was up), or would we talk to them with Popeye and Olive in the background?

I stared out of the window at the hospice grounds: the daphne blossoming beside the ornamental lake, the Japanese rock garden, the wheelchair-friendly walkway – all designed, no doubt, to create a feeling of peace. I wondered if Dot and Len had ever walked around the grounds together, whether they had found it comforting.

The nurse pumped handwash from an industrial-sized container, its smell of strawberry jelly quite nauseating. Once she'd washed her hands, she offered me my mug of tea. There was no going back now. I would have to follow her into the lounge; I'd have to tell Len that tonight his mum would probably die.

I should have prepared him better. And Steph, for that matter. I should have prepared myself.

'Dot told me about your guest house,' said the nurse, before taking a sip from her own mug of tea. 'What a wonderful idea.'

Folk talk of Macmillan nurses as angels, but I'd never much gone in for that. She clearly thought of me as a kindred spirit – a fellow do-gooder.

'Let's be getting on with it,' I said, taking a deep breath and then leading the way back into the lounge.

I headed straight over to Len and Steph, aware of the nurse following me. 'Come on, you two lovebirds,' I said. 'Budge up and turn that blasted thing off.'

'Yessir!' Len gave me a mock salute and turned off the power on the remote control.

'Can we see Mum now?'

'Yes, my dear, but—'

Len scrambled from the couch, pulling Steph up with him.

'Hold your horses. We've got plenty of time,' I said, patting the couch. 'Just sit down again for a moment.'

I noticed Len's hand tighten around Steph's, and they continued to stand there.

'Come on. Take a seat,' I said, moving to let them sit together. Len was almost as straight-backed as Steph, and he was so quiet that I could hear each time he swallowed. I wanted to say to them, 'All's all right when Maeve's here'. But I had to tell them the truth and it was best to get straight to the point: 'Your mum has taken a turn for the worse, Len. The nurse thinks she will die soon.'

Len said nothing. He just stared into space, blinking hard. Steph rubbed her hand up and down his spine.

'I'm so sorry, Len. Life can be rotten at times.' It felt inadequate but I couldn't think what else to say.

287

He took some deep breaths, rested his elbows on his knees and joined his hands. It took me a moment to realise that he was praying. I wrapped my arms around the two of them – Steph's shoulders so bony and his so soft.

After a few moments, Len made the sign of the cross: 'In the name of the Father and of the Son and of the Holy Spirit.' Then he clapped his hands together and said, 'Amen!'

The nurse – who had been sitting in an armchair pretending to be invisible – piped up: 'Listen, Len. I should probably warn you that your mum might look a bit different.'

On the day of Mum's stroke, no one prepared me for the sight of her. But as soon as I entered her bedroom and saw her lying there – her head twisted at an awkward angle, her mouth open, the breath rattling in her throat, her lips so pale – I feared that she was dying. I sat on the end of her bed, praying over and over for God to save her.

'Shall I take you to Mum's room now, Len? Would you like Steph and Mrs Maloney to come with you?'

Len nodded and we all traipsed out of the lounge, leaving the tray of untouched hot chocolates.

The corridor stank like a tart's boudoir. The pong of massage oils would be the last thing anyone would need when they were at death's door. No one could persuade me to spend my last days here. Then again, Len and Steph were hardly going to nurse me at Sea View Lodge. I tried to push an image of that fir tree to the fringes of my mind: its splintered branch smashed through the window, pine needles and slabs of plaster strewn all around.

Dot looked paler than ever: a large tangle of veins protruded over her bony elbow and the skin on her face looked as if it were pulled tight over her skull. It hardly seemed possible but she looked far worse than she had done just a week ago.

Len held his mum's hand and I noticed that her nails were coated with pearly varnish. No doubt one of the nurses or volunteers had got it into her head that it would be a good idea. The smell of nail polish must have made Dot feel awfully queasy.

Steph took hold of Dot's other hand, and I just stood there aware of my arms hanging at my sides. Not that she would have thanked me for pawing at her. I rearranged the yellow roses that sat in a vase on her bedside table, while she stroked Steph's engagement ring. The scent of the roses mingled with the smells of catarrh and sweat and over-stewed tea.

A scratchy sound came from deep in Dot's throat and I thought for a moment that she might die right then. But she was trying to say something. Len leant close to her and she made the same sound again. 'I love you too,' he said.

As soon as I got the chance to spend a moment alone with her, I would reassure her about my love for Len, but I couldn't bring myself to say it somehow in front of him and Steph and the nurse.

I'd have to nip out and call Zenka. She'd have to cancel this afternoon's quilting session that I'd arranged to do in the lounge of the Balmoral. Perhaps she could do her Zumba workout instead. The Mencap group wouldn't get bored with Zenka around.

'I'll give you some time alone,' the nurse whispered. 'But press that buzzer and I'll be straight back.'

The three of us sat beside Dot's sickbed in silence for a moment or two, until I realised that Len and Steph were relying on me to speak first.

The sight of the two of them galvanised me. I took a deep breath, and then leant towards Dot and said: 'He's so well loved, your boy.' I looked up at Len, who was listening intently, and I continued loudly enough to make sure he could hear: 'Steph and Dave and Zenka and me, we all love him so much.' I steamed on ahead, aware of Len's and Steph's eyes on me, aware that my voice would soon crack. 'He's taught me such a lot about love, has Len, things he learnt from you.'

God forgive me, but I hoped that Dot would die soon. Her eyes looked milky and it was difficult to know how much she was taking in. Despite what St John's might say about the wonders of morphine, poor Dot was becoming delirious. She clutched hold of Len's hand, staring at him intently and talking gibberish.

Len just stroked her arm. 'I'm here, Mum,' he kept saying. 'I'm here.'

To make matters worse, for some godforsaken reason the central heating in St John's was cranked up to its highest setting and no one seemed able to change it. The nurse had dug out a fan, which I angled towards Dot. And Len, Steph and I attempted to stir up some cool air by fanning copies of the *Visitor* in front of our faces.

After an hour or so, I noticed that Dot was covered in goosebumps, so I manoeuvred the fan away from her. But not long after that, she became clammy again. Try as we might, she always looked either too hot or too cold. By mid-afternoon, when I'd been up and down like a yo-yo to piddle around with that blasted fan, I was tempted just to leave it. But then a lowing sound came from deep inside Dot's body, so I mustered the energy to get up and change the setting yet again.

The nurse came in at one point, holding a tray of sandwiches. 'I popped into Thorntons during my lunch hour, and picked up these chocolate sticks.' She set the tray down, then soaked a swab with water and squeezed a droplet into Dot's mouth.

As Len and Steph melted their chocolate into their mugs of hot milk, just like Vincent had taught them, I imagined what it would be like to have him waiting for me in the car outside. But perhaps I couldn't have asked that of him – all the pain it would reawaken.

During this long afternoon, Len grew increasingly pale, and I watched, helpless, as he became more and more withdrawn and less and less himself – his only comfort silently paging through their wedding scrapbook with Steph.

I could see how the coming hours would pan out: the nurse and I would take turns to make hot chocolates or fetch glasses of water; the same old background music would play on an incessant loop; my mind would wander to the tarpaulin still covering my gable window, our attic rooms still blocked off; Steph and I would give Len some time alone with his mum; our backsides would get sore; the priest's visit would be a reprieve from the tedium as her death dragged on; we'd speak at times although there'd be nothing to say; and then we'd slip into silence.

CHAPTER NINETEEN

I drove past the Alhambra and the Midland and the Winter Gardens, leaving Sea View Lodge behind. As the grandeur of the promenade gave way to 1930s semis, and then hawthorn hedgerows and distant frosted fields, I felt a brief urge to turn back. Only last week, there'd been an article in the *Visitor* about a terrible pile-up on the motorway. Besides, Zenka might cause a disturbance at the Balmoral with her Zumba session; she might forget to take Len and Steph to their appointment with Father Pete; she might not give them enough time just to sit and grieve.

As the traffic slowed across the Lune Estuary, I looked down at the same muddy banks that I'd seen from the train on the day that Mum died. I had stared out of the window throughout the journey from Liverpool Lime Street, trying not to think about the way you sat in front of the mirror practising sounds that failed to form into words; trying not to think about the months that had passed since Frank had last kissed me; especially trying not to think about the phone call from Mr Roper telling me to catch the next train home.

It had been kind of Dave to offer to drive. I'd told him that I wouldn't have dreamed of asking him to make a long journey on his day off, but he'd said that he didn't mind driving when he had company; it was the loneliness of the long-haul deliveries that had begun to wear him down.

I had never been short of company even during those long years of weaning Dad off the booze and struggling to keep Sea View Lodge afloat. I'd dreamed for years of leaving Morecambe behind, but gradually I came to enjoy the banter of the builders who formed our main trade back in the seventies and eighties; I came to love watching Dad as he sat on the bench at the bottom of the garden, reading the paper and tamping tobacco into his pipe.

I hated to make Zenka so anxious but I had to insist in the end that this was one thing I must do on my own, that right now Dave would be more use helping with the funeral arrangements than traipsing across the country with me. *It's the grief*, I overheard her say. *Or the shock. She's not been the same since the ceiling caved in.*

My hands tightened around the wheel as I turned onto the slip road, hardly able to imagine how I could possibly merge the car into the traffic zooming down the M6.

Miraculously, I managed to get into the slow lane – where I planned to stay all the way down to junction three. It felt wrong, somehow, to be driving, wrong to be alive when Dot was dead.

I had thought that Mum was indestructible until the night of her stroke: her face twisted and her lips pale.

Part of me had still thought that Dad was indestructible right into his late nineties. Even when I called the GP, to make what would be his final visit, I didn't really think that Dad would die. He'd been ill before and always recovered.

I wanted to switch on Radio Four in the hope that the morning's news would drown out the memory of the branch crashing through my bedroom window, the thud of plaster and the roar of the wind. But I didn't dare remove my hand from the wheel.

Your harmonica was tucked into the breast pocket of my button-down dress, the weight of it bringing you back. My ears were full of your voice neighing. I could almost feel your hand grasping at my dress, almost see your hair cropped close to your head, almost hear that nun telling you to let go.

It had taken me almost a lifetime to fathom what you had perhaps been trying to say, and yet Vincent had understood all along.

A monotony of service stations and slip roads flashed by as I continued southward, past signs to Blackpool and Bolton and later still to Birmingham.

It was far too late for all of this now – far, far too late. But I pressed on, my memories raising you all from the dead, and I followed the signs to Coventry, getting increasingly anxious as I drew nearer to Vincent's home.

*

July 9, 1955

Dear Joseph and Maeve,

Please accept the profoundest of sympathies from all of us here at Mary Mount. You have been at the heart of all our meditations and prayers ever since the death of our beloved Edith. We will all miss her lovely voice at matins and her disarming smile. Bernadette, as you can imagine, is particularly distraught. The sight of her wandering around the medicinal garden alone is quite heartbreaking to behold.

God bestowed Edith with a talent for bringing out the best in others. Indeed, I have a sneaking suspicion that there might have been an intelligent young woman trapped inside poor Edith. Certainly, she gave us at Mary Mount at least as much love and care and wisdom as we gave her. Blessed, indeed, are the pure in heart.

I understand your desire to blame, but I pray that this letter might find you in a more peaceful state than that which we last encountered. With God's guidance, you will be reassured that we did all we could for Edith here at Mary Mount, that nothing could have prevented her soul from taking flight. A fatal seizure could have struck poor Edith at any moment. It was simply the most unfortunate timing, occurring as it did on the very night of her return here. We none of us know on what day the Lord cometh.

No good will come of self-hatred. You were right to send Edith back with us. You were in no fit state to care for her after all you'd just suffered at the church. We cannot hope to understand why we have been subjected to such pain, but be assured that God has a plan for each and every one of His children. He chose not to consecrate your marriage, Maeve. He chose not to return Edith to your care. Our Lord and Father chose, instead, to take Edith into His own divine embrace, to love and protect her in His own heavenly abode. It may be hard to imagine this now but I suspect that, in time, you will look back on your recent trials as a blessing. In any case, it is not our place to question His mysterious ways.

We sympathise with you in your time of grief but please understand that the spiritual and pastoral care of our family of Sisters and feeble-minded girls must remain at the heart of everything we do here at Mary Mount. After prayerful reflection, I'm sure you will agree that your behaviour during your last visit was inexcusable. Such emotional outbursts, while understandable, detract from the peaceful environment we work so hard here to maintain.

Assuming that you will acquit yourselves with decorum in future, the Sisters of Nazareth at Mary Mount will continue to extend to you our hospitality. Dear Bernadette, having no blood relatives of her own, would particularly appreciate your visits.

I have enclosed little Edith's personal belongings.

We pray that you might emerge from your dark night of the soul stronger and more godly.

Your devout servant,
Sister Winifred Aloysius

*

Father O'Reilly's words drone on in that clerical rhythm that you would have mimicked: *May we who mourn be reunited one day with Edith; together may we meet Christ Jesus*.

Dad and I stand with his drinking buddies and Mum's friends from church. I've spotted several of Sea View Lodge's regular guests, who've travelled from far and wide to ensure that you get a good send-off: honeymooners, families, civil servants from London. The nurse who let us discharge you is here, and your old Voluntary Visitor. They keep to the sidelines, not being Catholic, along with your fishermen friends. Frank wasn't at the chapel, but I'm still half expecting that he will show up. Despite myself, I ache for the scratch of his dark green cardigan, his scents of carbolic and smoke.

This is the will of my Father, says the Lord, that I should lose nothing of all that he has given to me.

Sister Anthony looks washed-out but the rest of the nuns wear such expressions of placid resignation that it makes me want to smack them.

As we make ready our sister's resting place, look also with favour on those who mourn.

She was *my* sister, I want to tell him, not yours or anyone else's. But some of your friends in blue pinafores are sobbing and there's a tiny part of me that's willing to share you with them. Bernie's gaze keeps darting all around as if she could look anywhere but at your grave.

We commend to Almighty God our sister Edith, and we commit her body to the ground: earth to earth, ashes to ashes, dust to dust.

Your grave is sheltered by the vast branches of a horse chestnut, its dark pink blossoms fluttering onto the white lid of your coffin. *This is not happening*, I think, just as I had done when Mum died. *This is not happening to us*. As the undertakers lower their ropes onto the velvet that covers the freshly dug soil, I feel a deep pang of regret. I should never have allowed the nuns to arrange your funeral in their chapel. We should have had Mass at St Mary's; the choir should have sung 'For Those in Peril on the Sea'; I should never have allowed the nuns to bury you in their graveyard.

Lord, you consoled Martha and Mary in their distress; draw near to us who mourn for Edith, and dry the tears of those who weep.

Sister Winifred stands opposite me across your open grave, intoning the responses. 'Lord have mercy,' she says, her hand squeezing Bernie's. She must have known that Mum was buried at Torrisholme Cemetery. We should never have allowed her to bury you here.

Now let us pray as Christ the Lord has taught us.

Bernie's eyes are fixed on the branches of the horse chestnut. I follow her gaze, unable to keep looking down at your coffin. A small owl is perched on the tree's lowest bough, its striped breast rising and falling, its eyes intent on our proceedings. As the rest of the mourners say the "Our Father", I keep staring at the owl. It looks perfectly comfortable up there, unfazed by the broad daylight.

Forgive us our trespasses, as we forgive those who trespass against us.

When Dad nudges me, I realise that it is my turn to throw a handful of earth onto your coffin, to swing Father O'Reilly's incense burner above your open grave.

It's only then that I see Vince with his father – the two of them standing right at the back of the crowd. 'What are you doing here?' I call out, the soil still in my palm. Even as I am speaking, I know that I am behaving badly, that you would be clenching your fists to your ears. And yet, I cannot stop myself: 'You're supposed to be with the regiment!'

He looks startled, his eyes beseeching me to stop.

I am still yelling at him although I am vaguely aware of the clatter of Father O'Reilly's incense burner falling to the ground, the sigh from Sister Winifred.

The branches of the horse chestnut shake as the owl ruffles its feathers – no doubt frightened by my noise.

'It's your fault,' I tell Vince, my voice cracking, the owl taking flight. 'It's your fault that Edie died.'

Vince nods slowly, and turns on his heel, the owl soaring far above him until they both disappear out of sight.

*

T'wit-t'woo, I love you true. Who do you love the best, Frank or Edie? Hush, little baby, don't say a word. Letters of thanks, letters from banks, letters of joy from girl and boy, receipted bills and invitations, to inspect new stock or to visit relations, and applications for situations, and timid lovers' declarations. New stock, tick-tock, tick-tock. And none will hear the postman's knock. Knock and the door will be opened. Seek and ye shall find. You'll come and find the place where I am lying, and kneel and say an 'Ave' there for me.

*

My hands still tight on the steering wheel, my back held taut, I drove into the retirement complex's cul-de-sacs and closes, and then backed the car out when I realised I'd taken a wrong turn. I skirted along the road parallel to the towpath, catching glimpses of canal boats, a thatched pub, dog walkers taking their daily strolls, and I slowed to a crawl to peer at the numbers on the doors. He couldn't live in that bungalow because he would never have installed a water feature on his front lawn, and the plastic Venetian blinds on that one could never have belonged to him. How could Vincent stand it, living cheek by jowl with other folk all waiting to die? Sea View Lodge may be a tumbledown madhouse but it had always been full of life.

As the road curved away from the canal, I spotted Vincent's home even before the number came into view.

Something about the raised vegetable beds told me that he lived there, something about the sage colour of his front door.

I still hadn't worked out what I could say to Vincent, although I'd been thinking about it since Christmas Eve. If he was out, I'd occupy myself until his return. But what if he had visitors? I didn't know what I'd do then.

I stalled the car, trying to parallel park. The shock of the engine's harrumph, the humiliation of being wedged diagonally across Vincent's road, the tension that had been building throughout the long drive – it all ruptured at once, tremors running down my limbs and tears streaming from my eyes.

It had all been a selfish exercise. Vincent had made it quite clear that he wanted to be left alone. Worse still, perhaps it was no more than a vanity project. Why should a man such as Vincent show any regard for an old woman who'd rarely set foot out of Morecambe Bay?

Lord knows how long I stayed there, slumped in my seat – not yet ready to face Vincent but not yet ready to turn back – the bonnet of my car jutting out into the middle of his street.

The next thing I knew, a knock rapped on the nearside window, and I managed to press on the car's horn in fright.

'What's going on?' he asked, as I opened the door, his tone concerned but not quite sympathetic.

'I'm sorry,' I said, taking a deep breath and pulling myself together. 'I drove down here to apologise.' Looking him full in the eye, I continued: 'I should never have said that you were responsible for Edie's death. It was so terribly wrong of me to lumber you with that.' I continued to look up at him from my seat in the car – not caring that my cheeks were no doubt streaked with mascara, that my hair would be in a terrible mess. I remembered instead the squeeze of Zenka's palm during our Christmas Eve meal; the way I'd held her gaze even as my eyes welled up.

He just stood there, putting his hands in his pockets and then taking them out, his old hesitancy returned. I was letting him see me, really see me, and he was about to turn me away.

'I blamed you for everything because I couldn't bear to blame Frank, or Dad, or myself.' Frank had been fond of Dad and Edie, but he was feckless. Vincent had been right all along: Frank had not been a man to rely on. But I didn't say any of this because Frank's name felt out of place, here outside Vincent's home.

He looked at me for a long while, biting his lip, his eyes kind now – just as they had always been.

'Thank you,' he managed.

I reached out to him then, and let him help me out of the car. We shook our heads at the sight of each other – two aged friends half laughing now, half weeping out here on the street – and then I spread open my arms and drew him into a hug, a hug filled with the scent of book jackets and the sandpaper rub of his stubble and the softness of his paunch. This is what it means to be known; I'd spent decades longing for this and yet Vincent had known me all along.

Things could have been so different if I'd just kept lying with him on the night of Mum's wake, if I'd just heard what he'd been trying to say. But I'd crawled out of our blanketed cocoon. *I will graduate, and I will marry Frank, and then we will care for Edie here*, I'd said, standing in the doorway, aware that my voice sounded robotic. *You will be Frank's best man, and you will never ever mention such a thing to me again*. He'd nodded slowly and got up, leaving me staring at the imprint of his body on the cushions.

'I thought you'd stopped driving?' he asked.

'I had,' I said. 'I still can't park.'

He laughed at that, and took the hint, taking my place in the driver's seat, turning on the engine and easily backing into the tight space. 'I was just about to indulge myself with a slice of *tarte tatin*,' he said as he locked up my car. 'Could I tempt you?'

Through Vincent's patio doors, I saw a baby grand in the middle of a room lined with floor-to-ceiling shelves of sheet music and records, books and CDs. A cocker spaniel barked and jumped up at the window. Vincent really must be lonely if he'd resorted to buying a mutt.

He opened his front door and the dog leapt into his arms. Vincent took my hand in his – the intimacy of his gesture unexpected; the roughness of his skin such a pleasure to me. He stroked my palm across his dog's flank. 'Rusty, Maeve is our friend,' he said, my hand rising and falling with the dog's breath, Vincent's fingers interlocking mine. 'Rusty was my Christmas present to myself. I've been so lonely since moving in here.'

There was no shame in speaking the truth. Perhaps it was Hélène who had taught Vincent this.

Rusty trotted obediently behind us as Vincent led me through to his conservatory, where a cane table and chairs stood bedecked with a bright green tablecloth, and wintry sunlight streamed in through the glass. His lawn backed onto the canal, icy willow branches weeping into the water.

Once he had settled me at the table, he crouched down to tickle Rusty's tummy. 'You were happy as Larry with Barbara, weren't you, Rusty?' he said. 'I was lucky to get you back.'

'Barbara?' I asked, attempting to sound nonchalant.

'Come on, you,' Vincent told Rusty. 'Into the garden. She lives around the corner – the place with the water feature on the front lawn,' he explained, as he headed into the kitchen. 'She's taken such a fancy to Rusty,' he called out, 'that anyone would have thought *I* was doing *her* the favour when I asked if she'd look after him while I was in Bruges.'

We fell into an easy silence as Vincent pottered around his kitchen, brewing coffee and plating up the *tarte tatin*. I relaxed into the cane chair, enjoying my first sight of crocuses this year, and still not quite believing that Vincent had let me in.

He returned holding a wooden tray, on which he'd set a large cafetière and the *tarte tatin*. I wondered if Vincent had baked it himself, if he was following his mother's family recipe or perhaps Hélène's. Her hands would have held that tray so many times over the years; perhaps she'd inherited it from her own mother.

Once Vincent had sliced the apple tart, and poured our coffees, I took your harmonica out of my pocket and handed it to him. 'Vince,' I said, remembering that this was what he'd asked me to call him when he first returned to Sea View Lodge, 'you said it wasn't right for this to be in your possession, but I don't think it's right for it to be anywhere else.'

He cradled it in his palms, looking at it with such affection that I knew it was in the right hands. 'Just before your wedding,' he said in the end, 'I suspected that Frank was seeing Cheryl again, but he promised me he'd ended it. It was only when Edie shouted, 'Cheryl horse!' and I saw the look on Frank's face that I knew deep down that he'd lied. He didn't have the guts to make a decision; he just let life sweep him along. I thought he told you afterwards – he said he'd sent you a note. But I handled it all wrong, Maeve. I'm not trying to make an excuse.'

I just shook my head. 'I was a fool,' I admitted. 'There's nothing more to it than that.'

'It was a terrible thing to do at that moment, a terrible position to put you in.'

I remembered exactly what he'd said when he came to Sea View Lodge after we'd all returned from St Mary's: *I care about you, Maeve; I care about Edie too.* And he would have cared for us, if only I'd been able to hear him. Somewhere deep down, I'd always known this. And yet all these years, I'd continued to tell myself that Frank had left because he couldn't forgive me for what I'd done to you; all these years, I'd insisted on believing that Vince had sabotaged my marriage out of spite. I'd just made an unwise choice in Frank: there was nothing more to it than that.

Vince and I sat in his conservatory for a long time, watching Rusty bound around the garden, a heron swooping into the canal to fetch fish for her young. I told him about Dot's death, about the way grief had made Len ravenous but put Steph right off her food; about how Dot and Zenka had been my only true female friends; about the gaping hole in my dormer window and the shaft of light that shone through.

We talked about the dark period after his daughter died, the way it had driven him apart from Hélène for a while, the two of them closing themselves off; the way, one night, he had spoken of their little girl's love of the funfair at Morecambe and said that he wanted to take their son there; how glad he was that he'd spoken because that trip north had brought them back to each other.

We slowly ate our slices of *tarte tatin* and, between us, we drained the cafetière.

'Do you think Edie knew?' I asked, as Vince turned over your harmonica in his palm.

He paused, his expression showing me that he knew exactly what I meant. 'I like to think she was trying to communicate with me but I don't know, Maeve. I just don't know.'

'I'm still trying to read her mind,' I said, as he placed second helpings onto each of our plates. 'Even after all these years, those phrases of hers keep popping into my head. I keep sifting them over and over, as if one of these days I'll learn to decipher them.'

'I don't suppose we ever know for sure,' said Vince, 'what anyone else is thinking.'

CHAPTER TWENTY

On the night of Dot's funeral, I dream that I am standing by the shoreline at dawn with a man at my side, a man who is Vince but does not look like him and I do not question this. The water creeps towards our bare feet and we watch as an owl flies towards the low-slung sun, which rises from the sea.

In the distance, Steph and Len are laughing and splashing and canoodling. And then a bruiser of a woman lumbers into the water, cradling you safe above the surf. I half recognise her creamy skin and close-shorn hair, and part of me worries that she'll notice us, standing there at the shoreline, that she'll expect me to remember her name; and another part of me longs for her to turn, to wade her way towards us, to bear you back across the waves.

*

Private and Confidential
Last Will and Testament
of
Maeve Maloney

This Will is made by me, Maeve Maloney, of 31 Marine Road West, Morecambe, Lancashire, LA3 1BY

1. Revocation
I revoke all earlier Wills and testamentary dispositions.

2. Appointment of Executors
2.1 I appoint Zenka Kazlauskienė to be my Executrix and Trustee.

2.2 If Zenka Kazlauskienė is unable or unwilling to act as my Executrix and Trustee or if she dies before proving my Will I make the following appointment instead.

2.3 I appoint David Greene to be my Executor and Trustee.

2.4 The expression 'my Trustees' means my personal representatives and the trustees of this Will and of any trust that might arise under it.

3. Funeral Directions
I wish my body to be buried in the plot with my twin sister, Edith Maloney, in Mary Mount graveyard.

4. Specific Bequest of Personal Chattels
4.1 I give all my personal chattels not otherwise specifically gifted by my Will or any Codicil free of all taxes and death duties to my Trustees as beneficial legatees:

I give to Stephanie Greene free of all taxes and death duties all my jewellery.

I give to Leonard Shepherd my banjo, piano and garden tools.

5. Gift of Residue
5.1 I give my Residuary Estate to Zenka Kazlauskienė and if Zenka Kazlauskienė dies before proving my Will then the following shall apply:

5.2 I give my Residuary Estate to David Greene.

6. Substitutional Provisions
If the above provisions for the distribution of my Residuary Estate fail then the following shall apply:

I give my Residuary Estate to Mencap, 123 Golden Lane, London, EC1Y 0RT whose registered number is 222377.

7. Charities
If at my death any charity to which I have made a gift does not exist the gift will not fail but my Trustees may pay it to such other learning disability charity with similar aims as they shall think fit.

Attestation
Signed by the above named Maeve Maloney
as and for her last Will in our presence and then by us in hers.

Signature of Testator: Maeve Maloney

Signature of first Witness: Sylvia Oglethorpe
Occupation: Solicitor
Address of first Witness:
Oglethorpe and Mullen
53 Princes Crescent
Morecambe, LA4 6BY

Signature of second Witness: Guy Mullen
Occupation: Solicitor
Address of second Witness:
Oglethorpe and Mullen
53 Princes Crescent
Morecambe, LA4 6BY

*

I tossed and turned for hours that night, still unused to sleeping in this room. I lay there thinking about Zenka and Dave curled up in the bed that Trish had bought; imagining

Len and Steph in their place too; aware all the while that Vince was just across the hall in the Crocus Room.

I got up in the end and went down to the kitchen to tackle the last of the washing-up. There was no point in hankering after a different past, but as I stood at the sink I thought again of Mum's wake, of how Frank had left and Vince had stayed. I couldn't help but wonder how life might have panned out had I listened to Vince, really listened, when he'd advised me not to rely on Frank.

The sound of the hot water must have woken Vince because I heard his footsteps making their way down through the house.

'You're awake too,' he whispered, as he came into the kitchen, although there was nobody to disturb.

He put the kettle on and fetched two mugs from the cupboard without having to ask where I kept them. 'You're worried about Len?'

Len had been so brave today, God love him, standing at the lectern. With his clean-shaven face and cropped hair, his eyes seemed bigger and bluer and more bewildered than ever as he prepared to give the eulogy.

He stood up there for so long, staring at the pipe organ, that I silently cursed Jennifer Tait for having persuaded him to speak. But he managed to recover himself enough to say: 'My mum taught me to make the most of life and to be the person I want to be. She helped me become a galanthophile and a gent and the gardener of Sea View Lodge, and she tried to help me become the husband of Stephanie Greene.' He paused then and caught Steph's eye. 'We're still working on that.'

'Mum,' he continued, before breaking down: 'You were the best mum I ever did have.'

Father Pete made his way over to stand next to Len. 'I think that says it all, Len. Your mum would have been so proud.'

Despite my best efforts, the memory of Len's courage caused me to well up. Vince put his arm around me – the weight and warmth of him giving me permission to cry. My tears were for Len, of course, but also for you and Mum and Dad. Even for Frank. I was crying too for Vince and me, for the few years we had left, for the privations they might hold, for all those decades I'd spent alone. But I was also crying for Dot: she'd meant more to me than I'd known.

There was something about Vince's proximity that made my tears seem right. Here, in the kitchen, Vince beside me and the night pitch-black outside, I felt as if someone had lifted the lid off Sea View Lodge – the sensation akin to the whip of the wind, making me acutely aware that I was alive.

My gaze kept straying to our old blue suitcase: I knew that I could now open it.

Steam rose from the spout of the kettle and the warm air filled with the scent of tea as Vince opened our caddy.

I rested my palm on the case's handle for a moment before lifting it.

'It doesn't half bring back memories, that old case,' said Vince, as he stirred the tea in the pot. 'Memories I wouldn't have chosen to own.'

'You said your mother had one?' I set down our mugs of tea.

'I remember my father packing her favourite things: a silk nightie, a monogrammed handkerchief, a tin of pomade, her typewriter.'

'Mine contains some of Edie's favourite things,' I told him, your name released from my mind.

I could feel him looking at me.

'And some other bits and bobs,' I went on. 'Just stuff from our youth.'

'Any old photos?'

That image of us slipped back into my mind: your mouth open wide in laughter, your eyes elfin, the water lapping at your toes, the froth catching in your curls, me holding you safe above the waves.

'Photos, old clothes, all sorts of paperwork.'

'Father didn't much go in for photographs – not after Mother went.'

I waited for Vince to say something more but he looked deep in thought, his hands cradling his mug.

'I packed this suitcase just after Edie died. It's not been opened since 1955.'

In the still of the night with Vince by my side, I knew I could prise open the lid of this suitcase. 'Would you like to take a look?' I brought myself to suggest. 'There might be some pictures from our youth.'

Vince helped me to set the case on the table. Sea View Lodge was so quiet that I could hear our breath. I counted to ten in French, my eyes closed, and then I tugged at the lid, which opened with surprising ease.

The gaping case released smells of mothballs and newsprint. My ocean-blue dress lay across the top, the stitching disintegrated and the hem hung loose, the folds of raw silk reminiscent of a woman fallen to the ground. I held it up at the shoulders, almost expecting to see the mermaid-coloured brooch that I'd once intended to pin to it. But, of course, I didn't wear that brooch on my wedding day – it was too full of the bathtub and the hospital and the sounds of your seizure.

'Oh, my dear,' said Vince, his eyes meeting mine, and I knew that he recognised the dress.

The underwear from Wood's was spread beneath it, hinting at the figure it should have clothed. My body had served me well, although it had thickened a little in the intervening years. I always imagined that you would have lost your fleshiness as you aged, just as I'd gained weight.

'I wandered off, that night,' I told Vince, needing to rid myself of the words, 'when I should have been bathing her.'

'I know, my dear,' he said slowly. 'Frank told me.'

The relief caused a sigh to escape from my body: Vince had known even the darkest, most closed-up part of me; he had known me and loved me regardless.

I coaxed open the tightly furled edges of newspaper, which had blossomed with spores of bruise-coloured mould: black and purple and green. 'If I'd looked after Edie properly, she wouldn't have been harmed.'

'It was a terrible thing that happened, Maeve. A terrible accident.'

My fingers uncovered first the mismatched crockery, then the Lancashire cotton pillow cases, the ivory-handled cutlery and the rose-coloured sherry glasses.

'If it wasn't for that, Mum might have lived; we wouldn't have sent Edie to the nuns.'

'You can't know that, Maeve. You did what you could with good intent and a clear heart. No one can do more than that.'

I paused before finally opening the box that the nuns had returned to us.

Everything was smeared in the China Red lipstick, which must have melted during a heat wave: a rusted tin of beeswax; the hymnal whose pages had warped. After you died, when I packed up your things with mine, I must have failed to notice that your harmonica was missing. I had tried never to think about Vince's proposal; it wouldn't have occurred to me that he had still been holding your gob-tin when he took his leave.

I expected to find your peachy silk blouse along with the lipstick and beeswax and hymnal, until it dawned on me that the nuns had dressed you in it to lay you out in your coffin.

I handed Vince a photograph album, and I began to sift through the folders and envelopes.

He paused for a moment at the picture of me in my full polka-dotted skirt and Frank in his uniform, both of us leaning against the new Ford Anglia, his arms draped around mine. Frank's skin had felt as warm and smooth as a pebble left out in the sun. But I could not remember why he was laughing, his head thrown back, a dimple right in the middle of his chin. I was turned towards him, my eyebrows quizzically tilted and my mouth open in mock disapproval. Dad must have made a joke from the other side of the lens.

We were so young, Frank and me, standing there with the sun rising behind us. We hadn't the slightest inkling of what life held in store.

'To think that he's dead,' said Vince.

'And the world continues to spin,' I replied, surprised by the truth of this.

Vince continued to turn the pages of the album and I continued to search through your files.

'Would you look at that,' Vince said, putting his glasses on. 'She was a real character, wasn't she, your Edie. That photo really captures her.'

He'd picked out that same picture of you that had kept coming back to me – the one of you paddling, your cheeks dimpled, your mouth open wide.

'You have the same laugh, you and Edie. Did you know that?' he asked, taking my hand. 'Something about your eyes when you laugh, it always reminds me of her.'

My eyes hadn't changed much over time – the whites hadn't yellowed in the way that you often see in folks of my age, the blue of my irises was still as bright as ever. Our eyes and our hair – the only things an outsider would see as identical.

The files contained the certification reports, letters from the Voluntary Visitor and Mr Roper and the nuns. It must have been me who sorted through your paperwork because Dad wouldn't have been in a fit state to order all this. The labels were in my hand although I could not remember writing them: *Personal*, *Medical*, *St Mary's*, *Mary Mount*. As I leafed through pages and pages of reports on you, and read reams and reams of letters, I expected to discover something, to learn something new about our lives. But once I reached the end of the files, I realised that I knew all their contents already – these memories I'd locked away in the shed. All along, I'd had everything I needed to decipher the truth of our past: I'd read and filed each and every document and I'd been holding them inside my body ever since.

CHAPTER TWENTY-ONE

I sat in the passenger seat with Vince's dog on my lap. 'There's a boy, Rusty,' I said, holding him close as Vince reached across us to slot a gift-wrapped present into the glove compartment.

He then nosed the car into a gap in the traffic, pulling away from Sea View Lodge. I stroked Rusty in an attempt to still the trembling in my hands, trying to remember how I'd reached Mary Mount that night, that night of my wedding. But all that came back to me was Dad saying: 'We've lost her, Maeve. Our grown-up girleen has been taken from us.'

And I forced myself to conjure up an image of his face that night: the toast crumbs and spittle caught in his beard, his bloodshot eyes, the way he'd wiped away snot with the back of his hand.

At the Gala Bingo, Vince turned from the promenade, leading us up out of town. What must Vince think of Morecambe, this man who'd once lived in Paris?

As he took left turns and then immediate rights, continued straight on at several roundabouts, and then took the second and third exits at several more, I felt myself getting disorientated. I was unsure how far we'd driven from the sea, whether we were travelling south or north.

I should have insisted that Dad and I spoke of you; each year on our birthday, I should have visited your grave. I should have knelt at your headstone, telling you about the past year: the children who came to the weekly French club I ran during the early years; Dad's slow recovery; the son of his friend, who had looked so crestfallen when I gave him the brush-off; the struggle to keep Sea View Lodge afloat; Steph's birth and my role as godmother; the time I almost wed the retired headmaster – just to be a married woman, just to be touched by a man – although I knew that he was only after free home help.

It had been yet another abandonment: the way we'd turned our backs on Mary Mount; the way we'd failed to utter your name.

'You know the way?' I brought myself to ask as we drove along a wide road flanked with fields.

'I visit my mother's grave every time I come back here.' He glanced at me before returning his gaze to the road.

The day I'd thrown him out of Sea View Lodge, Vince had mentioned that he still went to the convent each year. It was coming back to me now.

'She was buried at Mary Mount?' I asked, as we drove past a power station and up towards an American-style shopping outlet.

Vince concentrated on the traffic, slowing down to turn into a 1970s housing estate. 'I think all the inhabitants were buried there,' he said, parking up in front of a row of shops: a Co-op, a chippy, a post office, a betting shop and a florist. He seemed perfectly at home here and yet he was a man who had shopped in *boulangeries*, eaten in bistros and sent cards from the postbox at the Champs-Elysées.

'She was a nun?' I asked, the significance of his words taking a while to sink in.

Vince laughed as he fished a few notes from his pocket, but then he stroked Rusty and sighed. 'I thought you knew that my mother had been sent to Mary Mount,' he said in the end, his voice quiet as if he were worried that someone might overhear. 'That's how Father knew the nuns.'

'I don't understand.' All the rumours that had percolated

314

through St Mary's: she'd run off with a civil servant from London; she'd thrown herself off Central Pier; Mr Roper returned from the office one day to find all her clothes emptied from the dresser.

'Nowadays we'd call it a breakdown, I suppose.'

'I didn't know.'

'She was always drawing a bath or emptying a bath, running the water scorchingly hot. One day Father got home to find her covered in burns. He said he knew then that things couldn't go on.'

'Oh God, Vince,' I said. 'I'm sorry.'

Through the shopfront, I could see the florist making up bouquets.

'I didn't find out what had happened,' he said as we got out of the car, 'until around the time Father suggested sending Edie to the nuns.'

So that's why Vince and his father had been at Mary Mount on the day that we left you there. To think that he had carried this in him during the night of Mum's wake – that night when he had swilled tea leaves from china cups, his soapy hands brushing against mine. To think that he had carried this in him as his arms had drawn me close, as his damp hands had cradled my head to his chest, as his lips had kissed my crown.

'That's why your father was so keen for us to send Edie to Mary Mount.'

'He honestly thought she'd be best cared for there.'

'And it justified his own choice.'

'Yes, there'd have been that too.'

He must have been terrified about Vince's genetic inheritance. Perhaps that's why he'd been so keen to marry me off to Frank.

Rusty barked through the open window of the car.

'I always suspected that even if my marriage had gone ahead,' I said at the door of the florist, 'he'd have tried to persuade me to leave Edie there.'

'I don't think *that's* true, Maeve. I honestly don't think *that's* fair.'

He looked at me, his gaze sad but unflinching. And I felt suddenly thankful that Vince dared to say what he felt to be true, although he knew it was not what I wanted to hear.

I picked up the bouquets of calla lilies and angel's breath, while Vince paid the cashier.

There had been dozens of floral tributes at Dot's funeral. I hadn't realised that she'd known so many folk. The market-stall owners had gathered on the promenade to pay their respects to the funeral cortège, and they'd sent yellow carnations in the shape of Dot's name. It must have cost an absolute bomb, but I couldn't help feeling that it really was dreadfully ugly. I must leave instructions that I want no such thing. Then again, there's nothing sadder than a bare coffin.

I had been determined to keep Dad away from St Mary's even after he died. But it wasn't until the service at the crematorium ended that I realised how short and desolate a funeral could be without the ritual of the Mass. Neither Vince nor I said a word as we made our way back to the car. But once I'd placed the bouquets on the back seat and settled myself in the front, I placed my hand on his leg – the corduroy ridged beneath my palm.

He smiled at me, his face as open as ever, and I looked up at him, keeping my hand on his leg and feeling glad that I had dared to do such a thing. 'You still planning to go to Paris?' I asked.

He gave me a mischievous look, so my attempt at nonchalance had clearly failed.

'Do you think there might be any spare seats on your coach?' I laughed as I spoke, my hand still on his knee.

'I'd say there could be one with your name on it, Maeve Maloney, if that's what you're getting at?'

To think that Vince and I might finally get to speak French in Paris – in my eighties, I might eventually explore a bit more of the world.

'You read my mind, Vincent Roper,' I said. 'I can't think of anywhere I'd rather visit, or anyone I'd rather have show me around.'

'Thank you, Maeve. What a lovely thing to have said.'

We couldn't have been further from Paris as we twisted and turned through roads lined with identical houses: grey pebble-dash with damp porches and flat roofs. But even the houses here didn't look so decrepit as Sea View Lodge with her tarpaulin and blocked-off attic and *No Vacancies* sign.

Vince had to slow every few moments to drive over yet another speed bump or to circle yet another mini-roundabout. I had expected to recognise the approach to Mary Mount, but nothing was familiar. Eventually, we pulled into a drive, passing a playground with a rusting set of swings and a basketball post askew on its frame.

The drive led up to an NHS surgery, its sign rattling against the railings as the wind began to get up. When we got close enough for me to read it, I saw that it was called the Medicinal Garden. An unmade road ran up behind the surgery, its gravel balding in patches.

The air had been filled with the scent of lavender on the day you died – lavender and rosemary and mint.

As Vince's tyres crunched across the gravel, I realised that my palms were clammy.

It had been humid that morning; the midges had swarmed around us as Sister Winifred stepped outside to talk to Dad and me on the porch. I had been surprised to find her wearing chequered pyjamas rather than a nightgown. They came back to me all of a sudden, those pyjamas – of all the things to remember.

As the heavens opened, and Vince slowed the car to a crawl, I remembered that, through the dormitory windows I'd seen other women sitting up in bed that night, their shadows cast across the walls. One of them could have been Vince's mother.

I couldn't help but think, even now, that you might not have died if I'd let you move back home, if I'd never sent you to the convent at all. But Dad was drunk again and I was delirious with tears. You might have died in Sea View Lodge without your dad or your twin by your side. You might have died without anyone to reassure you that they were there.

The potholes quickly filled with rainwater, and Vince had to manoeuvre the car this way and that. We drove around a bend and then Mary Mount suddenly came into view. Like Sea View Lodge, a section of the roof had collapsed. But nobody had protected the convent with tarpaulin: its attic exposed to the rain and its glass panes smashed. A rag of curtain, whipped up by the wind, was flapping through the space where the parlour window had once been – like a trapped bird, trying to take flight.

We drove around the back of the convent, past where the rose gardens and laundry used to be. The graveyard was nestled into a dip in the valley, the headstones leaning into the hillside as if to keep balance, although this nook was protected from the worst of the winds.

The rain was still tipping down when I opened the car door, and I got half drenched even in the moments it took for Rusty to leap out and for me to open my brolly.

If Len and Steph had been with us, I would have sent them off to throw a stick for Rusty or to look for the graves of Sister Winifred Aloysius, Sister Anthony and Bernadette – although I didn't know poor Bernie's surname. Len would wade straight through the puddles, whereas Steph would skirt around them. There were advantages to the freedoms that came from no longer caring for them day in, day out – for one thing, I was no longer subjected to *The Sound of Music* and Radio Two – but I couldn't honestly say I preferred it.

I stood there, rain streaming down my brolly, water already creeping through the sides of my shoes. I'd expected it to come back to me – the location of your headstone – but, as I surveyed the graveyard, I hadn't a clue where to start. After your funeral, Dad and I could never bring ourselves

318

to step foot in the grounds of the convent – we never did see Bernie again, or any of the nuns.

Vince fetched the two bouquets. Without saying a word, he took me by the hand, leading me up the hillside, past the lines of nuns' graves.

A camellia half covered your headstone, Edie, one of its flowers in full bloom, raindrops clinging to its leaves, its petals a burnt orange like the colour of our hair.

Sister Winifred's words came back to me, there in the graveyard at Mary Mount: *an intelligent young woman trapped inside poor Edith.*

Vince stood beside me for several moments, the rain running down the slope of his nose. 'Your family would have been so proud,' he said tentatively, 'of what you've made of their home.'

I nodded, knowing it to be true.

'It must have taken a great deal of courage to remain still and draw the world to you.'

We stood quietly for some time before he edged his hand from mine. 'I'll leave you be,' he said, gesturing towards a headstone a few rows away.

I still yearn to read you, Edie, to understand what was going on in your mind. All I have are memories of your phrases and poems and songs; those objects you took to Mary Mount; that photograph of us. I'll never know whether you were trying to tell me something; whether there were things you wanted to say.

I bent to inhale the scent of your flower. 'Edie,' I whispered, holding aside a branch of the camellia bush and then running my fingers across the letters engraved in your stone: *Edith Mary Maloney (1933–1955), beloved daughter of Lillian (1902–1955) and Joseph, and sister of Maeve.* 'The waif to my stray.'

In those moments my whole life shrank to the damp moss and sandstone beneath my fingertips, the soil beneath my feet, and the perfume of the petals beneath my nose. All these years I've been yearning to read you; all these years I've been yearning for you to read me.

'It's doing rather well,' whispered Vince, helping me to straighten up, and then offering me the gift that I'd noticed in the car.

'You planted this?'

'My father,' said Vince, 'he did it. And that dark pink one for my mother.'

His mother's camellia was a few feet further up the hillside, its flowers facing yours. Perhaps Vince was right about his father: he had been misguided at times, but perhaps he hadn't been such a bad man.

As I edged open the wrapping paper, the rain began to lift. Vince explained that his mother had outlived Edie by a couple of years. 'The first time I came here,' he said, 'I brought all Maman's favourite books. But she was too sedated to read.'

I was holding his mother's copy of *Madame Bovary*, its cover dog-eared, its pages yellowed. Inside, I knew I'd find the passages that we'd underlined, the notes we'd made in the margins, the corners we'd turned down.

I held out my arms then and drew him towards me as I should have done all those years ago. 'Human speech is like a cracked kettle,' I quoted, 'on which we tap rhythms for bears to dance to—'

And Vince joined in, completing our favourite line: 'while we long to make music that will melt the stars.'

*

September 3, 1955
Dear Maeve,

I've hesitated to write until now for fear of intruding on your grief, but please know that you and your father have been always in our thoughts and prayers. Sister Winifred suggested that it might help us both if I share with you my memories of Edie's last hours. I only pray that this might give some comfort rather than add to your distress.

When I'm awake in the quiet of the night, asking the Lord why He didn't spare her, I wonder if you are also awake, if you are also thinking of Edie.

Bernie could hardly contain herself that night, when she heard Edie return, and I had to rush to keep up as she ran to her friend. Although Sister Winifred had been struggling to calm Edie, Bernie's embrace appeased her almost immediately. By the time we got into the parlour, they were singing 'Morning Has Broken' and 'Ave Maria' and asking for the gob-tin.

Edie ate two rounds of hot buttered toast, which I had cut into soldiers, and she drank a large mug of milk. She began to look rather tired – her top lip had turned bluish and her palms had sprung a cold sweat. But I didn't think it was anything an early night wouldn't cure.

I soaked Edie's sponge in rosewater and cleaned her clammy skin, then I dressed her in a new nightie and tucked her into freshly laundered sheets. She took a while to settle, so I kept her nightlight on and sang 'Speed Bonny Boat' and 'Hush Little Baby' until her lovely eyelashes quivered with the first signs of sleep.

Bernie's cries woke me some time before matins. I rushed straight to the dormitory, where I found Edie convulsing. Bernie was at her bedside, calling out for help. I made sure Edie's head was protected by pillows and that her mouth was clear, while Bernie fetched Sister Winifred. And then we all shielded little Edie from either side. I kept stroking her and singing her favourite lullabies, and Sister Winifred kept saying, 'We're here, Edie. We're right here.'

But the convulsions just kept rolling on, so one of the sisters fetched a damp flannel. I dabbed Edie's forehead and lips as she continued to fit.

When her seizure eventually exhausted itself, Edie did not come to. I shook her gently and spoke in her ear: 'Wake up now, my little one. It's time to wake up.' I thought I heard an owl call just as Edie let out a sigh, but Sister Winifred insists that I must be mistaken; it must have been a cockerel crowing. In any case, it was right at that moment that Edie's grip loosened, and her eyelashes stilled, and she did not draw another breath.

If you could bear to return here, Maeve, we'd love to see you and your father again. Bernie keeps asking after you both. If it is too painful to visit us here, perhaps we could meet you somewhere else?

I feel so blessed to have had Edie in my life – even for such a short time – and it is a relief to know that her presence continues in the life of her twin.

All my love and sorrow and sympathy,
Sister Anthony

*

It is six o'clock in the morning and the first light is cracking into the sky. Dad is sitting cross-legged on the gravel driveway of Mary Mount convent, unaware of the midges swarming around his head, his face a mess of snot and tears and drool.

I am battering with my fists on the door. 'Let us in,' I am screaming. 'For God's sake let us in.'

When the bolt eventually slides open, I ram my full weight against the door. But they are too strong for me: Sister Anthony bars my way and Sister Winifred slips onto the porch.

'Let me see her.'

'You need to calm down first, my dear,' she says, reaching out for me with her pyjama-clad arms. 'I'm so sorry,' she whispers, trying to still my trembling palms. 'We did everything we could to save her.'

322

I smack her hands away. 'Why didn't you call an ambulance?' I scream, ignoring her pleas for me to lower my voice. 'You let her die.'

I see that lights are coming on – first in some of the nuns' cells upstairs and then in the dormitory. Footsteps make their way through corridors; doors are opened and closed; one of the girls has started to wail.

'That's Bernadette,' Sister Winifred says. 'We'd only just got her back off.'

Sister Anthony steps onto the porch now, and whispers something in Sister Winifred's ear. Whatever she says seems to soften the older nun, who then approaches Dad. He is still cross-legged on the gravel, and he is rocking and groaning now. She sits down beside him on the ground, and takes him in her arms. 'You poor soul,' I hear her say. 'You poor, poor soul.'

The young nun looks pretty without her veil and yet this thought has no place at such a time.

When Sister Anthony takes me by the hand, I immediately collapse into tears.

'We did call an ambulance,' she whispers. 'But Edie had died by the time it arrived.'

'She was about to come home,' I sob. 'I was going to pick her up today. I was going to bring her back home.'

*

Home, James! My name's Edith Mary Maloney, Sea View Lodge, 31 Marine Road West. West or north-west, four or five, occasionally six later. Lundy, Fastnet, Irish Sea. But come ye back when summer's in the meadow, or when the valley's hushed and white with snow, 'tis I'll be here in sunshine or in shadow, oh, Danny boy, oh, Danny boy, I love you so.

323

CHAPTER TWENTY-TWO

'You're not coming to the Midland in that get-up,' Len told me. 'Steph always dresses up nice.'

To my knowledge they'd never stepped foot in the Midland, but I let it slide. 'Nobody's mentioned this outing to me. Are you sure you've got it right?'

'Dad says it's better to spring things on you,' said Steph. 'Otherwise you come up with an excuse.'

Vince coughed back a laugh, and I couldn't help but smile.

'That shirt's all right, Vince,' Len continued. 'But I'd change out of those cords.'

Len was wearing his boater, striped blazer and pink bow tie, and Steph was in her new tunic dress.

Vince caught my eye again. 'Quite right, Len,' he said. 'It's not every day I get to visit the Midland.'

'And today there's going to be a special announcement so we're all going to dress up smart.'

'Shh!' said Steph. 'Zenka says it's a secret.'

I was sick to the back teeth of secrets and announcements. And I couldn't help but feel that it was too early for Len to be painting the town red. We hardly had cause for celebration. But I knew deep down that Dot would have approved. I could just see her in her tie-dyed scarf and lime-green beads, swigging cocktails and laughing so heartily that the other customers would wish that their table were having as much fun as hers. And yet, the thought of entering the Rotunda Bar at the Midland Hotel was still enough to turn my stomach.

'Come on, Maeve,' said Steph, taking my hand. 'I'll help you choose an outfit.'

I had to give it to him, Len had done wonders for her confidence.

It was only as I followed Steph up the stairs that I realised I had nothing suitable to wear. If they'd given me a little more notice, I could have taken Steph to Debenhams – we could have sat on those high stools at the cosmetics counter as the Chanel girls painted our lips and dusted our eyelids. I might even have had my hair set at Janette's.

I opened my wardrobe door and contemplated the beige slacks, cream blouses and grey cardigans. Folk said that I'd aged well but no one ever complimented me for verve or *joie de vivre*. My life used to be so full of colour: the auburn of our hair, the salty blue of Vince's eyes, Mum's red, red lipstick. A fuchsia handbag or cobalt scarf would have given this old wardrobe quite a lift.

My button-down dress was always a safe bet but it struck me as rather dull for a trip to the Midland. I pictured myself in crimson crêpe with wide, wide sleeves. My hands rifled through outfit after outfit although I knew I owned no such thing.

Steph took several hangers off the rail and then replaced them. She seemed to have some kind of system although I couldn't quite fathom it.

'This one,' she said all of a sudden, pulling out a peacock-patterned blouse that I'd forgotten I owned, and then leaving me to get dressed.

Once I'd pulled the top over my head, I remembered why I'd stopped wearing this blouse. My stiff limbs could no longer reach to fasten the button at my nape. Vince must have helped Hélène in and out of her clothing countless times: his hands would have traced every notch of her spine as he unfastened each of her wedding gown's hooks from each of their eyes; he'd have levered up her hospital bed to allow him to ease her nightie over her head before sponging her with foam and then towelling her dry.

I sat at my dressing table, where I styled my hair and sprayed it with lacquer, ran a mascara wand though my lashes, and then painted my lips in the reddest lipstick I owned.

'You're late, you're late, for a very important date!' Len was singing and his footsteps were thudding down the stairs.

'You've a lot to learn, young man,' I heard Vince telling him. 'Never hurry a lady.'

I breathed in deeply and made my way out of my room, meeting Steph on the landing. We headed down the stairs hand in hand.

Zenka and Dave had arrived and were waiting for us in the hall. Mercifully, she was wearing a dress that almost reached her knees. 'Gorgeous!' she said, clapping her hands.

'My beauties,' chipped in Dave, and I could have sworn he had tears in his eyes.

We hadn't been short of compliments in our youth, you and me. Do you remember Mum calling us her *English roses*, Dad calling us his *beautiful waifs and strays*?

As Steph and I walked down the staircase – Len, Zenka, Vince, and Dave watching us from below – I felt as if I were Arletty or Bardot.

'If you don't mind me saying it, Maeve Maloney, you do look rather fine.'

Rusty barked as if in agreement with his owner, making all of us laugh.

I didn't mind him saying it one bit, although I could feel the blush rise to my cheeks and I was aware of the button unfastened at my nape.

Although Zenka interlocked her arm in mine as we stepped outside, a stranger would no doubt assume that we were a party of couples, that Vince and I were husband and wife. It would be quite something to walk along the promenade hand in hand with a gentleman – and not any old gentleman: this man who'd conducted at the Notre Dame Cathedral in Paris; this man who'd treasured your harmonica all these decades, packing and unpacking it each time he'd moved house; this man who'd been a good husband and father despite the trials of his youth. But, of course, Vince and I were not walking hand in hand: he kept to the kerbside – his cane tap-tap-tapping against the pavement, and I kept to the railings – my eyes on the tide that was racing in across the sand.

I took a glance back at Sea View Lodge. It looked the poor relation next to the Philpotts's home, whose slate tiles still glinted in the late-afternoon sun. On the day of Dot's funeral, Miranda had closed all her blinds and stood on the doorstep with the kids as the funeral car drove past. To think that someone who'd knocked down the wall between her kitchen and living room would do something so kind.

'All right, Len,' called out a man from the opposite side of the road. 'Taking Steph out on the town?' The man's wife joined him and their teenage sons – all of them decked out in matching football shirts. More fans spilled onto the pavement in front of the Boardwalk Sports Bar. 'Will we see you at Funky Feet next week?' Perhaps they took us for a family, just like them – a family stepping out for the night.

As we approached the skeletal fairground and derelict Polo Tower, Vince drifted towards me: 'We had some good times, didn't we? It wasn't a bad youth, all in all.'

'Best time of my life, those chorister days.'

He looked at me sadly then. He really had made a good marriage; he'd seen happier times in later years.

The story I've always told myself is one of a slow decline ever since the night of our twenty-first. But caring for Dad and Steph and Len and Sea View Lodge has given me my fair share of joy: singing along to Dad's tunes; stirring Steph's porridge; dead-heading the roses with Len; quilting with our guests.

'Things are looking up around here, don't you think?' said Vince.

The *Visitor* reported that the council was running the town on a shoestring so his optimism was bound to be misplaced.

He lowered his voice as we reached the stone jetty: 'Do you remember the night we all took a dip?'

I remembered treading water, my teeth chattering as I watched Frank prepare to dive. I remembered being surprised by the amount of hair on his chest, the smoothness of Vince's.

'How could I forget?'

I remembered Frank surfacing from his dive, and then holding me too tight, kissing me too hard – and for a split second I'd thought he might pull me under.

We all fell into silence as we reached the entrance to the Midland Hotel – its sweeping white curves and glass columns restored after years of dereliction.

Our footsteps echoed against the circular walls of the lobby and the chandelier of tubular glass glinted in the setting sun. Everything about it gave me enormous pleasure – well, except for the way the booths were upholstered in clashing pink-and-red leather.

I couldn't help but chuckle at the way Len dropped in *my fiancée* at every opportunity and I tried not to worry about where this might lead or what kind of announcement they had in store.

Vince sat beside me and the scent of his aftershave mixed with the saltiness of the olives and the fizz of champagne. Although he spoke mostly to Len and Steph, and I spoke mostly to Zenka and Dave, I was aware of the movements of his arms, his thigh just inches from mine.

Just then Len began shouting and waving, his voice too loud for the space. 'Will!' he shouted. 'Miranda!'

Who should have entered the Rotunda Bar but Miranda Philpotts and her husband? I must remember that he was called Will. He couldn't have appreciated quite what it meant to visit the Midland because he just wore chinos and a navy striped sweater, and Miranda had on tight jeans, albeit with a velvet jacket and heels.

'Keep your voice down, Len,' I said. 'We *are* in the Midland, remember.'

The Philpotts were making their way towards us now, and everyone else in the Rotunda Bar had turned our way.

'We're drinking champagne,' said Len as they approached.

Steph took a sip and then grimaced.

The Philpotts must have thought us very odd to be gallivanting when Dot was barely cold in her grave.

Len offered a glass to Miranda and another to Will.

'We've some good news,' announced Zenka. 'Miranda and Will have offered us an interest-free loan to get the roof shape-ship.'

'What?' I blurted out, spilling champagne over my hands as I thumped my glass on the table, only now realising quite how tense I had been about this.

'How generous,' said Vince, so genuinely relieved that I could tell he had been worrying on my behalf.

I scoured our neighbour's faces for hints of their motives. These same people had complained about our sing-alongs; they had painted their floorboards white.

'Dot would have been the first to raise her glass to that,' said Dave – his face flush with pleasure.

'To Dot!' the rest of them chimed, clinking their flutes of champagne.

I continued to stare at Miranda and Will until he began to look uncomfortable.

'It's in our interest,' Miranda explained, 'for you to get the work completed as soon as possible.'

She *had* painted over the graffiti on our front wall; she *had* lowered her blinds for Dot's funeral cortège.

Will changed the subject, asking whether I had been pleased with Len's spring-clean.

'His what?' I could only half concentrate on the conversation because my mind kept turning over an image of Sea View Lodge, safe and dry and proud once more.

'The potting shed,' Will explained. 'He wanted to surprise you by sorting it out.'

So that's how he'd managed to break the lock and

empty all our old things onto the back lawn. 'You rascal,' I said to Len, 'roping our neighbour into your potting-shed scheme.'

'Zenka took me to Lancaster to get the banjo restrung,' Len told Will. 'And Dave took all the rubbish to the tip.'

'We kept the cradle,' put in Steph. 'Cots are very expensive, aren't they, Len?'

I caught Will's eye and gave a shrug, almost believing the sentiment the gesture conveyed: *Que sera sera* as Mum was wont to say.

'We've Jennifer Tait to thank for this,' said Zenka. 'She gave an interview with the *Visitor* pleading for funds to save Sea View Lodge.'

She might as well have got me to wander around town with a begging bowl. But I had to give it to her, Jennifer Tait had succeeded where the rest of us had failed.

'She told them that you're a pillar of the community,' Dave explained.

Zenka winked at me and laughed. 'Little does she know!'

While the others continued talking, Zenka discreetly fastened my button. Here was my chance, and yet the subject felt almost too painful to mention. Yet I had apologised to Vince; I had told Dot that I would love Len as my own. 'There's something I'd like to tell you,' I said, taking Zenka's hand – her glittery nail varnish entirely inappropriate for a period of mourning.

I'd come up with all sorts of caveats to my will: Zenka would have to continue employing Len and Steph, cater to guests with disabilities and run Sea View Lodge with Dave. But in the end it had dawned on me that I could rely on Zenka, that there was no point in trying to control their lives from beyond the grave. 'I've left Sea View Lodge to you,' I told her, 'to do with as you please.'

She looked so stunned that it was difficult at first to know if she'd taken it in, but then she began to well up. 'Me?' she asked. 'Me?'

We owed the happiness of our childhood, didn't we, Edie, to the childlessness of an old maid. Mum would often place her palm above the fireplace in the parlour, close her eyes and whisper a prayer of thanks to the late Miss Wilkinson.

'You've been a good friend to me, Zenka,' I said. 'I know I've not always made it easy.'

She laughed at that, but then we both grew quiet, neither of us quite knowing what to say.

Just then some jive music started up. 'Let's show them how to Zumba!' said Len, grabbing Steph by the hand.

'We're in the Midland, Len,' I hissed, mortified that Will and Miranda were witness to this. 'You're not at Funky Feet now.'

But Len ignored me completely. He was already jumping all over the highly polished tiles, scissor kicking dangerously close to our table. Grief does strange things to folk.

Steph looked to her dad, who just said, 'Oh, what the hell?'

I'd never seen Steph move her body so freely; she'd got stage fright when she'd tried to perform with Mencap Musical a few years back.

The next thing I knew, Dave was up on his feet too, pulling Zenka with him – not that she needed any encouragement.

Everyone in the Rotunda Bar had turned to stare. Steph and Len, Zenka and Dave – they looked a sight, all four of them, their limbs jerking here, there and everywhere, their voices whooping and hollering.

The barman was making his way towards them. This was all we needed – to be manhandled out of the Midland Hotel. Surely he'd make allowances.

'We can Zumba!' cried out Len, and then didn't the barman go and join in, dancing as madly as the rest of them.

You would have been up there in a shot, scissor kicking just like Frank taught you. *I can play jive*, you'd call out, and you'd grab at folk, dragging them from their chairs. And slowly but surely you'd get most of them up, strangers the lot of them, dancing and laughing together.

Vince was standing on the sidelines now with Miranda and Will, clapping along with the rhythm. I joined them, taking the opportunity to offer my thanks to our neighbours – my deep and heartfelt thanks.

'Go, Len!' called out Will. 'What a mover!'

An elderly couple were looking on from their table at the far corner, tutting and shaking their heads. The sight of them prompted me to lean over to Vince. 'Do you remember how to jive?' I whispered.

He just raised his eyebrows and smiled.

'I'll bet we could teach them a thing or two,' I said, daring to take his hand.

And I led him onto the makeshift dance floor, surprised at how easy it had been to reach out and touch a man – this man, Vincent Roper.

'Maeve Maloney,' he laughed, twirling me around. 'You're one dark horse.'

We must have looked as demented as the rest of them – a pair of pensioners throwing our arms as wide as our stiff joints would allow; defying arthritic knees by shuffling our feet in time to the music; trusting our bodies to remember their old moves.

There was nothing I hated more than sentimentality, but I could almost imagine Dot looking down at us, hooting with laughter, proud as punch of her son.

The next thing I knew, Miranda and Will were dancing beside us. 'What a laugh,' she called out. 'I haven't had such fun since we had the kids.'

I'd been foolish to closet myself away all these years: the old friendships I could have sustained, the new friends I could have made.

Nigh on everyone was up dancing by now – the room full of smiles and laughter and even the odd tear. And although I was short of breath and my knees were getting sore, Vince's hand was in mine, and I was jiving in the Rotunda Bar at the Midland Hotel, and I could honestly say that I was having the time of my life.

One, two, three, four, five. I can play jive. Don't grab, Edie. Let go. Let's go! *Un*, *deux*, *trois*, *quatre*, *cinq*. *Que sera sera*, whatever will be, will be. Maeve and Edie are the snazziest twins in the seven seas. The future's not ours to see, *que sera sera*. Your Daddy loves you, so he does, his beautiful waifs and strays. Don't grab, Edie. Let go.

*

SAVE SEA VIEW LODGE

Sea View Lodge in Morecambe's West End is a guest house unlike any other. Disabled holidaymakers have flocked here for years and even some staff members have learning disabilities.

Hospitality runs in Maeve Maloney's blood since the proprietor, now nearing eighty, was born and bred in Sea View Lodge.

But storm damage has left the future of her guest house hanging in the balance. Unless the proprietor can raise the funds to replace a section of roof and get their timbers treated for wet rot, she cannot re-open for business.

Jennifer Tait of Lancashire Social Services describes Maeve Maloney as 'a pillar of the community' and Sea View Lodge as 'a very special place that offers community, hope and good cheer to those who most need it'.

'It will be a sad day for Morecambe if this shining beacon is forced to close', Jennifer Tait tells us. 'All donations, however small, will make a difference. Together, let's show that we care'.

You can donate today via www.justgiving.com/seaviewlodge.

*

The rose light of sunset reflected in the mackerel clouds above the Cumbrian hills. Despite the chewing gum on the pavement, the chip packets overflowing from the dustbins and the graffiti above the amusement arcade, I felt rather proud tonight to hail from Morecambe.

Will and Miranda were ahead of us chatting with Zenka and Dave, who were walking along hand in hand. They were getting as bad as Steph and Len.

Both Dave and Len seemed almost as out of puff as Vince and me. Dave hadn't half gained weight in the years since Zenka began plying him with pork trotters and dumplings and sheep's cheese. But Len glowed, whereas Dave looked well and truly shattered. He wasn't long back from a delivery to Aberdeen and the lengthy drives were beginning to take their toll.

I was about to follow them all into the Winter Gardens when Vince stepped forwards and held open the door. For the life of me, I couldn't fathom why those women's libbers had preferred to open doors themselves, walk by the kerbside, pull out their own chairs. What I'd have done for a husband to go out to work, mow the lawns and take out the bins, while I could have concentrated on cooking hearty meals and keeping the house spic and span. I wondered if Hélène had been a women's libber or whether she'd stayed at home and kept house.

As we stepped into the foyer, I breathed in the smells of popcorn and velvet and dust. I had to admit that the restoration was progressing rather better than I'd expected:

the mosaic flooring gleamed (although large boards still covered parts of the entrance hall), and they'd restored the downstairs bar (although they were using it to sell disposable cups of Pepsi and huge buckets of toffee popcorn).

While the others queued at the box office, I looked through the ice creams and chocolates. As I inspected the various sweets on offer, I caught sight of the teenage girl behind the counter rolling her eyes. I continued to take my time, eventually picking out a bar of Fry's Chocolate Cream for Len and a packet of Minstrels for Steph.

Just as Vince approached with my ticket, out of the corner of my eye I caught sight of someone I half recognised – an elderly woman with dyed-black hair and far too much make-up, a woman whose figure had admirably withstood the test of time. The woman was unmistakably Cheryl.

She was sharing a joke with a female friend, their heads thrown back in laughter. On the odd occasion I'd run into her over the years, her face had looked drawn, her features hard. She'd given birth to a whole brood, and Frank never did get his own garage, so she'd continued to work at the market – sometimes with a carrycot sat on her stall.

Frank's death must have given her a new lease of life. I'd spent so many years resenting Cheryl, persuading myself that Frank would have been a good husband if only he'd married me. But he was weak and fickle, was Frank: the grass was always greener. Cheryl and I had both been charmed and then spurned – that was clear to me now.

Vince did a double take at the sight of her but then, without saying a word, he placed his palm around mine and led me into the auditorium, hand in hand.

EPILOGUE

Today will go down in my memory as one of the most joyful of days, proof of a life I am thankful to have lived. Although Sea View Lodge has seen more than half a century of change, I never really believed that it could be witness to this.

Steph and Len ruled out Zenka's chicken and tarragon casserole and my coconut macaroons. Instead, the family from the Coffee Pot are cooking up vats of chicken korma and frying mounds of doughnut rings. The happy couple did at least allow Dave to string my hand-sewn bunting between the boughs of our trees.

After their long fight for this marriage, the waifs and strays of Sea View Lodge are well and truly ready. Some of our makeshift family are here with me at St Mary's and the others are still making their way to the church. I've spotted Angela and Caroline, the Misfits Comedy Troupe, and a few of the young carers from Manchester. It's a shame that the Brannigans can't make it – they're sunning themselves in Tuscany or some such place, and the poor folk at Mencap Musical have been let down at the last minute by their driver.

Zenka winks over at me from her spot in the front pew on the bride's side. There's a space beside her for Dave. I sit on the groom's side and Vince will join me later, both of us marvelling that we have survived to see such a day. Right now, he's at the front with Len, performing his duties as best man.

Vince will stay at Sea View Lodge for a couple of nights, and we plan to bore Dave and Zenka something rotten by watching *Les Enfants du Paradis* in preparation for our coach trip to Paris. They'll have the place to themselves for a few nights while I'll be with Vince up the Eiffel Tower; or listening to the choir at the Notre Dame; or watching cabarets in Montmartre. We'll have to spend a bomb on taxis as I can no longer walk very far. But I'm determined not to miss out – even if it means taking a walker.

For him, these places will be full of Hélène – where they met, where they first kissed, where they set up home; for me, they'll be full of the life I'd expected to lead. And yet, I will get to step foot on French soil and I will share the experience with my oldest friend.

Dave and Steph will have left Sea View Lodge by now, en route in the wedding car. They'll have driven past the Alhambra, the Midland and the Winter Gardens, past the lovely new restaurant on the eastern promenade. They'll probably have reached Hart's Ice Cream Parlour, which has been all spruced up of late.

Sea View Lodge will tick along just fine in my absence. Except for my quilting sessions, Zenka and Dave run the place these days. I'm sure our guests will put up with her Zumba class while I'm away.

Aspy Fella A Cappella are singing 'My Favourite Things' while we all wait for the bride. Although it is rather too noisy for my liking, I can't help but smile as the lead singer invites Len and Vince to take over. Len strums along on Dad's banjo and Vince plays on your harmonica. Several of the folk from Funky Feet dance in their chairs; Zenka is clapping her hands above her head; and even Jennifer Tait is tapping her foot in time. I can't say I like the woman, and she has sat herself rather too close to the front, but she's Sea View Lodge's greatest fan, and she's fought long and hard for Len's and Steph's right to wed.

As for me, my sore knees prevent me from dancing in the aisle, but I do find myself singing along. Old Mr Roper had been right when he claimed that I sounded like a crow, whereas you sang like a nightingale. Funny that I remember such things when I sometimes forget nowadays what Zenka served for dinner just a night ago.

Your lines from the duet for the Radio Mass cut through this hullabaloo: 'Thus evermore shall rise to Thee, glad hymns of praise from land to sea'. I can still hear your voices, you all freshwater and gusts of cold air, and Vince all crumpets and Mirabelle jam; I can still see the way your face opened into the widest of smiles as the congregation broke into applause.

I am already getting a lump in my throat: Lord knows how I'll get through today with my dignity intact and my mascara unscathed. I treated myself to a makeover at the cosmetics counter at Debenhams and don't want the effect spoilt before the nuptial Mass has even begun. At least I've tucked a few tissues into my new fuchsia-pink bag.

Just as the dreadful song is coming to an end, I turn to see my Steph, her arm interlocked with Dave's, the Philpotts kids good as gold behind her. She is wearing Trish's veil and no one would guess that she'd picked up her dress from Barnardo's. The white silk shows off her jet-black hair, its shade perfectly matching her bunch of snowdrops from our garden.

'Wow!' calls out Len above the hush of the church.

Vince looks over at me, our shared smile full of grandparental pride. This man is both the same person who walked out of my wedding and a different one, I realise, and I find myself offering up a prayer of thanks for the return of this man who has always known me, this man I have finally come to know.

And even as the wedding march starts up, I am fishing for my tissues and then dabbing at my eyes.

THE STORY BEHIND THE STORY OF OWL SONG AT DAWN

My nearest and dearest may be unfathomable at times but I can always read the minds of my friends on the page: it was this realisation that propelled my own desire to write.

My grandma, although she's been dead for years, still holds sway over my imagination. She lived off the state pension but managed to wear fur coats and visit the hairdresser every week; take in stray cats; treat us to milk loaf and strawberry splits. But her life had been irrevocably damaged by the death of her eldest son and the disintegration of her marriage – unforgivable for a 1950s Liverpool Catholic.

Perhaps it's down to her that I find myself so attracted to broken things: derelict funfairs; tatty vintage dresses; people whose surface resilience hides their distress. Maybe this is why I created in *Owl Song at Dawn* an elderly woman, both proud and brave; why I offered her one last chance to heal.

To the outside world, my sister Lou might well look broken: her cerebral palsy was detected in 1983 and a name put to her autism far later. The doctor who initially diagnosed her told my parents to focus their love on her twin, Sarah, and on their eldest daughter, me; put her in an institution; forget there'd ever been three.

If only that doctor could see us now: Lou leading her way onto the dance floor, throwing back her head in laughter, singing along to the lyrics; Sarah and me following in her wake.

So which of us is really broken: Lou, who elbows her way between couples, getting the men to dance with her; or me, who looks on, half in apology, half in admiration?

This question really struck home several years ago, back when I first got the idea for *Owl Song at Dawn*. I had heard about Foxes Hotel, a seaside guest house staffed by people with learning disabilities, so I booked in for a long weekend and journeyed down there alone. One night at dinner, I got chatting to a married couple at the next table, both of whom had Down's. 'Could you not find anyone to come with you, love?' asked the wife sympathetically.

It's this encounter that got me thinking about what love really looks like and who gets to see it. Maeve in *Owl Song at Dawn* may have been fêted as the cleverest girl in town but it takes her until she's nigh on eighty to appreciate the love that Edie, her 'severely subnormal' twin, may have spotted all along.

The voices of people with learning disabilities have too long been silenced, their stories written out of our collective memories. Until I began research for this book, I knew very little about the way the Nazi's had tested out their murder methods on thousands of people with disabilities. My discovery of Britain and America's dark flirtation with eugenics came as a shock to me. I was, of course, already familiar with the distressing tales to come out of asylums, but I discovered that there was a parallel history that remained even more firmly locked behind closed doors: the secret attempts by so many post-war families to bring up their disabled children with tenderness and humour and love.

In the process of deciphering the characters in *Owl Song at Dawn*, it's my sister's mind I've been trying to read. Like Edie, Lou has only a narrow and quirky range of phrases, but her love of words is unbridled. I strive to become a more fluent interpreter of her language, and live in the hope that one day the world might finally turn its ear.

ACKNOWLEDGEMENTS

I am fortunate to count among my friends many talented writers, who have consoled me during tough times and multiplied the opportunities for celebration.

Emily Midorikawa helped me to detect the very first strains of *Owl Song at Dawn* and listened so attentively to its every variation that it often felt as if we were singing a duet. I am so proud that the cover of our next book will feature our names side by side.

Antonia Honeywell and Wayne Milstead critiqued more drafts of this novel than could reasonably be expected of any friend. And Circle of Missé Retreat – run by Wayne and Aaron Tighe, oftentimes with the kind assistance of Ben Bywater and Alison Mordue – has offered me time and again an enchanting space in which to write.

I also owe a debt of gratitude to Sarah Butler, Edward Hogan, Patricia McVeigh, Elizabeth L. Silver and Wendy Vaizey, who have open-heartedly entered into my worlds – both on and off the page – and welcomed me into theirs.

Alison Burns, Clare Jacob, Emily Pedder, Deborah Phillips and Ashley Taggart all gave their time and expertise, providing invaluable insights and support.

This collegial spirit was fostered by my writing teachers. I often find myself returning to the astute advice offered by Sally Cline, Louise Doughty and Michèle Roberts. And I am especially grateful to Jill Dawson, whose mentoring and friendship have extended well beyond her tenure at the University of East Anglia's Creative Writing programme.

The wisdom and diligence of Linda Anderson and Derek Neale of the Open University lent me the stamina required for the long haul, and the generous-spirited responses of Stevie Davies and Fiona Doloughan moved me to tears.

The intellectual, artistic, practical and financial support of the OU gave me the time, space and guidance I needed to write this novel. I have also benefited from the support of other fantastic organisations: Arts Council England; Byrdcliffe Artist in Residence program, the Royal Literary Fund and Writers' Centre Norwich. While staying in Foxes Hotel – a hospitality academy for people with learning disabilities – I dreamt up Sea View Lodge. My residency at Sunnyside Rural Trust – a social enterprise that trains people with learning disabilities and autism to work in horticulture – introduced me to a group of poets who have shaped this novel immeasurably. I am also indebted to my students at New York University – London and on City University's Novel Studio, as well as all those I have taught elsewhere over the years.

I couldn't ask for a better agent than Veronique Baxter, who, with the assistance of Laura West, Nikoline Eriksen and the team at David Higham, has made so many of my long-held literary dreams come true.

Thanks to my editor, Lauren Parsons, for hearing the owls that sing at dawn, and to Tom Chalmers, Lottie Chase, Lucy Chamberlain, Robert Harries, Jessica Reid and everyone at Legend Press for being so willing to open their ears.

Long before my life became graced with publishers, agents, literary organisations and universities, my family inspired in me a love of books. I wish I could share *Owl Song at Dawn* with my cousin, Nic, as I will with her sister, Gin – both role models and fellow readers, whose kindness and confidence in me never wavered.

Finally, my sisters, Louise and Sarah: it's a privilege to share a life story with you two. And my parents, Phil and Elaine: thank you for filling our lives with stories; believing – sometimes against the odds – that we could tell them; and loving well enough to allow us to do so in our own ways.

COME VISIT US AT
WWW.LEGENDPRESS.CO.UK

FOLLOW US
@LEGEND_PRESS